PR

BY
NANCY LEONARD

Cosmo Publishing
UNITED STATES OF AMERICA

May 2023

ISBN: 978-1-949872-83-5

Special thanks to Elizabeth Thorpe, my editor, who has provided endless levels of quality education and support, my writing group: Judith Collins, Pat Hauschildt, Ginger McNew, and Amanda Leonard without whose encouragement this book would never have evolved, and Terry Persun, for always having my back and pushing me forward. Special thanks to Margie Yellow Kidney, my Blackfeet editor, for numerous Blackfeet details and for her friendship.

For Tristan and Noel

PART I

What's the old saying? Money can't buy happiness. Well, it can't buy trust, either. I believe I'm a good man. But I'm wealthy beyond measure. Every woman I meet finds out. Every woman who knows the truth can't be trusted. Can a woman love me if she doesn't know me? Can she love me if she does? This is the catch 22.

Charlie Curchin

CHAPTER 1

CHARLIE

AN UNUSUAL GUST of fresh oxygen makes me pause so I take a minute to clean a layer of sweat and grime off my face with a red bandana and catch a breath. Montana in late September with a forest fire roaring on your flank is damn hot.

"Charlie? Can you take water down to the guys cutting brush?" Howie asks. "I'm whacked and need a break."

"You got it. And I'll stay down and help finish the line. A couple hundred yards and we'll have this baby hooked."

I head cheerfully down the dirt path with two plastic containers, each with forty pounds of water. It's the hottest part of the day, after four in the afternoon, with no additional fresh breeze to stir the air. The temperature in the sun must be well over 120 degrees. After living the past two days in wind-blown ash, I'm about as dirty as it's possible for a human to get.

There's something macho about being miserable, filthy, and exhausted. The transformation amuses me every time I climb into a well-deserved shower. I enter encrusted with dirt and ash and come out, eventually, looking like myself. Only after the war with elements has been won, do I allow myself to start thinking about showers, food, and women. The order varies.

In one week away I'll be completing my rookie season as a member of the Lolo IHC, a local Missoula Hotshot unit, and elite forest-fighting crew. I'm proud to have qualified, and prouder still that I seem to be good at it. But staying humble is an absolute necessity. The fire can beat you, fast and sure, and there's no replay button. Also, I've been accepted as an ordinary guy, which I love. I come from big money and it's common for guys like me to be kept outside the crew—segregated from the rest. I don't feel that. I've worked doubly hard to do more than my share to earn my place. I've also endured not-so-gentle harassment and come out the other end mostly intact.

I'm supposed to be the reasonable twin, the one my mother can count on not to keep her up nights worrying. She knows I have a level head on my shoulders, but I also know she'll have researched this organization and with typical thoroughness. Even so, I probably should have passed on this. Although we're twins, Todd and I are non-identical, both tall with the family reddish-brown hair, his several shades darker than my own, and with completely different personalities. Mom has more than enough anxiety dealing with Todd, the reckless one, the one continually upping the challenge and the danger. Each mountain has to be higher and steeper than the one before, each wilderness more isolated, and each helicopter ski trip more challenging. We all worry.

But I have to follow my passion, too. I'm twenty-five and need this wildness to contrast with my professional world. I like the muscles the work produces and the battles with nature. And I don't have to go to the city gym during fire season, that's for damn sure.

Reaching the line, I yell "water boy," alerting people to pause for a momentary break.

"Hey, Spoon," answers Walt. "'Bout time for refreshments. It's hotter than hell in this oak jungle. Glad you've lowered yourself to join us."

Walt is my best friend on the crew, and I smile and roll my eyes at his friendly jabs. Spoon is his nickname for me, inspired by my silver-spoon background. Most of the other guys ignore my unusual family situation, but Walt loves harassing me with it, mostly because he knows it's a touchy issue.

"Came to hide out in paradise like the rest of you raccoons. All I see are the whites of your eyes behind the ash."

"You blend right in," he says. "With your red face you look like another spot fire."

I grimace good naturedly at Walt's poor attempt at humor.

"Those gorgeous baby-blues still stand out," he says. "But don't worry. I won't out you with the ladies later."

"How much?" I ask.

"Depends on who you're hustling. High stakes and you'll have to make it worth my while."

Everyone knows I try to keep my background secret. And

mostly, unless they're too drunk, they hold back that information from a potential conquest in an after-hours bar, allowing me to be my ordinary charming self and let passion flow.

The line of fourteen Hotshots had been spread out over a four-hundred-foot section of trail, but now they all congregate for a short break. I've bonded strongly with this group over the summer. The twenty of us, including supervisors, live, eat and train together in addition to the real business of firefighting. One thing that distinguishes us is we all cover each other's backs, no exceptions.

Pinky, our crew boss, got his name by being repeatedly covered with pink mud that can save our collective ass from time to time. When danger reaches a critical point, a tanker can drop fire-retardant, either on the head of a growing fire, or directly on a crew. If they can find us.

Pinky's radio comes to life, and we hear him groan, "Oh, shit. I'm tired of eating crap. Yes. Fine. We'll beat it north to the creek bed and hunker down on the south bank."

He clicks off his radio and yells loud enough for all of us to hear. "The wind's picked up. We're at risk here, and the I.C. wants to drop some of my favorite goo."

More collective groans.

"It's a quarter mile. No one wants to risk our beautiful bodies. Double time it, guys and gals."

There's more good-natured grumbling as we pair up—the usual drill.

"Stay together," Pinky continues. "We have time. There's fifteen of us now, including our water boy."

I smile to myself. Pinky's an A-1 squad boss, and always knows who he's responsible for.

Starting to breathe denser smoke, I feel the wind change then stow my shower fantasies to focus. I don't want to trip on the rough ground and become someone's problem. The fire's roar is building on our right. I've heard worse this summer, but I like it well ahead of me, not on my flank with the wind changing. We keep double timing it.

The creek bed is just ahead. It's mostly rocky and dry this time of year, but there's a little water standing in pools. We group together with Pinky as he has us count off in random order. "One, two…"

"Twelve," I call out in my turn.

"Thirteen," sounds another voice.

"Fourteen," calls one of our ladies. Then nothing. We wait.

"Count out again," yells Pinky. We quickly repeat the verbal count. Fourteen again. "Damn it, who's missing?"

"Walt," someone yells. "He was right behind me."

The roar from the fire is louder now. For the first time I can see flames towering from the direction we just left. Where the hell is Walt? I should have checked before I took off.

"Hunker down. Be ready to deploy shelters," Pinky yells above the noise. "Rosko, you're in charge. They know where we are. Stay close together. Mud's on the way. Three minutes. I'm going back for Walt."

"Pinky, I'm with you." I yell.

"Stay put, Charlie. He can't be far. I don't want you caught out."

Pinky disappears into the dense smoke. Damn it, Walt. The season has been going so well. Where the hell are you?

"Two minutes till mud drop," yells Rosko. "The damn dragon turned again. It's headed straight for us. Shelters at the ready. Close together so the pilot can see us."

We do as we're told. This is the first time I've been in a serious situation. With the wind shift, the air is suddenly full of whirling smoke and embers. I'm anxiously hoping the tanker can find us to make his drop then stand behind Rosko, trying to prepare myself. With few exceptions, once you shelter up, you give up all control. You either live or die in there. I'm starting to feel strong heat now and start taking shallow, rapid breaths, afraid to take a deep lungful of the heated air.

"That's enough. Shelter up," screams Rosko at the top of his lungs.

Shaking out my foil tent from the pouch, I put my feet in, and pull it over my legs, back and head. I can feel my heart pounding. The roar of the fire is now very close. Shelters can take severe heat but not direct flames. Sweat rolls down my back and it's not only from the heat. We've been trained to do this, but I'm shaking. There's no guarantee.

The heated waves of air cause my shelter sides to flap back and forth as I strain to hear Pinky's voice above the roar of the fire. I'm reminded of a time when Todd and I were sleeping in a heavy canvas tent in our back yard and how scared we were. The tent collapsed in a similar high wind, crushing down on top of us in the middle of the night. We hung onto each other and screamed. We were probably seven or eight.

Suddenly it's becoming so hot in here that I'm crazed to escape, trying just to hold on. It's much worse outside. I'd probably die.

Louder than the roar of the fire, I hear the drone of the tanker, the life-saving sound. I try holding my breath.

A long fifteen seconds later my shelter is partially collapsed by the heavy retardant settling over us. The fire sound is suddenly diminished. I collapse in relieved gratitude that the pilot knew what he was doing. And I'm worrying about Walt.

We're trained to wait until the guy in charge gives us the go ahead to climb out.

Finally, I hear Pinky yelling, "Thought I couldn't look any worse, but this is a new low. Climb on out of those shake and bakes."

I scramble out, seeing a disgustingly dirty group of firefighters. We're so obscenely ugly, dripping the red goo, that we all start laughing. Walt is standing next to Pinky, shaking his hand, so I guess there's a story there.

"At least they don't make us pay for the hot water and soap," Pinky remarks. "That'd be a deal after breaker for me."

Standing in a hot shower four hours later, I'm in a more peaceful frame of mind, letting the water pound my head and shoulders. Soon I'll be headed back to school, completing my MBA, but plan to continue my pilot training. I earned a license to fly helicopters last winter and originally planned to come out here next summer as a chopper pilot instead of a ground grunt. But to my surprise, I've loved being one of the crew, digging dirt on the fire line, being one more guy cracking nervous jokes when things get dicey. On the humor subject, during our run to safety, Walt caught his foot in a hole, couldn't get loose, and had to rip his foot out of his boot. He was limping out with only a sock on one foot when Pinky found him.

After graduation I'll be absorbed back into the family conglomerate, Curchin LTD, from which I spend most of my summers trying to distance myself, hiding out in ash and generic western bars. Stretching my neck, I settle in to enjoy the hot water just a little longer with a sleepy smile on my face.

I'm finally out and wrapping a towel around my waist when Walt leans his head in the shower room door. "Spoon, there's been a call for you."

"Ever go back for your boot, Hop-A-Long?" I ask.

"Stuff it, Charlie. Listen up, it was Charlie 2. He said it was important and to call home immediately." Most of my friends know we go by Charlie 2 and Charlie 3. Grampa was a Charlie, also. Simplifies things.

Crap! I mutter to myself. All I want now is to collapse into some cozy bar booth and start celebrating, being a conquering hero with some local lady who likes firefighters. Taking a few seconds to wriggle my damp body into a pair of jeans, I pull out my cell and punch in our home number.

Dad answers, almost breathless. "Charlie? Listen. Todd's disappeared. His plane went off radar in south-western Alberta."

I have to swallow several times before I can think. "Where's Hugh? Is he coming?"

"He was the first person I called after I tried you. I just heard back from him. He's in the air now, piloting the 550."

"Where is he?"

"Flew the advance team to a meeting with the State Department. Stayed on in DC to hold the plane for their return. But now we'll get the team back commercial or send John."

"Can he function?" It goes without saying that Hugh deeply loves Todd. He's also my best friend.

"I asked him that. He told me he'd compartmentalize."

He can do that. Special forces training kicks in. "What should I do?"

"Get yourself to Calgary. We'll meet at the airport there. Mom and I are waiting here at home for Juli."

"She knows then."

"She knows. I sent Stosh for her. I insisted she not drive. You know how she gets."

"Dad, I love you. Tell Mom."

"Just get yourself to Calgary," He pauses. "I love you, too."

I'm struck for the umpteenth time that all the wealth in the world can't protect you from being thrown to your knees. A mythical giant is hitting me over and over with a huge bludgeon. I can't move. I can barely breathe. The beating continues. I hope I can keep breathing. I'm not sure. I want my brother. I want my self-centered, wild man of a brother, more than I can bear.

CHAPTER 2

JULI

STOSH IS WAITING at the curb at the soccer center as I race to the car hauling my gear. He's our rock—gardener, mechanic, engineer, do-anything-asked, in addition to being my dad's best friend, and another father figure to all us kids. Glancing at him, he shakes his head. No news. It's a long twenty minutes in the mostly deserted, dark streets before we turn into our driveway. Stosh has tried his best to give me hope, but when I finally started sobbing, he had to pull over and hug me. There were tears in his eyes when I leaned away.

He pulls up to the front portico where Mom and Dad are waiting. Jumping out before the car comes to a full stop, I manage a few steps before I'm stopped by my purse strap caught on the car door. I pull frantically on it, give up, and leave it dangling. "Dad?"

He rushes to me. "He's only been missing a few hours, Sweetheart. You know Todd. At worst he's probably hiking out of somewhere. We'll find him." It only takes one look at Mom's face to know, despite his words, she's worried sick. But maybe... Nothing could possibly happen to Todd.

* * *

Several hours later, we sit silently as Stosh maneuvers the car through the airport traffic into the private plane holding location. I have a cut starting on my lower lip where I've been chewing it in anxious frustration.

During the drive here, I've been constantly texting Hugh, our adopted brother since babyhood and our primary pilot. He landed twenty minutes ago and is currently occupied overseeing the refueling of our jet. We're dropped off at the side of it, and rushing to Hugh, I'm enveloped in a bear hug. Mom and Dad say a few emotional words to him then hurry up the stairs. Hugh is a study in contrasts—close-cropped, dark curly hair with the professional military demeanor he developed during his Special Forces years, alternately combined with overblown adolescent humor. Tonight, the humor is gone.

"Hugh," I cry. "Is he alive? Will we find him?"

When he says nothing, I fall apart again. "Oh no," I moan. "No!"

Grabbing my arm, he half-drags me up the steep stairs, then inside to the cockpit area, shutting the door. "Listen," he says, holding my shoulders tightly until the tornado of my rage burns itself out. "Listen to me, Juli," he says again. "We've got to get a hold of ourselves. We need to plan. Not go crazy. Get it... For your mom and dad?"

I collapse into his arms and sag against him.

"Maybe we'll find him," he adds. "We won't give up hope." He shakes me gently. "Lots of people survive crashes. Todd is a good pilot. He'd set it down if he could."

After several moments, I look up at him, taking a final deep breath. "Okay, Hugh. Just stay with me. Okay?"

"Okay," he agrees, "I promise." Then adds, "But stay with me, too."

CHAPTER 3

CHARLIE

THE ENTIRE FLIGHT to Calgary I've been torn between extreme despair and outrage that Todd's putting us through this again. He's always lost in avalanche country helicopter skiing, disappearing while hiking alone without an itinerary, or trekking in the Middle East with terrorists in the neighborhood. Then, after providing the family with several days of nauseating fear, he turns up. When he reappears this time, I'm going to punch him in the gut. I swear. Anger feels better than terror.

Grabbing my carry-on, I take my place in line, standing wedged in the tight aisle, repeatedly sighing as I wait for passengers ahead of me to deplane. It took time to get out of fire country and wind my way through a couple of connecting flights. It's after midnight when I finally emerge, and to my surprise Dad and Mom are both waiting for me. My heart sinks. They must be really scared. Dad probably hasn't been in an airport waiting room in twenty years. Mom's holding it together, but just, her color is grayish.

"Tell me," I say, putting my arms around Mom then looking at Dad.

"Todd flew Lufthansa from Ankara to London. He spent several days waiting for our plane to be available. He called from Heathrow Wednesday afternoon. He was picking up the G150. After a few hours of stop-over and rest in Gander, he was planning to pilot it out to see you." He sighs, then adds, "He was headed for Missoula. 'One more joy ride before school starts,' was the last thing he ever said to me. That plus, 'I love you, Dad.'"

"Did he file a flight plan?"

"It called for a second stop in Saskatoon for fuel. He said he'd sleep there if he was tired."

Dad's shoulders start to shake. Wrapping our arms around each other, we hold each other tightly. My shoulders are shaking, too.

I know what Todd was doing. Our mutual birthday is in two days. He wanted to share a few beers to celebrate.

Dad tries to talk, then is forced to stop.

Several moments pass before he can proceed. "On record, the plane stopped in Saskatoon to refuel Tuesday evening, then took off again about nine. He never made it to Missoula. He should have landed around eleven that night. He was going to surprise you." He pauses. "I should have waited up to hear, but it was one in the morning in Philly."

At this point Mom starts crying softly, but hard enough that people lingering in the waiting room turn to stare before drifting away. She's now standing slightly apart, staring out the window with her hands balled tightly at her side. I catch Dad's eyes on me. We think alike. We're realists. He's the one who knows. The odds are horrible. If he were alive and okay, he'd have called. He would have known how worried we all are. We never miss check-ins when we pilot. Never. But maybe he's survived far into the wilderness out of cell phone reach. My mind switches back and forth between hope and despair.

"When I got up yesterday," Dad continues, "there was no message. I put all our guys on it, cell phone tracking, flight plans, radar scans… There's nothing, Charlie. Nothing. I keep hoping I'll get a call—that he had to walk out of somewhere…"

"I should have put my foot down," Mom says, vehemently. "I should have said no to this last trip. Trekking now in the Middle East for God's sake." She's crying harder now. "But how could I say no? He could talk me into anything." After a shaky breath she adds, "but he made it all the way to Saskatoon. We checked."

"I know, Mom," I say. "It's not just you. He got around us all."
We just spoke about him in past tense, I think, cringing with dread.

"What's being done? What can I do?" I ask.

"Canadian search teams are already doing flyovers in fixed wing aircraft. But it's such a large area. There's no signal from the locator beacon. We can't understand that unless he went down in water. We just don't know. We're hiring every private plane and helicopter available and bringing in more. The search area is so rugged. He wasn't flying a straight line to Missoula. It's another mystery. He wasn't following his flight plan. He seemed to be joy riding over the Canadian Rockies when he dropped off radar."

"Todd doesn't play by the rules," I say.

Dad nods. "They lost him about an hour west of Saskatoon. As close as we can narrow it down, he's in an area of 20,000 square miles. Even that's iffy. They have a search grid set up, and they're trying to triangulate his cell phone. Nothing on that yet."

"I can't just sit around. I want to take a helicopter up, Dad."

Mom gasps and I understand. "I won't go alone. My flying skills are only fair. I'll go up with Hugh. Be another set of eyes."

"I'm going, too," Dad says. "I can't stay on the ground and wait. Mom will go up, too. We'll all fly on to Banff now. We'll use it as our search base. We have people arranging aircraft."

I look around. "Where's Juli?"

"Hugh's on his third walk around the airport with her. She starts to get frantic if she stands still, so Hugh is staying with her, walking off her nerves."

"And Tina? Is she coming?"

"She'll fly out tomorrow morning in one of the small jets. She needed to get her family organized, then pack. She's planning to coordinate the search effort—man the search facility."

I glance over at Mom, catching her with a furious expression. Surprised, I reluctantly turn back to Dad. "Is Tina holding it together?"

"She seems to be handling it," he answers, "but I just talked to Phil. He admitted he keeps finding her in the bathroom crying."

He stops as Mom suddenly grabs his arm. "Enough of this," she says emphatically. "No more crying."

"Mom?"

"He's going to be found alive, Charlie," she says tightly.

I nod with my best possible smile. Maybe she's right. I need to have hope, too. Todd is my other half.

I hear a distant scream and moments later Juli streaks through the crowd, throwing herself into my arms.

CHAPTER 4

CHARLIE

IT'S BEEN ALMOST two weeks since we began our search. Our whole family has spent countless hours in the air, looking until we're blurry-eyed. I've been biting my fingernails down to nubbins, which I've never done, plus currently existing in an almost constant state of nausea, aggravated by the constant jolts of the helicopter that never bothered me before.

We admit to ourselves that we're looking for wreckage, even wishing for some smoke from the crash site, or more hopefully, a signal fire. The area is so vast, plus a weather front came through on the second day, suspending the air search. The storm dumped inches of drenching rain, cutting visibility, and masking anything smoldering. Periodically, I've been piloting one of our two Sikorsky helicopters to give Hugh a break and resting my eyes from endless scanning. I'm racking up flight time and competency.

It wasn't until the second evening after we learned of Todd's disappearance that I called Meg. I've long since stopped thinking of her as Hep, Todd's name for her since they were kids. I put it off, and put it off, but finally the impulse to call jabbed me every minute, plus the news media finally got a hold of the story. I didn't want her to find out that way. I punched in her number, took a very deep breath, and waited...

"Hey, Charlie. How's the Hotshot?"

"That's what I need to talk to you about, kid. Where are you?"

"What's it to ya?" she said. She hadn't really heard my voice yet.

"No, seriously. Are you alone?"

"No, Mom and Dad are here. I'm home for the weekend?" Her voice had changed, sensing something.

"Meg, listen. You should know... You need to know..."

I heard a sharp intake of a breath.

"Todd is missing. His plane appears to have crashed. Somewhere in the Canadian Rockies."

I waited for a response. Nothing.

"Meg...?"

It was several moments before I heard a response, her voice a whisper. "When? Is there hope?"

"Of course," I said, trying to keep my voice steady. "We're all looking. It's the second day and we... Well, it's a lot of territory to cover."

No response.

I could tell the line was still connected but there was only silence. I held on... Finally, I heard what might have been low moaning... Then nothing.

* * *

I've tried to hold on to hope, but as the weeks wear on, we've all had to deal with the reality that we may never find Todd. My fire season is over. The additional rain we had last week up and down the Western Rockies ended it. I'm personally trashed, anyway. We're all washed out of emotion. Juli held it together for three days than started screaming in her sleep and never really stopped. Dad got her some drugs. I'm on autopilot. It's typical for me to hold things together while the heat is on, then have a private meltdown. I'm still holding on. Barely. I frequently make fists to prevent my hands shaking.

We're under the final gun now because a cold front is moving down from the Arctic, bringing with it the first major snowfall of the year. If there are any signs of a crash, they'll be obscured under snow, probably until next May. If my brother is somehow still alive, this is our last chance. I've dealt with the probability of his death. What I can't stomach is the possibility he's been hurt, can't move, and is helplessly waiting for us to find him. I shove that image away repeatedly. It makes me physically ill. I've been questioning whether my gut would tell me if he were dead. Twins have this second sense about each other. I keep thinking some part of me would know if he... Nothing.

I've had a lot of time to think up here, endlessly scanning the lower foothills and higher rocky slopes for anything out of the ordinary. Once, a long time ago, Todd and I were the same, little boys growing up in oblivious luxury with parents who provided us with every need, including unquestioned stability. Until one night when I was eight.

* * *

It was a family tradition on Friday nights that we could bring sleeping bags and sleep on the floor of our parents' bedroom at the foot of their bed—a night of indoor camping. We watched kid movies on their TV, ate junk food, and brought books to read. That night was the following Saturday night, and I returned to search for my favorite book which I'd left in their room the night before.

It was late that night, after ten, and I had just crawled under their bed to retrieve my book, when my parents came bursting into the room. They were fighting. They were usually careful to avoid serious disagreements when we were around, but that night they thought they were alone. My mother was yelling, something about how my father never took her opinions seriously, how he looked down on her. I think I remember her saying *trophy wife.*

Dad was yelling back. It escalated, their voices getting louder and louder. I was terrified. Finally, the word that all kids dread was thrown out. My father said it. "Do you want a divorce?"

The fighting stopped. It was hideously silent. I waited. My father asked again, "Well, do you?" It seemed hours but was probably only a few minutes until I heard my mother finally answer angrily, "No."

"Fine," Dad yelled. "Let me know if you change your mind." Then he stormed out of the room.

Mom followed him out, slamming the door so hard that the room shook.

I don't know how many years later I got that incident in better perspective. Parents do fight. And if they're careful, kids don't hear much of it, but my world had changed. Maybe, if I'd heard them fight more often, it wouldn't have been such a huge event. I learned for the first time that love is not always enduring, and it can be fragile.

I never told anyone about that night, except Todd, but I know it changed me on some deep level. My brother and I looked at the world differently from that night on.

* * *

Hugh's back at the controls and I'm pushing hard to focus. *Todd*, I think, *give us a sign*. Help us. I don't know if we'll be able to fly tomorrow. Hugh and I have decided to make one last pass along the Northern Rockies between British Columbia and Alberta, following the crest of the Rockies southeast toward the US border. It would be like Todd to want a last look at the Provincial Park.

We had to stop once to refuel near Jasper and the afternoon lengthens when I see something out of the ordinary. It's a section of blackened trees up against the northwest side of a glacier.

"See that, Hugh," I say, pointing. "Can you make a pass right over that area?"

"Roger that."

We fly over in minutes and Hugh hovers at one hundred feet. I can easily see part of a fuselage and pieces of two wings torn off a white private jet. Most of the pieces are very small. The nose of the plane doesn't exist. It looks like it went straight down into the ground. My eyes fill with tears. We don't say anything, but Hugh points to a flat area an eighth of a mile from the grove of burned trees.

We land and clamber out of the helicopter, steeling ourselves as we race to the scene. It's quickly apparent that this was not a survivable crash, but I call out his name several times. I can't help myself. My screams turn to meaningless sounds and Hugh pulls me into his arms. It's only after several minutes that I can pull myself together and try a call to Dad who's at the search center base in Banff. It's wilderness but we're high up and not too far from civilization and I have bars.

"Dad," I manage, "we've found the crash site, but there's no one here. It doesn't look like he could possibly have survived it. We can't find a body."

Hugh motions me over to the side of the remaining fuselage, pointing down at the ground. There are huge bear tracks, probably of a grizzly, and what looks like blood that has drained into the dirt.

"I'm pulling up my G.P.S. coordinates," I say to Dad. "If you can, get up here?"

"I'll try," I hear him say.

"It'll probably be impossible tomorrow due to the weather front." Taking a ragged breath, I read off our location coordinates.

It's been fifty minutes with the sun hanging low over a ridge of mountains to the west when we hear the rotors of a large helicopter approaching us. Hugh shoots a flare over the glacier to direct them in, avoiding any fire risk. In minutes the flight crew and Dad are approaching us.

As Dad comes up, I throw my arms around him and shake my head. "Nothing. No remains."

He nods.

I indicate to Hugh to fill them in.

"We've looked," he says. "Nothing but animal tracks. It's probable that Todd's remains were dragged off. It's obvious what happened here. The crash was violent, not survivable, and it started a fire. The prevailing wind blew the flames up against the glacier. It didn't start a big ground fire, even in those very dry conditions. It just burned itself out in three acres or so. It was amazing Charlie even saw it."

"Have you searched the area thoroughly?" Dad asks.

"We've covered every inch in the last hour," I say. "No physical remains that we could find, just part of an old ball cap and one shoe. We've searched inside a full half-mile perimeter. The underbrush is very thin up this high and we could see easily. All we found were animal tracks. Lots of them."

"Charlie," offers Hugh, "I'm absolutely sure his death was instantaneous with the crash."

As we speak, there's a shift in the wind, now coming strongly from the north, and colder by ten or fifteen degrees in the last few minutes. We're at medium-high altitude here, over 5,000 feet.

"What should we do now?" Dad asks.

Hugh looks at me.

"We can put our minds at rest. Todd isn't suffering somewhere alone. He's gone. For me, I'd like to spend this last half-hour of daylight being with Todd, and then say goodbye."

"What about authorities?" Dad asks.

"I know crash investigators will want to look at the site, but that may be impossible until next spring. We could have two feet of snow here by tomorrow morning and six feet in a week."

Hugh nods in silent agreement.

Before we leave, I take pictures. Dad's crew takes many more, documenting everything we can. At the end, Dad and I sit near the wreckage on an old tree trunk, listening to the wind whip through the alpine firs. I'm holding the well-worn Phillies cap to my cheek. It smells like Todd.

* * *

Tina had a long phone conversation with Phil and her kids just before we took off and has been in a deep sleep in the back ever since. She told me she was exhausted to her soul. I'm sitting with Juli in the mid-section, passing the time until we get back to Philadelphia. She's the best athlete in the family, taking out her intensity by playing on a women's semi-professional soccer team. She has my auburn hair, which she manages in a wild mass of disarray or worn in a long pigtail which she unbraids, then braids when she's stressed.

Juli also inherited Todd's daredevil genes and, unlike the rest of us, never considered the possibility that anything could happen to him, or any one of us. She's the most deeply shocked, taking undetermined weeks off from their pre-season tour. She says she feels hollowed out.

My invincible sister is so wretched that I'm trying to stick with her, lessen the time she broods. We're both trying to find topics far away from what we can't bear to think about—that our family will be forever altered and diminished.

"So, Juli. How's your love life?" That's usually a safe topic. It's usually great.

"Every guy seems like the last one." She mutters unhappily.

"You're not thinking of settling down, are you?"

"We've talked about this before, Charlie. Especially with losing…" She swallows. "I'd like someone I can count on, and I'm not talking about just showing up for dinner out. Somebody like you or Dad." She manages a half-smile. "Someone with some depth."

"I know you're feeling vulnerable, honey, but you've got time, and so do I before we descend into middle age."

"It's even worse for me than you. Everyone knows who I am, and that I'm ridiculously rich—just another privileged, spoiled brat." She looks sideways at me to see if I'm rolling my eyes. "God, they even talk about the family fortune on ESPN. How will we ever know if we're really loved?"

I grimace. "Maybe we should just live it up for five more years, have plastic surgery, change our names, and get jobs in an upscale shoe store." Glancing at her, I don't see a hint of the smile I was hoping for.

"Listen, Charlie," she says, gripping my hand so hard it hurts. "Promise me you'll take care of yourself. You're the only big brother I've got now."

"Same back at you, sweetheart. You're the wild woman. Promise me, too? Okay?"

"I promise," she says seriously. "And I mean it. I don't think we have to worry about Tina. As long as the Internet functions, she'll be fine indoors."

"Still, you never know," I say. "I'll tell her to be careful, too."

We sit silently for a while. "So," she asks finally, "what happened with Angela? I haven't heard you mention her recently."

"She's gone," I reply. "Started pouting when I didn't take her into the city for expensive evenings. We went to a wedding together two months ago and I overheard her bragging about how many corporate jets her boyfriend's family had—how we have them named alphabetically. I hate that. I really do."

"Let's make a pact, Charlie. If we don't find great people in a few years, we'll help each other."

"You won't need it," I encourage. "But sure. I'll help."

"That's good," she says, closing her eyes with a ghost of a smile.

That makes me feel a little better, but I'm putting up a good front. I'm strung tight as a drum.

* * *

It's raining hard when Hugh lands the plane in Philly. I never give safety a thought, not with Hugh at the controls. He doesn't take chances. Ever. We sit quietly together in the plane as Hugh finishes all his post-flight duties. None of us wanted to leave him alone or maybe we simply need him with us, and that includes Mom and Dad. He seems so tough. We all lean on my best friend.

We've remained the closest of friends, the five of us: Juli, me, Hugh, Todd, and Meg. I've called her several more times during the search to keep her informed. She needed to know. She has been deeply in love with Todd since grade school.

"Juli?" I ask.

She looks up at me.

"Meg is going to be down there at the car. Do you want...?"

"No," she says. "I can handle her now. It's... It's my turn."

Our family SUV is parked sixty feet away as the outer door of our plane is opened. Stosh gets out in the rain, holding an umbrella over a woman's head. I steel myself as Juli hurries down the steps, runs over, and grabs Meg, both dissolving into each other's arms.

They stand clutching each other in grief. Even though I knew how much she loved Todd, the intensity of Meg's grief surprises me, matching Juli's and mine. Meg's sobs overwhelm the background noise of the rain. Mom and Dad join us. Todd's life impacted so many other lives. The rain increases, becoming a constant drumming. We're getting drenched, but it seems necessary and appropriate, a ritual we need to complete our absolute misery.

Tina's husband, Phil, and their two little boys rush to the plane to greet her. He whisks them quickly away in a separate car.

CHAPTER 5

JULI

AFTER THE ANGUISHED drive from the airport, the family lingers around the kitchen table of our family home on the Main Line, trying to eat some of the food that Molly, our housekeeper and adopted second mother, keeps placing in front of us. Meg was minimally comforted with shared anguish and just taken away. She's my best friend. I don't remember when she wasn't another sister. We spent our entire teenage years as a two-person being, shifting back and forth between our two houses, sharing endless sleepovers, talking boys. There was never any doubt she was planning a future with Todd. We used to plan strategy of kidnapping him for her, ending with laughing hysterics about what she'd do with him when she got him that left us gasping.

Now I wonder oddly when I'll be able to tolerate seeing her and her wretchedness again. I've been trying to recover, put this behind me a little, push it under. But seeing her at the airport brought back how much we've lost. Despite that, I make a silent resolution to call her often, to do something merciful for another human being.

"I wish I had a wife," mutters a voice behind me.

It almost makes me smile, it's so out of character for my playboy friend. "A joke, Hugh?" I ask.

"No," he says as I turn to see him blinking his eyes rapidly.

I put my arms around him.

* * *

It's been several weeks since we found the crash. I'm finally off the pills Dad gave me, flushing the remainder of the bottle down the john in disgust after finally sleeping through the night. Often though, I purposefully hide out beyond the pool, sit on the ground with my back to one of our giant maples, and howl out my anguish.

I scream his name, beat my fists on the ground and sob. But I guess I'm better. I can talk to Mom and Dad about Todd now.

Now that I'm climbing out of my own fog, Charlie worries me. He appeared relatively normal for the first week or so, then started falling apart. As I got better, he got worse. Maybe he held himself together for me. But now he's a ghost. He wanders around the house, speaking only when spoken to. Dad tries to discuss school plans, and all he gets in response is a blank stare as if he didn't understand the question. He doesn't cry, that I've observed. His lifeline seems severed. I can tell he's lost weight. His clothes are beginning to hang on him. We have to call him for meals, and then remind him to eat.

I always thought of him as the calm, stoic member of the family. Knew he'd fill Dad's shoes when the time came but now, I wonder if I'm not stronger. I called Meg to ask how she's doing, and to see if she had any ideas of how to get Charlie to move on a little. She concedes she's doing better, too. Admitting it feels like a betrayal, but we have to go on. We're all worried about Charlie.

Hugh's Porsche pulls in the driveway. He's just back from his first long business flight since Todd's death.

"How'd it go?" I ask.

"Okay. Fine. It was good to get back in the groove. Nothing too challenging. Heathrow is almost a home airport."

"I talked to Meg about Charlie. We're worried."

"No change?"

I shake my head. "What should we do?"

"Counseling? Maybe? I needed it once and it helped… A lot."

"I've been afraid to bring everything up again. But letting Charlie alone...? It doesn't seem to be working."

"Let's get him out by the pool. See if we can break through."

"I'll get him."

I clued in Molly, who brought out drinks, then left us alone. Hugh nods at me to start. Taking a deep breath, I begin, "Charlie? Is it getting any better?"

He looks at me as if I've struck him. "Better?"

Apparently, it takes him some time to process the question. Hugh and I wait.

"I'll be fine," he says eventually.

"Charlie?" Hugh asks. "Are you burying this? You're allowed to grieve."

"Grieve? Grieve?" he says, suddenly exploding in anger. "And just how do I do that, Hugh? I'll never see Todd again. Am I supposed to scream for a few days, then get over it?"

That does it. Standing up, I stomp over to Charlie's chair and grab his shirt. "I'm mad at the world, too, Charlie. You won't forget him. I won't forget him as long as I live. But I've lost you, too. I need you."

"I'm not here now," he says coldly, rising abruptly, wrenching away, and beginning to walk toward the house.

"Then get your ass back here," I say, and start pounding on his chest.

Over and over, I hit him. He doesn't defend himself. The blows get weaker as I tire, but I need him so much. Finally, as I stand in front of him, he slowly puts his arms around me.

"Okay, Juli," he says softly. "Okay. I'll come back."

Hugh joins us. "It's all I can do to move ahead, too. But I am. If we hadn't loved him so much, it wouldn't be this hard."

"It's almost impossible," Charlie says in a flat voice.

"One step forward. One step then another," Hugh says.

Charlie looks down at me. "Juli?"

"I'm here."

"Hugh?" he asks, almost as if he's surprised.

"We're both here," Hugh says. "You can count on that."

He sighs over and over, finally adding, "I guess that'll have to do."

* * *

It's been another two weeks, and Charlie is finally moving forward. I can see the effort it costs him, but I almost caught him smiling yesterday. It was a weak, pathetic smile but I'll take it. He finally formalized registration for winter classes on the homestretch for his MBA. He was way over the deadline, but they made an exception; everyone knew of our family tragedy.

Tomorrow I'm flying to the Bay area to talk to a recruiter for the professional women's soccer league. They approached me and I'm interested. It's not a done deal, but suddenly I want to get back into the mainstream.

Just as I start upstairs to pack, I hear the doorbell and listen as I always do to see if anyone else is getting it, then head into the front vestibule, almost colliding with Charlie who's also approaching. One of Todd's old hookups, someone I detest, is tapping her foot on our entryway.

"Hello, Juli."

"Hello, Laura."

"I… I need to talk to your father."

"Because...?" I ask, rather rudely.

"Todd and I had a business arrangement, and I want to see if the family will honor his commitment."

Charlie had halted just behind me and now steps into view.

"Will you share this arrangement with us?" he asks.

"Yes. Well… I wanted to start a business, and he offered to advance me $20,000 to get it off the ground."

"Was he sober?" I ask.

She gives me a dirty look. "Just let me speak to your father."

"I don't think so," Charlie says. "Not till we hear details."

"I want to start a boutique in Westfordshire Square. Todd said he'd help."

"And how would you like to verify that?" Charlie asks coldly.

I'm familiar with my brother's tone of voice. He's on a precarious edge.

"Is the family honorable or not?" she continues. "I'm making commitments."

"Paperwork?" Charlie mutters, his voice rising.

"It was verbal," she acknowledges, glaring at him.

Charlie suddenly steps in front of me, takes her by both shoulders, and manually spins her around facing the driveway. "If I ever see your ass near my home again," he growls, "I'll make you regret it. Now get off our property."

"Get your hands off me," she screams. "I bet I'll have bruises. You'll be hearing from my lawyer, or maybe the police."

Stomping over to her aging sedan, she flings herself in the

driver's seat, slams the door, then splatters an arc of gravel as she escapes.

Despite my having the same impulse to throw her off the property, Charlie surprised me. In any kind of normal situation, he would have handled this with brutal sarcasm. It makes me recognize how brittle Charlie remains.

"Charlie? Are you okay?"

He looks at me with a pained expression. "I just friggin' couldn't stand it. Trying to take advantage…"

I put my arms around him. "It'll be okay. We're going to make it through this."

He gives me the old wry smile I love. "Where'd you get this new self-control?"

I smile back. "You just didn't see it. I had my fist cocked to punch her. You just beat me to it."

"Damn straight," he says. "We could have taken her out and a dozen more like her."

We're both really smiling as we walk back in the house.

CHAPTER 6

MIRANDA

FEBRUARY FIRST, and I'm still basking in my recent acceptance at Georgetown Law School, I'm eagerly waiting for my big sister, Rena, to make it home. We'll be together for a long weekend before she returns to New York as an official understudy in a new off-Broadway play. She should be in rare form. Dad just called to make sure we'd all be home for dinner because he has a surprise for us girls.

Rena blows in the front door, already looking like a Broadway starlet—flaming red hair and a body that gets noticed. "So," she begins, "what's Dad's big surprise?"

"Haven't a clue. Mom swore she didn't know, either. I just talked to her on the phone from Aunt Bev's."

"When's she coming home?"

"She said she'll fly in Sunday afternoon before you go back to be sure not to miss you."

Rena swings one gorgeous leg over another after settling on the couch. Even at home she's continually positioning herself in some dramatic pose. She says she can't help it.

As Dad's car pulls in the driveway, Rena grins at me. "Guess we'll find out soon."

"Glad you're both here," he declares enthusiastically, bounding in the door. "Guess what?"

"What?" we both say together, humoring him.

"What would you think about going to a big-deal reception at the State Department tomorrow night? White tie, very prestigious event. Music, lavish everything, and every V.I.P. in town." He grins. "Plus, gorgeous, available men. You can practice your social skills."

"Why are you going?" I ask, knowing this is several pay grades above his mid-level position with the National Security Agency.

"Our section head is in Europe and my boss has the flu. Besides,

Alan thought you girls might like to go hob-nob."

"Oh, we would," Rena responds, then looks at me for confirmation.

"I'm in," I add enthusiastically.

"Great news," Rena adds before making a dramatic exit. "I can practice my seduction skills."

Dad and I laugh together. We know she's only partly kidding.

I settle myself on the couch with Dad as he puts his arm around my shoulders. I've always been in sync with him. We think alike and are much more down to earth than Rena who takes after my more melodramatic mother.

"You'll love this," he says. "The head of Georgetown Law might be there as well as influential politicians and international business leaders."

"What's the big occasion?"

"Haven't you heard? The Secretary of State just resigned, poor health, and John Douglas, my old boss, was just nominated to temporarily fill his seat. I'll know most of the people he'll be taking with him to State so I can introduce you around. I wasn't kidding when I said everyone will be there—even younger generation up-and-coming types."

* * *

Rena and I are 'well-turned out' as my grandmother would have said. Rena is wearing a body-hugging silverish dress that shows off her assets, which are considerable, and I have on a new black silk cocktail dress, which makes me feel sophisticated. Rena helped me with my hair and makeup, and I feel glamorous; for me anyway. Still, I plan on spending a lot of time across the room from Rena. In direct competition it's no contest.

We hand over the car to a white-coated attendant and join the assembly inside a somewhat intimidating State Department building. I've been to several Washington social events but never anything approaching this. I was in this complex once several years ago on an organized tour. The reception is being held in a formal diplomatic room, cleared of any furniture except for subtle seating in various clusters around the perimeter. An enormous rose-colored carpet provides an aura of intimacy, despite the massive interior which is adorned with numerous dark-red marble columns with Corinthian headers, surrounding the circumference of the area. A small orchestra commands one end of the room and a lavish bar area is staffed nearby.

Rena comes alive, almost like switching on a lightbulb. This is her element. She is immediately surrounded by a crowd of interested men who are happily entertained by stories of her budding acting career.

My eyes turn toward the entrance. Two men enter. Both are tall with penetrating blue eyes and the same thick hair, obviously close relatives. The older man has significant gray mixed in with the chestnut color. For the first time this evening, I'm personally intrigued by a young man. "Who are those men just arriving?" I ask Dad, who happens to be standing close by.

"You have good taste," Dad responds, smiling at my obvious interest. "That's Charles Curchin and his son, also a Charles." He pauses. "Charlie, I think. Wanna meet them?"

To answer, I start walking in their direction and hear Dad chuckling behind me.

As we approach, I hear a welcoming voice. "Tony Flynn, if I remember correctly. And who might this young lady be?"

Dad steps over to shake the older man's hand. "I'm surprised you remember, Charlie. It's been some time." He subtly urges me forward. "This is my younger daughter, Miranda. She's just been accepted to Georgetown Law."

"Well, well. Good for you, young lady. Tony here is obviously proud."

Despite everything, I'm surprised at the astute memory and easy graciousness of the older, obviously very influential man standing before me. It's a beneficial talent in important people. He puts his hand warmly on the shoulder of the younger man. "This handsome fellow is my son, Charlie 3. I'm Charlie 2. It helps me not to get confused."

I smile back. I bet almost nothing confuses Charlie 2. Turning my attention to his son, I find him smiling warmly at me.

"Very pleased to know you, Miranda. Congratulations." I smile helplessly up at him. When I don't say anything, he continues, "Georgetown is top tier. Do you have any idea what type of law you might be interested in?"

I shake my head. My usual talkative nature has deserted me. "Um... Uh, I'm not sure yet."

"That's best," he comments. "Leave yourself open to be inspired."

"Charlie is getting his master's degree from Wharton Business School. He's just finishing his last year."

Dad laughs. "And with another proud father."

"Just right," Charlie 2 agrees. "Just right." He continues, beaming proudly at his son, "Then he'll go overseas—to Eastern Europe, specifically." He turns back to me. "We develop real estate interests in that part of the world."

I nod automatically, trying to think of something compelling to comment. In addition, I'm closely observing Charlie 3. He's polite, pleasant, acting perfectly appropriate, and completely unengaged. Much to my amazement, I'm disappointed. This is a guy I'd like to know better. Much better. But I can't think of anything to draw him back into the conversation. Just as we're about to move on, Rena rushes over.

"Charlie Curchin," she says, obviously addressing the younger man. I watch as her eyes twinkle openly at him.

"Ah," Dad says. "My other daughter, Rena. She's a budding actress."

"Not budding as fast as I'd like, but I love the drama of that world. No pun intended."

Rena is obviously not having the same jitters I am. I groan to myself, expecting that Charlie will be immediately interested, and that will be that. But no. He seems exactly as he was with me, friendly and distant.

Fairly soon they move away. Charlie is immediately taken over by a variety of younger friends who enthusiastically engage his attention. His father goes his own separate way, joining his own friends and associates.

I move to another side of the room and am immediately approached by a man I know from the NSA.

"Miranda," he begins. "Do you remember me, Carl Thornburg? Your wonderful dad and I worked together on a project for the foreign service some years ago. You've changed."

I smile. "I think I was fourteen or fifteen then. Of course, I remember you. You haven't changed at all."

"I ran into your dad last week and he let me know you girls would probably be here. But you're the one who's changed. You're gorgeous! All grown up. And going to Georgetown Law, I hear. How wonderful. It's my alma mater." He looks around the room. "Come with me. Rubin Conklin is here. You may know he's the current Georgetown President. Let me introduce you. He'd love to know an incoming law plebe."

* * *

Rena and I have had different experiences. I've had many intriguing talks with fascinating influential people, while she made the rounds of the younger guys, danced a lot, laughed a lot, and has even found time to give me several enthusiastic thumbs up. I smile back at her with a thumbs-up.

Throughout the evening, I frequently searched out Charlie 3 from a small distance. He was always gracious, and constantly included in amiable conversations with friends. Still, although others were laughing and joking, he never seemed to completely relax. Many women tried to spark his attention, but no one seemed to provoke a connection. I suppose he has a serious relationship elsewhere. It would be amazing if he didn't. Still, there's something mysterious about him, something restrained. Once I had an opportunity to closely pay attention to him, standing adjacent to him while he was engaged in another conversation group. He stood quietly, interacted politely, and smiled warmly. But if momentarily unattended, it was if a veneer melted away, exposing another person altogether; a man who was uncomfortable in this setting tonight with these happy people—someone who really wished he were somewhere else—who was making a major effort to seem engaged.

I laugh to myself. I'm probably making this whole thing up. No denying I'm infatuated. I wish I'd been more together when I had my chance earlier. There are many questions I'd like to ask him.

If I was a little older, a little bolder, I'd go over and try to unlock the mystery.

But of course, I don't.

Some hours later, Dad and I have time to discuss the evening. Rena has already gone to her room, and we're slouched together on the sofa in our rec room.

"Well? He asks. "What did you think of all that?"

I smile. Dad generally doesn't ask trivial questions. "Okay. From my point of view, it was a window into a world I'm trying to enter, but also a caution. Everyone seemed to have an agenda— wanting something or selling something in a very pleasant way."

He laughs out loud. "You never disappoint me. That's what politics is. Generally transactional. What can I get from you and what do I have to give in return? Friendship? Loyalty? Persuasion? Not sabotaging my efforts... It goes on and on." He turns to me. "Is this a world you want to be a part of?"

"Maybe."

"You know what I mean. There are many wonderful things you will be able to do with a law degree. Just don't fall into something without a lot of thought. You have lots of time, just as Charlie Curchin suggested" He gives me a close look. "You liked him. Didn't you?"

"Yes! I *liked* him. 'Course he wasn't interested."

"I might be able to explain why."

"Go on..."

"It wasn't the place to go into all that, but several months ago his twin brother died in a plane crash. They were extraordinarily close, and I don't think he's over it. In fact, I was surprised to see either Curchin there tonight."

"I did notice something was off. I was going to ask you about it."

"I don't know either man well. But obviously they're quality guys. Charlie, the father and businessman, is known for his honesty and reliability."

"Where did you meet him?"

"I worked with him several years ago. They were developing commercial interests in Romania, and he requested some background checks on specific business owners. It was an informal request, but as I alluded to before, The Curchin Organization has always shared common information that overlaps with our governmental oversight. Scratch my back... And all that."

"He was friendly. Kind."

Dad gives me a look. "As was his son."

I sigh. I can't help it. "Yeah. Maybe I'll run in to him again when I can think of something to say."

"I noticed. Tongue tied. A first for you. Hmm?"

Yawning, I stand up. "Love you, Dad. Keep an eye open for future opportunities. Will ya?"

"For political advantage?"

I smile and head up the stairs, planning on searching the Internet.

Minutes later I'm in pajamas, curled up in bed with my phone. I punch in Charles Curchin. Up comes Charlie's dad, of course, same name. I try Wikipedia.

Pictures of the family and family bios follow: Charles Brower Curchin II, son of the founder and namesake of Curchin Limited. Anna, his wife. Charles Brower Curchin III, and two sisters. Finally, Todd Shipton Curchin, missing, presumed deceased, twin brother of Charlie.

I type in Todd Shipton Curchin and see Charlie. No, it's not Charlie, but a younger similar version. There are old family pictures of the entire family and several of the twins at various ages from toddlerhood up through college years. It's just over five months since Todd disappeared in a flight over Canada. He was piloting a private jet before it crashed in the Canadian Rockies. The plane was found, but no body.

What follows is a description of the plane fragments, located after an exhaustive search, just before heavy winter snows blanketed the mountains. Charlie in a search helicopter followed leads and hunches for weeks, finally locating the crash site near an obscure glacier.

I lie quietly, thinking about the sadness I observed in Charlie. I can't imagine searching for days on end for a beloved brother through thousands of square miles of wilderness.

As I settle into sleep, I wonder if I'll ever encounter Charlie Curchin again, realizing I have one more thing I can't talk to him about.

ASH

As I go through the security process, I smile. I usually don't give it a thought anymore, but the first few months I was in a cold sweat, half expecting that someone in mirror shades would throw me against the building with my face slammed against the wall. I'd be handcuffed behind my back, thrown into a windowless van, and driven God-knows-where to no-man's-land to disappear— Permanently.

CHAPTER 7

CHARLIE

IT'S BEEN TEN MONTHS since the plane went down. The investigative team finally got to the crash site as the snow melted enough to expose the wreckage. The professionals have been going over the site bit by bit. It hasn't been pleasant, bringing it all up again, and some of the results are unsettling.

Two major findings. There was a small fire, possibly an explosion, inside the back of the plane, prior to the crash, severing the horizontal stabilizer cables. Todd wouldn't have been able to fly the plane. They're doing more tests to determine whether it was it an electrical fire, a secondary explosion, or even an incendiary device carried on the plane. After all this time, and the extreme weather over the winter, physical residue is minimal.

The other odd thing was there were no black boxes found, even after an extensive search of an enlarged area around the crash site. They're completely non-destructible. It was heartbreaking not to have some clues to explain all this. Maybe we'll never know more than we know now. In the back of our minds is the possibility that it wasn't an accident. Without more proof, it seems meaningless to rehash that, but it grinds on me. Dad and I talk about it but haven't wanted to speculate again with Mom and the girls. The investigation's been hard enough on everyone. Unless something more specific turns up, we'll keep it between ourselves.

I finished my MBA on schedule and am currently spending the summer out West with my old Hotshot team. It's my first fire season since Todd's death and for the first few weeks, memories almost overpowered me. Walt and most of the crew from last season seemed to struggle about whether to bring it up or avoid painful topics. There were uncomfortable silences. Finally, though, I was pressured to talk about it all. I'd been having trouble sleeping, even relating to the crew, but finally, Walt cornered me.

"Enough, Spoons," he said. "We're all tired of tiptoeing around. You might as well tell us how you found the plane and how you felt..." He paused. "How you're dealing with it now."

And so I did. At that evening's campfire, I put myself through the whole thing again. The horror of not knowing during the search, the agony of finding the wreckage, and my struggles to find happiness in ordinary life with the giant hole left in my heart.

Of course, it helped. I began to feel like one of the team again. Old friends relaxed and shared my grief. Unfortunately, one new team member awakened other feelings, providing the current disaster I'm trying to live down.

As a welcome reprieve, I've taken a few days off from firefighting to fly home. Dad has arranged an afternoon planning council at our alternative corporate headquarters, the large dining room table off the kitchen. We're a privately owned company and can forgo formalities. With the family plus a small board of directors and administrative heads hurriedly assembled, we're meeting today off the public radar. Before the business meeting commences, I know Dad intends to share additional information we've learned about Todd's crash, officially laying it to rest with our closest associates.

A large mug of coffee in hand, he calls the meeting to order.

"As you all know," he begins, "Todd flew commercial from the northern area of Georgia near the Russian border, with a scheduled stopover in Istanbul, then on to London. He hadn't been on a business trip, officially or unofficially. He was hiking with friends." He pauses for a sip of coffee and a deep breath.

"From London he piloted our plane, uneventfully as far as we know, to a final refueling stop in Saskatoon, Alberta. It gave me some peace of mind when we verified that he did top off tanks with jet fuel rather than try to make Missoula, landing on fumes." He clears his throat. "It would have been harder to live with—that he simply ran out of gas."

I silently agree. Todd had several near misses for just that stunt. Several people nod.

"So," he says, taking another deep breath, "on to other things. We've been broadening our interests in the Middle East for over six years. But I admit I'm unsettled."

He takes a few seconds to look at each person around the table. "I'm considering extricating business interests from that part of the region—the latest expansion. It seems increasingly obvious that no one on the planet can predict what will happen over there or can manage it. Therefore, I'm proposing we sell those positions at a significant loss to a government subsidiary. Let them take the risks."

Everyone is silent for a few minutes thinking. I know Mike Petrov will be disappointed, having put a lot of time and effort into developing those potential corporate partnerships and connections.

"Charlie, I understand," Mike says. "I believe there are huge profits to be made if... And that's the obvious question... If the whole region doesn't blow up. The thing that keeps me up nights is that we'll get an intricate corporate structure in place, more monies invested, when hostile political leadership will emerge, cut off negotiations, and nationalize our business. Obviously, it's your call. There are repercussions either way we go."

"Tina?" asks Dad.

My older sister clicks on her computer and graphs appear on a big screen. "I put together the data you requested. On graph one, the red line shows the expenditures we've put into the Middle East area in the last three years and projected future expenses. The blue line is projected revenue. The financial outlay has been relatively small but will grow exponentially over the next two years. It will take approximately two additional years to start turning a profit. This is a good time to make this decision, before expenditures start to accelerate."

"Juli?"

"Dad, I don't know enough to have a professional opinion except to say I'm nervous about everything over there. I watch the news like everyone else. I have Muslim friends who are terrified that relatives will be threatened or trapped over there. I say, get out."

Dad smiles at Juli, "I need gut impressions, and you usually have well-thought-out gut impressions."

"Anna?"

"I vote with Juli. There was a disturbing association with Todd's accident that I can't put my finger on. We've talked it to death, but let's move our focus to other regions."

Dad turns to me. "Charlie 3? This is your area."

I smile. I'm always Charlie 3 in formal meetings. "I think we should restructure so that our interests lie completely west and south of the Black Sea. Can you pull up a map of the region, Tina?"

She does.

"I'm fine with the Balkans, but anywhere east or north of there is experiencing increased unrest. Ukraine is already a military disaster. Besides, Western Europe and Russia are using it as a bargaining chip for political maneuvering. Turkey, obviously, we'll need to work with, but I don't think we need additional partnerships there. And I want to add that Mike has done a magnificent job in those areas I recommended. We can build on the relationships he's formed. Mike, I'll work with you on that anytime you're ready."

Dad turns to the two most valued vice-presidents, Gloria Whitworth, who is responsible for researching economic and political trends, and Tom Campbell, head of the legal division. "Tom? Gloria? I know you got my memo. Any new thoughts?"

"You know what I think, Charlie," Gloria adds. "You've been reading my assessments. It's a hornets' nest. I like to sleep nights, too."

Tom shows the thumbs down sign, a man of few words, even though he heads the entire legal team.

"I guess no one is galloping in to rescue my plan," Dad says. "Alright, this whole operation was my idea. I take full responsibility. Let's pull the plug. Mike, I've wanted you further northwest as Charlie 3 said. Get back to me in a few weeks with an outline and a tentative timeline."

"And Mike," I add, "my fire season will wrap in eight weeks

or so. I've finished my degree so I'm flexible. How about setting up a tour of the remaining region around October first? We'll take Gloria along for comic relief and meet with all our contacts. Let them know, face to face, what our plans are. I don't want them to have to guess, worrying that we're pulling their carpet out, too."

"Damn it, Charlie 3," Gloria says. "You know Hugh provides the comic relief. I'll be along for sophistication and seduction if needed."

We all laugh because Gloria wears jeans most of the time, has a husband and two kids, and would rather hike with a backpack than seduce anyone. She has multiple, invaluable functions. Humor is only one of them.

* * *

Everyone's gone except family. Juli left a while back on a date. The rest of us are relaxing, feet up, and finishing the last dregs of Dad's post-meeting martinis. I smile at him. "Don't look so glum. No one expects you to be invincible. If we never stretched out, we'd never progress. Besides, I thought it was a great idea, too."

"Charlie, you were nineteen when I thought this up. But, okay, this must be your fault." He smiles affectionately back at me. "And thank for taking the time. It's the height of your fire season."

"Sure. Hugh's flying me back early tomorrow."

Mom stands up to give me a hug before retiring. "I'm glad Juli could make it home for this. She said to tell you she'd be back early. She's out tormenting poor Doug."

I smile. Doug's an old flame but spending time with me was the major reason she came home.

* * *

Several hours later, Juli and I are sitting on the side of our lighted pool in the darkness, sipping gin and tonics, and dangling our feet in the brilliant, aqua-blue water. It's hot in Philadelphia in August.

"I'm glad Dad brought it all to a head," I say. "The world economy is teetering on the brink and we're still in relatively good shape.

Let's stop burning through our cash and hunker down until things stabilize. I don't see a clear path ahead. That's unusual for me."

"You're going to be good at this, Charlie. You're decisive and supportive of the team at the same time."

We silently watch the pool cleaner robot, circling endlessly.

"How's it working out with Doug?" I finally ask. "Type one or type two? Hot or brilliant?"

"One," she grimaces. "I run all over him. He's charming, but boring as hell."

"Jules?" I ask. "Why not try your intellectual equal for a change?"

"It's hard to get that right. The smart ones want me to grease a slide into the family business. I hate that and call them on it. They get mad and... You know. I get tired of the battle."

I sigh, our old dilemma.

"What about you?" she asks

"Right now, I just want to get back to firefighting."

"And western bar country. How's the redneck disguise holding up?"

I groan.

"What happened?"

"I thought I had a real thing going. Gretchen Summers, nice girl, smart, one of the Hotshot recruits. We'd been dating most of the early summer. I decided to start enlightening her... About our assets."

"How'd she handle it?"

"Turned out she'd known all along I wasn't just another guy earning graduate school tuition."

"So...?"

"I asked her about her plans. She said she was hoping I'd encourage her to move back east to be near me."

"Okay. That's reasonable."

"Then I asked her what she thought I did back here, and she got mad. Said I was playing a game with her—setting her up to lie. She said she'd known almost from the start I was part of a huge corporation, a family business, and that I'd boogie on back there, put on my pinstripes, and transform myself."

"How did she find out?"

"She said she asked people on the crew. Said she wanted to know something about me before she got more seriously involved. Then she asked me if I'd heard of the Internet."

"Damnit."

"Yeah, well… I told her she should have asked me directly and she got upset. She said I should have leveled with her early on." I pause. "And then it got really nasty." Glancing over I see her grimace.

"I told her I felt like I was being managed. 'Fine,' she threw at me. 'When you get my part scripted, let me know'."

Juli doesn't comment so I continue. "It went downhill from there. Now we're hardly speaking." Grimly, I move my feet in endless circles in the aqua water.

"Charlie," Juli finally asks, "how do you know Gretchen wasn't one of the special ones? Maybe she just didn't know how to let you know that she knew. You're overly sensitive about all that. How can any girl win?"

"I ended up seducing her back and milking the relationship for sex, all the while wondering if I wasn't the real problem. I really liked that girl, but I didn't trust anything she said. It wasn't working and I finally dumped her. Now she'll hardly look at me. She accused me in front of the crew of being a rich asshole. Maybe I am."

"No. You're stuck. Just like me." She gives me a hug. "I'm sorry."

"I don't like being a jerk, and I really don't like the life of a monk."

"See. I told you last fall this was going to be a problem. From my perspective, you never gave her a chance. One small lapse of judgment and you're out of there. You always react like that. What if the love of your life makes a mistake on a bigger scale? Are you going to close up and run? You're going to have to trust someone someday."

I keep twirling my feet in the blue water. "Have you called Meg back?" I finally ask her. "She called yesterday."

"Now, there, Charlie. She's special. Even you can't doubt she loved Todd."

I nod. "Even if he didn't reciprocate. It's been ten months and she can barely talk about him."

"She's in New York, for God's sake. We talk often. After your fire season is over, we owe it to all of us to keep up the connection. Let's fly down there."

Suddenly I feel deeply lonely.

"I've never felt anything like she felt about Todd," Juli continues. "I'm beginning to think it's not in me."

"It's in you. You're the most passionate person I know. It'll probably blow you out of the water when you least expect it."

She gives me a sisterly loving look. "Thanks. I mean it."

"You're welcome, kid."

She gives me a kiss on the cheek, stands, and heads back into the house.

I'm quiet, thinking for a long time. What if Gretchen cared about me the same way Meg cared about Todd? What if I threw it away? That's past repairing now. I sigh regretfully. Thoughts of Todd and what I've lost painfully intrude. It comes to me that I can't bear any more loss. I can't risk that.

And looking back, I realize I've never allowed anyone inside my wall. Not really. Not yet.

ASH

Glancing over my shoulder, I laugh at myself. No one notices or cares if a nondescript man with a lousy haircut, dressed in sweats and running shoes, stops at a concrete bench in the local park. It's been a month since I last sat on this bench. The slot beneath the concrete seat is almost impossible to find—small and overlaid with some sort of moss that has become part of the deteriorating cement. I feel underneath the seat and find the slit, then pull out the plastic insert with the tiny note inside. On it is written one word. "No." Someday the word will be "Yes," and I'll know my world is about to change. I sigh with mixed relief and disappointment.

CHAPTER 8

MIRANDA

MY LAST CLASS was over at noon, and I'm free and enroute in my beater Honda, returning to our family home in Silver Spring, Maryland. I have tomorrow and the next week off and am looking forward to a relaxing family spring break. Then it's back to classes for the stressful final push to complete my first year at Georgetown. Rena may be able to make it down, too, for a shorter visit. Dad is encouraging us both to meet a Blackfeet Native American who he'll be mentoring in computer security at the NSA where he works.

He's paying a debt to a soldier who saved his life before I was born. I've heard the story many times. When Dad was a naive kid, just out of college, twenty-odd years ago, he was sent with his army unit to Kuwait, unfortunately just days before Saddam Hussein invaded the country. He would have died there except for a fellow officer who was killed protecting him. In the intervening years, he's become close to the two sons of that man. This computer guy, Lew Black River, is a good friend of those sons. It's convoluted, but I understand it helps Dad feel like he's giving something back to the man who died.

Supposedly Lew, who grew up on the Blackfeet reservation in Montana, is an untrained genius. Dad hasn't met him in person and can hardly wait.

Should be interesting to say the least. Dad has let us know that the guy is thirty and has hardly ever been out of Northern Montana. He may be relatively unsophisticated was the way Dad put it. He explained that this young man could use a little friendship and encouragement in this high-pressure world. At least my clothes shouldn't intimidate him. I'm still dressed in student casual and, with my long brown hair and dark hazel eyes, could probably hide out on his reservation and not be noticed.

Rena, on the other hand, will probably scare him to death. She's a seasoned New York City sophisticate now, and the embodiment of gorgeous. I'm grinning to myself as I pull in the driveway, picturing a warrior-chief, sitting on a wild mustang. Well, we'll see.

Grabbing my backpack, I hurry in through the back entry, and head toward the voices in the living room. A very tall man stands up formally as I enter the room. No wild horses. I'm the one under-dressed. He's wearing expensive casual clothes, khakis, with a navy-blue cotton shirt, and has a styled haircut that shows off his midnight black hair. He's also good looking with a friendly smile as he holds out his hand. This guy is extraordinary!

"Hello," he says. "I'm Llewellyn Black River. Please call me Lew."

"I'm Miranda," I answer, smiling back.

"This is my younger daughter," Dad says. "Miranda, we were waiting to see if you wanted to take in the sights of the capitol with us. Lew will tour the NSA tomorrow, but I thought this afternoon we'd be tourists and I'll take him out for a nice dinner."

"I'll need a few minutes to change," I say. "Is Mom still having a girl's weekend?"

"She'll be back Saturday night after exhausting herself shopping. Rena will be home tomorrow on the five o'clock train."

Good. I'll have him all to myself for a day before Rena arrives. Then I smile at myself. I met this guy five minutes ago, and I'm already feeling possessive. I run up the stairs to change into a simple, maroon wrap dress and flats, then take a little extra time with my make-up. I hope that Mom won't have had a lot to drink when she meets Lew. She can occasionally get loud and laugh too much. Surprisingly, I want him to think well of my family.

* * *

We've spent a lovely afternoon touring every familiar monument and landmark, and Lew is so excited he's made it fun for us all. He's enthusiastically observant, not making any effort to appear cool, while making small self-depreciating comments about himself and the smaller world he came from. It has the opposite effect. I plain like this guy.

"Look at that," he says. "All those pink trees. It's a fantasy world."

"It's the National Cherry Blossom Festival," I explain. "I see it every year and it always thrills me."

"Can we stop?" he asks. "All those pink petals are falling in the wind. It's snowing pink. I want to walk in it."

Me, too.

We pile out of the car and wander around in the pink world. Lew grins like a six-year-old, holding his hands out to catch petals. So do I.

He's been entertaining Dad and me with stories about Montana and life on the reservation, including humorous stories about when he was a kid, then suddenly he gets serious.

"I'm feeling like ghosts from my past are here," he says.

Dad and I look at him quizzically.

"Yeah," he says. "Did you know our last tribal chief died right here?"

"In DC?" I ask.

"He came back with a delegation to try to retain tribal lands in 1903. While he was here, he got sick and died of pneumonia. I suddenly feel his presence."

I feel goosebumps. "One of our chiefs died of pneumonia, here, too. President William Henry Harrison died in 1841 after only a month in office."

Lew looks at me. "Not so different after all," he says.

"No. Not so different," I say, smiling up at him. "Give me more details about Montana."

"The thing that's so different," he begins. "The thing that will take some getting used to here, is the humid air. Reservation air is fresh and dry with the wind constantly blowing. It's so unspoiled. So... boundless. I don't mean to insult you, but I miss the austerity. I'm not expressing it very well."

"No," I say. "I know exactly what you mean." We smile at each other again.

As we drive around the capitol, Dad provides Lew with historical perspective and global perspective. I'm surprised what he already knows, despite what he admits was a limited education. He's interested in everything, integrating information like the human computer he seems to be.

Meanwhile, I remember what Lew told me about his home. His descriptions make it seem like a foreign country to a city girl like me. Lew's pride in the dramatic beauty of the mountains and the Northern Plains is captivating. Our family vacations have been to cities, crowded tourist areas or to visit relatives. I've never spent time in the wild areas of the United States. The wide-open spaces begin to intrigue me.

Dad's splurging by treating us to an upscale Georgetown restaurant, Giorgio's, which specializes in rack of lamb, steaks, and good wines. I can tell Lew is making a constant effort to blend in, but Dad and I have encouraged him so much he's beginning to relax. The wine list is eight pages long, bound in thick maroon leather, and is over the top, even for me. We all laugh about it, asking the waiter for recommendations.

After a lingering two-hour dinner with a variety of courses, Lew and I top it off with Irish coffees. I don't get much time alone with Dad and am enjoying that, too. We have the same sense of humor and kid around a lot. Lew fits in like we've known him for years. Dad finally drives us back home, telling Lew he'll see him tomorrow morning for the grand tour at the NSA.

"You must be exhausted," I say. "You've had a very long day."

"I know your father must have told you I've hardly been anywhere outside of Montana. I'm reasonably sure I'll make a complete fool of myself tomorrow. Definitely rezzed-out."

"Rezzed out?"

"You know—unworldly. Unsophisticated."

"You're no fool," I smile. "That's obvious. You're already awesome."

He silently smiles back.

"Would you like something to drink? Dad's got a decent bar."

"Maybe a beer?"

We decide to change back into jeans first, regrouping in the kitchen. Despite myself I'm charmed. I put on some soft music, and we settle on our old couch in our rec room with a fire in the fireplace.

"Tell me more about your home, Lew."

"To me it's the most beautiful place imaginable. Glacier National Park, 'The Park' as we call it, was built up of hundreds of millions of years of sedimentary rock, stacked up, layer upon layer, in stripes of gold, red, green and gray. Glaciers formed the almost vertical walls as they gouged out valleys."

I close my eyes to imagine the picture he's painting.

He goes on, "Ice and compressed snow moved down from the highest elevations, forming frozen conveyor belts. As they melt, they make aqua lakes that form the headwaters of our rivers."

"Have you always lived there?"

"My ancestors lived on the plains and in the park since our tribal history began. We had to give away the park, though."

"Why?"

"We were starving. The buffalo were killed off. One winter over six hundred of my people died. Those remaining alive traded the park to the government for food to survive."

I'm horrified and gasp.

He looks at me with a funny expression. "You never heard about that?"

"I never realized... I mean... I guess I should have known something about that."

"I didn't mean to upset you. Where I come from, everyone knows the history."

"You're a born storyteller. I'm caught up in it all. I want to see it. It sounds so rough and remote."

"As beautiful as the park is, I love the reservation land even more, especially when there's a big storm coming in. In the late fall and winter the wind roars across the high plateau."

"Is it dangerous?"

"It can be. It's still a very isolated area. Curtains of snow blowing horizontally across the northern plains in the winter is as wild a thing as you will ever see."

He looks like he's considering a private joke. "What are you thinking?" I ask.

"Just that I usually don't talk this much. I hardly recognize myself."

"Keep talking. You paint vivid pictures. It's hard to believe it's the same country I live in."

"You're a good listener. You bring out a new side of me." He smiles to himself. "I have a lot of talkative friends. I rarely get a turn."

"You said you have many great friends."

"In a wild country, you need friends to depend on. Yes, I'm a very fortunate man."

"Your friends are the lucky ones."

He gives me a surprised look. "That's a very nice thing to say."

I smile at him. "It's pretty obvious, Lew." I hesitate. "Don't misunderstand me, but you're not part of this world."

He gives me a close questioning look.

"I'm not explaining what I mean. I'm sorry. I mean, um … That I can't quite imagine you pumping gas down near Victoria Circle and buying groceries at the co-op."

"Actually, I do both. I bought groceries five days ago and filled my truck up with gas just before I left."

I realize I'm blushing. "I hope you don't think I'm…"

He grins. "No. I'm kidding. I don't quite understand where I fit in either. Someday I'll tell you about Lizzie. She took me to buy new clothes so I wouldn't stand out like a poor Indian. And encouraged me to get a good haircut. "He pauses. "I'm not sophisticated, Miranda. But I'm a good person. I'm so fortunate to have this opportunity to learn."

"Who is Lizzie? Is she your girl?"

"No. No. She met my friend, Win, last winter and they fell madly in love. She came out from the civilized East." He laughs. "Cleveland, as a matter of fact, to be with him. I'm lucky to know her. She's become my good friend. And as for me... Well. No woman now."

We're quiet together for some time, watching the fire.

Lew finally says, "This huge city—everything. You, even. I'm overwhelmed."

"You've got a big day tomorrow, Lew. I'm excited for you. Just remember, they're the lucky ones." I slide over near him and put my hand on his shoulder. He turns his head toward me, and I kiss him gently on his lips. He gives me a surprised smile.

"What?" I ask.

"I like it here in civilization. I don't feel like such a stranger after all."

"Good," I smile back. "That was the point."

"Could I try that one more time? Just to be sure?"

I turn around so I'm cradled in his arms and turn my head up to him. He lowers his lips to mine, kisses me, then moves my hair to the side with his fingers, and covers my lips again with his.

I reach up and gently pull him to me, closing my eyes. When I open them, he's looking down at me. "You're beautiful," he says, smiling gently.

"So are you," I answer. This guy's simple expressions move me. But I see his eyes are drooping, his smile melting away, as his own eyes close.

"You're exhausted," I say, gently pulling away. "Let's curl up on the couch just for a little while more and watch the fire."

We slouch comfortably together, but in several minutes, I look over at him. He's fast asleep. I gently pick up one large hand and turn it over to see his palm. It's callused. I can see him doing hard work or riding horses out in that fresh air he loves so much. I softly replace his hand and smile at his boyish face, relaxed in sleep. I place a small blanket over him and head up the stairs.

When I checked on Lew an hour or so later, he'd gone to his room. It's late, after midnight, and I'm having trouble falling asleep. I have two overlapping thoughts. One, I want to know this guy a lot better. And two, that damn Rena is coming home tomorrow, and I sure hope she doesn't like him.

* * *

Dad and Lew have already left by the time I get up, so I spend a nice day, padding around in my socks, raiding my parents' refrigerator, and doing a little homework. I'm really looking forward to seeing Lew and hearing about his day. I catch myself thinking about him often.

Finally, about six, I hear Dad's car in the driveway. I hear laughter and see Rena running up the front steps. She looks knockout fantastic, and has her arm locked in Lew's.

"Shit," I say under my breath.

I meet Rena in the kitchen. "So, what's your impression of this guy?" I ask.

"Totally yummy," she says. "My God. I'd love to play games with him. You know, cowgirls and Indians. That's one hot guy."

"Seriously," I say. "Did you like him?"

"He's not very worldly, but it might be fun to... Orient him. Yes, seriously, he's a very nice guy and different, and adorable. You're not interested, are you?"

"Would you hold off if I was?"

She laughs. "Probably not unless you were really interested. You only just met him, right?"

I sigh. "Yes, I only just met him. Besides, I blend into the woodwork when you're around. I've got no dibs..." As I say that, I'm kicking myself.

It only gets worse. By half-way through dinner, I know I've lost this battle. She's as interested as I was yesterday, and Lew is defenseless. Rena keeps touching his arm and he grins back like a deer in headlights. He's been talking excitedly about meeting all the bigwigs at the NSA, revealing that he felt more or less comfortable with them. I'm quietly proud of him. Dad says he more than held his own with the intellectuals there; had ideas that surprised everyone he talked to. He was encouraged to target coming to work there. Enthusiastically encouraged.

By nine this evening, Lew begged off and collapsed upstairs.

He's one worn-out Blackfeet. I can only imagine the contrast with his life before. He told me he runs a small computer parts store and for excitement tries to keep several nephews out of trouble.

Rena has invited Lew up for a visit to the Big Apple and he's accepted. They're taking the train up tomorrow and he'll stay overnight. I'm surprised how sad I feel, like I lost a close friend. I find Dad's eyes on me. I look back at him and wince. Dad always knows what I'm thinking. We both shake our heads at each other.

* * *

Dad and I are sitting in the rec room alone, watching an old Alfred Hitchcock movie, Rear Window, the following evening. Mom got back mid-afternoon and has gotten a play by play of all the romantic intrigue. She can hardly wait to meet Lew, especially since Dad told her about our sisterly rivalry. I patiently sat through Mom's shopping triumphs from her girls' weekend in Atlantic City, and the latest family gossip, before she headed upstairs with armloads of packages.

Since then, I've pretended to watch the movie, mostly staring off into space, when Dad interrupts my thoughts.

"Why so distant, Miranda?" Dad asks.

"To tell you the truth, I had a strong connection with Lew."

"I was deeply surprised by him," Dad admits. "I've talked to him on the phone, of course, but he has an amazing intellect." He turns to study me. "You really like him, don't you?"

I sigh. "Part of it is I've always felt restless in the East Coast super-civilization culture. I'm wondering what it would be like to live in the West."

"You've got two more years to go for that law degree. Then you could go anywhere. If I were you, I'd jump at the chance. If you don't, you'll always regret it. Unless you meet the love of your life in the meantime, of course, then you'd have to negotiate."

I've gotten quiet again. I'm trying to decide if I want to go back to school early since I've lost. The movie is winding down, and when I look up, Dad is staring seriously at me again.

I glower angrily at the floor. "I'm sick of Rena grabbing anything she wants."

Silence.

"I know. I know. She wasn't aware I was interested. I hardly did myself." I'm still scowling.

He moves to sit next to me on the couch, putting his arm around me. "Let me tell you what I know about Lew. Paul told me that he's been more or less in love, very one sided, with the younger sister of a friend since they were children." He waits until I look up at him. "He has almost no experience with the wiles of women. He's a tree waiting to crash. But he's going to learn fast. Women are going to fall all over him, so be patient. Be his friend. He really is going to need one in this voracious town. Bide your time, my darling daughter."

I take a minute to fully take in what he's saying. Finally, "I'm in love with you, anyway."

"I know, sweetie."

CHAPTER 9

CHARLIE

I THROW MY PULASKI, an axe handle with an axe head mounted across from a small shovel, behind my shoulders and stretch until I feel the joints pop. It feels great. I feel great. I'm a pretty happy guy. The forest floor of north central Montana smells of old fir and spruce needles, baking in the hot sun. Although I'm an administrator by job title, I keep in shape with my crews as often as I want. And I want out of my cage often.

Dad has officially released me from corporate responsibilities until October first, except for occasional board meetings. That means I'll have three and a half months of relative freedom to live an almost anonymous life. Even with my limited time allotment, I've ascended to a position of some authority in the wildland firefighting world. I work under the umbrella of NIFC (nif-cee), the National Interagency Fire Center, also simply referred to as Boise, its physical location. The organization acts to coordinate and disperse firefighting resources for the entire country.

The United States is a giant chessboard on which we shuffle and coordinate men, material, aircraft, and other resources, depending on national fire flare-ups and anticipated problems. It used to be limited to wildfire management, but now it's expanded to encompass any national emergency event, including earthquakes, hurricanes, tornados, and floods. I could joyfully work at this full time but am currently juggling both of my parallel careers.

Last year, I precipitously fell in love with Lizzie, a girl I could have married—a personal catastrophe. Trouble was that she was in love with another guy. It was the worst thing that ever happened to me, except for losing my brother. I've been forced to admit I put them into the same universe of pain. But it's been long enough that I'm beginning to look around. I want to love a good woman and have her love me back. It seems so simple… And so elusive.

Today, though, I'm enjoying my freedom. I worked out during the off-season and am capable of hiking to mountain tops and back in good time, carrying heavy gear. I've currently joined one of our Hotshots teams, headed by my old friend, Jack Lambert, the manager of the Louis and Clark Hotshots. He knows I like to be familiar with as many of the crewmembers as possible. You never know when a personal connection will make a difference in an emergency.

I sat Jack down after my relationship disintegrated with Lizzie, pleaded with him to allow me to remain an ordinary guy—not a target, to please keep my background a secret. Wealth can make you paranoid. Few understand, but until you've walked in my shoes… Anyway, he agreed. Now I'm just Charlie from NIFC, nice to know you—the way I like it. But it's a hard secret to keep, especially with the Internet.

Not everyone is on site yet. It will be two more weeks before the stragglers check in, many still fulfilling winter obligations. We've just finished another eight-mile training hike in the mountains with fifty-pound packs. Everyone kept up, even enjoyed it. There are fourteen of us, sitting together on aluminum folding chairs in the ready room, as Jack introduces me. It's the usual mix of eleven guys and three women. Two of the ladies I know from last year, Hannah One and Hannah Two, as I refer to them for the obvious reason. Plus, there's a recruit who has just joined us, an athletic girl who looks like she could outrun me. I always liked the type.

After the briefing, I walk up and introduce myself. "Hello. I'm Charlie Curchin. I understand you're from the Chicago area. Attended Loyola, if I remember right."

"Yes. I'm Kay. Kay Nordland."

"So… How did you end up here?"

"You want the long or short version?"

I size her up. She's got short black hair and the greenest eyes I've ever seen. I quickly glance at the whole package. "The long one. Over beers?"

She smiles back. "Suits me."

* * *

We've settled into a booth at the Hungry Bear Tavern in downtown Great Falls with the traditional western décor: branding irons, old saddles, a collection of spurs. There's a frayed basket of unshelled peanuts on each table with shells littering the floor. Kay gives me a warm smile. I'm being pursued; friendly girl, very friendly, and smart and nice, and it's early in the fire season. I have a reputation for dating a different girl each year—a summer romance if you will—complete with ash, grime, danger, and hot showers afterwards. It's a lethal combination. And I'm willing to settle for that this year, too. But not many know that I'm looking for a lot more.

"So, tell me your story," I say after a swig of my beer.

"I'll show you mine, if you show me yours," she says, but blushes and I find myself grinning and intrigued.

"I'm sorry," she says. "I have a weird sense of humor. But that's only fair."

"Sure," I say. "You go first."

"Okay. I'm from Oak Lawn and have three older brothers. That's probably why I'm so tough. All the rest of my family are happily setting up families and finding houses there, driving into Chicago once or twice a year for some big event. I wanted something more."

"This is nice country," I say. "Northern Montana. I'm hooked permanently. I'd like to buy some land out here eventually. Maybe have a cattle ranch."

"You too? I'd like to settle out here and raise cattle."

"You're kidding."

"Nope. I've got one more year of college then I'm moving. Besides, I like cows."

"Why did you decide to try the Hotshots?"

"It was the most exciting thing I could imagine. I knew I could do it. I can outrace the entire South Side. Okay, your turn."

The old problem. No way I'm going to tell her the whole truth. I settle into telling part-of-the-truth mode. "Okay. I'm originally from Philadelphia. I have a degree in business, but I love fighting fires. It's like your cow thing. I set my mind on going for it. Now I love it. It's what I want to do. For now, anyway."

"Family?"

"Two sisters and Mom and Dad. We're close."

"Do they live in Philly?"

"Yeah. Nice old city."

She allows me to drift away from my personal story. We have more beers, then a few more. I'm getting loose and relaxed. We decide to get some dinner. She offers to share the bill. I automatically insist on paying, then immediately regret playing the rich guy role.

"Trying to impress me?" She smiles. "Nice welcome, though."

I laugh it off. I'm having a very good time. Kay's smart and funny and has started leaning against me. Not pushy—just the right amount of very interested. I suggest we have a real drink back at my room.

We decide to try pay-per-view back in my motel room. I'm pretty sure where this is going and I'm happy about that. We got an expensive bottle. I paid. Surprisingly, she didn't comment this time. Even more surprising, I decide I like this girl. I haven't been interested in any serious way since Lizzie and I ache to find a girl who I could trust to gradually get to know me. I'm in control of my head tonight, simply hopeful this might turn into something. That would be unexpectedly nice.

We watched a good thriller and are turning to other things. I'm having a great time. I've been laughing so much my stomach hurts. I'm a little drunk. She, even a little more so. The expensive bottle is gone, money well spent. We're playing strip poker without the poker. We're calling it "pokerless." It takes some creativity, or what passes for that when you're inebriated, but it's going well. I'm usually not in situations like this, but I'm winning. She keeps saying she's winning, and we laugh some more.

Eventually, I sober up a little, rolling her over on her back, my legs on either side of her, and look down at her. We haven't really gotten to it yet, but we're close. One more lost hand of pokerless...

"Kay," I ask. "Do you like me?"

Her silly look changes. "Yeah, Charlie. I really do."

"You sound surprised?"

"Well, you're handsome as all get out, and not an asshole."

"Yeah, well... And why might I be an asshole?"

"Gorgeous guys are usually jerks."

"Have you played pokerless with many?"

"Nope," she giggles. "You're the absolutely first."

"Hmm?" I murmur, nibbling on her ear. "Who else is usually an asshole?"

"Oh, for heaven's sake, Charlie. Rich guys are usually assholes."

I feel a small chill and look down at her. "Is that why you were surprised you liked me?"

"I... Well, I... Damn it, Charlie. Sort of." I can tell she's still drunk.

"Just how rich did you think I am?"

I can tell she's getting annoyed. "You're a billionaire, Charlie. In case you didn't know."

I'm having less fun now. I roll my leg off her.

"Tell me. I want to know. Why did you come up here tonight?"

"I...?"

"I'm not upset. Please tell me."

"You're good looking and smart, and I thought I'd like to see what developed. Honestly. Why such a big deal?"

"And you knew I was rich?"

"Everyone on the planet knows that."

* * *

I'm trying to give her the benefit of the doubt. I know my problem. We didn't finish our game last night. I couldn't get back in the correct mood. But I might give it another try. She's hot and she's probably right. Probably the whole planet knows. I've got to cut people a little slack. And she seemed very disappointed.

I'm about to walk out to the shed to check on some chainsaws delivered this afternoon when I hear Hannah One and Hannah Two talking just outside the door.

"I like her, too. But I'm glad it didn't work out with Charlie."

"It was funny listening to her talk about pokerless when she got home last night. I'm going to try it. I wonder if Charlie would make it a team sport?" (laughter)

"It was sort of unfair to him, though. She's engaged to that guy from Chicago."

"She said she forgot to mention it. Just wanted to play around a little."

"Strange. I get the feeling that she's engaged until something better turns up."

"She let slip she wanted one more try for big money before she gives up and settles. She was pretty drunk."

"Yeah. I really didn't like that. Cold. Then she made like she was kidding, but I don't know… And Charlie's part of our family after last year."

"Charlie's a grown man. I'm sure he's had plenty of women pursuing him. But still… I really like Charlie. He's too good for her. I'm glad he didn't go after her."

"She was really bummed."

"And you know the other weird thing. She kept saying, 'I hate friggin' dirty cows, anyway'."

Coldness descends. My wall has gone back up. Maybe I will ask Kay out again. But next time, I'll use her.

ASH

*This morning I followed the standard procedure one more time,
pulled out the plastic pouch, and inside was "Yes." It's all coming
due. Scanning the grounds carefully, I moved to the secondary
location on the other side of the park, pulled out the loose brick in
the public restroom exterior wall, and there lay the microchip in
a tiny container. After experiencing the gamut of emotions: shock,
fear, and excitement, I'm finally sitting quietly with a stunned grin
on my face—At fucking last. I've waited so long—five patient
years after being upgraded to highest level operative, keeping
in excellent shape that I've hidden under larger-than-necessary,
casual clothes. I'm ready.*

*Back in my apartment, I've read the expanded dossier from the
microchip. It appears there's a serious threat, a Blackfeet Indian
of all people, recruited from a reservation in the obscure Montana
wilderness. But he's been noticed. He's hacked into some of our
most sensitive databases—taken everyone by surprise—used our
technology against us. He's on our radar—one Lew Black River.*

CHAPTER 10

LEW

PULLING INTO MY assigned parking slot at the apartment,
I turn off the motor and instead of jumping out mindlessly, I sit
quietly. I need a moment to put my life in perspective. Looking
back over the last two years, I hardly recognize myself. Every time
I go home to Montana, I reorient my friends to who I am—reassure
them I'm the old me with a new cosmetic shell.

I am changed though. My thoughts and language are different.
Who I am has almost caught up with who I've been pretending
to be—someone who knows his way around DC, and the NSA. I
have a GPS in my car, but rarely need to follow its commands. This
has become my world. I love the culture and diversity of people

I encounter daily. I'm about as far from Browning, Montana, as the moon once seemed to be. Still, I know there's a sub-level of sophistication and manipulation in the nation's capital I'm totally unaware of. Political considerations seem second nature to most of my new friends, but they go right over my head. Playing complex mind games to get your way seems so inefficient.

There are endless opportunities I never knew existed. I have Tony to thank for all this. If he hadn't taken an interest, I'd still be ordering cables and printer ink cartridges in my tiny shop, wearing an old Browning Indians sweatshirt, and getting a haircut in my mother's kitchen, allowing her to see my face occasionally. My best friends would be the same friends I've had since diaperhood, Win and Willie, and I'd probably still be pining away over Willie's sister, Tashi.

Win and I go back the farthest. We played as babies in Two Medicine River at his great grandmother's tiny lodge by the water. Most of the time we got along without pants, spending our days shooting tiny arrows with tiny bows she made for us. Birdy was her name. She was one of the last great old ladies of our tribe, born sometime in the 1890's, and was a great storyteller. We'd run ourselves into exhaustion then fall asleep in the shade of a willow tree with her telling us stories about the old buffalo days she'd heard about from her grandmother. You can't buy friendship like that.

I love those people deeply. We don't talk about it, but we know. We're brothers in every sense, and sisters, too. The Blackfeet reservation is my center and always will be. But now I have the whole world.

Money and women are part of it. I'm trying to spend money. I'm making five times as much as I did on the res and even with the high prices here my wants haven't kept up. Stuff mostly complicates my life, but I love my black-metallic BMW, M3 convertible. Win laughs at me. He's getting married and I'm getting a hot car.

I'm a slow starter. I have the tiniest apartment in D.C. crowded with two computer tables of tech gear, a couch facing the decent fireplace, and a double bed behind a wooden screen separating the two areas. It's not cluttered, and I keep it clean. The two things I brought from home are my grizzly-bear rug spread out in front of the fireplace, and an oil painting of Two Medicine River by my friend Bruce. Women don't seem to mind the simplicity, and the rug gets a lot of use. They love my car, too.

Which brings me to my favorite topic, women. They're everywhere. It's like going into a car dealership and all the cars want to buy me. A while back, Tony and I even had "the talk," which was amusing since his oldest daughter was one of the "individuals" he was continually cautioning me about. In addition, he knew it. The talk consisted of a variety of warnings of how a naive, attractive (I flatter myself), Native American totally out of his element, could be taken advantage of by sophisticated East Coast divas. He first had to explain what a diva was. And second, he had to explain how being taken advantage of could be such a bad thing.

Other than having tiny unintended warriors running around, I have yet to figure out his point. So far, no warriors that I know of, and second, life is spectacular!

Tony has mostly given up trying to temper my evolution. He values the entertainment value of stories I bring home too much. I don't mention any names, which is fortunate since several stories involve Rena. She showed me the ropes, metaphorically, and I'll always be grateful. She was my first introduction to the vast East Coast world of wine, women and song, sophisticated nightclubs, and seductive dinners at midnight. She incorrectly believed I'd be her exclusive property for as long as she wished, but she wasn't exclusive back. And I had thirty years of pent-up emotions to deal with.

I lie awake at night, often not alone, and grin with the wonder of it all. The cultured, classy women I encounter don't seem to mind that I'm lacking the subtleties of social refinement. It's not as if I'm a country hack. I'm a quick learner. Women enjoy my company and I theirs.

I've finished my degree in computer security. The NSA funded it, integrating it with my work schedule. It's like putting on an expensive pair of shoes that you don't have to break in—comfortable and beautiful. Now I want to justify all the confidence people have shown in me. I believe I'm ready.

Tony has become the father I never had. Mine died when I was eight, but he died for me long before that, buried in alcohol and disinterest. Tony started out being my mentor and has turned into my best friend back here.

And, of course, there's Miranda. I'm holding clear water in my leaky hands, and if I'm not careful, I'll let her slip away. She's my other best friend. I should try to tie her down if I can. As much as we both try to suppress it, we have chemistry and affection going far beyond friendship. If I'd had a normal life of women in my early years... But the temptations here are so numerous that I get distracted, still making up for lost time.

She's buried herself in temporary relationships, too, working hard in law school. We see each other every couple of weeks, watch old movies in the family rec-room, and talk successes and failures with the opposite sex, biding our time. I haven't kissed her since that first night long ago. Rena's blatant sex appeal moved me in another direction. And then there were so many directions. I'm convinced that if I started kissing Miranda again, I wouldn't stop. And I'm not quite ready. We've skirted our attraction very successfully, neither of us quite willing to risk the friendship we share. I avoid looking at her lips.

Tomorrow, I meet my new boss and department head, Ross Clopton, assistant director of Middle Eastern security and liaison with counterintelligence. He asked for me, specifically, and I'm honored. His entire region is becoming progressively unsettled with Syria's catastrophic revolution and Egypt's instability, let alone Iran and Pakistan's hostilities. Iraq is progressively leaning toward Iran and Afghanistan teeters as usual toward chaos.

Fortunately, the U.S. has become more energy independent and could convert significantly to natural gas usage if the shit hit the fan. The power balance of the old-world order is disintegrating before our eyes and that means global scrambling for power. My job will be to help monitor and protect against cyberattacks which are occurring with frightening regularity. I'm smart enough to know how little I know, but I'm getting perspective quickly. That's why Ross wants me.

* * *

I'm on time for my 9:00 meeting with Ross and only a little nervous. I've met him several times before and am constantly surprised how young he is for his level of responsibility. He just turned forty and looks even younger, with thick dark brown hair and eyes reflecting his sharp intellect.

"Come on in, Lew. Good to see you again. I'm delighted you decided to join my team."

"It's an honor, sir. It's what I wanted most."

"Please call me Ross. I like informality and I don't want you to be careful with me. I want honest impressions and ideas, not what you've figured out I want to hear."

I look down briefly and smile despite myself. That's why I wanted to work with Ross. He has that reputation.

"Do you have a plan for me?"

"Yes. I hope you don't mind some traveling."

I shake my head. "No. I'd love it."

"Good. I'm sending you out with Will Nelson. He's getting too old to be on the go so much. I want to groom you to share his job. Possibly, take it over eventually. As you know, Iran and Russia are two of our most pressing and sophisticated cyber threats, along with China, of course, and North Korea.

"Iran is expanding her dominance in the entire Middle East region and, together with Russia and the Saudis, they control much of the oil flow in the area—Russia to Europe and Iran though the Strait of Hormuz." He pauses for a breath. "And of course, there's the Israelis, changing alliances and leadership every other minute."

He pauses to see if he's lost me yet and I nod encouragingly. He hasn't. "Seriously, sir. I do get the picture. I've had great tutorials."

He continues with a smile. "We're monitoring information constantly, but it's a young man's game. Global hacking moves too fast for us old guys. That's why we're so glad to have you. I'm also sending Aamad Navissi with you as interpreter and bodyguard. It never hurts to have some physical security. He's a tough guy of Iranian heritage. Speaks the language fluently." He scrutinizes my face with a speculative look. "Intimidated yet?"

"No, sir. Ross, sir." I say forcefully.

"I've read your dossier, of course. You're Blackfeet, I understand. Can you ride a horse?"

"Yes."

"Well?"

"Very well."

"That may come in handy. Are you a warrior?"

Apparently, he's trying to hide a grin. "Well, sir. I haven't lifted any scalps recently, but I'm looking forward to it. By the way, where am I going?"

He frowns. "You don't need to know."

I grimace.

Ross laughs abruptly at my discomfort, then grins broadly. "Kidding, Lew. I'm absolutely delighted to have you on board. Dolly will give you a call about tickets and timing, but I'm expecting you to fly out to Istanbul with the crew early next week. Plan on two weeks relatively incommunicado, and we'll have an extensive debriefing when you get back." He becomes serious, "And that location actually is confidential."

I nod.

"Enjoy the long weekend."

We shake hands. "Thanks, Ross," I say. "And by the way, I wasn't kidding about the scalps. I have a collection."

As I walk out of the room, I glance back at Ross who's looking at me with an expression of someone who was caught off guard and resist the impulse to close the meeting with a horizontal forearm swipe, a Blackfeet exit. He's probably had enough warrior exposure for one day.

Well, nice. I've got at least three days before I have to leave. I'm hoping Miranda is coming home and I'm looking forward to connecting with my nephew, Tommy. I decide to head over to the NSA software engineering section where he's starting a summer internship. I don't see enough of my nephew. He's usually in school in New York or hanging at Charlie's house in Philadelphia during school breaks. I got a text he's free this morning and was hoping to get together.

I jog over to the software development building, then text him, getting an instant reply, "5 min unk". It's humid today in early summer, already in the high eighties, so I find a bench in the shade with a breeze to wait for Tommy.

"Oki, Uncle Lew!" I hear yelled out of a third story window.

"Be right down."

It's been a year since the car accident. Once Tommy got over the shock of losing his lower left leg and serious depression, there's been no holding him. Charlie, in fact Charlie's whole family, took him under their wing, got him state-of-the-art medical rehabilitation and spectacular tutors, and he's now well on his way to taking the world by computer storm. Plus, he's one gorgeous kid. He always considered Win a role model, and they look a lot alike. Women swoon. He even wears his hair long down his back like Win. He gets looks walking around campus. And charming is his middle name. He gets that from me.

Charlie got involved with our family of friends, attempting to help Lizzie, while simultaneously trying to entice her away from Win. It was early on in Win and Lizzie's relationship, during a troubled period, but it was a lost cause. They were married last November. But as I've gotten to know Charlie these last few years, I've learned he has heart. By that I mean he shows loyalty and honor which we Blackfeet treat with highest respect.

I know the value of a surrogate family, which the Curchins are providing for Tommy. His father, my ex-brother-in-law, was a worthless drunk. I filled in some of the parenting role, but the Curchins have been extraordinary. Charlie and Tommy have become brothers in the native sense, despite the ten-year age difference.

And I know something else. Charlie needed a brother. He was a twin. Four years ago, his brother disappeared in a plane crash somewhere in the wilds of western Canada. His body was never found, just some wreckage. I don't know the family well, but Tommy shared that history. Also, that there were rumors of sabotage related to international business dealings. I've searched the Internet and never found any specifics. Details were somehow expunged. All I really know is that Charlie and Tommy have become family, and I couldn't be happier for both of them.

"Oki, Hairy Noser." Tommy's usual greeting. It's an affectionate label, indicating you originate from down near Heart Butte in the southern part of the reservation. The Black River band comes from that area.

"Oki, aapiita." (Hello, sit down.)

65

"Nice to hear a little Blackfeet," he replies. "Aahsaapinakos." (Good morning.)

"Kikataiistsokinnih?" (Are you hungry?")

"Aa, niitsiksisstsokin?" (Yes, I'm starved.)

"What else is new? Come on, I'll buy you breakfast."

We walk across the complex to a cafeteria and settle in. "How do you like D.C.?" I ask.

"Love it, especially the museums and the girls."

"I'll bet."

"Yep. Every day is another opportunity." He gives me a knowing look.

"Just don't overdo it." I say, smiling in agreement. Tommy is ten years younger than I am, but I feel like we're in the same emotional place with women. There are distractions everywhere.

"Boy, that's rich coming from you. How are you coping with the Flynn females?"

"Trying to keep my head above water as usual. I'm using you as my primary role model."

He laughs, then adds, "No, seriously. How's Miranda?"

"One more year in law school. I've almost got her convinced to come out to Montana—try living out there."

"She'd love it. Hmm? How old is she?" He glances at me. "Maybe it would work."

"She's twenty-four and keep your hands off her."

He looks at me closely. "That's only five years difference. When she's thirty I'll be twenty-five."

Giving him a cold fixed stare, I cross my arms.

"This is really bothering you, isn't it? If you like her that much, what are you waiting for?"

"You dirty south-sider," I mutter uneasily. "I've been thinking about it."

Tommy gives me a satisfied grin then changes the subject. "How do you like the new job?"

It takes me a moment to refocus. "No details, but I'm flying overseas next week. Big new world. We're two lucky 'Injins'."

We nod agreeably. "How are the Curchins? I ask, finally. "Have you seen Charlie?"

"He's busier than hell with family business. And the weather projection is for a bad fire season this summer, maybe one of the worst in years. 'Course, they've all been bad recently."

"I've been following it."

"Mom called. They had a big fire on the res near Cut Bank again—grassland fire, like the one they had earlier this winter. Unusual east wind. Ran twenty miles before they could completely get it under control."

"Anyone hurt?" I ask. I know most of the people out there.

"Not this time. They lost two farmhouses and outbuildings. Some stock that couldn't outrun it. Coulda' been a lot worse..."

"Win and his network...," I say. "Phone trees and alarms."

"Yeah. They called people. No one's been killed the last few years. Win's system put a stop to that. If they get enough notice..."

"Browning and Heart Butte are exposed, but the Chief Mountain Shots would be on it."

"Anyway," Tommy adds, "I haven't seen Charlie since spring break. I'm flying up soon. He's still there. Why don't you come?"

"Maybe. But with this new job, I'm low man. Looks like I'll be out of the country for a while."

"Well, think about it. I'd invite Miranda, but you'd probably kill me. Besides, I don't want her to meet Charlie. You and I have enough competition."

"Yeah. I don't like that idea much. Oh. I forgot. Tony wants you to come for dinner this weekend. Give him a call if it works out."

"Great. I'll have a chance to hustle Miranda," he says, punching my arm as he stands up. Despite myself, I can't help glaring at him, making him laugh out loud.

"Niitakkotamattsino," (I'll see you later) he says, hurrying off.

I remain brooding in my chair. My kid-nephew has once again made me consider my future. My life is so fine now I'm reluctant to rock the boat. And Miranda is only twenty-four. More than enough time to let her grow up a little, have some fun. But I've learned "fun" is hard to manage—to get just right.

PART II
MODERN DAY

CHAPTER 11

LEW

I'VE BEEN WORKING under Ross Clopton for a year, and it's been everything I hoped it would be. My degree is finished. Fast-tracked was an understatement—twenty-four credit hours a quarter. I rapidly advanced beyond the course work, becoming technical development support for other students. Once I learned the new languages, it was easy.

Just as I arrive for an impromptu meeting with the boss, two suits come out of the inner office. Dolly catches my eye and waves me in.

Ross surprises me by meeting me at the door with a smile and a handshake. "Come on in Lew. Thanks for coming so quickly." Poking his head around the corner, he adds, "Dolly. Hold my calls."

As I walk in, she winks conspiratorially me. Dolly's completely predictable—comfortable nondescript clothes, mid-fifties, and salt and pepper hair worn short. It's her eyes that set her apart, always brimming with intelligence and highlighted by expressive eyebrows. I've known her long enough to know she's invaluable to Ross. She supplies the added benefit of mothering me, calls me 'darlin' with a bit of a southern drawl. If I have enough notice, I bring her flowers. I didn't have time today. Something's up.

"Sit down, Lew," Ross says, beginning to talk before I can settle into a chair. "I've been discussing your work with some of the men heading software development. I understand you've been working with them to create an integrated global monitoring system. They say they've never seen anyone who can simplify complicated, multi-national, data—see patterns out of smoke screens. They're impressed, to put it mildly."

Ross doesn't intimidate me, but I feel newly deferential. He's just been promoted to section chief—a very big deal. "Yes, sir," I say. "It seems so obvious to me. I'm constantly surprised everyone doesn't make the connections."

"Well, they don't, Lew. And when the biggest of big boys go back over your work, they corroborate the sophistication, and are astounded by your systems' simplicity. How did you learn to do this?"

I shrug my shoulders.

"We've talked about this before, but you keep upping your ability. And for God's sake, call me Ross. If you're going to be the boy wonder, you can at least do that."

"I'm pumped, too. I've been given the freedom to explore multiple databases and play around. Free think, I guess they call it. I'm having a blast. And I contribute at the same time. It's a dream come true." I smile conspiratorially. "I can hardly wait to get to work."

He shakes his head in disbelief.

"I don't know how I learned to do this. Patterns keep developing and forming bigger pictures."

"Well, as you know, they've just named me section chief in charge of Middle East cryptanalysis and international security. I'm taking you along with me unless you have any reservations?"

"Was that a pun?" I love Indian jokes.

Ross grins back. "No, I wish I'd thought of it."

"Anyway, I'm thrilled, Ross. Is Dolly on board?"

"Is the sun coming up tomorrow? Welcome to the team. And one more thing. I'm putting together a select group to attend a multi-national symposium in Turkey in about a month. You'd be low man again, Lew, but you're coming on strong, and this problem just keeps growing exponentially. We want to develop a training program we can share with our Middle Eastern allies on averting and countering hacking sabotage." Then he adds, "Without giving away all our trade secrets. Are you interested?"

I grin broadly.

"Okay. You got along well with Aamad, right?"

"He's the best.""

"Then get ready for a major trip in four weeks, about three weeks duration. We're bringing in our guys from all over, even South Korea and Iran for the time being. Of course, it's China we're really worried about, and North Korea is working with them to make trouble… And the damn Russians. It gives me a headache, to tell you the truth." Leaning forward, he looks me squarely in the eye, then adds, "For God's sake, listen to Aamad. After the last trip he admitted you didn't take your personal security seriously enough." He lowers his voice. "We're not playing Cowboys and Indians here."

"Yes, Ross," I say, grinning back.

"Okay. Okay. We'll talk the day before you fly out. And take some serious time off to clear your head before the trip. Just let Dolly know."

ASH

It's almost unbelievable what this Blackfeet is doing. He's gone beyond what I personally understand and can predict. The big boys are freaked. He's singlehandedly managed to jeopardize all our intricately set up monitors and security systems. Everything of theirs is protected and firewalls are coming on so fast we can't reconfigure them. In some ways it's comical. All these high-level geek wonders, and it takes a novice, aboriginal whiz kid to flummox everyone.

They're starting to talk about taking this guy out. Or as an alternative, getting their hands on him. He could be very valuable under our control. You can always turn people. Torture aside, bravery counts for nothing if family members are threatened. It shouldn't be difficult to abduct him if it came to that, but I'm hoping I'm not the operative they have in mind. That takes a muscle mentality. I'm more of an information harvester. Well, I'll see what the power guys want. It appears my first exotic trip may be to Turkey. Grinning ironically, I fantasize... It's too bad I can't level with my friend Brad, my cultivated civilian coworker. He'd love the stories.

CHAPTER 12

MIRANDA

A LOT OF CHANGES have happened in the last few years, the most significant is I got my law degree from Georgetown. It's been a long pull. I'm ready for my adult life to start. I finished an internship in DC but turned down a job offer. Mom and Dad have been encouraging as long as I can be self-supporting, "while I'm finding myself." (Dad's words.)

Sighing with deep contentment, I bask in fall sunshine on the Sanders family ranch, seven hundred feet above and overlooking Two Medicine River. The sun has dropped low enough that its reflection makes the river glow in a band of shimmering silver flowing east.

I've come here to Montana with Dad and Rena for a reunion of Lew's large extended family of friends near Browning on the Blackfeet Indian Reservation. Lew's headed back to the Middle East in several weeks but got permission for significant R and R first.

Dad feels a deep connection with several people here. He's come to renew a kinship with what has become a second family. Rena and I have come with dissimilar purposes. She wants Lew back. It's been satisfying watching Rena's evolution with Lew. She started out treating him like a lovable lap dog. But somewhere in the last two years, he's become his own man, desirable in his own right in the D.C. social scene. Women constantly drift in his direction. I'm adequately nice looking, but attractive girls are a dime a dozen in Georgetown, as opposed to tall Native Americans with a sensual, welcoming look. He's moved on, been involved with a variety of other women. We haven't talked details. And he's a gentleman.

Frankly, Rena squandered her relationship with Lew. It served her right. I never approved of the way she treated him. Plus, Rena's career is stagnating in smaller theater groups off Broadway. It's not improving her peace of mind. She's very talented, but there's so much competition, and her dream of being a stage star is dimming. We discuss it often—her realistic appraisal of her fading career. She's looking for someone to expand her life outside of the theater world. That's when she focuses on Lew.

Contrasting with Rena, I'm out here for myself and won't be going home. I intend to see what kind of lawyering job I can get with some help and encouragement from Lew's family of friends.

I recently ended a fairly serious relationship with one of my fellow law students—my passion and interest simply stopped developing. Jeff was a typical corporate-lawyer type with a predictable career path. I wanted something defining in my life other than a four-thousand-square-foot house in Georgetown. Plus, I'm sick to death of Washington political infighting, the swamp as they're beginning to call it. I'm getting out before I get sucked in for good.

Lew and I have happily become important to each other as best friends. The old physical attraction is still there, but well buried. We've seen a lot of each other over the last two years, mostly at our Silver Spring house, laughing about our various love lives and blunders.

Lew has become the son Dad never had, spinning stories over our backyard barbeque, and watching guy movies together that Mom and I would rather pass on. They follow the NFL in season, and Washington Wizards basketball. Lew played basketball in high school, admitting he was the star center forward. He describes it as back in the buffalo days.

This afternoon I've met dozens of Lew's friends, including Sam and Paul Thomas, the sons of the man who gave his life saving my dad, and Lizzie Sanders and Win, her husband. Together, they are hosting this reunion. In addition, Lew's biological family is here, including his mother, Pauline, along with his sister, Carol, who is Tommy's mother. It was an honor to finally meet them. I feel adventurous, an evolving western version of myself, meeting fascinating people, many ways removed from self-impressed intellectuals. Lew loves the irony. He's turning cosmopolitan while I'm going country. We have such a valuable friendship; I'd have mess it up with romance. There would be so much to lose and often you can't go back if it doesn't work out. Besides, I'll be out here. He'll be back there. There should be opportunities of many kinds.

While making the rounds, I've explained to anyone who will listen that I'm looking for work in Great Falls, Missoula, or Helena, hoping to get a job as a legal assistant or lawyer-temp position, while I study for the Montana state bar exam. Charlie Curchin is pursuing me, not in a personal sense, but to take Lizzie's place at the local BLM, Bureau of Land Management, field office in Great Falls. Through Lew, and Tommy of course, I know of Tommy's close relationship with Charlie and his extended family in Philadelphia.

It's ironic. At the age of twenty-one, when I was introduced to Charlie, I was immediately infatuated by him to the point of becoming a frozen silent statue. It's been many years, and I've thought of him from time to time, wondering what happened to him, and if he found peace with his brother's death. For several of those early years, I even hoped I'd run into him, randomly searching for him in crowds. Now I laugh at myself, suddenly presented with my fantasy, finding that he's an ordinary, flesh and blood, man.

When we were introduced that long-ago night, Charlie didn't notice me. I'm not the kind of woman who blows people out of the water at large gatherings. Charlie, on the other hand, is always noticed. I've learned since that big money doesn't come close to describing the family assets. Charlie's family controls a multinational conglomerate based on the East Coast. But here, in a setting of friends, away from the undercurrent of being pursued, he's approachable. I'm enjoying the relaxed, comfortable atmosphere to get to know him.

Charlie wants someone training over the winter to assist the main dispatcher. Al Monroe, apparently a beloved curmudgeon of a guy, is looking to switch to back-up in a year or so. Lizzie had a baby last week, ending her career as assistant dispatcher for this summer fire season. She intends to work back into the job part-time next summer, and it would be a good way for me to earn living expenses while I look for something in my field. And who knows? Maybe someday Lizzie and I could share the job permanently if Al quits down the line. It all sounds incredibly exciting, and I could easily combine it with legal contract work. The possibilities out here seem endless.

With baby Paulie in her arms, Lizzie has been teasing Charlie about recruiting hot women for his job openings. Charlie is agreeing with her, saying he's unselfishly doing it for Al's benefit, making everyone laugh. I understand he competed seriously for Lizzie's affection, several years ago. I also understand he's probably not completely over her.

Many of the people here are couples, so we unattached people have formed a group of our own. In addition to Charlie and myself, Katherine Donovan and Tommy stand together talking to Lizzie. Katherine had been introduced earlier as a mystery guest. Turned out that Sam Thomas decided not to attempt to seduce her four years ago in Oregon, which started a chain of events bringing us all here tonight, over thirty people, now a family. I love things like that.

Tommy and Charlie's unusual closeness gives me insight into

Charlie's character, although he doesn't need any more help to keep me interested. Despite his wealth, Charlie has turned out to be an affable, sensitive guy. Katherine is attracted, too. I can tell she knows absolutely nothing about him.

Lew walks over to join us, putting his hand on his nephew's shoulder. Lew is attractive, but Tommy is beautiful. He reminds me of Win, Lizzie's husband. Both are men that would make you stop on the street, turn around, and stare. The term 'chiseled features' comes to mind, and with their long black hair, hanging down their backs, they're coupled with savvy intelligence. Surrounded by intriguing new friends, I'm having the time of my life. I notice Dad glance my way frequently, smiling, enjoying my happiness. I'm getting a kick out of surreptitious knowledge of Charlie's background, trying not to disclose that I've met him. Between Tommy, Charlie, and Lew, plus using Two Medicine River as a backdrop, I've been admiring the views.

We settle in, laughing at stories of Lew's reservation exploits, Tommy's effort to use Win as seduction role model, and even Charlie's failed effort to lure Lizzie away from Win in earlier days. He describes his past effort as a bumbling attempt. I bet he wasn't bumbling at all, but it's obvious to all that it was a lost cause.

Tommy, helpfully, is offering Charlie advice on how to successfully get women, especially considering his earlier failure. For a twenty-one-year-old, Tommy has a great sense of humor, and Charlie can laugh at himself. Charlie pulls out a pen, telling Tommy he's going to take notes on his forearm.

"Okay," Charlie says. "But keep it simple."

"Alright. First, always look them straight in the eyes and smolder."

Charlie writes down *smolder*. "I'm afraid you'll have to demonstrate."

"Okay. Come here Miranda."

I walk over to Tommy's side and smile up innocently. Tommy leans over, opens his eyes wide, and looks down at me through incredibly thick lashes.

"My God," I say, putting the back of my hand to my forehead so that I appear to swoon.

"Let me try that," Charlie says.

I walk over to Charlie, giving him the same smile.

He looks down at me, but I start giggling, then really laugh, then laugh harder. "Oh, dear," I say, then start laughing all over again.

"No. No. No," Tommy interrupts, rolling his eyes. He approaches me, giving me the Tommy look. This time I totally appear to faint, falling flat out on the ground, apparently unconscious.

By this time, everyone is laughing hysterically.

"Damn it, "complains Charlie, helping me up, "I've failed at smoldering. What's next?"

"Well, most important, is to act hard to get, especially with really beautiful girls like Katherine or Miranda." Charlie writes *hard to get* on his forearm as Tommy continues, "When they come around, you act disinterested, like sex is the farthest thing from your mind. If they try to get you alone, you fend them off by introducing them to a friend, who you suggest might be interested. Then you allow them to be taken away by your attractive, helpful, and virile friend, preferably a Blackfeet warrior, and you continue to ignore them. It works every time."

"Let me get this straight," says Charlie. "If a gorgeous, hot female wants me, I give them to you."

"Pretty much."

We all smile at Tommy.

"What can I say," he says. "I was born with animal magnetism."

Hugh McManus, the Curchin corporate pilot, strolls over. Rena also joins us and is introduced around. She pauses as Charlie is introduced, finally saying, "You look familiar. Are you from Philadelphia—the Philadelphia Curchins?" I can almost see Charlie sigh to himself. "Yes," he admits, "same family."

Charlie and McManus exchange looks of regretful resignation. Wheels start turning in Rena's head as she settles in. She's not going anywhere now, and it changes the dynamic of the group immediately. Charlie leaves to talk with Win, while I decide to take a walk alone down a winding dirt path along the bluff edge. There's no hurry. We're going to spend the night in the bunkhouse in the barn.

Walking over to tell Dad where I'm going, I find Paul and Sam talking to him. They point out the trailhead that's supposed to lead down to a pool, and offer to go with me, but I've been talking non-stop all day, and welcome a little alone time to get the feel of the land.

Eventually, I turn and wave at the distant gathering before disappearing down the dirt path. It's after six and still sunny but cooling off faster than I anticipated. The huge grassland fields have been mowed and hayed recently, illuminating a gently rolling mesa that glows a golden color in the slanted light. Breathing in the aroma of cut dried grass, I feel the gentle wind on my bare forearms, my hair blown restlessly in the breeze.

It awakens a new emotion in me. I feel very far from home. The haze in the evening light gives the land a deep orange glow toward the uplift of the Rockies, adding to the feeling of the magic of this world. I feel like holding up my arms to the sky, feeling so much a part of it all. I do it. I've never felt this way in my life, finally taking several steps forward to the edge of the bluff, which drops off sharply, falling many hundreds of feet to the contrasting landscape of the riverbed below.

Who am I? I don't feel at all like I felt inside the beltway of DC. Could I come out here and belong? Abruptly, I want it all, as surely as I want to breathe air. I'm young. I can decide to live anywhere. Why not live in this beautiful land where I feel a part of the earth and the sky? I will.

I hear a horse coming in my direction. It's Lew, riding bareback on a big chestnut horse. He looks so much at home, in bare feet and tattered jeans—so relaxed, so different, so native. He turns sideways on the horse with both feet dangling on the same side, grins down at me, then slides off, holding the reins in his hand.

"Hi, I came to get you." He takes a close look at me. "You okay? Are you crying?"

"Lew," I say, "I'm overwhelmed. I love it here. I don't want to leave. It's maybe where I want to spend my life. I wondered if I'd feel this way."

"Miranda," he says, as puts his arm around my shoulder. "It's my people's land. It's a part of me—my center."

I turn to look at him, feeling his emotion.

"This land is the ashes and blood of my ancestors. I feel honored to be part of it. This is where my story begins. If you forget who you are or where you come from—you're a horseless wanderer. These mountains remind me I'm a direct descendant of the niitsiitapii, the real people."

We stand there silently, watching the sun slowly disappear behind the jagged backbone of mountains.

He smiles at me. "Ready?"

I nod.

He grabs a fist full of the horse's mane, vaulting easily onto his back, then flattens out his foot, his hand reaching for my arm. "Put your foot on top of my foot and I'll lift you up."

I do as he says. Suddenly I find myself sitting behind him on the horse, giggling. I've ridden before as a kid, but never bareback and never holding onto a guy's chest for support. I grin happily to myself.

"Hold on," he says, and we take off on a slow canter.

I tighten my arms around his waist as we head home, looking back down the valley to the river twining below.

"Two Medicine. Our family river. Beautiful, huh?"

"Yes," I say, breathing in the wild aroma of dried grass in the wind, duplicating the strong emotion I felt before.

As we pull up to the group, everyone yells greetings. Win asks Lew if he found a white girl on the plains to snatch. Lew yells back something at Win in Blackfeet—iikiitammiksistsiko—they both laugh. Lew's friend Willie laughs, too.

Charlie is watching me with a quizzical, interested look. Really interested, and I grin back at him. It's been a great day.

As I remove my arms from around Lew's chest, I'm aware that something meaningful has changed. I've put off serious fantasies about Lew for a very long time. I'm used to fighting it off, but...

Our eyes meet intensely while he steadies my arm as I slide off his horse. With imperceivable cues, Lew backs the horse several feet, turns him abruptly, and begins a slow canter toward the barn. My eyes follow my warrior-friend most of the way.

When I have an opportunity, I ask Lew what he said to Win in Blackfeet.

He laughs. "I said something to the effect of 'It's a happy day.' And 'I wonder if the guest lodge is free'?"

"Well, is it?" I ask, getting an enigmatic look in response.

* * *

Several hours later we're all sitting on Win's long porch, some of us in chairs, some of us on the edge of the deck with our legs dangling over the edge. Win has a huge fire burning in the firepit at the bluff edge.

Two people have eluded me. One is Curchin's pilot. Once I even kidded him about avoiding me, and he laughed, almost said something, then hurried away. I'm probably exaggerating a conspiracy.

My second failure is not spending time with Vinnie Long, an elderly lady with white curly hair, who to my untrained eye seems to be a hub around which this entire family of friends revolves. People are practically standing in line to talk to her, and I didn't want to intrude. Once I caught her studying me. She broke out in a broad smile and waved. I'll keep trying.

We're all sipping something, coffee, beer, wine, things in flasks, harder stuff, and listening to Sam play soft end-of-evening music. Bruce is strumming softly while Sam embellishes with picking. It's magical. I want this evening to last forever. It's been the best day of my life. I've fallen in love with the area, the close group of friends who have accepted me, and something more—all my buried feelings regarding Lew have surfaced again.

Dad, Rena, and Lew are flying back to D.C. tomorrow afternoon. I'll be talking more to Charlie about dispatcher training and starting to look for a job seriously next week. I'd love to find something in Great Falls, so I'll start there first, but plan to make a list of law offices to canvas in the next few weeks. Willie's girlfriend Susan works as a legal assistant at a firm in Great Falls so that's the obvious place to start, plus I could fit in some dispatcher training at the local BLM office.

Walking over, I sit down with Dad. I'll be saying good-bye to him and Rena for a while. I wish I could ask Rena to keep an eye on Lew, but it would be disingenuous. Underlying it all, she sincerely cares about him. A lot to consider. I take Dad's hand in mine as we sit quietly.

"Pretty nice place," Dad says eventually.

"I feel like I belong here."

"Then I'm glad you discovered it."

We sit together in companionable silence with Dad still holding my hand. Finally, he says, "I'll miss you, baby. It's hard to let you go."

"I'm pretty old for a baby."

"Not to me," he says quietly.

We linger, silently contented. "What are you thinking about?" I ask him, finally.

"Katherine Donovan and what Sam said about her starting all this, three years ago, with a chance meeting. He's wrong, of course."

I smile. "Yes. It really started before I was born, in Kuwait, didn't it?"

"Exactly. If I hadn't joined the army to get college money... It goes back and back."

"You know I love Mom, but we've always been special, haven't we?"

"Yes, and don't worry. I'll keep an eye on Lew for you."

"Hmm?"

"Oh, don't look so innocent. You know what I mean. I was watching when you came riding back with him. Go ahead and fool yourself, but you can't fool me."

I sigh. "Maybe. I'm leaving behind a whole world of competition."

"No one knows what the future will bring. But if you're interested, you might mention it to him—something for him to think about when he's back in civilization. It's obvious that you love it out here. He does, too."

"All right," I say reluctantly. "I'll look for an opening."

"You do that." He smiles mischievously.

I stand up, rolling my eyes, and look around. Charlie catches my eye and motions me over to where he's been sitting with Lizzie and Win, who are just getting up to leave. Lizzie gives me a hug while

Win favors me with an alluring smile. Which I appreciate. Lew says he can't help it. Women swoon. He's blindingly attractive. Lizzie leaves to help in the kitchen as I continue to watch Win as he goes over to build up the fire.

"So, what's your plan?" Charlie asks, interrupting my train of thought.

"Oh… Um. Serious job hunting. And you?"

"Well," he says, "this fire season is almost over. First of next month, I'll transition back to the family business." He studies my face. "I'm guessing you know something about my background, as much as you've tried to hide it."

"Yes, Charlie," I admit. "I know who you are. I've even met you once years ago. I was a bland face in a sea of gorgeous women at a reception at the State Department."

He nods. "Yes, it's easy to miss the diamonds in the rough, not that you're rough, but my assets get in the way." He sighs, deeply. "That's one of the reasons I love it out here. I can be myself. Sometimes, I even meet people who don't know my family connections. I'm sorry you know who I am. It colors our getting to know each other."

I smile at him.

"Yeah. Yeah. I know. A lot of people would like my problem."

"Charlie, we can be friends, and I appreciate the job idea you mentioned earlier. I'd like to talk to the people at the BLM." I pause. "Unless you want to renege because you think I might use the advantage."

"Of course not. Are you going to be staying out here?"

"You know Susan? She keeps an apartment in Great Falls. Everyone chips in to use it. I'm going to pay a full month's rent. Use it as a base while I explore jobs."

"I know the place. I… I was there when I was involved with Lizzie," he smiles.

"She's truly amazing, isn't she?" I ask.

"Yes. I'm satisfied to be a part of her life as a friend. Win's fine with it." He sighs, almost inaudibly. "Obviously, I'm no threat."

I'm quiet for a while. Charlie finally asks, "What are you thinking?"

"She's so beautiful. I don't know if I've ever known someone as beautiful as she is, who's also beautiful inside."

Charlie allows himself a second of a sad smile. "I talked to Win about it once. He said she was self-absorbed when he first met her, but having her sister almost die enabled her to value what was important."

We both look over at her holding tiny Paulie. "What about her connection with Bruce? Several people have referred to their deep friendship."

"You should hear his story. I'd tell you now, but it would take a long session over some beers to do it justice. Speaking of that, I'm leaving here after breakfast tomorrow, but I'm staying around for most of this week. How about we get together for dinner tomorrow night in Great Falls? If you'll be down by then?"

"I've got a ride down tomorrow afternoon."

"I'll fill you in on the friend family history. Meanwhile, I'll find out when Jack Lambert is available to talk to you about the job."

"Sounds perfect. What time?"

"I'll pick you up around six-thirty."

Despite what I said, having a meeting/date with Charlie is a little daunting. I hope we know each other well enough that I can act naturally. Bigger-then-hell wealth is intimidating. And there's the old attraction.

As I get up, I see Lew watching us, so I walk over to him. Time is passing and I may not have many opportunities to say anything. And I haven't a clue where to begin.

"It's been a lovely day," I start out. When he doesn't say anything, I add, "Every single person is special. Fascinating."

"It'll take you some time to know them all, but you're getting the general idea."

"Is it going to be hard going back?"

"I love both worlds now," he says, turning to look seriously at me. "I'll miss you, though. We've been close friends."

I nod. I'm out of words. What can I possibly say?

"Are you tired?" he asks. "Do you have energy for a short walk?"

"Of course."

"Wait a minute. I'll get a blanket. The Milky Way is amazing out here."

We walk out to the east until the farm lights are far behind us in the distance. Lew stretches the blanket on the ground, and we lie down.

He puts his arm under my head. "Look up," he says. "We Blackfeet call it the Wolf Trail. Can you see it? It resembles a trail left by a wolf pack. Makoi-yohsokoyi in our language."

I've seen the Milky Way before, but this is beyond comparison. It's glaringly white and you can see the bulge in the center of the galaxy like pictures in an astronomy textbook. For the first time in my life, I can see the dark areas of stardust clouds blocking some of the center. We're quiet as we see several shooting stars.

I sigh audibly in the darkness at the beauty. "I'll always see the wolf trail from now on."

"We've been friends from that first night, long ago," he says. "It's three and a half years now. I'm different and you've grown up."

I smile into the starlight. "I remember you well back then. You were so honest about how overwhelming it was. You were so truthful. Most people would have tried to fake it."

"Of course, Rena was especially welcoming." I can see him grinning in the starlight.

I grin, too. "Yes, you were putty in her hands if I remember correctly."

"You were pretty nice yourself, Miranda. I remember you kissing a poor, frightened Blackfeet."

I take his hand in mine in the darkness, smiling to myself, remembering.

Lew is silent for a time, seeming to organize what he wants to say. Surprisingly, he rolls toward me on his side as he pulls me gently to him. His warm lips press down on mine. I've been denying my desire for such a long time that I break into tears.

"I'm sorry," I manage. "I don't know where that came from."

"Mira," he says softly, his pet name for me. "Have I waited too long?"

"I... What?"

"I've needed some time to...experience some things."

I'm silent. The silence stretches out.

"Oh, what the hell," he mutters, and draws me against him. He weaves his large hands in my hair. His lips open mine, urgently. My hands reach up around his neck as I press my body's entire length against his hardness. The pull is so strong it astonishes me. It's hard to keep my head. If I don't stop now, I'm not going to...

His hands move up to my breasts...

"Wait, Lew."

"I want you, Mira." His voice is husky. "I have wanted you."

"Let me think..."

He pulls a little away from me, waiting for me to explain.

"You just can't spring this on me out of nowhere. I need to understand where you're coming from. You're too important to lose if... I mean... I couldn't bear for us not to be friends. I've depended on it for so long and never appreciated it."

"I don't turn you off, do I? Tell me now."

"No, you don't..."

"Easy to say."

"Do you want me to prove that isn't true?"

"Yes."

"Jeez, Lew."

"You think it was easy to come on to you? After all this time?"

"No, but..."

"No. I need to know. I don't want to risk our friendship, either." He pauses.

I wait.

Finally, he continues, "I'm not a cultured, subtle easterner... But here's my point. Either let me know you want me, or I'll go back to the status quo." His finger traces my cheek. "Your move," he murmurs in a low guttural voice.

"Lew," I almost wail.

Silence. Shaking my head, I try to gather my thoughts.

Sitting up abruptly, I unbutton my blouse, reaching behind me to remove my bra, then lean over him, taking his head in my hands as I press my breasts to his lips.

He groans, kissing them, as I delight in the sensations he's eliciting. "Is that an answer?" I whisper.

"That'll do, Mira," he murmurs back in that same sensuous voice.

Putting his hand behind my head, he looms over me. The pleasure of seriously making out with a guy I've been trying not to fantasize about for years shocks me with its intensity. Pulling him to me, I press myself against his hard chest. I want all of him, and reaching down to touch him, it's obvious he wants me. My friend is a beautiful man. An aching sound comes from somewhere inside me as I pull him tightly against me, massaging my hands up his long bare back. It's obvious where this is leading. "Lew," I manage, trying to breathe, "Do we want to do this?"

"Yes."

Trying once more to slow this down, I say, "You're going back to the East Coast."

His lips move lower.

"Ahh," I moan as he nips my belly. "And I'm planning on staying out here."

His lips move up to my breasts again.

"I mean…" Sensations begin overwhelming me. "Jesus, Lew." I try to catch my breath again. "You said you needed to experience things. Are you done experiencing?"

"Are you?" His hand moves lower and lower.

"Come on," I whisper loudly. "You know what I'm getting at."

He pulls a little away then bites my lower lip.

My body reacts strongly and I'm getting frantic. "Tell me. Are you interested in me as an experience or a lot more?"

"You know you're a lot more."

"Okay. But… Are you going back to D.C. to resume your lifestyle?"

"I don't know. I hadn't thought about that until four seconds ago." He stretches my arms over my head and leans back over me, his lips brushing my neck.

"Lew. Stop! I don't want to be a one-night stand. Even for you."

He finally leans back, taking a deep breath. "Well, me either. What about you? Charlie certainly seems interested."

"What the hell does Charlie have to do with anything?"

"I've been watching him. He's coming on to you. Are you ready to turn him away? Have you agreed to go out with him?"

I don't say anything.

"Well...?"

"We're going to meet tomorrow to discuss an employment option."

"Is that what they call it now?"

"Damn it, Lew. You're distracting me. I thought we were discussing us."

"We are. You might as well spill it all out. What do you want? Do you want me and just me?"

"I... Like you said, I hadn't thought about it."

"Okay. You want to wait to do anything, until you decide?"

I sit in a stupefied silence.

He moves away, shifting back. "Let me know when."

"That's not fair to put it on me. You're the one who changed everything."

"Well, you didn't seem to mind a few minutes ago when you were taking off your clothes. Ex...cuse...me for thinking you agreed."

"You... You..." I mutter. "Who the hell do you think you are—God's gift to womanhood?" I glare at him. "Yeah. I'll let you know. When hell freezes over."

"Fine."

"Fine."

He lurches to his feet. "I'll leave the blanket. Enjoy the view."

I hear his footsteps echoing away from me in the dark. I sit there naked from the waist up in the darkness and wonder what in the hell just happened.

* * *

Damn him. I'm sitting on my sleeping bag in the tack room silently fuming. I can't believe the whole conversation as I replay it over and over in my mind. It's almost dawn and I've slept very little. I've never seen Lew like that. Never. He's generally so mild mannered, and to have him turn on me. Crap. I hardly understand it, myself, but I keep coming back to the fact that I was right. We shouldn't do anything until we're clear about what we want, especially in our own minds. To be honest, I know exactly what I want. I want him. As I finally calm down, I come to the realization that he was so angry because he wants me, too. I can't come up with any other explanation. He wants me and was jealous.

Dad's asleep in the lower bunk with Rena in a sleeping bag on the top. I've been lying on a thick foam pad on the floor. After rolling over for the zillionth time, I start crying. Trying not to wake either of them, I muffle the sound, and try to get some sleep.

I did sleep a little because I'm abruptly awakened by muffled laughter in the main barn. Rena and Dad already seem up and gone to breakfast without waking me. Several men sneak into the tack room to get saddles and other gear. Sitting up in my sleeping bag, I find Win carrying an armload of various tack, motioning vigorously that I should get moving. Glancing at my phone, I see that it's just after seven, and quickly scoot into the tiny bathroom to wash my face and brush my teeth. When I emerge, I find the main center hall is now full of men, calling to each other, saddling horses, and playfully jostling around.

I catch Win to ask, "What's going on?"

"We're having a male bonding event—early morning ride and play 'Injuns'. Uncle Billy brought up some of the family herd yesterday. We're going to gallop around and raise hell."

"Okay?"

"Watch and see," he says.

Lew gives me a sardonic smile. He looks like he didn't get much sleep, either.

The horses are taken outside by the impassioned horsemen of the group: Lew, of course, and Win, Willie, Paul, Bruce, and Tommy. Pots of red, white, and black paint are passed around, then used to put lines and designs on their faces while howling with laughter, playing. Win, Tommy, Willie, and Lew put handprints on their horse's rumps and zig-zagging streaks of paint. Win dips his hands in the red paint and slaps Bruce and Paul's faces and chests with it.

I don't recognize Lew. Half of his face is painted black. Everyone now is bare-chested in the cold morning air. Some of the guys wear distinctive blue beaded necklaces. Paul and Bruce swing into their saddles while Lew, Willie, Win, and Tommy vault onto their horses bareback. The horses are milling around, crowding into each other, as the men scream war whoops.

By now everyone has gathered on the grass in front of the house to watch.

Win and Tommy's long hair is blowing in the wind. Paul has untied his hair from a short ponytail. They all look different, even a little scary, as they yell. Lew's horse rears up in the air followed by Win and Willie's horses. Lew looks at me as if to say, "Hot blood, huh."

Yeah.

Suddenly Win yells something in Blackfeet, 'Ki' and Lew answers him, 'Kagau', as they all sweep out of the immediate area.

Susan is standing behind me. "Wow," she says.

Next to her is Bruce's mother, Sophie, who is hiding tears. I wonder why.

The horsemen are so different from the civilized men I met in the last few days. Lew is showing another side of himself I never imagined. Win, Willie, and Lew grew up on the reservation as best friends from young boyhood. Lew told me that Win is unparalleled as a rider, in a class of his own. But Lew is majestic on a horse.

As if on cue, the men start riding around and around in a progressively larger circle as Tommy rises to his knees, then to his feet, finally standing up, balancing on his horse's back. He's an amputee, for God's sake. Lew, Willie, and Win drop off one side of their horses, hanging precariously by a bent knee, yelling war cries.

Straightening up, they gallop off to the east down the ridge trail. Diminishing sounds of laughter and war-like noises drift back to us on the wind.

I'm stunned and stand motionless for some moments. Finally, I walk over to Sophie and ask, "Are you okay?"

She smiles at me. "Watching Bruce like that, part of caring crazy friends…" She sighs. "It's wonderful. Beyond words."

There is so much I don't know about the people here. They need a semester orientation course for newcomers.

Crossing the yard to the main house, I find the kitchen and volunteer help, getting put on a fruit salad detail. After much chopping and piling up of food, we all sit down on the porch with coffee to await the return of the warriors. Dad comes over and sits down next to me. "Well," he says quietly, "did you get an opportunity?"

"Yes. It was a total disaster."

Dad grimaces. "Damn. Every time I get into social issues with you girls it turns into a mistake of global proportions. I'm sorry."

"Don't sweat it, Dad. I'm sure it was a good idea. I just blew it."

"Do you want to talk about it?"

"Never in my life."

Dad pats my knee. "Oh, well, no matter what, he'll be back east with me. I don't want to lose my football buddy."

I punch him. We wait.

At last, I see them appear a mile down the bluff trail galloping full out. From a distance they could be an Indian war party from the eighteen-hundreds. It's unsettling. They're here in minutes and stop at the porch laughing and talking with everyone. Lew rides over to where I'm sitting and motions to me, stony-faced.

I stand up and walk over. He flattens his foot and reaches down for me. I get a sudden feeling he's staking his territory. Despite myself, I glance over at Charlie, who's not particularly happy, watching us. I'm glad I know how to do this. I let Lew lift me up and we ride off. I'm outside myself, a woman on a horse with her man. The thought astounds me.

In minutes we're near the pool. Lew ties his horse to a tree, then we walk the three hundred feet to the swimming area. He still looks like a wild man with the black face paint.

"Did you get any sleep?"

I look down. "Not much," I say, frowning.

"There's no time left," he says, "so I might as well say this. I'm glad you weren't turned off. And..."

I'm still looking down, and I'm feeling angry again. I don't say anything.

"For God's sake, say something, Miranda."

I turn angry eyes toward him. "I friggin' didn't know what to say last night. I was confused about what I wanted and how to go about it. But that was no excuse for you stomping off like that. You... You jerk."

"Is that the best you can come up with?" he growls at me.

"Okay. You smug, chauvinistic, self-indulgent, asshole."

"Better. Anything else?"

"You…" I look up and see him beginning to grin. I haul back and slug him. But my heart isn't in it. I hide a smile. Then I kick at him, several times.

"I hate you," I say.

"Me, too," he says, and pulls me into his arms. I settle in to feel his bare chest against me. The imminent separation looms.

I'm exhausted and bewildered. "We've wasted some valuable time," I manage.

"I'm sorry, Mira," he mutters. "I blew it."

"No. I blew it."

"You did not. I blew it."

"Damn it. I blew it."

"What are we going to do with each other?" he says, pulling my face up to him for a serious kiss.

Responding to his urgency, I close my eyes.

Pushing me up against a tree, he presses against me. I don't stop him this time as he groans into my mouth and moves his hand down my belly. I hold my breath. But abruptly, frustratingly, he stops himself. "This is a big deal, Mira. Let's hold on. I'll be back out here for two weeks at Christmas."

"Get your fill of experiences before then," I say. I'm joking, but I'm waiting for him to argue against that.

He sighs. I can tell there's something he's not saying. Disconcertingly, he gives me one last lingering kiss, takes my hand, and literally starts pulling me back toward his horse.

This morning has been confusing, but there's one thing I'm not confused about. I love being on the back of a horse with him. It's so…stimulating. My hands stroke his bare skin, moving my fingers around his chest, fingering his blue-beaded necklace.

Suddenly he pulls the horse to a stop. We're halfway back. "Stop it, Mira," he mutters, "unless you want me to take you back to the pool."

"And what if I do."

I'm leaning against him so I can feel, more than hear, another deep sigh. "I have to handle *a business arrangement* of my own first. Back in DC.

My hands pause. We sit there motionless on his horse for several minutes.

"You mean you came onto me when you...?" Anger doesn't begin to cover it.

"Damn it, Mira. We've been close friends for a long time. I never expected I'd feel so strongly. So suddenly. I didn't know how to handle this. I got carried away. I'm sorry."

"You're sorry? You're sorry? I almost scream. "For what...? That you led me on? That the seduction didn't work? What?"

"Look," he says. "It was seeing you out here in my world. I could imagine you living here, being a part of it. It shocked me. I suddenly started to imagine... And..."

"No, damn it," I'm crying now. "What really shocked you was Charlie coming on to me. You were friggin' jealous. Admit it. Talk about being self-centered." I'm sputtering.

"Mira. Stop this." He's angry now.

"You bastard. Well, just go back to your business arrangement. See if I care."

He glares back at me, kicking his horse so suddenly I have to make a frantic grab for him to keep from falling off on my ass. As we approach the stable, I slide myself off before we completely stop, storm through the center hall of the barn, stomping past Paul and Sam in the tack room, who give me a surprised look. Continuing into the small bathroom, I slam the door more loudly than I intend, lock it, and bury my face in my hands. I can hear Lew storm into the barn a few seconds later, grumbling loudly, and adding a string of expletives. Then I hear low laughter as Sam says loudly, "Women troubles."

After what seems like a long time, there's silence in the barn. Pulling myself together, I grab my hairbrush and find my face is smeared with black paint. I'm mindful of the fact that everyone else saw the same thing. Moaning with embarrassment, I wash my face, then walk out of the bathroom.

I'm downcast. No one is waiting for me.

Most people remaining are relaxing, drinking coffee, or cleaning up. Lew is sitting off to the side, staring off into space. Getting some food, I settle myself on the grass next to Dad, leaning back against his leg. Neither one of us says anything. More people start leaving for parts unknown. Plans have been made for Thanksgiving and Christmas holidays. There have been over thirty-five people coming and going. Someone kept track.

Dad taps me on the shoulder and says quietly, "Not getting better, huh?"

I sit there glumly and shake my head.

"Honey, look at me."

I do.

"You've cared about him a long time, haven't you?"

I wince and start to fidget.

"Listen to me. He's going to realize soon you wouldn't be so upset if this wasn't important to you."

"I have no idea what's in his head."

"He cares deeply about you. I know that."

I look over at Lew and sigh.

"You got your message across. He's no idiot. Even if you weren't terribly skillful in delivering it, I'm glad you said something."

"He's a piece of crap." I say, putting my head in my hands.

"Look, honey. You can't influence everything. You've put a lot of thought in to coming out here to live. Quit messing your mind up over Lew and enjoy it. It's a beautiful place."

It takes a moment before I nod. "Dad, what would I do without you?"

He slides his arm around my shoulders. "Come on. Take a walk with me before we have to go."

Charlie, who apparently has been watching us, approaches with an inscrutable expression. "I'll see you this evening," he says, loudly enough for Lew to hear. Smiling, he hurries to his car.

Taking one final look at Lew, who's now actively scowling into the distance, I walk off with my dad.

CHAPTER 13

MIRANDA

CHARLIE AND I are looking at an older truck for me before we have dinner—a very older truck. I found it on the Internet, and it sounded perfect. It's a classic old Ford from the early fifties, dark green, with a huge metal grill in front. I can see myself tooling on down the road in it with a blade of grass in my teeth.

It's got charm and the old farmer assures me it will chug on forever if I change the belts occasionally. There's plenty of room under the hood so I can work on it easily, he says. That was not a big selling point for me, but I acted as if it was. Charlie kept nodding seriously as if I'd probably change the oil tonight. Obviously, the retired farmer knows how to maintain vehicles. He has all the records from the day he bought it in 1953, a stack of papers two inches thick.

Charlie laughs at me when I kick the tires. "Looks good to me," I say.

"Me, too," he says. "You're not going to get very good mileage, but that dinosaur should last another forty years, besides, you look good in green. Can you drive a long stick on the floor?"

"I have no idea, but how hard can it be? Will you show me?"

I'm now bumping and lurching down the road. They hadn't heard of power steering when they built this baby, but I'm learning to work with it, plus it's going to be great arm exercise. After Charlie's coaching, I'm finally getting the hang of it. At least I can drive well enough to get back to my apartment. Charlie is behind me with his hazard lights on. That's overkill. I'm not that bad. Besides, I see him laughing in the rearview mirror as I grind the gears at a stoplight.

We decide on beer and the biggest, baddest burgers in Great Falls and if we die young who cares. We're starting a second round of drinks when I ask, "So what happened between Lizzie and Bruce? They seem like close friends now."

"Didn't Lew ever tell you any of it?"

"We didn't talk about unpleasant things out here. Mostly funny stories about the guys, horse racing, pranks as kids. I know Lizzie's sister Ellie used to date Bruce years ago, and that Lizzie forgave him for something bad he did to Ellie."

He smiles. "Then there's a lot you don't know."

"Lew didn't want to go into it until I knew the people better. He said it wouldn't be fair to them. It's all a bit of a mystery."

"You can tell Bruce is accepted, even loved now, so I'll start with that. He did something almost unforgivable and went to prison for it. He redeemed himself by saving Tashi's life, almost losing his own in the process."

"Tashi? Willie's sister?"

He nods. "Confused yet?"

"Nope. What did he do to deserve prison? He seems so softhearted to me."

"He tried to kill Ellie and nearly succeeded."

"What!"

"The bottom line is that he almost murdered Ellie in uncontrolled rage after a life of psychological abuse by his Svengali-like father. Somehow Lizzie was able to forgive him and encouraged him to build a new life. There are all kinds of extenuating circumstances, but he's completely changed."

"How could everyone forgive him?"

"You can see how much Tashi means to everyone. She'd be dead if Bruce hadn't saved her. She was trapped in a crevasse, freezing to death."

"Unbelievable. Do you trust him? Can you be sure he's completely changed?"

"Who knows what any of us can be driven to in our deepest, darkest self, but I've never encountered anyone trying harder than Bruce has. It's awe-inspiring when you know what hell of a home life he came from."

"His mother seems so normal, so compassionate. How could she let that happen?"

"She was brutalized, too. Dominated for decades."

When I don't say anything, he continues. "Big money and

power used to destroy… It can crush you. I've seen it. Bruce's early life was wretched. The total opposite of mine."

The conversation has gotten so serious, that I take a sip of beer, looking silently at Charlie.

"Sorry, I don't usually get so introspective."

"I'm grateful you're letting me know you."

He appears to study me as he has several times before, making me feel slightly uneasy. To change the mood, I ask, "How do you come into the picture?"

He can't help a soft sigh. "I met Lizzie when she and Win were having a rough time several years ago. I was attracted, to put it mildly." He smiles with some discomfort. "Win had disappeared… For several months. Another long story. I should have known at the time it wasn't completely over between them. I shouldn't have interfered…" He takes a sip of beer. "But I did," he says, smiling sheepishly. "When it ended, I stayed on. I'd sort of fallen in love with the whole family."

His vulnerability is endearing. This is obviously a painful subject, but I have to ask, "Do you still love her, Charlie?"

He takes a moment, deciding what to say. Finally, smiling wryly, he says, "Truthfully? I suppose I do. You know, I didn't spend that much time with her. And she loved Win so much I never had a prayer."

I'm surprised at his honesty.

"Did you get to know Vinnie?" he asks, obviously changing the subject.

"Not really. I should have tried harder, but loving friends always surrounded her. I couldn't elbow in. I understand it's some sort of a rite of passage."

He nods. "She told me once that being a life-long friend is as strong a bond as marriage. I don't exactly believe it, and she obviously said that to make me feel better." He sounds wistful. "But it did help." He looks into my eyes. "Vinnie is the glue that holds us all together. She brings out the best in people." He smiles ironically. "But only after she determines you're worth it. She decided Bruce had a good soul, and that was enough for everyone. Amazing really."

We sit quietly for several minutes before he says casually, "I haven't been seriously interested in anyone since then. I've decided I need to try harder. I've been sulking long enough. And I've gotten to the point I have to remember to feel bad."

"That seems like a good sign," I say. "I hardly know you, but you seem like an extraordinarily good man." I smile warmly at him. "You should look around. It's a cold world out there, and winter's coming on."

"Are you suggesting yourself?" he says lightly.

"You mean, sort of a burnt offering? No, Charlie. Find a girl like you."

"Like me...?" He seems confused, then slides closer to me in the booth and puts his thumb under my chin. "If by any chance I was interested, are you available? I watched you and Lew. It seemed to me that there was a lot of tension there, let alone the smudged face paint."

I wince with embarrassment.

"Seriously, I don't want to be the second man out again."

I flush. "Don't mess with me, Charlie. I'm not in your league and you know it."

"Damn it. That was exactly what I meant up at the ranch. I knew it would be difficult to be merely a normal man with you. And you haven't answered my question."

"All right. If you press me, Lew and I have been friends, very good friends for years, and are circling each other, considering more," I admit. "That's a good way to describe it. We've never talked in detail about people we're currently dating. When romances blow over, we laugh together at our failures." I allow a little anger to show through. "He just admitted he's seeing someone back east. And after putting some uncomfortable pressure on me out here. He didn't volunteer to end it and pursue me." I pause and look away. "But if he did, I'd be tempted."

I moan almost inaudibly. "I can't believe I'm telling you all this. I guess it's because you leveled with me about Lizzie."

"So, you admit you like him, but you're not involved."

I sigh. "Yes, I like him, and we're not involved."

"But how important...?"

"Let's quit this, Charlie. I'm done talking about Lew. I'm getting uncomfortable and I'd like to call it a night."

"What does that mean?"

I grimace. "I'm beginning to feel like a piece of meat you're about to devour."

"What in the hell are you talking about?"

"I'm sorry. I'm not making any sense to me, either. Please. Can you just take me home?"

"Yes, I can do that," he says stiffly.

He throws some money on the table, and we walk out.

With an annoyed look, he mutters, "I'll get the car."

We drive home in silence. Charlie gets out and walks me to the door. We still haven't said a word.

"I wish you'd tell me why you're running away," he finally asks.

"I feel like you're playing with me. I don't feel equal in this contest."

"Miranda, you don't feel equal. That's the whole problem here. If I were a typical struggling jerk, it wouldn't bother you if I tried to find out if you were available. That's all I was doing." He touches my face gently, looking into my eyes. "I don't want to get hurt, like any guy. I like you a lot. More than a lot. In fact, you're the first girl I've seriously considered letting into my life since... Well, you know."

I turn to him, biting my lip while considering what he said. He really is something special. My eyes drop to his lips. We stand there on my little porch for a long time.

Finally, I say. "Do you want to come in for a drink?"

"I thought you'd never ask," he replies softly.

We walk in, and I head over to light a fire in the small fireplace. It's getting chilly at night now.

"Let me do that," he offers.

I go into the kitchen to open a bottle of wine.

When he's finished, he comes over and sits beside me on the couch. We take a token sip of wine then set the glasses on the coffee table. Even to me it seems like a waste of time. Slipping his arm around my shoulders, he gently pulls me toward him. He really is a beautiful man. *Oh, just enjoy it,* I think to myself. His lips are warm and unrelenting. Positioning my hands on his chest, I slowly move them up and around his neck. He murmurs my name, "Miranda, lovely Miranda." His lips move lower, caressing my neck.

His hair falls into his eyes. I reach up to move it aside and am drawn to his remarkably blue eyes. His lips draw my attention, and I give up the fight. With my tongue I touch his through his open lips before he pulls me down on the couch so that we're lying stretched out together.

He becomes not a rich man, not a better man, just a man who wants to feel some warmth on a cold fall night. I want that, too. He slides his hands up my back outside my shirt. He feels so good, and more than that, I'm beginning to believe he's sincere. He's lonely. He really likes me. It also dawns on me this is not a game to him.

I look into his eyes as he smiles at me. "I'm amazed by what you're making me feel," he says. "It's been a long time. I like the feel of you in my arms."

"I'm beginning to believe you, Charlie. I'm not going anywhere, not tonight."

He starts to slowly unbutton my blouse, then hooks his hand underneath my breasts. I run my fingers through his long reddish hair until he grins at me.

"What?" I ask.

"I'm glad I put my chips back on the table. This is working out better than I expected."

"I'm a cheap drunk, and you're very tempting. I'm fighting the urge to see how far I can get with you."

"I'm curious myself."

"You seem rather willing, if you don't mind me saying."

"No. No. I'm really a hard case," he says. "You're going to have to try a lot harder. I'll just lie here and see if you can get to second base."

I giggle. I lean over him and feel my breast flatten against his chest. "I bet I can get your shirt off in ten seconds."

He looks up at me. I see his smile fade into something else. There's a little anxiety there as well as desire as his eyes narrow.

"This is harder than you can imagine. It's hard to chance this. I've built some walls against being used." He sighs. "I wish you didn't know who I am."

"It's hard for both of us."

I can see him apparently struggling with himself, pulling back a little.

"All I know," I say finally, "is that for this night I'm sharing it with you. I would feel empty if you left. I've been trying to bury my fear, too. I give up. Please kiss me. And don't stop for a while."

He forcibly takes me in his arms and starts kissing me. And caressing me. I forgot to put some music on. I hear his breath, his sighs, and the cold wind tapping a branch, and rattling on the window. I pull him closer to me.

"You're so beautiful," he says at last. "If I had to leave now it would be painful. I need your warmth. I've been out in the cold for a long time."

"I love to watch you in the firelight, Charlie. But I need a flaw here, just to make you seem real." I take his hand and kiss the back of it then put his thumb in my mouth and circle it with my tongue.

He stifles a groan. "I have plenty, Miranda, and I'll create more if that's what you want."

We lie there until the embers dim with our arms around each other. I remember the Blackfeet phrase Lew taught me, 'iikiitammiksistsiko'. It's been a very good day—and I need to stop thinking about Lew.

"Charlie? Do you have to do anything tomorrow?"

"I was going to save the world from total destruction. But I can put that off. I'd rather spend it with you. Why?"

"I was going to play hard to get, but it seems insincere. I admit it. You're incredible."

He grins at me. "Covering your body with kisses for twenty-four hours sounds about right. Who knows? Maybe the world can get by on its own."

I reach up and grab a handful of hair and pull him down on top of me then laugh at my own audacity. "You bring out the lecherous woman in me. I want you, and I can't believe I just said that." I moan with embarrassment.

His eyes darken. "I'll take whatever you'll give me, but I warn you. If you unleash me, there's no telling where it will end."

"I'll chance it, Charlie, for tonight, anyway."

"The hell with the consequences," I hear him mutter to himself. "Caution is for the faint of heart."

* * *

It's been a wonderful ten days, maybe the best in my life. I'm being wooed. Charlie is leaving to resume his business interests on Wednesday, and he's putting pressure on me to come along and meet the family. I have two dresses with me and believe me, they are nothing special. I'm fighting this off, hard. I don't understand his insistence. Charlie says it's just a date. They're having one of his fleet of corporate jets pick him up. That's not a date, that's an international event.

We can spend three or four days together then they'll fly me back out here, alone in the jet. It's ridiculous. I've been having fantasies of holding a knife to the pilot's throat and having him fly me to Caracas with Ben Affleck. I've definitely seen too many thriller movies recently.

The fall sunny days have been stimulating to a new romance. It's sweater weather and dramatically wild up in the mountains. Charlie knows the area well from his fire-fighting connection. He used to fly helicopters himself but hasn't kept it up, so today he arranged with a pilot friend from the Missoula fire base to take us on a wilderness tour. His friend stayed with the helicopter with instructions to allow us privacy as we picnic by a crystal aqua lake. I keep searching for Charlie's flaws without success.

I smile to myself. I've turned into the aggressor. Charlie's been holding something back. He said he doesn't want to pressure me physically while my *friendship* with Lew is unresolved. Maybe in both our minds.

"Tell me again why I need to meet your parents."

"Don't be silly. You don't need to do anything. You have several law firms interested, and Jack already wants you for the dispatcher position. You're going to choose something in a few weeks. I can show you my world before we both get swept up earning a living."

"But Charlie, I'm happy with you here in Montana. I still think of you as a boring regular guy. Isn't that what you want?"

"I want you to know my other life because it's not what you imagine. You expect a hundred-room resort-mansion with female servants in short black uniforms with frilly white aprons and a butler." He laughs to himself.

"What?"

"We do have Stosh, but he's fifty-seven and has been with our family for twenty years. If we tried to dress him up as a butler, he'd roll around on the floor laughing. My parents are real people. Think about it, Miranda. Okay?"

I cram a huge piece of sugar cookie in his mouth, kissing him as he laughs and chokes. "Okay, I'll think about it."

CHAPTER 14

MIRANDA

I WAS CONVINCED. When Charlie turned on that movie-star smile, what could I do? The flight is luxurious. I pad around in socks on a thick carpet just because I can. Charlie said this is one of the two family mini jets, and today Charlie and I are the only passengers. Our pilot is again the same elusive man from the reunion. As before, he keeps our contacts brief and professional. Strangely though, on several occasions when Charlie went up to discuss flight plans, I heard strong laughter coming from the cockpit. Charlie confessed that the pilot, Hugh, has a strange sense of humor and is under strict orders to behave himself, then refused to explain what he meant.

We've landed at Philadelphia International Airport and are currently headed in an ordinary taxi to Charlie's home near the Main Line. I was expecting a stretch limo, but he explained he was pretending to be normal, then added he'd rather die than be seen in one. I've given up feeling overly nervous. He says they rarely use more than one fork or spoon, so I guess I'll survive. Charlie also made the point that he hasn't seen a cup and saucer since last Thanksgiving. Like everyone they use mismatched mugs, featuring things like "World's Best Grandma."

The houses change from normal, to big, to really big, to really rich. Even the trees look wealthy, looking like aging Grande dames, supporting heavy umbrellas of leaves, which form a canopy covering the residential street, making it appear like a tunnel. The local avenue is dotted with old-fashioned, tulip-shaped glass streetlamps. We pass seriously over-the-top places with huge, manicured lawns, set far back from the street. At last, we slow, approaching a brick structure that supports a heavy iron gate, now swung open—the formal entrance of a long, curved driveway. A traditional iron fence rims the entire property with sharp spikes on the top. Just as we turn in the driveway, an older woman jogs by with a golden retriever on a leash, enthusiastically waving to Charlie, who waves back.

"Lois," he explains. "Our neighbor."

Inspecting the house, I find it a more reasonable size and dimension than I expected. The red brick structure has six large wooden-framed windows on the second floor, spread out evenly, and highlighted with painted white wood and dark green shutters. The floor level is elevated above the ground with four steps leading up to a large veranda area. The roof extends over a covered drive-through area supported with white wooden pillars.

Charlie pays the cab driver and comes around to open my door.

An attractive, dark-haired woman in her mid-fifties rushes out to meet us. "Hi Miranda," she says, almost breathless. "I'm so pleased to meet you." She holds out her hands, then takes mine in both of hers.

"Obviously, Miranda, this is my mother, Anna. Mom, this is Miranda."

It isn't obvious. She's wearing rumpled tan slacks, and a simple long-sleeved cream t-shirt. Her undisciplined wavy hair indicates she only occasionally runs a brush through it.

"Charlie lied to you. I need to get that out of the way first. We have two additional family members, not one—Stosh and, of course, Molly, who's also my best friend. We're sort of a co-op."

What a funny way to start. I smile helplessly at her.

"Charlie told me he was trying to downplay our lifestyle. Anyway, Stosh, as my son told you, does everything in the world: chauffeur, gardener, plumber, and keeps Charlie 2 company, mostly watching sporting events. They wager the outcomes, but I'm not allowed to know how much. Molly is our cook, housekeeper, and my confidante. I follow her around, helping her clean, so that she'll listen to my opinions on everything. Charlie 2 gets tired of listening to me." She stops for a breath.

Charlie laughs. "Jeez, Mom. Give Miranda a chance to get a word in edgewise."

Now I'm grinning. "I was worried I wouldn't have anything to say. But maybe I could just clean around behind you, cleaning behind Molly, sharing ideas?"

"Absolutely. I hope you don't have too many opinions, though."

I'm stunned. I really like Charlie's mom.

"When's Dad getting home?" Charlie asks.

"Soon. He's galloping home to meet Miranda. He couldn't wait. And I tried to put off Tina but no luck."

"Where's Stosh?" Charlie asks.

"Soccer. Maddy's playing."

Charlie turns to me. "His six-year-old granddaughter. It's the end of the world if he's not there, or if he's even late. I was wondering why he didn't pick us up."

I'm beginning to get nervous, again.

Charlie notices and puts his arm around me. "My family is hopelessly, over the top, friendly. I know that's not what you expected. We need lessons on being cool."

"You don't need lessons on anything, Charlie." We smile intimately at each other.

Anna smiles happily at both of us. "Come on in."

The house is clean, but happily cluttered with books, technology, art projects, and gardening supplies. It's a home. An older lady, wearing skinny jeans and a similar long-sleeved t-shirt as Anna, comes rushing out from the kitchen. "Hello, I'm Molly. I was throwing together some snacks. You must be Miranda."

"Very happy to meet you," I say.

She also looks very pleased, smiling broadly at me, while rushing over to Charlie for a quick kiss.

"Anna, why don't you take Miranda out to the back patio, and I'll bring drinks," Molly offers.

"I'll carry the tray," Charlie adds.

Charlie's mom and I leave through French doors, which open onto a sloping mowed lawn with huge trees that appear intentionally placed as art objects.

"You're trying to hide it," she says, "but I can tell we're not exactly what you expected."

"Charlie may have told you. I do know a little about the family…" I search for the right word, "business. But you don't seem all that different from my family in Silver Spring. It is surprising."

"We keep a low profile," Anna admits, "and mostly we're a

family of ideas and relationships, not possessions." She smiles, adding, "We tend to come on a bit strongly. I'm sorry about that. We're happy for Charlie, that he's interested in someone. He's been *not interested,* for a while. Tell me a little about yourself."

"Well, I just got my law degree from Georgetown, but I don't want to be the traditional urban attorney. My parents have encouraged me to explore alternatives." I smile. "And my Dad was in the military. He wants me to have experiences."

Before she can respond, loud voices are heard in the house. A striking, older man barrels out to join us. He looks as I remember him from several years ago, maybe with more gray hair, but with the same piercing blue eyes. Behind him follows an attractive, expensively dressed, female corporate type with an auburn pageboy. Charlie trails, third in line, carrying a tray, glaring at her in an exasperated way.

"Sorry, Charlie. She might as well get all the pain out of the way." She turns to me. "I'm Tina, Charlie's older, protective sister. I'm here to make sure you aren't going to eat him alive."

"Tina!" responds Charlie. "This is intimidating enough without you scaring her to death."

"Miranda doesn't look a bit scared," Tina smiles warmly.

I smile back. Charlie's sister is a little overwhelming, but I like her.

"Don't let the rest of my family frighten you," interrupts Charlie's dad. "I'm the normal one. Please call me Charlie, too. Or rather Charlie 2." He holds up two fingers.

I shake my head. How can I feel awkward in this group? "Okay. I give up. You were right, Charlie. This was a very good idea."

"How about food?" Molly interrupts loudly from the kitchen.

"Molly was Tina's nanny thirty-some years ago and never left," Anna explains. "She takes care of us, and we take care of her. The same with Stosh. His kids are grown and his wife travels so he's here a lot."

"And you, Molly? Do you have another family?"

"This is my family. These kids are my kids."

Charlie smiles broadly. "That's the reason I turned out so well. I have two moms."

I settle into a comfortable chair, feeling relaxed enough to put my feet up on an ottoman.

"I've already told everyone about your new move to the Wild West," Charlie says.

"I was just telling your mother my plan not to be a big-city lawyer, at least not now. I want some adventure and wide-open spaces."

"That sounds uncomfortably familiar," grumbles Charlie 2. "I guess us old nose-to-the-grindstone guys will have to deal with it. What do your folks say?"

"They've been encouraging. If I'm self-supporting, they say go for it."

Sometime later, after putting my small suitcase in my assigned bedroom, I heave a sigh of relief, finally enjoying a moment of quiet. My guest room is an oasis of white, dominated by a dark wooden, four-poster bed with an ivory lace covering, positioned on waxed hardwood floors. The only contrasting color in the room is an enormous green glass vase filled with red and yellow zinnias.

Tina had walked me upstairs to show me the way, telling me funny family stories that always seemed to involve her younger sister, Juli. Surprisingly, Hugh, our elusive pilot, often took part, often causing near disasters.

* * *

We've had a great visit. Charlie and I are currently lying out on a blanket under a tree, drinking some of Molly's lemonade. I've been here for three days and feel comfortable wearing jeans and un-ironed cotton shirts like everyone else. Most of the time, I forget this is a financially extraordinary family until someone takes a call from Singapore or Switzerland or Brussels and makes a low-key decision, negotiating multi-million-dollar international contracts with apparent nonchalance. Charlie seems oblivious to my amazement.

I adore Stosh Turkovitch, who immigrated from Poland as a small child. Every day, he brings me fresh-cut flowers from the garden. Over at the pool, Stosh wraps a towel around his granddaughter, Maddy, then they both head this way.

"We'll all miss you, Miranda," he says, as they settle down on a corner of our blanket.

"I'll miss you both, too," I say, laughing at Maddy, whose teeth are chattering loudly.

"She refuses to get out until she's shriveled and blue," Stosh explains. "I'm babysitting this afternoon."

"I'm not a baby," she says. "I'm six."

"I agree," Stosh tells her. "You're very grown up."

"I'm hungry," she says.

"Well, hope to see you again soon," he says, getting up.

"Me, too," I smile, adding, "Stosh, the flowers were really special. Thank you."

He smiles. "Come on," he says to Maddy. "I know where the chocolate chip cookie jar is."

"Bye, Miranda," she says.

"Bye, Maddy."

She waves, then pulls on Stosh's hand as he smiles down at her. We watch as they cross the lawn and enter the kitchen.

"Are you sure you don't mind flying back alone on Sunday ?" Charlie asks.

"It's exciting, to tell you the truth, a story to tell my grandchildren. But it's going to feel very lonely out there without you." Carefully putting my empty glass on the grass, I attack him, kissing him in a way that emphasizes my point. We enjoy each other, stopping just short of embarrassing anyone watching from the kitchen window.

"Are you about ready?" he asks when I stop assaulting him.

"All packed. I should call Dad. It's about two and a half hours from Philly to Silver Spring?"

"If we can get out of here in an hour, we should be there around three. Miss some of the rush-hour traffic. It's Friday so it will be worse than usual."

"My parent's house is close to the Four Seasons—ten, fifteen minutes."

"But the traffic between their house and the hotel will be brutal. The hotel is only a mile from the White House." He pauses, studying my face. "I should get current with my helicopter pilot's license. It would be nice to fly us directly to Silver Spring. College

Park Airport is only a few miles from your house, right?"

I glance at him humorously.

He smiles, wryly. "Okay. I looked it up."

"So, what would it take?"

"Less than you might expect. I'd need a new flight physical from a doctor authorized to do that, and probably ten hours with an instructor to get back in the groove." He takes my hand. "And why not? It'll be something to keep me out of trouble back here. Then I'd need to fly often enough to keep my hand in."

Despite myself, the benefits of the lifestyle affect me. I'm trying to keep it in perspective, separate from Charlie, himself.

"Are you excited about the party tonight?"

"I am. I love talking to anyone interesting. And like your mom, I have a lot of opinions. After meeting your family, advising our President and the Leader of China should be a piece of cake."

"The guest of honor will be disappointed, but I don't expect they'll make it, although they should talk to you sometime and get ideas how to run their countries."

Charlie's mom walks over to us across the lawn, carrying a small box. "Hi, you two. I understand you're going to Mort's party at the Four Seasons tonight. I thought Miranda would get a kick out of wearing some diamonds. Don't if you don't want to, dear, but they're just gathering dust in the safe." She opens the box. Inside is a simple, but elegant, diamond necklace and matching earrings.

I gasp. "How beautiful. I can't even pretend I wouldn't love to wear this. And the nicest thing, Anna, is it's a vote of confidence in me. I'm very grateful. Yes. I accept." I get up and give her a hug.

She laughs and leaves.

"Charlie?"

"Mom really likes you. That's obvious. It makes me very happy."

"You were right, of course. Your family is wonderful."

"I wanted you to know them. I haven't brought a girl home very often in my life. It's been special for me, too."

* * *

Four hours later we're sitting in our family living room in Silver

Spring. Dad and Charlie already knew each other from Montana so he concentrated on putting Mom at ease. She responded by being her usual gracious self, making Charlie feel welcome, asking about the job search, my new truck, and meeting Charlie's parents. She left moments ago for her part-time job at our local library, giving me an enthusiastic thumbs-up on the way out the door with a huge smile. We'll come back here after the reception to spend the night.

We have over two hours before we leave so we're still loose and hanging out. Charlie hung his tux in a bag in the closet by the front door. I'm guarding the box with the diamonds in it on my lap for safe keeping when I hear footsteps on the front porch. A familiar voice calls out, "Oki, Tony. Thought I'd drop by... Whose hot car...?"

Lew bursts through the front door then stops dead in his tracks. "Miranda?"

"Hi Lew," I say.

He hesitates, then, "Charlie, what are you doing here?"

"Taking Miranda to a party before she flies back to Montana on Sunday."

"Oh..."

"Sit down, Lew," Dad interrupts. "I'm glad you stopped by. They just drove down from Philadelphia. If you'd been an hour later, you might have missed them."

I'm wondering what everyone in the room is feeling. I'm uncomfortable, even guilty, and I'm not sure why. "Anything new here, Lew?" I ask. "I haven't heard a word. Not even a text since you left."

Lew looks pre-occupied. "Things have been complicated. Lots I can't talk about. I'm going overseas the middle of next week and... And..."

The conversation stops. Everyone, including Dad, seems frozen. Charlie tries to say something generic, "So, how's the job going...?" Then he stops, too.

Lew eyes seem tortured. Suddenly he looks straight at me. "What are you doing here...? Back here?"

"Visiting Charlie's family and Dad."

"You should have let me know."

"I didn't know I had to have permission?"

"It's not permission. It's..."

"Why does it concern you?"

"Your welfare always concerns me."

"What are you talking about? You've got a business arrangement of your own. You told me that. It's my life, Lew."

Charlie and Dad look like they're watching a play. I realize, dimly, that there's something here going on with Lew that I don't understand.

I can see tension in his eyes, something beyond anger or jealousy. No one says anything as Lew visibly fights an inner battle. He looks back and forth between Dad and me.

He sighs. "I've had death threats, Mira. One of them may involve you."

Charlie gasps. "What are you talking about?"

"Death threats?" I ask.

"They started before the trip to Montana. Threatening only me. But since I've been back, I've received two more. One threat included *a friend*."

I'm terrified for him. "Why? Is it your job?"

"What does security say?" Dad asks. "Do they know who's behind it?"

"They don't know, Tony. The notes are all they have. As you know, I've been concentrating on Middle East terrorist networks." He glances fearfully at my face. "Obviously, it's threatening something consequential; or exposing a broad organization by a shadowy larger player. I was coming over to let you know."

"My God, Lew," I say.

"I want you gone, Miranda. Now. As soon as you can arrange it."

"That's crazy. We're just friends. We haven't talked for weeks. You have someone back here. Why me?"

He looks at me a long time, considering his answer.

Finally, he admits, "We don't know who could be in danger."

"Miranda was flying back to Montana Sunday morning, but we should bump that up to tomorrow," Charlie says grimly. "She's going back alone, but I'll be with her until she's on our plane."

"Hold on," I interrupt, turning to Charlie, then to Lew. "I have a say in this. I can't see how this involves me."

Lew glances out the front window and quickly scans the area as if he hadn't heard me. "Don't leave her alone," he says to Charlie. "Not for a second." Then he adds, "Even back there, Mira, watch your back."

He looks so scared that I finally become frightened. "Dad. Should I be worried?"

"Describe the notes. What did they say?" Dad asks.

"All the same. Block letters on generic white typing paper. No prints. Someone was careful."

"So...?" I ask. "Specifically, what...?"

"The first two said, QUIT NSA and a drawing of a skull. The last one said, QUIT OR DIE – G-FRIEND, TOO."

"That was it? Nothing else?"

"Nothing."

"Who do they think G-FRIEND refers to?" Dad asks.

I can see Lew get even more uncomfortable.

"It could be any ex-girlfriend, my very-recent ex-girlfriend, or..." he pauses, looking at me, "my best friend."

"But...? What are the chances I'm at risk? I really think..."

"No. I agree," Dad interrupts. "We should get Miranda out of here. I've been working for the NSA for five years. I've never heard of anything like this."

That silences me.

"No one is seriously worried about Miranda," Lew points out. "Except me."

We try to digest this.

"Terrorists are getting bolder and more dispersed worldwide," Lew continues. "Terror cells act independently, so monitoring the original communication links is almost useless." He shakes his head. "Everyone is hacking everyone. We're the most worried about the Chinese and the Iranians. Or maybe the Russians are behind this or they're acting alone. It's odd that there were no other specific demands."

"They were specific enough," Dad mutters. "Have they set up surveillance?"

"They're pushing me to accept a bodyguard. I'd hate that." He sighs. "If these threats are meant to soften me up, they're working. It's killing me that Miranda might be caught up in all this."

"Okay. Fine," I relent. "I'll fly back tomorrow. But we're staying here tonight like we planned."

"Good enough," Lew agrees, then asks, "What are you doing tonight?"

"We're going to a very upscale party at the Four Seasons. I thought Miranda would get a kick out of it," replies Charlie.

"Who knows you'll be there?" Lew asks me.

"My parents and the people in this room."

"You didn't have to make a reservation?" Dad asks.

"No," Charlie replies. "I know the people organizing it—family friends. Over-the-top retirement party. We won't have a problem."

"How about if I come and hang out. Keep my eyes open?" Lew smiles innocently. "Besides, I love mingling with blue-bloods."

I suspect he has a more personal interest. And what about this ex-girlfriend? I catch Charlie looking at Lew with less than total enthusiasm. Unfortunately, there's no gracious way he can get out of it.

"Sure," he says grudgingly. "It's black tie. Is that a problem?"

"I'll try not to embarrasses you," Lew says, smiling pointedly at Charlie. "Can you let the gatekeepers know?"

Charlie pulls out his phone and sends a text. "Done."

"Fine," says Lew. "I'll be lurking around in the shadows."

"You do that, Lew," agrees Charlie.

I give Dad a look. Despite the scary news, he's hiding a smile. I wink back. I'm in love with everyone in the room. This could become a major problem, but I've gotta say, I'm enjoying this. I've been a shrinking violet most of my life. Maybe it's my time in the sun.

"I've got to get dressed. See you later tonight, Lew."

"Yeah. I've gotta go and iron my best hoodie." He smiles jovially at Charlie and is gone.

ASH

Bloody hell. I want out of this amateurish fiasco. Some higher-ups are obviously panicking. After all these years, this very instant, I'm supposed to drop everything at my cover location, possibly never to be heard from again, make up some flimsy excuse, hustle to the Four Seasons, find an ambush point, and kill Black River. My handlers know I'm primarily an information gatherer, not a trained assassin. He must be threatening something crucial.

The last time I even fired a weapon was six months ago at a gun range. Still, I'm an excellent marksman, and they know it. It's in my dossier. But damn! Obviously, I'm expendable. No thought for my safety, escape route, anything. The powers-that-be, whoever they are, have many opaque layers to protect themselves. At least they didn't order me to kill myself outright if I was caught... Yet. Besides, it might have put a damper on my enthusiasm.

CHAPTER 15

MIRANDA

I'D CALLED RENA just before we left Charlie's house in Philly, thinking she might be available, but she was stuck in New York and couldn't get free. She would have been in her element at the Four Seasons and loved to see Lew in a tux. She asked for a picture.

We're just getting out of Charlie's Audi RS7 as a parking-lot attendant hurries over to take the car. I've been here before, but not like this. Charlie is beautiful. I'm used to seeing him in t-shirts and jeans, but tonight he looks like James Bond. I keep looking at him. Despite myself, I'm dismayed. I can't imagine attacking this guy like I did on his back lawn several hours ago. It's just not possible. I wouldn't want to get him dirty.

He's been making a fuss over me, too, and I believe it's sincere. I'm wearing my best dress, the same simple black silk cocktail dress, and tonight the diamonds show off the low-cut neckline. I feel beautiful. Maybe it's shallow but wearing a gazillion-dollars' worth of diamonds does increase your self-confidence. And Charlie keeps bending over to kiss me. That increases my confidence, too.

Glowing in the evening dusk, the venue is all crystal and fire, highlighted by the most striking tiered chandelier I've ever seen. Shimmering silver translucent curtains cover most of the walls, and floor-to-ceiling glass allows us to look out over the lights and monuments of D.C. Twenty-four-foot-high glass sliders are open in the warm night air, leading down two steps to a large pool with glass balls, gleaming inside with candlelight, floating in the water. A food buffet dominates one end of the large expanse with heavy brocade tablecloths loaded with exotic food. Other tables are crowded with fragile sparkling crystal goblets and other assorted glassware, adjoining a bar staffed by deferential, white-jacketed attendants. Probably close to a hundred three-foot-tall white candles and banks of white roses line the center open area.

"It's so beautiful," I say. "There's no point in acting cool. Thank you for bringing me."

"Thank you for allowing me to share it with you, Miranda. Without you here, it's just scenery." He bends over, puts his arms around me, and gives me such a long public kiss. I'm embarrassed and very pleased.

"Come on," he says. "Let me introduce you to some friends." A six-person orchestra is playing understated music as I'm taken around the room. There are probably two hundred people here and I can name a few—several politicians, celebrities from interviews on TV, reminding me of the very first time I encountered Charlie. I smile to myself, remembering that night when I disappeared into the woodwork.

People are dancing and mingling. I've been engaged in several provocative conversations, and even offered a job interview at one of the most influential law firms in DC. Charlie has had his arm around my waist much of the time, which is uncommon in this room, and I've danced with several young men who have been trying to redirect my interest.

Scanning the room, I notice a tall familiar guy, leaning against the wall with his arms crossed, studying me with a wry smile. I can guess what he's thinking. "Enjoy the dream world, Babe."

Pointing him out to Charlie, I leave him to continue a conversation with some CEO, then make my way across the crowded room.

"You look beautiful, Mira," he says, softly. "Diamonds suit you."

"You're stunning, yourself." And he is, wearing a perfectly fitted tux. "I can't believe how you look."

"One of my business arrangements from the past encouraged me to buy it and I'm glad to put it to use." He smiles. "'Course, I wouldn't want to embarrass Charlie, standing out as a hick from the reservation."

"You're the most intriguing guy in the room. Look at all these women ogling you."

"I have noticed, Mira, when I'm not looking at you. You look so much at home it frightens me."

I study him carefully. There's seriousness and maybe some anxiety behind the carefully chosen words. This is Lew. We've been teasing, even tormenting each other, but we both know we're risking something valuable.

"Come on," he says. "Let's show them an Indian war dance."

He pulls me into the center of the room where other couples are dancing and proceeds to give the assembly instructions on the finer points. He's an incredible dancer, as I knew from before. We whirl around the room, while others give way to watch. I can feel their eyes on us and hear the conversation din diminish. He gives me a seductive grin as we finally leave the floor.

I have the idea he's toying with me. "I can't continue this, Lew. Are you involved with someone or not?" I'm fighting to keep my voice very low to avoid attention. "I need to know now." I lower my voice even more to a whisper. "My relationship with Charlie is evolving. Tell me the truth."

His eyes rise to look over my shoulder.

Unexpectedly, a hand appears possessively around my waist. Turning my head, Charlie is scrutinizing Lew closely.

"I didn't need to worry about our friend here," he says. "I've had half a dozen women asking me if I know you: rich, single, interested, women. See anyone you'd like an introduction to?"

"No, Charlie. Do you wish I did?"

"Yeah. I'd like that. A lot."

They look each other squarely in the eye. I don't see obvious dislike, but I do see them facing off.

A longhaired blonde comes up to us. "Hi, Charlie. Care to introduce me to your friends?"

"Hello, Charlene. Sure. This is Miranda Flynn and Lew Black River. Miranda just graduated Georgetown Law, and Lew's our friend, originally from Montana. He's a computer geek."

I see her give Lew a blinding smile.

"This is Charlene Van Ryan. She and I grew up together. Went to kindergarten way back when."

"Would you like to dance?" she says to Lew, not wasting any time. "I'd love to hear about Montana."

"My favorite topic," Lew replies.

He gives her a seductive Lew smile as I correspondingly see her melt. Damn it.

* * *

I've had a wonderful, dreadful evening. It's forced me to confront the reality of being in love with two men. It was infuriating that I couldn't get Lew to answer my pointed question. Maybe he's also involved with two people, and I'm one of them. The sensible thing to do is go back to Montana and see what evolves. And, most frustrating of all, admit that I can't control anyone but myself.

I won't easily let this evening go. It's threatened my vision of the future. Beyond the clash of cultures, the growing antagonism between Lew and Charlie is obvious. On some basic level I need to value Charlie for himself, not the trappings. Lew's been happily dancing with that affluent blonde who's obviously interested. She'll be here and I'll be out there. My head is spinning. Both men comfortably inhabit both worlds—my old one and the new one I'm trying to enter. I'm not at ease in either.

"How are you doing, Miranda?" Charlie asks me.

"It's been a dream, Charlie. I've been Cinderella, but I want to go home, take off the diamonds, and kiss you in my bare feet. It's been enough."

"I've had a lifetime of this, Miranda. I'm happy you've had this night, but I can't tell you how good it makes me feel to hear you say that. Let's go."

"Let me say goodbye to Lew. Can you give me a couple of minutes?"

"Yes, Sweetheart."

I smile and kiss his cheek. That's the first time he's called me that. I go near to where Lew is dancing and stand smiling at him. It takes several minutes for him to extricate himself. "We're leaving, Lew. I… I need, to say goodbye."

"I've been evasive, Mira. Forgive me," he says, suddenly completely serious. I can't encourage you. I want you far away from me."

"I need to know, Lew. What I asked. Please?"

He stands there, suddenly, like he's holding himself together, a pained expression on his face.

"You know how I feel," he whispers. "Do I have to say it? Be patient."

Be patient? Is he kidding? Is this conceit, fear, or something else? I suddenly feel bereft at the lost opportunity.

Tears form in my eyes. We stand there looking at each other. Finally, I say, "Take care of yourself, Lew. If anything happens to you…"

"I'll call you the minute I get back from Turkey. I promise. Go start a wonderful life in Montana."

He turns, walks back over to say a few words to the blonde, then walks rapidly out of the room.

I turn, watching him go. Charlie is just walking up behind me, making me jump. He wraps his arms around me.

"Are you ready?" he asks.

"Yes."

We say a quick goodbye to several of Charlie's friends, stop to get my checked coat, then walk through the main lobby of the hotel toward the exit. I'm feeling like "The End" just flashed on a movie screen, but that thought is interrupted by raised voices coming from the entrance. We're halted at the doorway where a small crowd has congregated.

"Please wait," a uniformed doorman cautions us.

Looking past him, I see the flashing lights of an ambulance, just arriving near the front entrance. Several police cars, all with lights flashing, pull up to surround it.

"What happened?" Charlie asks.

"It may be a while before you can leave, sir," the man replies. "We've had a shooting incident."

Coldness descends. Looking toward the center of where police and medics are gathering, I can make out the long-tuxedoed legs of a man on the ground. *No!* I think. Zooming round the doorman, followed immediately by a scrambling Charlie, my worst fear is realized. Lew lies on the ground in a pool of blood that seems to be coming from the back of his head. The blood is increasing at a steady rate on the driveway.

Dropping to the ground, I plead, "Lew, I'm here. Hang on." His eyes flicker and open slightly. Charlie drops beside me. Lew's bloody left hand reaches up to grasp Charlie's lapel, pulling Charlie close so he can hear.

"Get her out of here."

He allows his eyes to close and drops his hand. Ambulance attendants start elbowing us out of the way, quickly supporting Lew's head in a neck brace, then lift him onto a stretcher. "Where are you going?" Charlie asks urgently. "Which hospital?"

"Who are you? Who is he?" One of the ambulance paramedics asks.

"I'm Charles Curchin, a friend," Charlie replies. "Your patient is Llewellyn Black River of the NSA."

"Washington Hospital Center," one of the men replies, as Lew's stretcher is hustled into the ambulance.

"We'll follow you in," Charlie yells after them.

Charlie's pulls me rather roughly to my feet. I'm hustled back to the front entrance of the hotel, shielded by his body. "Keep her in here," Charlie says to the doorman, "if you value your life." He turns to me. "I'll get the car. We'll go to the hospital." Briefly talking to an attendant and retrieving his keys, Charlie takes off running toward the garage.

* * *

It's Friday night in Washington DC, a very busy night for a trauma center. Charlie is holding my cold hands in his. We've been here an hour and I'm terribly scared. I haven't said more than a few words to Charlie while we wait.

A kind-looking older doctor in scrubs comes out to talk to us. "Hi, Charlie. Good news on your friend."

I look up at Charlie and start to cry.

"Miranda," says Charlie, "this is Dan Blankenship, head of neurosurgery here, and a very close family friend. Thanks for ruining your evening and coming so fast."

"It was my pleasure, Charlie. More to the point, if the bullet had been another half inch to the right this would have been a tragedy. It looked much worse than it was." He smiles at me reassuringly. "Head wounds are messy. He has a groove in the bone on the side of his head, but he'll be fine. We want to do a few repeat scans, just to be sure." He smiles at me again. "We're thawing him out. We prepped him for emergency surgery in case we needed to go in, but fortunately we didn't."

"Do you suppose...?" I start to ask.

"Sure. He's just about awake," He interrupts. "If you want to go in for a few minutes? It shouldn't hurt him."

I smile at him through my tears.

"Thanks Dan," Charlie says. "I owe you one."

"No, you don't," he says. "I love giving good news."

We walk into room 201 and see Lew with a huge white bandage wrapped like a turban around his head. He has one IV going and an oxygen tube, but, otherwise, looks pretty good.

"Hi," I say.

"I knew you'd show up, damn it."

I find a chair next to him and take his hand.

"I'm going into a war zone in the Middle East for three weeks and I get shot at the Four Seasons." He grimaces. "Go figure."

"How are you feeling?" I ask.

"Pretty good. I can see two of you, though, and even more diamonds."

"The doctor said you dodged a bullet. Well, almost dodged a bullet," Charlie remarks.

"I have a very hard head. I'm mostly concerned about my tux. It's only the third time I've worn it. I hope they can get the blood out."

"Lew, for God's sake," I say. "That's what you're worried about?"

"No," he says, suddenly serious. "It's you! They weren't kidding and you might be on the list. You're getting her out of here, Charlie?"

"She had to see you first. We have a police escort back to her house. I've arranged for the plane early tomorrow. Police will stay outside Tony's house tonight, then escort us to the airport. Sometimes it does help to know people."

"What did the doctor say about the trip to the Middle East?" I ask.

"He wants me to wait a week, but unless something unexpected turns up in my head I'm good to go home tomorrow."

"What about security, Lew? I'm scared to death."

"They're providing around-the-clock protection here and a bodyguard on the trip over. I'm impressed. I don't think I'm worth all this, but I guess someone does."

Lew's eyes are drooping so I know we have to go.

"We'll be half the way around the planet from each other," Lew says to me, "so I won't be able to keep an eye on you. Watch your back, okay?"

I can only look at him.

"At least you'll blend in, with the turban," Charlie says.

"You know better, Charlie. That's India, not Turkey."

They shake hands and I kiss Lew on the cheek, gently, and we're gone.

An hour later I get a text. "Thank Charlie. Tux getting cleaned."

I lean over and show it to Charlie, my own personal bodyguard.

He smiles. "He's really attached to that tux."

"He grew up poor, Charlie. It's a big deal to him."

"I know," he says.

* * *

I'm delivered to the plane early the next morning and turn to Charlie. "Don't wait too long. I miss you already."

"That's very nice to know, Miranda. I'm going to try to make it out in three weeks. My poor father needs some encouragement. He's been very patient with me. Call me the second you get off in Great Falls."

Hugh McManus, now dressed in a dark blue pilot's suit, approaches us. "If the young lady is ready?" he says, with a completely inappropriate grin.

"Give us a minute, Hugh," Charlie grins back at the pilot, who walks back to the plane.

"This is very hard," I say. "Maybe I should reconsider DC?"

"It's too dangerous, honey. Go. I'll be out soon."

One last passionate kiss and I'm handed up the stairs of the plane. I pause at the door and turn. He's looking up at me with an undecipherable expression.

Moments later I'm still standing at the top of the stairs at the door of the plane. Charlie is standing below the steps with a quizzical smile on his face. I've been daydreaming. I walk back down the steps and throw myself into his arms.

"Miranda," he says, "think of me. No one has, for a very long time."

"Hurry back to Montana," I say, helplessly, then run up the stairs, find my seat, and sigh dejectedly several times.

My pilot walks out of the cabin. He still looks very professional from the waist up, but instead of traditional long pants he's changed into khaki shorts. He looks amazingly like a misplaced postal worker.

"Call me Hugh," he begins. "I didn't know if you remembered my name. I'll be your pilot again this trip. We're the only ones onboard. The flight is about four hours long. If for any reason you have an emergency, call me. I can put the plane on autopilot." He smiles, humorously. "Try to make it a real emergency, though."

I smile back at him.

"If you want to talk or you get lonesome, push this button and I'll talk on a two-way intercom. No pilot jokes. I've heard them all before. You know, like how many pilots does it take to change a light bulb?"

"How many?" I ask in confusion.

"Two," he says. "One to hold the bulb steady and the other to fly the plane around in circles."

I give him a horrified look, then laugh.

"Don't worry," he says. "I'm a better pilot than a comedian. There's food and drinks in the closet refrigerator and use the microwave if you'd like."

"Thanks. I'm going to pretend I'm a queen or something."

"Go ahead," he says. "All fantasies are allowed. And if you're tired, there's a bedroom in the back. Although," he continues, "it's hard to imagine Charlie motivated you to stay up late. Still..." he pauses for dramatic effect, "I suppose anything's possible."

I stifle a giggle—a surprisingly personal comment about his boss.

Abruptly, he laughs. "Damn. I promised Charlie... Oh well. And wait until I turn off the seatbelt sign to move around. If there's strong turbulence, I'll check on you. We'll be taxiing out in a few minutes."

I give him a big grin.

"Enjoy," he says. "It's nice flying people who don't take this all for granted."

"I bet Charlie's nice to work for."

"Yes. He's a class act as an employer and a friend."

"How long have you known him?" I ask.

"We three guys went to grade school together. We almost got kicked out of third grade for kissing a girl behind the gym. The only thing that saved us was she was an older woman. Fifth grade, if I remember correctly."

He seems to wait for me to make a comment. I'm guessing the other of the three guys was Todd, but I don't want Hugh to know that I know about him. Not until Charlie and I can discuss it.

"I get the feeling that you and Charlie share quite a past."

He hesitates again as if there's something he wants to say, then adds, "Let's just say we want to remain men of mystery."

Still looking for a chink in the armor. It's harder than I could have imagined leaving Charlie. Despite his protestations of a perfect life, there's the family tragedy buried below the surface. I almost talked to his mother about it. Maybe next time I see her.

I believe, now, that there will be a next time. The plane is starting to move, turning toward the main runway. I look out the window and see Charlie, still standing on the tarmac with his hand raised. I wave wildly as he disappears behind the plane. He said three weeks. I've never looked the family up on the internet since that long ago first encounter. I buzz Hugh.

"Hi, Miranda. What's up?"

"Hi. Just wondering. Do we have internet on board?"

"Gogo."

"Gogo?"

"It's a wireless provider for aircraft. You won't need a password. Just select 'Gogo'. Can you wait till we're away from the airport? Ten minutes will do."

"Thanks Hugh."

"You're welcome. Let me know if you want to hear the one about the chicken and the pilot crossing the road."

"Gotcha."

I bet Charlie and Hugh were holy terrors in the third grade. It's obvious now that they are best friends. There's so much to think about these last twenty-four hours. I talked to Lew just before we left for the airport, and he sounded normal. They're going to let him loose this afternoon, but he's bored already. I was talking to him with Charlie sitting next to me. Even if he hadn't been there, I don't know what I would have said to Lew. He's been uncharacteristically elusive about a lot of things, including how he feels about me. And then to be actually shot...

Now that I have some time on my hands, I need to do some soul searching. I've been so caught up in my newfound social success, there remain many things that need serious examination. There's mortal danger involving Lew, and I seem to be connected. Plus, I'm personally involved with him. Dad's convinced I've been nearly in love with him for the last few years. If I'm honest, Jeff, my recent ex-boyfriend, was a safe choice. Sub-consciously, I knew I wasn't going there in the long run. I might as well face the fact that I've been waiting for Lew to have a little fun and be there for the home stretch. Lew cares. We've been close to the lip for years and it's spilling over fast. The only thing I hadn't counted on was Charlie.

I still worry it's absurd for him to be interested in someone with my ordinary background. It doesn't last long, though. With a dad like mine, I had to be quality. I have a great education and a very good mind. Charlie has said he feels privileged to be with me. I don't have big money behind me, but Charlie insists that's an asset.

He is a beautiful man. At the Four Seasons last night, it was as if the room stopped when we came in and I know it wasn't me that stopped it. Many of the female eyes were on Charlie, at least the first part of the evening, until it seemed he had no interest in anyone but me.

It's been five years since I last looked up the family, inspired by our first meeting. It's way over ten minutes so I log in and punch Charles Curchin again into the search engine. Pictures of the family and family bios follow. Some details I remember. Charles Brower Curchin II, son of the founder and namesake of Curchin Limited, Anna Coral Curchin, wife of Charles II and literary agent – retired. Children: Charles Brower Curchin III, currently a vice-president in charge of real-estate acquisitions in the Eastern Europe, Tina Curchin Davidson, vice-CFO of Curchin Limited, wife of Philip Davidson. Julia Lee Curchin, professional woman's soccer player, and finally, Todd Shipton Curchin, deceased, twin brother of Charlie.

I sit quietly in my seat, remembering the sadness, the unusual sensitivity, I've observed in Charlie. Very soon I need to talk to Charlie about it. So far, he's decided not to share that experience, a fault-line running through his life. It explains why Hugh paused a few minutes ago, waiting to see if I knew, silently questioning whether Charlie and I had talked about it.

It makes me more aware that I don't want to hurt Charlie. Ever. And I don't ever want to hurt Lew. The indulgence of being involved with these two wonderful men dims a lot. I know Lew's life hasn't been smooth either. His father drank himself to death when Lew was in grade school. He loves and loves intensely. I've seen him with his friends.

If I disengaged from Charlie, it would hurt him deeply. He's let me inside his world and under his shell. He's taking a risk. He doesn't pretend to be a tough guy.

Not that I want to disengage. I'm falling and falling fast. If Lew has hesitations about developing our relationship, maybe it would be best if I don't push it. Maybe I should let him stay a friend. And the decision could be taken out of my hands. I'm probably an idiot to believe I could have either one of these beautiful men. But Charlie seems to have committed himself, for the time being anyway. We haven't had sex yet. It was coming last night, but a bullet changed those plans.

Never in my life have I allowed these kinds of musings to go on, but I feel the need to get my life in focus. Sitting quietly in my seat, I stare out the window, trying to put all that's happened in some perspective.

It's been another half-hour and I'm still unsettled. I'm going to do everything I can to protect Charlie's feelings. His fear of abandonment is understandable. I want to be with him, to tell him I know. If I asked Hugh to turn the plane around, would he do it? Is it my plane or Charlie's?

I buzz Hugh.

"Hi Miranda. Got an emergency?"

"Not exactly. But I was wondering… Who directs this plane? What if I wanted to turn around and go back?"

"Got a light bulb to change?"

I giggle. "No Hugh. I just wondered."

"I'm yours to command."

"Really?"

"Yep."

"Hmm. Okay. I'll let you know."

"Know any knock-knock jokes?"

"Bye, Hugh."

Boy, that would blow his mind. It would be ridiculous. Crazy. When in my life could I do something like this?

I buzz Hugh.

"Hi Miranda. Have you decided about the light bulb?"

"Yep. I want to change it."

"Do you want to think about it for a few minutes?"

"Should I?"

"No, don't think. It would be great fun."

"Hmm? Where are we, Hugh?"

"Bypassing the approach to O'Hare. About twenty minutes east of Chicago."

"Change the bulb, Hugh. Do you know where Charlie is?"

"He's still in DC. I was supposed to fly back there and leave the plane. We were going to drive back to Philly together tomorrow."

"Then do it."

I feel the left wing dip. Hugh leaves the intercom on long enough so I can hear him laughing. I really like Hugh.

CHAPTER 16

MIRANDA

AS WE TAXI into Dulles International, Hugh buzzes me. "Hi Miranda. Should I give Charlie a heads up?"

"Do you know where he is?"

"Nope. It's Saturday. You want me to call him?"

"I don't know... Maybe he's got another girlfriend? Now I'm scared."

"Miranda. I don't know much, but that's not a problem. He's nuts about you."

"Aren't we supposed to be landing about now in Great Falls? Won't he know where you're calling from?"

"No. Close enough to the time of the scheduled landing. I was supposed to check in for further instructions when I got there. I'll see where he is now." I hear a devilish cackle over the intercom. "We'll sneak up on him. This will be great."

"Can I come up and listen in when you call?"

"Sure. Just let me pull into our holding area. I'll buzz you in about five minutes."

I'm beginning to feel like a guilty teenager. Maybe this wasn't such a hot idea.

"Okay, Miranda. Punch 543 into the lock box and come in."

I do as I'm told. 543.

"Hi. Ready?"

Reaching over, I grab his arm. "Maybe we should just get out of here?"

"Don't be silly, partner-in-crime. I haven't had this much fun in years. I can hardly wait to see Charlie's face."

He searches my anxious face until I nod, then hits Charlie's contact button. It rings and rings.

"That's odd," Hugh mutters. "It went to voicemail. I'll call Anna and see if she knows where he is." He hits another number.

"Hello, Hugh. Anna here."

He puts the call on speaker. "Anna? Where's Charlie? I was supposed to touch base."

"He just called. He went back to check on Lew at Washington Hospital Center, arriving just minutes after his friend was attacked again." Her voice rises. "Can you believe it? Right there in his hospital room?"

My blood freezes. Hugh sees my face and asks, "Is he going to make it?"

"I don't know any details. Where are you?"

"Long story. I'm back in DC with Miranda. We'll get a taxi and meet him there."

Hugh and I race to find a taxi, leaving my luggage on the plane. He takes my arm, pulling me through the outer airport. Suddenly he comes to a dead halt and turns to face me.

"Damn it," he says. "Charlie's going to kill me for bringing you back here. This is a war zone. Promise to stick with me every second, Miranda. Promise me now, or we go right back to the plane."

"I promise, Hugh." We both look at each other. The fun is off the joke. My mind is reeling.

Five minutes later, we're on the way. In fifteen more, we're racing up three flights of stairs to Lew's room. An intimidating man at the door with a bulging shoulder holster stops us, checks our I.D., then calls into the room for verification. Lew's face is covered with new bruises and one of his eyes is partly swollen shut. A man from housekeeping is sweeping up broken glass while Charlie stands wide-eyed, near a vinyl chair by the window.

"Miranda?" he explodes. "What the hell?" He looks at Hugh.

"My boss told me to turn around. What could I do?" Hugh admits, looking self-conscious.

"I missed you," I say meekly to Charlie.

"Jeez, Miranda." He hurries to me, pulling me into his arms. "It's crazy here. I'm being a second bodyguard until more FBI guys arrive." Lew's original bodyguard was hospital security, totally unprepared for what happened.

At this point, Lew's eyes open a slit and he sees me. "What the hell?" he says, echoing Charlie. "Why aren't you safe in Montana?"

"I... I'm sorry. I took the pilot hostage and forced him to bring me back."

No one's laughing. Not even Hugh.

"It was a whim." I grimace.

"Well, get your ass back on that plane," Lew growls. "Charlie...?"

"Damn it. He's right. This is insanity here. The only thing, Lew... The dead guy... You said he mentioned a woman. What if someone follows her back to Montana?"

Lew and Charlie stare at each other.

"Slow this down." Hugh says. "Tell me exactly what happened. Every detail."

Hugh's not telling jokes now. His voice has changed. I'm beginning to understand Hugh isn't just a pilot/postal worker, but it's hard to tell. The Curchins don't seem to have normal job descriptions for employees.

"I'll tell them," Charlie says to Lew. "You rest."

Lew nods, letting his eyes slowly close.

"Lew was considering checking himself out when a man strolled in. He wore a hospital badge, had a stethoscope around his neck, and carried a medical chart. The security guy stepped out to take a phone call, at which point the 'doctor' shut the door, then asked Lew whether the same *young lady* would be picking him up. Lew didn't answer. He was immediately suspicious. The man turned to leave, then suddenly raised a gun with a silencer attached. Lew dodged and rolled off the bed, while the guy got off one bad shot. Lew kicked his IV stand in his direction, then tackled him. It was a miracle Lew got to him before he got off another round. They fought and Lew finally got him under control and..." He looks at Lew. "And he snapped his neck."

Lew cracks his eyes open to see my reaction, then winces.

I gulp. "You killed him?"

"I'm Blackfeet, remember. Take no prisoners. Actually, we do take prisoners, but I didn't take the time to torture him or take his scalp."

There's no sign of joking. Or remorse.

"I should have left him alive to question him. I wasn't thinking too clearly. It was the drugs, and I was in survival mode. Stupid."

My mouth is open. Do I know this man at all?

"Must have been quite a fight," says Hugh. "Wish I'd been here."

Lew smiles weakly at Hugh. "Yeah, it was satisfying. Now I lived through it."

"Hugh was Special Forces in Afghanistan." Charlie says. "Takes one warrior to appreciate one."

"What are we going to do about Miranda?" Lew asks. "All kidding aside..."

I look at him, having absolutely no idea which part of our conversation was kidding. "Do about me...?"

"Having you return to Montana without a bodyguard." Lew answers, looking at me. "Charlie?"

"I'm not even sure about Silver Spring," he remarks seriously. "Her entire family could be at risk."

"I'm horribly sorry, Miranda." Lew says. "You may be in serious danger."

"You're the one dodging bullets," I manage, then collapse onto a nearby chair.

Charlie moves quickly to my side. "The Special Forces guy will switch from pilot to protection mode. You're moving to our house, Miranda." He glances at Hugh, who nods affirmatively.

"I can't do that. I'm not jeopardizing your family."

"You probably didn't notice before, but our house is a fortress when we need it to be. We have complex overseas interests. Occasionally we feel the need to protect ourselves." He glances at his friend. "We have some... family history I haven't shared. Hugh functions as head of our security team."

"I also do windows and gutters," adds Hugh.

"We put up with his terrible jokes. That's the downside," laments Charlie.

"Lew. Were you hurt badly?" I ask.

He answers with his eyes shut. "I still had IVs in. It slowed me down. But, no, I'm okay. Hit my head a few times. There are a lot of sharp edges in this small room." He hesitates. "Honestly, the guy was no pushover. It was close," he admits. "I'm not used to fighting for my life." He seems stunned.

"I'll give you a minute," Charlie says graciously, and leaves.

I move over and sit on the side of his bed. "Win told me at the reunion that he'd only seen you upset several times in your life, but when you got angry you had big medicine, was the way he put it."

"I've had my moments."

I'm so thankful you have that side of you, Lew. I'm glad you killed him."

"Really?"

"Why? If you hadn't, you'd be dead, my warrior friend. It surprised me. That's all."

"Well, well. Maybe you'll do okay in the Wild West after all."

"Did you have doubts, Lew?"

"Lean over and give me a kiss. I'll let you know."

He reaches over, IVs and all, winding his hand in my hair and pulls me toward him. This is not a peck on the cheek. I can't help it. I'm lost in it.

"Don't give in to Charlie's persuasion too easily, Mira," he murmurs seriously. "I'll have my day yet."

"I'm trying, Lew," I manage as he lets me go. "Watch yourself," I say, in desperation. "If anything happens to you... I don't know what..."

"You, too, darlin'," he says slowly, unhappily.

As I walk into the hospital corridor, the weight of the day descends. I've been halfway across the country and back, and now this. Charlie, with a worried expression, leans against a nearby wall, talking intensely on his phone as Hugh jogs down the corridor toward the exit. At the same instant, Lew's new bodyguard calls out to another intense man, who's running down the hall toward us. Together they head into Lew's room. My world has changed.

Charlie clicks off his phone. "We're headed back to our house," Charlie says. "I called Mom. She's furious. She'd shoot the bad guys all by herself if we let her."

"Honestly?" One more surprise in a day of surprises.

"I want you where I can keep an eye on you. We're going to drive home, and Hugh will fly the jet up. But first, he'll contact your dad and offer him a flight up to Philly. We're guessing he'd want to help make plans for all this. Even so, they'll probably beat us home with the traffic."

I should be participating in what to do, but for a little while I'm letting Charlie do the heavy lifting. I'm incredibly relieved he thought to involve Dad.

Heading down the hall, two additional security individuals are briefing hospital employees at the nurses' station. After several deep sighs, I turn to Charlie. "Why didn't you encourage me to get to know Hugh before the first flight? He's fantastic. Complicated."

Charlie shakes his head. "You've only scratched the surface. He's capable of anything, especially to harass me. Streaking. Anything." He hesitates. "I had to pay him off."

"What were you laughing about in the cockpit?"

"He was renegotiating. Threatening me with horrible things. I won't tell you what."

* * *

As we pull in the driveway, Charlie points at Hugh's silver Porsche parked around back. "Hugh made it. He's probably tormenting Mom with pilot jokes. The worst ones involve successful exploits with loose women. She loves him, though. Another son."

I wonder when to bring up his lost brother. *Not now*, I think. I can't wait to see my dad and hurry inside. A lot has happened in the twelve hours since we said goodbye this morning.

Dad stands to give me an unusually strong hug. Having a daughter possibly threatened by a killer is unusual for him, too. And now there have been two serious attempts on Lew's life. Rena has been told to stay in New York, and Mom was encouraged to arrange a visit with her sister in Indiana.

We've reassembled in the Curchin living room, with Dad keeping his arm snugly around me on a couch. Stosh has joined the group, along with Tina, and Charlie 2. This feels like a war council. The only family member missing is Charlie's younger sister, Juli, who's on the West Coast playing soccer. She's the one I most want to meet, but that will have to wait.

Hugh sits next to Phil, Tina's husband, who I've just met for the first time. He writes articles for economic trade papers in addition to being a stay-at-home-dad for Charlie's nephews, Billy and

Scotty, and appears somewhat separated from the chaos. I think he's here to manage the kids.

I've never seen Dad rattled before. He's now extremely concerned about me, and Lew. The second attempt on Lew's life was so unexpected and deadly. Hand to hand combat in a hospital room? Unbelievable. Dad's flying back to DC when we're done here, probably with me in tow, needing to be convinced that Lew is safely protected. There are now three company men camped outside his hospital room. Lew's trip to the Middle East has been put off until the NSA reassesses everything.

That I've been caught up in this has put us all on edge. I'm really scared for the first time. This is crazy. What if I am the G-friend? Nothing seems impossible anymore.

"I'm still not in agreement," Dad interjects. "Miranda is my responsibility. None of you Curchins are connected to these threats. We'll go back and let the company handle security. This is not your burden."

"Tony," says Charlie 3, "responsibility aside, I'm not letting her out of my sight until we get some clarity here? I'll fly back with you if you don't want her to remain here. God-awful things are happening, and big government organizations don't respond quickly enough. I need to know they're completely on top of this."

"I agree, but…"

"Mr. Flynn," interrupts Charlie's dad. "We've had serious international threats in the past, and the family has dealt with them professionally. You can explore that with my permission. We have high-level security on the property. You just aren't aware of it. I trust Hugh with my family's life. I have before. We have additional agents Hugh calls in if he feels we need them. Stosh is also trained. Why not let Miranda stay here at our house for a few days until you feel confident things have been sorted out? When the situation allows you to feel secure, Hugh can fly her down to Silver Spring or back to Montana."

Dad looks at me, still unconvinced.

"And besides," he continues, glancing at his son, "I don't want Charlie 3 to have a stroke or anything."

That brings a small smile to Dad's face. He's quiet for a few minutes, thinking.

"Yes, I see your point. All right. Even the professionals at the home office are shaken up. You need to understand how big a cog in our national security wheel Lew has become. Let's just say everything possible will be done." He looks at Anna. "Are you absolutely sure you want to take on this risk?"

"Mr. Flynn," answers Charlie's mother, "you don't know me at all, and I don't know Miranda well. But I do know that she is worth all the effort and resources we can bring to bear. My son is correct. She's become very special to us all. Let us do this."

I swallow hard and give her a look of astonishment. She's still staring intensely at my dad.

A few moments pass. "Alright. If you're going to be responsible for my daughter's life," he says finally, "you should at least call me Tony."

"Good, Tony," Anna says.

Dad studies my face. "You're positive?" he asks. "Are you sure you want to stay?"

"For now," I say, then admit. "I feel safer here."

"Then I'd like to go back to DC and check on Lew," Dad says. "He's all alone."

"Jack Fort, our other primary pilot, will fly you back," Charlie 2 affirms, pulling out his phone. "He's on call. He knows we might need him."

Charlie 3 adds, "Tony, we'll be with her constantly with excellent surveillance. We'll call often to share information."

Pocketing his phone, Charlie 2 confirms, "Jack will be at the airport in an hour. There's a taxi outside at your disposal. Just tell him to go to Gate 18-C."

"I'm grateful," Dad says, standing. "Keep me in the loop." He and I share a last lingering hug.

Charlie's dad also stands up. "I'll walk you out."

He's back in a few minutes. "I'm impressed with your father. Charlie told me he's a quality guy."

I nod. "I know how worried he is. And he loves Lew. Dad's very solid in emergencies. The whole family shields my mother.

I'm sure she was delighted to escape to Indiana. Dad hasn't even mentioned me in this mess. She'd have to be tranquilized."

"You might be surprised in a real emergency," Anna says. "Until you're tested you never really know. She might handle it better than you expect."

"Or maybe worse," I say. "Hopefully, I won't find out."

In a quiet moment, I consider what Mom's take on all this will be. She's been easy to dismiss because we hardly ever discuss serious issues. Her eyes glaze over if I try. But she's one of the most loving people I know, unfailingly supportive of me and the friends I crowded into our house during the early years. She and Dad married very young. She spent a couple of social years at college and gratefully dumped the effort. They've been happy, but I know Dad goes elsewhere for intellectual stimulation. She appears to let him make all the serious decisions, but rather than debate things directly, manipulates him with carefully chosen disinterest or excessive worry. He knows that's the way she operates. I sensed only relief she'll be in Indiana, leaving him free to concentrate on what's happening with me.

Charlie comes over to sit next to me on the couch, taking my hand in his. The men and Anna discuss the security system, including motion-sensing cameras that activate floodlights, projecting images onto multiple screens in a security room off the kitchen. The front gate is now closed, with new pass codes activated for the entry and house. They proceed to discuss several communication technologies and weapons on the property. I'm impressed with how often Anna is asked for opinions and her shrewd advice freely offered.

The world of extreme wealth is still new to me. I'd never considered the problems and the downside. Family matters are carefully avoided or alluded to that I wouldn't have noticed if I hadn't read about the family on the Internet this afternoon. A mental list of questions is developing to ask Charlie privately when the time seems right.

Hugh has moved center stage in site security. This side of him fascinates me. Charlie filled me in on the road trip up. He's in his early thirties, spent two years at Emory before dropping the effort to go directly to Army flight school. He then spent six years in the military as a Special Forces helicopter pilot, including three tours overseas, before joining the Curchin family organization and fulfilling a variety of roles. His overdeveloped sense of humor disguises a quick intelligence and organizational aptitude. I watch Hugh and Charlie relate as close friends and equals.

I'm beginning to lose my ability to concentrate on details as the meeting ends. Tomorrow is Sunday and we'll meet for brunch at ten. After saying goodnight to everyone, Charlie walks me upstairs.

"How are you managing?" he asks.

"I'm still mostly worried about Lew."

"I'm hoping this is overkill, myself," he says. "Before, it seemed unlikely you were implicated, but after this morning at the hospital… I'm glad you're here where I can be sure you're safe." He stops at the top of the stairs. "Miranda, do you have any idea how important you've become to me?"

"Yes, Charlie. I do. And I am scared. I'm glad I'm here."

"And Lew?" he asks.

"Can we go back to your room, Charlie?"

I've been here before, of course, during my visit, but now I want his arms around me when I answer that question. His large bedroom is at the end of the corridor and very different from mine. It's a man's room with dark tan walls, a great sound system, and a Hudson's Bay Blanket draped over his bed. Old sports medals hang on the wall, plus various pieces of well-used sports equipment lying around: a baseball mitt, several soccer balls, two chipped lacrosse sticks and a built-in stack of cubbyholes with very used sports shoes. There are some personal items, including a framed picture of eagles Charlie drew in the third grade and a small yellowing photo showing two young boys, one playing drums and the other an electric guitar, in a junior high school band. The drummer was Charlie.

In addition to this family home in Philly, I now know he has an apartment in New York City and a personal beach cottage that he uses on Chesapeake Bay near DC when he doesn't want or need to be downtown. Plus, he's mentioned a Curchin family apartment in San Francisco, even a corporate flat in London. I try to not dwell on all that. I'm ready to be back in Montana, away from all this harsh reality, including the wealth.

Walking into his room, Charlie closes the door and locks it. We kick off our shoes and lie together on the bed. The old feeling of disbelief comes over me as it often does when I'm with Charlie. I roll toward him on my side, sighing as I touch his face. "About Lew...," I begin.

"Yes."

"I'm going to do the best I can to explain how I feel about him, but then I don't want to talk more about it. Unless something changes."

"Miranda, I don't want to put you on the spot."

"No. You need to know. Lew is very important to me. I don't think he knows what he wants now. The truth is that I'd been waiting for him to be ready. I've been 'biding my time', as Dad pointed out. We've never had sex but..." I pause, trying to decide how to explain. "But recently... I've been tempted." I take a breath. "And I didn't count on you, Charlie. I hardly know you, your past, and your weak points. I have mine, as well. You don't know me. Not really."

I pause again to organize my thoughts.

"Miranda, please..."

"Listen, Charlie. I can barely breathe sometimes when I'm with you. I'm trying to keep my expectations realistic. You're making it very difficult."

He moves against me, our bodies molding together. We've been careful, both of us, each afraid for our own reasons. He moves his hands behind my back and presses me against him, hard. I feel the clenching of the muscles deep inside me. It almost hurts. "Charlie," I whisper. "I desperately want you."

"My love," he murmurs.

My love. The words are so powerful. I'm rolled onto my back, looking up into his eyes as he hovers over me. I can't disguise my desire. It's in every part of me, in every look, every touch I give to him. His head drops to my neck as he caresses me with his lips, his hands moving to my breasts. I want to give him everything. No matter the consequences, no matter the future. The feeling is so overwhelming my throat locks up and I feel my eyes filling with tears.

His breathing has gotten rapid, but I hear him groan and suddenly roll off me. "Miranda."

My name has become a plea.

"Yes," I whisper.

"I don't want to make any mistakes. I want you to be sure. I don't want to seduce you then have you regret it. I'm in love with you. I want you settled on how you feel about Lew and me, before…"

The pull is so strong. I want him, but I understand. It would devastate him if I slept with him and then went back to Lew. I need to know if I would… If I could. My breathing slowly returns to normal. "Don't leave me, Charlie. I couldn't bear it, not tonight, not after all that's happened."

"You can count on that, Sweetheart. I'm not going anywhere. I'll be as near as you'll have me. Take a little time, for both our sakes."

He wraps his arms around my body, pulling me to him. How can I not love this man? It's like fighting off gravity.

We lie together for hours, talking, sharing thoughts, touching each other, trying to contain our longing. I find myself laughing at nothing, mock punching him from time to time, even choking back tears at the kind of love language that you don't want anyone else to hear.

We're quiet for some time until I finally ask, "Charlie, tell me about Todd."

I hear an abrupt low gasp. Then a period of silence, and finally a deep sigh.

"Since you asked, I assume you know we were twins. We were as close as two brothers could be. We had the same interests. We both loved the outdoors, sports, that kind of thing, but I was the quiet one, the careful one. Todd, on the other hand, loved danger. It became his role, entertaining us. Mom always thought he should be an actor—that or a stand-up comedian. As we got older, he brought home great stories about his adventures, always pushing limits." Charlie sighs. "It was almost as if he felt it was his duty to risk his neck." He seems to drift away remembering.

"I saw his picture," I say softly. "He looked like you. He was beautiful."

It's some time before he can continue.

"He seemed invincible to everyone except Mom. She was a very lenient mother, but Todd worried her. Dad and I would reassure her, but we started to become apprehensive, too. That's one problem with wealth. You can have all the toys; all the adventures money can buy. As long as we did well in school, it was hard to deny us anything."

"What did he love to do? What did you?"

"I mostly kept my desires reasonable: flying lessons, ski trips, hiking with friends. But Todd needed a constant escalation of danger."

"What was the worst?"

"It was all worst. He had to push every safety limit. Looking back, we should have seen it coming, tried to temper him. But it was like trying to put a leash on a tornado. And he was so charming, so relentless."

Walking to a dresser across the room, Charlie retrieves a small flat box from a top drawer, and sitting together on the bed, we open it. Inside are thirty or so pictures of the brothers, alone and together, and an old baseball cap zipped in a baggie. Quickly, I can tell the difference, even as little boys. Todd had a thinner face with narrower eyes that seemed always to be partially closed, as if he had a secret he didn't want you to know about, a barely contained devilishness.

There are pictures of tiny boys with big baskets on Easter egg hunts, rafting on rivers, playing on the beach, climbing rock outcroppings, sailing in tiny one-man sailboats. One picture stands out, taken on a rocky beach somewhere, with a beautiful dark-haired young girl. All three look about fourteen with their arms around each other. There are several of both boys with arms over each other's shoulders, laughing with beers in hand, almost grown men, the college years.

The last few are apparently photos of a plane wreck, but it's hard to tell, the debris is so unrecognizable. The pictures tell the story. Charlie and I sit there silently.

"It was impossible not to love him, his wildness. He took all of us along on his ride and then it ended. It was five years ago and sometimes it feels like it was yesterday. That's one reason it's hard for me to let go, to love. It can be lost." Removing the ball cap out of the baggie, he begins turning it over and over in his hands.

Finally, he turns to me. "That's why I stopped flying helicopters. I flew one with Hugh looking for Todd until we found the wreckage; two long weeks. The plane had burned, starting a fire of several acres. That was ultimately how I spotted it. Afterwards, we looked and looked for his body, wanted to bring in search dogs, but didn't have time. It had rained hard before we found the plane, obliterating any tracks, and we assumed wild animals had carried off any remains. Deep snow started that night, ending the investigation until spring."

"But didn't you fly helicopters for the fire service?"

"I tried for a season but every time I piloted a helicopter, I'd be reminded of searching for Todd, and get overwhelmed with depressing memories. Finally, it just didn't seem worth it until you inspired me," he smiles at me. "And it's been a long time, five years this month."

"Your whole family is wonderful, Charlie. You were right of course. It's impossible not to feel at home. Your mother especially. She constantly amazes me. I couldn't detect one flicker of suspicion or disapproval. She's as easy to care about as you are." I smile. "Obviously, the sun rises and sets with you."

"No games. What you see is what you get. No one messes with Mom." He laughs. "Or Dad, either. It's worked well in his business dealings. His transparency is refreshing to a lot of jaded money types. No one is afraid to do business with him."

"What pleases me most, is how forthright your mother is. I come from a household in which we anticipate how Mom is going to maneuver us into getting what she wants. Dad and I make it a game. But it's exhausting."

"I suspect that's why Mom liked you from the start. You're pleasantly direct, like she is."

"How did she deal with Todd's death?"

"She's never completely dealt with it. If you asked her today, she's still imagining he'll turn up somewhere with amnesia or something." He smiles indulgently. "Dad and I don't push it. She doesn't seem tormented, so we let it lie."

"And you, Charlie?"

"I adored him. Someone like him won't walk my way again."

"Why is the old baseball cap in the baggie?"

"I found it at the crash site. It smells like Todd. I keep it like this and occasionally, when I especially miss him, I unzip it and take a little whiff."

I pull Charlie back on the bed with me. "Let me fill that empty space a little."

"It's wonderful," he says, "just having you here. I've never talked with anyone outside the family about Todd. It wasn't hard with you, Miranda. Fill me some more."

Charlie and I lie together, wrapped in each other's arms. Despite what Lew's desires and my conflicts are, I'm feeling I've made my choice. I want Charlie, in every way possible. It's only my fear of hurting him that's holding me back. Soon, though. I want to constantly touch him, and I do. My hand keeps swinging his way. I brush my hip against his. I'm lost in him. And he's the one who's looking at me like he can't believe he's with me.

* * *

A few minutes before ten the next morning, I join the assembled family at the heavy old oak table beside the kitchen. Charlie's dad puts his arm around my shoulders, and I feel like it's to tell me that he's happy I know about Todd.

The table is apparently the family boardroom with the added advantage of being close enough to the kitchen sidebar that Molly can easily keep it well supplied with food. Not much surprises me about this family anymore, but having your ex-nanny involved with war plans is still amazing. Molly has good down-to-earth suggestions and is listened to. Tina and Phil won't be here, but everyone else is. Hugh sits unobtrusively some distance away, his feet up on some ancient footstool covered in faded needlepoint, pensively stirring a mug of coffee.

A doorbell rings and Molly goes to answer it. She comes back accompanying a slender man about fifty, wearing a generic gray suit and an artificial smile. Charlie 2 approaches him to have a few private words, then accompanies him in to join us.

"Everyone," Charlie's dad begins. "This is FBI Agent Bagdonavitch. He's requested the opportunity to corroborate details concerning the attempts on Lew Black River's life."

After settling stiffly on an offered chair, the agent begins emotionlessly. "My colleagues in DC spent two hours interviewing Lew Black River and Mr. Flynn late last night. I've been forwarded the transcripts of their conversation. I can't be forthcoming on details involving Lew's national security work."

He's become very serious. "The most critical unknown is how Lew was targeted initially at the Four Seasons. After that first incident, it would have been easy to trace him to University Hospital, but no one can figure how it became known he'd be at the hotel in the first place." He scans the room. "Who knew he'd be there and when?"

Everyone looks at Charlie and me. "Let me," Charlie says. "It was a last-minute decision. The event started at eight and I texted Lew's name to be included on the list of attendees at about six. The text went directly to the event organizer, a Miss Harding. The only other people who knew he'd be there were Miranda, Lew, Tony Flynn, and myself until I personally notified the Four Seasons. I suppose it's possible my phone was hacked, but assuming he was the target, the assassin had only several hours lead-time. Miranda and I were there until about eleven-thirty. We started to leave about the time Lew was shot. By the time we retrieved our coats, it had already happened."

"Assuming he was the target?" the agent asks. "Who else could have been a target?"

I look at Charlie who nods at me to continue. "I've also been... We don't think so, but..."

"Yes, Mr. Flynn spoke of that. We're considering the possibility the assassin was there to target you and had an impromptu opportunity to get to Lew. I was told the notes threatened two people."

I freeze. Charlie notices and takes my hand.

145

"Miss Flynn," the agent asks, "did anyone else know you were going to the Four Seasons?"

"Only my sister in New York. I called her to see if she could come down, but she was busy and didn't have enough time to get there."

"Do you and your sister get along?"

"Of course," I blurt out. "We love each other. She couldn't possibly be involved."

"Does she have any axe to grind with Lew?"

"They dated in the past but not seriously. No, they're friends. Family friends."

"Have they been... Intimate?"

"Possibly. Probably. In the past. We've never spelled it out to each other."

"So, she could be jealous."

"Not like that. It's not like she would go out and hire someone. This is crazy. She's an ordinary sister who likes to buy shoes!" I'm raising my voice.

"Has she ever shown any violent behavior or tendencies?"

"No, of course not. She cried for days when her goldfish died."

"Okay. Sorry. We have to probe every possibility. Somehow a person with a sniper's rifle got to the hotel location in time to set up an ambush and an escape route. Then someone trailed the ambulance, or got additional information, and targeted him again at the hospital. This is complicated and sophisticated. In addition, he got access to Lew's hospital room number, which was not given out to anyone except you, and Mr. Curchin, with Lew's permission." He turns to face Charlie. "Mr. Curchin, how do you and Lew get along?"

Charlie hesitates, taking some time to consider his answer. "Lew has interest in Miranda that goes beyond friendship. Miranda and I have a new relationship. Clearly, we are rivals. I'm telling you this so that you don't find it out later, assume I didn't level with you."

"I have several uncomfortable questions for you, Mr. Curchin. Would you prefer to discuss them privately?"

Everyone in the room is taken back. Charlie 2 interrupts in a cold professional voice, "We've been very accommodating, Mr. Bagdonavitch. We'll need a lawyer present if this is to continue."

"Dad. It's all right." He holds up his hand. "I have nothing to hide." Charlie stares coldly at the agent, "Ask your questions."

The atmosphere has become progressively strained.

"I'm familiar with your brother's violent death five years ago. The case is still open. You were investigated around that time for aggressive behavior. Would you illuminate the previous event? And... Are there episodes in your past, particularly involving your brother, that I should be aware of? Other violent incidents?"

Charlie glares at the agent. I've never seen Charlie angry, let alone hostile, making a visible effort to control himself. "I cherished my brother more than any other living person. I detested the woman involved in the complaint you're referring to. She wasn't harmed. She was deplorable; tried to extort money after my brother's death." Now he is openly glaring at the agent. "You can search anywhere, ask anyone. Dig until hell freezes over. You'll find there was nothing between my brother and me except love. And as far as Black Water is concerned... I don't need to assassinate competition."

The agent studies him gravely. Finally, he nods at Charlie 3 and says, "I regret having to ask these questions. We're just starting our investigation. You should know that Mr. Black River has become a key figure, monitoring sinister foreign interests that threaten national security. Further protection of him will be coordinated with the CIA and FBI, in conjunction with the NSA. He's a unique and special individual. I wouldn't be doing my job if I didn't pursue every possibility."

Everyone takes a deep breath, including the agent. "I may have some questions later," he says, "but I'm finished for now. Excuse my bluntness. I have Lew's safety in mind, and additionally that of several young ladies. You must realize everyone is supremely concerned after two assassination attempts." The agent turns to Charlie's father. "Thank you for your cooperation. We'll share relevant information as we can."

"Miranda is our highest priority," Charlie 2 emphasizes. "I hope it's understood anything impacting her safety needs to be communicated to us immediately so we can protect her." He continues, "I'm going to have my legal team contact your lead investigator to ensure that." He pauses. "The family has nothing to hide. We have security apparatus here and overseas to assist your investigation if that becomes necessary."

The agent stands and nods gravely around the room. "I get the picture. We'll be in touch."

Molly walks him back down the hallway to the front door.

We sit there silently until the door opens and closes.

Standing abruptly, I stammer, "I'm so... So sorry. I should have gone with my father. This is causing you so much trouble."

Charlie 2 starts to say something.

Urgently, I add, "Please. I won't stay here. If you could just have Hugh ..."

"Who do you think we are?" Charlie 3 interrupts indignantly. "Just a bunch of rich wimps?"

"What?"

"I hate it when you don't treat me like an ordinary guy. Damn it, Miranda."

"I..."

"Do you imagine you're inconveniencing the conglomerate, or something? Do you think you're not important enough to protect because you're not some filthy rich, society woman?"

"That's enough," Anna breaks in.

"No, Mom, Damn it. Either Miranda realizes she's become the most important person in the world to me. And I'll do everything to protect her or... Or..."

"Or what, Charlie?" I say softly.

"Or... I don't know."

I walk over to Charlie and put my hand on his arm. "Okay," I say quietly. "I give up. You can protect me."

"Okay, then," he says heatedly.

"Okay."

"Well, I'm glad we got that settled," declares Charlie 2. "I need some waffles to calm my nerves."

We've finished brunch, and I know the routine by now as I help Anna rinse and throw dishes in the dishwasher. Molly scrubs the few pans. Hugh collects trash as Stosh makes more coffee in the fanciest coffee machine I've ever seen.

"Miranda?" asks Charlie 2. "Do you have the foggiest idea what's behind all this? Don't give away any national security information, but what in the hell does Lew do?"

"He hasn't told me anything specific. All I know is that he's gotten very good at intercepting certain international viruses that are being imbedded to take down systems in the US, hacking into what could be used to blackmail or paralyze our government. That's all I know. I don't even know which countries are involved."

"This computer vulnerability has been coming on for a long time," Charlie 2 says. "It's been escalating exponentially since Todd died. Our company facilitated several real estate contracts, using Turkey as an intermediary, and bypassing Russia, but hacking interference became such a problem that we sold our subsidiary interest back to the government. They have better security protection. I never regretted that decision. Only government sophistication can deal with those issues. Lew must be something. Hasn't he only been working for them a year or so?"

"Two years, really. Even during the period when he was finishing his degree, he was cutting edge. It's amazing, knowing where he came from. That's where I met Charlie, on the Blackfeet Reservation in northern Montana. It's the most beautiful country I've ever seen, but very remote, not exactly a hub of technology. Lew's probably a genius to have evolved there."

"Well, he's important enough for someone to want him out of the way," Anna says, standing up. "Your dad is safer with you up here, too. He needs to separate from Lew quickly. I'm sure he knows that."

I glance over at Charlie as they turn to leave. He's trying to hide it, but I know it doesn't thrill him to have me talk about how wonderful Lew is.

I've been waiting for some time alone and finally have an opportunity to ask, "What was that about this morning, between you and some woman...? When Todd disappeared...?"

"Todd had many relationships of minimal depth. Weeks after he died, one young woman tried to convince us she was owed money. I lost my temper, badly... Threatened her, then physically ushered her out of the house. She caused some trouble for us, and it happened at a very vulnerable time as you can imagine." He laughs. "To tell you the truth, I probably prevented Juli from doing jail time. She was standing with me, ready to kill that same witch. I just got there first."

"You tried to tell me, Charlie. Wealth can cause trouble." Hesitating, I finally ask, "Tell me something about Juli. All the stories of wild adventures seem to include her. What's she like? Is she like you?"

He shakes his head. "No. Much more like Todd was—fearless, aggressive, and impulsive. She loves deeply but has never come close to sustaining a long-term relationship." He sighs. "Same as me, I guess. Trusting is always an issue."

He stares pensively at me. "I keep expecting to wake up, but you're still here. Maybe I can start to believe it."

"Believe it," I say, staring into his eyes until he breaks out in a grin. Then I add, "Tell me something more about Juli so I can know her."

"Hmm? Alright. When Todd died, I lost myself. Nothing helped. Several weeks after he died, I was deeply broken. Couldn't eat. Couldn't sleep. Everyone tried to help me, but I was unreachable." He grimaces, remembering. "She was relentless, for several months. She checked in constantly, shared her own pain, helped give me hope. I decided to live."

"Charlie..."

"I love her because she cares so much."

"Then I'll love her, too."

* * *

I need to finalize a job. It's been six weeks since my summer internship ended, and my funds are not endless. I'm ready to work. The consensus is that I would be safer in Montana and it's time. I've arranged in person job interviews in Great Falls with two law firms the middle of this coming week. Charlie also needs to work. Even Charlie 2 is dropping hints about him earning his keep. It now seems incredible, but I feel at home with the whole family. Tina has dropped by for dinner and was warm and encouraging. I finally talked to Juli on speakerphone with Charlie. I liked her a lot despite the vague feeling that I was being screened in an interview. And I remembered what Charlie had told me.

Charlie and I are going to try and wait two and a half weeks. Hugh is going to return me to Montana tomorrow. It's time. The security machine has pushed me down the list of targets.

He and I are sitting on well-used padded lounge chairs, placed side-by-side on the back patio, holding hands. It's getting cooler now, mid-October weather, and the sun is setting earlier. Our legs are covered by a frayed wool red plaid blanket exactly like one we have at home. The trees in the back yard, several huge oaks and maples, are really turning color now, deep reds and bright oranges and gold. Stosh has been mowing with a big leaf collector and someone in the neighborhood is burning piles of fall leaves, producing that fall aroma. It's the best time of year in this part of the country and I'm relaxed and very happy.

"I'm so glad I came back here, Charlie. I believe I could fit in with your family."

"My hope was you could know that."

I can't imagine what could spoil my emerging devotion. My man. I stop and laugh at myself. I'm beginning to believe it might be true.

CHAPTER 17

LEW

"ARE YOU SURE you feel up to this trip, Lew?" asks Ross. "I doubt the world will collapse if you put this off another week."

"No, I'm ready. From what the briefing people tell me, the company elites are already in the air, or close to it. I feel fine. Not even a headache." I say, simultaneously demonstrating my Blackfeet warrior stance. "I know what I want to present. Let's do this."

"I'm not going to make fun of your fighter ability; not after your recent encounter," he says seriously. "And you can rest on the plane. There's a bedroom in the back. Use it. You'll be tired from the time zone change. Turkey is about as far around the planet as you can go."

"It's nice to know you care," I smile at him. Despite the reality of Ross evolving into an NSA superstar, he and I have always gotten along easily.

"I do care, Lew, and it's not just because you're enhancing my career," he says, more seriously than I would have expected. "Everyone has been briefed and for once the mission is clear and defined. I'll wait for you to get back for the debriefing. We'll keep air communication to logistics." He leans over his desk to shake my hand. "Be nice to the Turks. We don't have many friends left over there. As you know they keep communication open with our adversaries which is becoming invaluable. And for God's sake, try to stay out of female entanglements. I don't want to wait ten years to get you exchanged for some foreign operative."

"Got it. I have enough trouble handling entanglements here."

"I know that. I have my sources, including Clancy's daughter with a broken heart."

He gives me a look like he really does know. Crap.

"See you when you get back," he says, smiling broadly.

* * *

I glance out the window of the military plane taking me to Turkey from Ramstein Air Force Base in Germany. Below me is the Strait of Bosporus which separates the Eastern European portion of Istanbul from the Asia section. Egypt has become a stable western ally. Lebanon's a disaster now. God only knows how that's going to sort out. Jordan is reliably in the Western camp while supporting hundreds of thousands of refugees. The Saudis under MBS give our entire government a constant headache. We're trying to work with them but not appear to be condoning atrocities and push them into the Russian sphere. Plus, they have significant internal pressure to keep both the zealots and moderates happy, and the problem of younger generations of royals costing them untold billions. Who knows how that's going to evolve?

For the near term, Turkey is reasonably friendly, although a less reliable partner than earlier years. The U.S. has extensive covert connections set up in Turkey along with the largest State Department security structure in the area. There are five thousand US military personnel at Incirlik Air Base where we'll be landing. I'm also aware we keep significant tactical nuclear weapons at the base. Still, I was here last year and feel comfortable enough.

Shaking my head, I admit several years ago, I wouldn't have been able to find these countries on a map.

I'm traveling with my trusted companions, Will Nelson and Aamad Nivissi. Will is in his usual position, flattened out in the seat across the aisle, asleep with Ambien tablets. Aamad and I are playing cribbage.

Long hours in the air have provided an opportunity to consider my life. After thirty years of relative calm on the res, the broader world has come crashing down on me. Despite exaggerating my Blackfeet upbringing here for dramatic effect, I've been a low-profile techy guy. My most nefarious adventure of the distant past involved *borrowing* some of our neighbors' horses with Willie and Win, decorating them with war paint for the local summer pow-wow, and riding them in the local parade. I was fourteen.

My life now consists of life and death intrigue, women at risk, and assassination attempts on my life. The big guys have brought in heavily armed bodyguards with planners orchestrating my every move. To be frank, as much as I try to appear cool and calm, I'm as flummoxed as I've ever been in my life. I've accepted I won't be going overseas often in the near future. I'm too expensive to protect, and too valuable. I've been able to identify mid-and-long-term national threats; even better, develop creative counter measures.

Turkey is central enough that various operatives and planners can congregate in person to discuss my ideas. Wireless communication can be hacked with dire ramifications. I smile to myself. Several years ago, 'dire' and 'ramifications' were hardly part of my working vocabulary."

"Earth to Black River," my cribbage pardner interrupts, bringing me back to reality.

"Sorry. Sorry. I was daydreaming."

He stretches his neck with an amused grin. "I need a break, anyway."

I'm incredibly lucky to have Aamad as a traveling companion and protector. He works out continually, and can provide lethal force if needed, both with weapons and martial arts skills. Plus, we've become great friends. He doesn't stand out in a crowd, especially in this part of the world, until you see his eyes. They're crackling with intelligence and perpetual humor, which he unleashes at me.

Aamad functions as my social guidance counselor, pointing out every wrong move I make with women, and is very strategic as far as the ladies are concerned. He's as calculating as I am a bumbling novice in the cosmopolitan world. So far, he's primarily berated me for obvious mistakes, mostly involving Miranda. After listening to my protestations for over a year of why I haven't leveled with her about my feelings, he finally pointed out that modern-day females are our intellectual equals. In addition, they are equally powerful, and really don't like being kept out of the loop, however well-intentioned. I know that. I do. But in Blackfeet culture, or maybe rural male culture, protecting women for their own good overwhelms my modern outlook.

Even before this situation, I didn't want to get Miranda involved. And to be honest, until this mess with Charlie, I was still having a whale of a lot of fun playing the field.

When I was becoming aware of Rena's multiple relationships, I became obsessed with an aggressive lady I met at a party in my apartment building. We had a brief affair which flashed hot and flamed out. Stephanie wasn't the kind of woman you want to make plans with, plus she abruptly moved to New York. The crowning glory was she and Rena met. Before you knew it, they became roommates. The convoluted drama provided a lot of comic material for Aamad, and a lot of discomfort for me. I imagine they spend long evenings over glasses of wine discussing my shortcomings. Like I say, it's been a learning curve.

I wasn't entirely honest with Miranda in Montana. There is someone in DC as I implied. Leanne knows much more about my line of work than Miranda does. Her father is a company man, one of my superiors in fact, and extricating myself is going to be a little tricky. Not that I can't do it. Besides, her father doesn't want me within a hundred miles of her now. It won't damage my career. I'm beginning to know my own worth, but it's something I want to handle well. I owe her that.

But as Aamad points out, "Get with it." This whole situation with Miranda has been excruciating. I thought I had time until I saw Charlie focus on her at Win's ranch. I could almost see the light bulb go on in his eyes. God damn it to hell. He has all the sophistication I don't and was smart enough to drop everything to go for her. My stomach turned over when I saw them together at Tony's. I've been such a fucking idiot. Of all the people I don't want to compete with, it's Charlie. And I need to put this out of my mind for the next two weeks.

Aamad breaks into my thoughts by pointing out the window. It's just after sunset and the lights on the grounds illuminate the immensely beautiful Sabanci Mosque on the banks of the Seyhan River as the plane makes its final approach to the US Air Base. I feel a long way from home but energized in this exotic part of the world. Strangely, with my dark hair and eyes, I stand out less in Turkey than I do in DC. In some ways, the underlying tribal society here is comparable to the culture of my ancestors a hundred and fifty years ago, continuing forward to modern times in Blackfeet country.

Similarly, modern urban development and technology are

encroaching and changing people's lives. The high-rises here look boringly similar. Scores of them have sprouted up over the last ten years like mushrooms. The newer part of Adana is sprawling, not nearly as beautiful as the older sections of the ancient city, but vibrant with youthful energy. People from all over the world gather here, interacting freely in this uniquely secular country. Unfortunately, authoritarian trends are being exacerbated here like much of Eastern Europe.

We're met by a State Department official and driven to the Adana Hilton. It's eight P.M. local time and I need some time to organize and focus my thoughts before my short opening discussion tomorrow morning. I hope I can get to sleep soon after dinner, but the time change has thrown me. Ross has told me he's staying up very late so he can hear my major presentation the day after tomorrow in real time. He said that as if it was supposed to make me relax.

The Hilton is impressive by anyone's standards. They've put me on the tenth floor facing directly across the river with a breathtaking view of the Mosque. Dropping my duffle, I step out onto the lanai in darkness with the lights of Istanbul spread out before me. The dry desert air is unique. Each desert city has its own distinctive flavor. I can almost smell the kabobs from the stalls in the outdoor market, hear the vendors calling. Again, for just a few seconds, I feel very far away from everyone I love and feel a shiver despite the heat.

* * *

The morning meeting went well. There were almost forty people in attendance from Europe, the Far East, and the neighborhood of Middle Eastern countries. We spent most of the time prioritizing a daily schedule of seminars presented by a variety of specialists including myself. This afternoon we'll get an overview of world hacking dilemmas which will get more specific as the two weeks progress. I had an individual indoctrination meeting with Aamad and several security personnel with strict instructions not to ever, and they emphasized ever, go out without a major team of bodyguards. Downer. The last time here I was a nobody, roaming around with Aamad, ignored on the streets as another everyman.

We've spent the second morning with general discussions of various strategic situations. I'm to address the entire assembly this afternoon at 1:30. I've never talked to a group larger than an ordinary classroom and I'm exhaling deep breaths just thinking about it. Will says to remember I don't have to solve all the world's problems, just bring out concepts they may not have thought of. And, anyway, I'm a rookie so no one has high expectations.

Thoughts of Miranda often distract me, desperately hoping that Charlie is stuck in far-off Philadelphia. I'm up next. Focus! I tell myself.

I've been standing awkwardly at the podium, trying to decide if I should lean on it, and then clear my throat several times. "Ladies and gentlemen," I start out—forget what I was going to say—then fumble with my notes one more time.

"Ladies and gentlemen. As you know, the president has signed a directive for the NSA to develop a program targeted at our allies, protecting them from cyberattack, and enabling them to take anticipatory action against imminent threats. You can assume, as I do, that nothing I present is adequately protected against hacking or wiretapping, so specifics will be given on a country-by-country basis in person to representatives and their tech support teams. This will be merely an outline of general topics, and a summary of qualifiers to general statements." My dry throat locks up. "Um? Questions so far?" I choke out, finally remembering to look up. The room has gone absolutely quiet. Either I've got their full attention or everyone's asleep.

I manage to swallow a half glass of water in one continuous gulp before continuing. "The two countries most prone to cause immediate problems are Iran and North Korea. Russia and China have more sophisticated cyber hacking networks, but it's not in their current economic interest to disrupt our infrastructure, either physical structures or cyber security. Anything that would damage us would threaten international trade and loan repayments. Unfortunately, the world balance does not remain static. At any time, bad actors could use chaos to weaken us. Iran and North Korea have everything to gain and nothing to lose by causing us problems. Anything that weakens us threatens our resolve to maintain and increase sanctions. We will provide firewalls against unanticipated aggression."

I look up again. People are honest-to-God taking notes. Several prominent men in the front row nod and smile encouragingly. *Whoa, cool*, I decide, squaring my shoulders before I continue. "As many of you know, the Iranians were successful in hacking into the Saudis largest state-run oil producer. Luckily, it didn't disrupt oil production, but the benefit of preventing this on a larger scale is obvious. In response to that, the NSA is developing hardware and software programs for just that purpose. We will be providing training and even joint cyber war-games for a variety of scenarios."

I go on to descriptions of various systems on a general basis and a schedule for this week's sub-groups to discuss various networks and how each region of the world will be integrated into a coordinated defense system. After almost an hour, I thank everyone for listening, and step gratefully away from the podium. I'm immediately shocked by loud applause. It rocks the room and goes on for some time. Several influential people hurry over to congratulate me, holding out hands to be shaken.

Several minutes later I get a vibration on my cell—Ross back in DC. "Lew, I just listened to your presentation on closed circuit T.V. Just wanted you to know you nailed it."

"Thanks, boss," I say.

"No. Listen," he says. "I mean it, Lew. Well done. Very well done."

"I'm just glad it's over." I admit, then add. "To tell you the truth, I surprised myself."

I hear him laugh before he continues. "Well, the pressure's off until the next major session on Friday and the individual training sessions next week should be a piece of cake for you. You're not responsible for the infrastructure of the computer programs, just the strategic implications. My instructions are to relax and listen and learn. We'll talk later. Again, great job!" Just before he clicks off, I hear a parting shot, "And for God's sake, behave yourself."

Back in the room at four in the afternoon, I'm exhausted but pumped. Just the chance to interact with these brilliant, responsible people is awe-inspiring. Will has been beyond supportive. He told me he'll begin turning over some of his duties to me. His stomach has been bothering him and his doctor wants him to rest for a month or two. He has no fear of me overtaking him. He's too good a man, having thirty years of experience to draw on. We're going to be a great team.

I'm pacing around the room. What I want is to get out of the hotel and explore Adana, go to the carzi for kabobs, and absorb the culture. Except for exotic music in the lobby, I could be home in Baltimore. And I'm a fresh air kind of guy.

"Nope," admonishes Aamad. "Don't even think about it. I'll have some local food brought in and tested for poison."

"Oh, come on. That's got to be overkill."

"Bisho'ur," he says. "After that speech, you're even more on the international radar. You have a big red target on your chest. If you give me any trouble, I'm supposed to call in the serious suits with the mirror glasses. They aren't any fun at all."

"Okay. Okay," I say reluctantly. "I'll behave." I've learned two words in Farsi from my bodyguard-friend. Bisho'ur,' which means idiot. And kos'khool, which Aamad uses when I'm completely out of line. Literally, it means dumbass. There are several more descriptive phrases that he emphasizes with gestures. He lets me guess at the translation.

"Atta boy, Lew. We're stuck with pay-per-view. Let's see if we can find some exotic dancers with gems in their navels. We're both getting combat pay. You're going to be rich."

* * *

Closing in on the end of the symposium, I'm satisfied with what we've accomplished. I'm a contributing member of a design team that may do something significant on a world scale. Late at night, lying awake in my hotel room, I try to figure out how a kid from the res was transformed into a player. But when I feel my ego getting out of control, I remember my friends, especially Miranda, and imagine what it would feel like not having people who care.

I'm mentally exhausted. This has been the most intense thing I've ever experienced, frightening at times, starting with people trying to kill me back home. The security folks have me looking over my shoulder constantly. No more creative thinking. I'm done in. Will, who's been involved at this level for a decade, has helped me cope with the emotional drain. He supplies alcohol and humor, admitting he's a little put out no one's ever tried to kill him. "Puts me further down the pecking order," he grumbled, then admitted dodging bullets in a hospital room is for younger guys, and it wouldn't have done his ulcer any good, anyway.

On a more serious note, he suggested that after the debriefing, which he informs me will be intense, I take a week or two off to get the ordinary world back in focus. He said Ross will insist on it, and I agree. My head's a mess, and I need to straighten myself out before I move ahead.

When I've had some decent sleep, I'm going to concentrate on Miranda. The thought keeps surfacing that it may already be too late. She was standing in front of me, begging me to level with her, and I thought I was protecting her by keeping her out of this world. I should have learned something from Win on that topic. He stood a good chance of losing Lizzie with the same crap, and with the same White Boy. We've talked about it. Damn it all to hell. I'm going to clear my head and try to develop a plan all the way back to the states.

Aamad pokes his head in the door. "Lew. They want us locked down from now on. We'll be leaving for the airport around six tomorrow morning."

"Gotcha," I yell back, smiling to myself. I'm not leaving here without one quick trip to the carzi. I love the open-air markets and have a mental list of presents to get for people back home. Plus, I want a dozen kabobs from the street vendors. I'll take a big swig of pink stuff and if that doesn't work, I'll recover on the plane.

Tousling my hair, I put on dark glasses and a rumpled shirt which I leave untucked, then peek carefully into the hall. No one I know is around. With my dark skin and hair, I'll blend in. Feeling like a disheveled James Bond, I make a quick right turn, quickly reaching the stairwell. Ten flights down and I'm hailing a cab. As it pulls out of the hotel driveway, I turn in my seat for a last look. No one is running after me, waving their arms. Feeling smug, I look at my cell, six PM. It's roughly a fifteen-minute trip. I should make it back by seven-thirty. They probably won't even miss me.

I've been dropped off in the more modern building section of the bazaar and walk toward the outskirts. This carzi is unique, less touristy than the grand bazaar in Istanbul, and all the locals frequent it. It has the feel of a large Indian pow-wow in Montana. The farther you get from the building structures the more primitive it gets. It spans over a square mile and the entire area is filled with wonderful smells of spices and cooking meat aromas and a unique background noise.

The men laugh and yell constantly with women's high-pitched voices dominating the bartering, waggling their tongues to get your attention. Flat tables are everywhere, mounded with everything imaginable: spices, rugs, dried fruit, brassware, and exotic woven materials. Covering the tables are translucent muslin awnings, filtering the sun and fluttering in the breeze. Then there are the smaller pushcarts, increasing the farther out you go from the central section, with older boys shoving them and hawking their goods. Here I can feel part of a foreign land.

The colors on the tables blend red, orange and browns with bright blues of cobalt and turquoise. I'd love to take Miranda here. A few camels and horses are tied to various stalls, even small flocks of sheep and goats. I'm wedging my purchases in my backpack, mostly nuts and spices, and trying to choose some silk for Miranda, when I'm grabbed from behind.

Aamad is glaring at me. "Damn it, kos'khool. He's almost shaking me. "I knew you'd be here somewhere. I've got six guys out looking for you. Everyone's frantic."

I gasp. "Jesus H. Christ, Aamad. You scared me to death."

"Fine," he says. "We're fuckin' even. Now start moving out of here."

"Okay. Okay," I say. "Just let me pay this lady."

While he scans the crowd, I hurriedly hand over some coins and turn to start moving. Aamad's become a frozen statue with blazing eyes. Leaning over, he mutters, "Listen up, God damn it. And pay attention. You're being followed and we're a half-mile from the car." He grabs my arm. "Don't look, but there's three guys, two dressed as Arabs. They have guns under their robes."

"Where?"

"A hundred feet to the right, over by the big fig tree." He grabs my arm. "Start moving off to the left. It's the wrong way to the car, but we can circle 'round once we get to the main route. There'll be more people. You're way too far out."

I do as he says but he stops me, still holding my arm. "Damn," he says, "they're moving with us, starting to cut us off. And I can't see any of my boys."

I glance over, easily spotting the three guys moving parallel to us. For the first time I feel real fear.

"Listen to me, Lew. This is damn serious. I don't want you taken hostage."

A coldness wells up in me. I'm traditionally cool under stress and start looking for escape routes.

"Pay attention," Aamad mutters. "I'm gonna run directly at the three guys, brandishing my gun. They're between us and the main path to the car. When I do that, wait a few seconds and run like hell. Veer a little off to the right, then sprint up the main drag. They probably won't shoot into a crowd."

"You're crazy, Aamad. I'm not sacrificing you." The pleasant atmosphere of the market has turned grim and gray.

"Look, Bisho'ur. You're my responsibility. They'll fire me if I let anything happen."

Underlying his bravado is fear and concern. Desperately, I look for an alternative.

"Aamad, can you ride a horse?"

"What the hell are you talking about?"

"Well, can you?"

"Yes, sort of."

"I'm going to sprint for the gray horse tied to that vendor's stand, the one with the crowd in front of it. The bad guys will be surprised. They'll follow me away from you. I'll jump on the horse and gallop back through them, shooting in the air so they'll know I'm armed. I'll pull you up behind me and we'll ride like hell back toward the car. Give me your gun."

"ARE YOU CRAZY!"

"No. No. I do this kind of stuff with my friends at home all the time. I'll pass you on your left as you face me. Just link arms and I'll pivot you up behind me. Just go with the flow."

"Over my dead fucking body."

"Damn it, Aamad. If you don't do this, you'll really be dead. I'm not leaving you. Do it, unless you have a better idea."

He gives me a long look and rolls his eyes. "Oh, dear God!" he says, slipping me his gun.

"On the count of three," I say. "One—two—three!" I whip around and race toward the horse. I have about three seconds until all hell breaks loose. I reach the horse. Luckily it has the reins only draped over another rope. I fly onto his bare back, whip him around, and gallop hell-bent toward Aamad. It works like a charm. Bullets start to fly as I whip Aamad up with me. "Hold on!" I yell. Both scrunching down, we gallop toward the main entrance with Aamad holding on to me for dear life, dodging scrambling people as we go. Close to the car, we leap off and run for it.

Two company guys, seeing us, get the general idea we need to beat it out of here fast. We dive in open doors, and in seconds, the car is zooming away from the crowd. Aamad and I are yelling. I'm not sure what Aamad is yelling, but I'm yelling Blackfeet war whoops.

* * *

The debriefing is going in a different direction. Aamad and I are sitting in a large conference room with Ross, Ross's boss, and Ross's boss's boss and seven other guys, including an Under Secretary of State. They all been asking questions and giving one-word frowning opinions. I've just finished going over the whole thing for the second time. No one is happy with us. There is absolute silence in the room.

No one knows what to say. We sit motionless. Moments pass. Finally, I wince. "I'm really sorry," I say, mostly to break the silence.

Ross leans across the table at me and growls, "Damn it, Lew. You are not Indiana Jones."

"I guess I shouldn't have gone to the bazaar."

"You've been the target of two assassination attempts and you're in the Middle East and you want to go SHOPPING?"

"When you put it like that..."

"And you, Aamad. You're officially demoted to... I can't imagine anything low enough."

"Look," I say seriously. "He... Um... I managed to escape. I'm a Blackfeet. Stealth is my middle name." I look around. No one is laughing. I try again. "He was willing to sacrifice his life for me. I'm not going anywhere without him."

"Fine, Lew. But he goes back in for extensive retraining. You guys are too close. You've got to... Goddamn it, cooperate. It's not just that you're extremely valuable to the entire program. I don't want you killed or taken hostage. You were fucking lucky! Goddamn it, Lew," he says again, "you must have some idea what shit could have been done to you. Blackfeet warrior or not, I doubt you would have fucking survived it. They cut people up, you know. Hack off body parts. As it was, four operatives looking for you didn't make it back to the hotel for hours. We had more people out looking for them. It was..." He pauses for emphasis then roars, "A major fuck-up!"

I cringe. That was a lot of expletives from Ross. "You're right, sir. I really am sorry. And scared."

He continues to glare at both of us. "Aamad? Can you be professional enough to justify continuing?"

"Yes, sir." He says contritely.

Several lengthy sighs later, Ross continues. "All right, then. Aamad, get down to security and sign up for a refresher course on maintaining objectivity. Lew, download the torture video and watch it over and over. Both of you take a week and a half off. I expect you back in the office a week from Monday at nine."

He glowers at us as we smile meekly back.

"Now get out of here."

"Yes, sir," we say in unison.

We walk out of the office with as much dignity as possible then slump against the corridor wall.

"He was pissed," I say. "No more 'call me Ross'."

"His neck would have been in a noose if I'd let you get captured.

I'm sorry, Lew. The whole thing was my fault. I'm supposed to explain reality to you, make you behave. You're just a dumb smuck from the res. I tend to forget that at times. It is my job."

"You're right, Aamad. And you could have been killed. I couldn't live with that. Maybe we are too close. You're such a damn nice guy."

"I'm too charming for my own good." He shakes his head. "So, big guy. What are you doing next week? Have you had time to think about it, between being flogged by the boss?"

"Yep. I'm going to my apartment and get twenty-four hours sleep. And I need to have a long talk leveling with Leanne. It's only fair. Then I'll see if I can repair things with Miranda."

"How's that going to go? With Leanne, I mean?"

"She won't be suicidal, but I'd like her to think breaking up is her idea." I sigh. "Anyway, her dad will be pleased. He wants her as far away from me as possible. Can't see that I blame him. I keep involving people I care about, being the wattsa' pssi schmuck that I am."

"Good luck with that, Lew. I'm headed home to take my turn at changing diapers."

"You're a lucky guy, Aamad. 'Course, you know that. I'll text you if I'm in the area."

He slaps my arm affectionately then hurries off. I stay leaning against the wall, adjusting. Hmm? First, I'll call Tony and find out where Miranda is. I'm hoping she's in Montana. What I'm really hoping is Charlie is still marooned back here. I groan with embarrassment on how I left it. Why don't I just tell her what I feel? Beyond that, I'm exhausted. I'll try sleeping first; right after I buy a plane ticket and send Ross a fruit basket.

Ash

I'm mortally afraid for the first time in my life, and for my sister and my nephew. Another operative approached me in person. It was a threat, oblique but unequivocal, that my failure is putting us at risk. He's informed me this assignment is to be concluded immediately. No more botched attempts. The dead hospital assassin, an experienced muscle man, was made to look a fool, as was the entire enterprise. Public failure is never supposed to happen. Word gets around in our clandestine world, and we can't afford the loss of face. Then there was the Turkish debacle. In desperation, and luckily for me, they assigned more "experienced" men. I'm still shaking my head at how that went down. Plus, Black River should be guarded like gold now.

"Do whatever it takes." I now have unlimited access to extra operatives, trigger men, men who don't know anything about anything, but they get money for blood. I'll be trailing the Blackfeet around, looking for opportunities, which is why I needed to quit my current job. Afterwards, I'm to blend into obscurity. Spooks can't afford real friends, although I'll considerably miss Brad. He's hosting me tonight for a farewell barbeque. I'm surprised how down I feel about that. When I was recruited, I never anticipated the loneliness.

CHAPTER 18

LEW

A STRONG WEST wind alters the plane's course slightly, making the approach to Great Falls airport more directly from the east. We'll be landing just after sunset. I'm as excited as a kid to see my Rocky Mountains and ancestral home. I keep pointing it out to my companion, a FBI guy who is somber and humorless. I suspect Ross chose him personally. It's late October so a thick blanket of snow covers the mountain slopes, extending almost to the widening valleys below. A big weather front is coming in tomorrow afternoon and I'm hoping to get on a horse and watch it roll in from the north.

I've been reassessing many things, including my last conversation with Ross, attempting to convince him to allow me to come home unescorted. I wasn't kidding about my mental status. I'm still a mess.

* * *

"Please, Ross," I pleaded. "I'm as strung out as I've ever been in my life. Plus, I...um...have a personal issue—a big one. I need time at home, alone, no bodyguards, to resolve some things."

That was a serious speech from me. It sobered the boss. That and the fact that I was almost in tears. "Lew," he said, with more compassion than I've ever seen from him, "We almost lost you."

I grimace. He's trying to keep me safe.

"I know, when you signed up..." he went on. "Well, I know you never imagined all this. Honestly, neither did we. But here we are."

I stared him down for the first time in my life. "I won't have a bodyguard at home. It won't work. No."

He lowered his eyebrows. No one ever says no to Ross. I could see his face getting red.

"Listen," I said, "you don't know the res. Everyone knows everyone, for generations. We watch out for each other. The police are our neighbors, our family members. I'll let them know. The whole reservation will be my bodyguard. Please, Ross. Please." I was almost begging—clearly not myself. It was pretty obvious.

He sat at his desk, doing the usual thing he does when he's undecided in a bad way—folded his arms across his chest and tapped his right upper arm with his left index finger. Minutes passed. I waited him out.

"All right," he said, finally. "You will fly under an assumed name. You will have one of our company men drive a circuitous route to the airport, and you will keep a low profile from this moment on. You will have a bodyguard 'til the second you step off the military jet, and I expect you to arrange friends to meet you at the plane, including your police-friend. Then slink around at home and dress like... Well, however you used to dress before you were... *Discovered.* Slouch. Don't make eye contact with strangers. Get it?"

"Yes, sir. Yes, Ross, sir. I promise. Thank you. Thank you." I rushed over to him. It was way too intimidating to hug a frustrated, exasperated boss so I did the next best thing—fist-bumped his upper arm until he told me to, "Damn-it-all, quit it," while sighing in resignation.

* * *

Blackfeet heritage is not past to me. Several hundred years ago we were doing hideous atrocities to enemies and having them done to us. It was a survival necessity. I'm a hundred percent Blackfeet and that's part of who I am. Civilized men are not far removed from 'kill or be killed'; one vendetta or one war removed as recent atrocities in Eastern Europe have shown. I'll have to reflect more on that sobering idea.

I did watch the torture videos as Ross suggested. It was sobering, sickening. I was supremely grateful I didn't have to endure that kind of thing, let alone die, for God's sake. Stupid. Stupid. Even worse, I put Aamad at risk, although he keeps apologizing to me for the same thing.

The more pressing issue is Miranda. It took me halfway around the planet to get my predicament in focus, and as soon as I landed, I called Tony; pleaded for honesty. It was awkward but I know he told me the truth. He said he'd known all along Miranda and I have cared deeply for each other. He even admitted encouraging her to talk to me about it at the reunion at Win's. Stupid jerk that I am, I squandered that chance, plus the honor thing—ending it with Leanne first. Then I got caught up in Charlie being involved and got frantically jealous. I'm groaning with frustration. I want her more than anything I've ever wanted in my life.

I allowed an opening and Charlie stepped right through the door ahead of me. Apparently, Charlie is flying to Montana to visit her this weekend. Tony leveled with me. Miranda is very involved, was the way he put it. He admitted it may not be possible for me to do anything at this point. He also said he's doing nothing to influence Miranda on this. It's too important and it's her life. He laughed and said he'd probably mess it up anyway... Something about a poor track record.

What he didn't say is that he likes and admires Charlie. And I've been banking on Tony as a future father-in-law. What in the hell have I been waiting for? I guess I'll lay my feelings on the line with her. Two and a half years of friendship ought to count for something. Shouldn't it? I'm renting a car at the airport and called Miranda just before I got on the plane. I ached when I heard her voice. She's agreed to see me tonight. She said she has something to tell me.

I'm trying not to floor the gas. I've been thinking about what I want to say, and it all sounds incredibly simple-minded, even to me. Parking the car in front of her apartment, I take a deep breath to steady myself. She's Charlie's girl now. What I'm considering is beyond any definition of fair play. But I want her back. That's the blunt fact. If I do what I intend, I'll be blatantly attempting to seduce her. Just so I understand the truth. I sit one more minute to steady myself then walk rapidly to her door and ring the bell.

The door flies open. "Lew," she says, "Dad called about Adana. I can't stand this…" And she throws herself into my arms, crying.

I had expected a Dear John conversation, but here she is in my arms. It shakes me to my core. She's warm and sobbing, and I realize all over again that I want her so much I can hardly breathe. "It's okay, Miranda. I'll be more careful," I say. "I promise. I promise." I tip her face up to mine and kiss her deeply, bending her body to mine.

We hold each other for dear life until she gasps and says, "Lew. Lew. Please, let me go. I need to tell you…"

I release her and she starts crying all over again.

We're sitting on her couch, having my Dear John conversation, but somehow it seems to be killing both of us. I keep apologizing over and over. If I'd had enough courage, smarts, sophistication, or sense this wouldn't have happened. She says she's in love with Charlie and, no, they haven't had sex yet, but she wants to. He's coming out in three days.

I'm frantic but trying not to completely lose it. "Miranda," I say, as calmly as I can manage, "I love you. I think you love me, too. Can't you wait a bit? Give me a chance to do the things, to say the things, I should have before. This is not first come, first serve. This could be your life forever. You owe it to yourself to be sure."

"That's what Charlie told me, to take the time to be sure. And I was sure; right up to the second you walked in my door." She starts crying again.

I feel like crying myself. If I was a good, really good, human being, I'd vacate the premises and fly myself right back to DC and watch torture videos. Having my ears cut off seems almost tame with what's going on here.

We sit in silence, me battling with myself not to reach out and pull her to me. "Listen," I say. "I have an idea. We're both a disaster. Let's just have sex twelve times tonight until we're bored with it. Then I'll give up the contest and go back to DC."

She gasps. "That's it. Perfect! I hadn't thought of that." And I finally get a weak smile.

She turns to me. "Besides, I want to see if you've learned anything about women these last two and a half years."

I take her in my arms. I've never in my life kissed a woman I've been absolutely sure I love. I feel so protective of her. I want to show her how much I love her. But, on top of everything, I really don't want to mess up her life. This is not about sex, it's something much more.

I kiss her deeply. Echoes of the distant past flood my head with emotions. I want her every way a man wants a woman. I want to take her away and hide her. Damn it. I want her all to myself. All these years we've played around this feeling, never quite letting it be born. I'm kissing her because to not kiss her would end me. At the very least, I want her to know the depth of my feelings, so she can judge in the cold light of day.

"Miranda, listen to me. I've loved you so long. It came on so gradually that I didn't recognize it. But I do. This has nothing to do with Charlie. I love you. If Charlie is the love of your life, I'll have to deal with it. But it's not too late. Both of us want you to make the right choice."

I take a deep breath to ask the question I've been framing in my mind for hours. "I'm going to ask one thing. Come up to Win's ranch tomorrow with me and I'll show you the wildness that's a part of me. You don't know me, my heritage. Maybe it will scare you or put you off. I come from a very poor family, across the universe from Charlie's family. If you don't choose me, then I'll live with it." I'm trying not to plead. "But will you come? We'll ride out to meet the storm come in. Remember, I told you about that wildness that very first night."

I can see the angst on her face. Several minutes pass.

"Yes, Lew. I'll come."

"I'm going to Jeremy's tonight. I don't want to seduce you…" I smile absurdly. "Of course, I do, but I want to play fair." I roll my eyes at myself on that one. "I'll pick you up tomorrow at eight, okay? Unless you want to have sex twelve times first?"

"Tempting," she sighs, "but no. Kiss me once, then I'll see you tomorrow."

I gently take her in my arms, wondering if she feels how hard my heart is pounding. God! I hope I've learned something in the last two and a half years. I have a feeling Charlie knows something. An unsolicited vision of my historic past appears—a graphic image of me scalping Charlie. I force it under. *Just kidding*, I think to myself. On the other hand, maybe he has graphic images of attacking me with a squad of bluecoats.

CHAPTER 19

MIRANDA

LEW JUST LEFT. My legs give out and I slide to the floor with my back against the door and bury my head in my arms. I'm positive I'm not the first person in the world who is probably in love with two people. But how could this have happened? Isn't love supposed to be the most wonderful thing in the universe. I'm sick. Every time I go over my choices, see what I could have done differently, I can't come up with a thing. On paper Lew blew it and I should... But after all the years of almost loving Lew and to have it handed to me...?

On top of it all, there's no one the planet I can talk to about this. Dad admits he always makes things worse and he's a guy for heaven's sake. My mother's advice is something I stopped taking in grade school. My sister has let it be known that she'd settle for leftovers, so I can't begin to talk to her about this. I have two close girlfriends, but they've barely heard of Charlie, and having Lew as a love interest after some of our various missteps and catastrophes... I'd sound like a lunatic, even to myself.

Damnation! I finally stop crying, get up off the floor, and start pacing. It dawns on me that since I haven't a clue what to do, I'll try being honest with both men. See if they were sincere about me taking some time. In the meantime, despair is slowly being replaced with indignation at the situation Lew put me in. On the other hand, it took everything I had not to take him up on his satiation idea. I wonder how many times...?

I need a drink, badly! And that honesty thing is hard to pull off. Can't a girl have a little mystery? Oh, hell! It's only been six weeks since I met Charlie. I'm due to start my new job at a Great Falls law firm on Wednesday, and I can hardly focus beyond this second. How can I be expected to have any perspective? And I think the real Dear Abby is probably dead and I couldn't get an answer back by eight tomorrow morning, anyway.

* * *

Promptly at eight the doorbell rings. He's grinning down at me with the typical Lew grin that I love. "Hi, how did you sleep?" he asks.

"Perfectly well," I say, "after 3:00 a.m. or so."

"Me. too. I'm ready to show off my family and our dramatic Montana weather."

He's not touching me, so I guess our boy has learned something, after all. I badly want him to. It's a two-hour drive from Great Falls to Browning. His mom and sister will be waiting for us with breakfast.

"This is the first time I ever brought a girl home," Lew says. "I've warned them that we're just friends, but they've heard me talk endlessly about you for years, so I'm not sure they believe it."

"That'll make all of us then," I say.

Abruptly, Lew pulls over to the side of the road. "Oh, crap. I was going to play hard to get, but I'm terrible at stuff like that." He turns and gently takes my cheeks in his hands and lowers his mouth to mine.

I feel my body tighten. I don't say anything, but I don't pull away.

"I couldn't help that, Mira. I just couldn't. Let's go. Mom's waiting."

We pull up to a modest two-story frame house that could've used a coat of paint fifteen years ago. The front steps tilt precariously to the left, leading up to a covered porch. Before we can get out of the car, a small boy of about nine races up to the driver's side and literally starts jumping up and down. Lew manages to get out of the car before being physically attacked. He picks the boy up and throws him over his shoulder, head down, with the boy shrieking with delight. "This maniac is my nephew, Frankie, Tommy's younger brother. Frankie, this is Miranda."

"Hello..o..o..o," Frankie says, as he's bumped along on the way to the house, still over Lew's shoulder. The front door opens. Two women come out to greet us, both tall with shoulder- length dark brown hair.

"Hello Miranda," says the older woman. "You've been Lew's good friend for so long. Welcome."

"Grandma and Mom have been cleaning the house for three days. They won't even let me sit in the living room," interrupts Frankie.

"Hello," says the younger woman. "Come on in. Breakfast is ready."

"This is my mom, Pauline, and my sister Carol," Lew says.

"I'm so glad to finally meet you. I also know Tommy well. He's been at our house with Lew often. He's charming, like his uncle. Impossible not to love."

"Doesn't he know it," says Carol. "Tommy's trying to live up to his uncle's local reputation. When Lew's not around, I'll fill you in."

"She's heard most of it. Besides, Carol. When did you ever need an excuse to remind everyone how challenging I was?"

It's obvious this is a loving family. When I look at Frankie, skinned knees, scrubbed face and scruffy hair, I imagine Lew as a kid, growing up in this house.

"Frankie has my old room," Lew says, turning to the boy. "What's up? I've been here five minutes and you don't want to know what I brought you?"

"Mom told me if I asked, I couldn't have it," Frankie says. "She's trying to civilize me."

Lew pulls out a rectangular package with an Apple logo on it.

Shrieks as Frankie starts hugging Lew. "An iPad! An iPad! Thanks Uncle Lew. You're the best!"

"Don't even say it, Carol," Lew interrupts. "I can't even imagine how to spend my money. Besides, with Tommy and me gone, you'll need Frankie for tech support. Gotta keep him current. Computer skills are the family ticket to fame and fortune."

Carol gets up and gives Lew a huge hug. "We owe you so much, Lew. Tommy is flying through his courses."

"He owes most of that to Charlie and his family," Lew says.

Observing Lew smiling at his sister, I have some idea of the rocky start both Tommy and Frankie had. And it cost Lew to bring up Charlie like that.

Later, we're driving out to Win and Lizzie's on Heart Butte Road after a long stay with Lew's family. "What wonderful people. No wonder you turned out so well. Carol's fantastic."

"There's ten years age difference," he says. "Carol was seventeen when she got pregnant with Tommy and the kid who got her pregnant never amounted to anything. He came and went for years, hanging around, doing odd jobs, just long enough to get her pregnant with Frankie. Then he took off."

"What happened to him?"

"We found out not long ago he died in a bar fight down in Colorado. I never told you."

"Your mother held it together."

"You know the story of my dad who wasn't there. Somehow, Mom managed to keep us a family, fed and loved through the tough years. She worked two jobs until Carol moved back in with her, working to help out. When I was fourteen or so, I started getting jobs fixing computers."

"How did you learn to do that?"

"Scrambling on my own. We had no money. I kept calling tech support or asking teachers. On Saturdays, I'd hitch a ride to an Internet café in Cut Bank and the old guy who ran it helped me. Everyone helped me, mostly to get me out of their hair. But, throughout it all, I had love. Carol was almost a second mother because Mom was working so hard." He glances at me. "Not exactly Charlie's upbringing."

"No," I say. "Not exactly." I turn around in my seat to face Lew. "I never heard the whole story, Lew. No wonder you're so close to them."

"Mom seems good. She's working for a large animal vet and loves it. But I worry about Carol. She's never had a break. She's only forty. Maybe I can help her. I've never thought to offer before. My life has been changing so fast I can't keep up with it. It's no excuse, Mira, but that's been part of my problem with you."

"No one could be critical of you, Lew. You've done the impossible. You can be excused for being human. You're the most loyal person I've ever known."

"Maybe that's something to build on," he says.

"Maybe," I say, and take hold of his hand.

"You know what else I had," Lew adds. "Do you have any idea how important Win and Willie have been? Win's father was a father to me until he died. They held me together during some very dark times. And they made me want to live up to what they knew I could be. That's very powerful. I couldn't let them down."

"Do Win and Lizzie know what is going on with us?"

"They've wormed some out of me. I've tried my best to be vague, but when you get to know them, you'll realize it's hopeless. You'll see. They don't know you well enough to give you a thorough grilling, but it's coming."

"I remember Win's sister, from before."

"You don't have to worry about her. She's quieter than the rest of us. And I don't know if she'll be around. She's always coming and going, hauling horses."

Pulling off the main highway, we drive through stubble of hayed-off fields. Passing the older house, no one seems at home. Alice lives there with Win's mother, Sarah. There are no mature trees near Win's new house, set closer to the bluff, a quarter mile further down the two-track road. Only two small saplings, newly planted, are staked against the ever-present wind. Win's truck and Lizzie's Subaru are parked outside. I haven't been here since the reunion in early September. Now the house looks battened down for the winter. The wooden porch chairs have been stored somewhere with many cords of dry wood added on the leeside of the house near the fireplace chimney. Next to the massive pile is a large door providing access to the inside.

Win and Lizzie come out on the porch to greet us, Win carrying Paulie, now a pudgy seven-week-old armful.

"He's huge," I say. "Is he eating steak and mashed potatoes?"

"Almost," Win says. "He's a bruiser. Gonna take after his uncle Lew."

"Lucky kid," Lew says. "Hopefully, he'll get my looks, too."

"Sorry," Lizzie says. "He looks just like Win's baby pictures."

Lizzie and I smile at each other. It goes unsaid that Win is just plain gorgeous.

"So...," Win says. "Going out to watch the first storm of the winter blow in?"

"It's my thing," Lew replies.

"When we were kids," Win adds, "Lew always rode out to the rise where he's taking you. He'd sit there for hours, watching the weather fronts move in. The more violent, the better."

"I'll see what Miranda's made of," Lew says.

"You've ridden before?" Lizzie asks. "Lew said you had some experience."

"If riding seven or eight times as a kid counts. Definitely went through the loving-horses stage, collected plastic horses, and built barns and fences for them. I spent years trying to convince Dad that we could keep a horse in our garage."

"You're going to ride my mare, Silk," she offers. "Gentle as they come. Win wouldn't let me ride anything excitable, especially since I was pregnant. She'll take care of you. She's unspookable."

"That so nice of you, Lizzie."

"She needs the exercise. Win rode her around yesterday to remind her how to behave."

"You won't have a problem," he adds.

Lizzie smiles. "Have fun. I put out an extra coat in the barn to be tied on the back of your saddle. It's warm now but Win says the temperature might fall thirty degrees in an hour as the front crosses. We'll have hot food and cocoa when you get back."

"Or something stronger," Win adds.

We walk the eighth of a mile to the family barn to get the horses, then I settle myself on a bale of hay to watch Lew saddle Silk, a medium-sized, ten-year-old mare, gray with a black mane and tail.

"Let me help you up, Mira, and I'll get Cloud."

"You're going to ride Win's horse?"

"He insisted. That horse never fails to make women swoon. Told me that's how he got Lizzie."

I can see he's kidding. Partly. Lew leads Cloud out with just a bridle.

"You're going to ride him bareback?"

"Nothing like a hot horse in cold weather to keep you warm," he grins, vaulting on the tall black quarter horse's back. "We'll walk to loosen up the horses and see how it goes for you. We can walk the whole time if you want. I want you to feel safe."

I sit comfortably on Silk's back, then follow Lew out of the barn into the warm sunshine. It's around sixty degrees with only a light breeze blowing steadily from the west. "You're sure the storm is coming?" I ask.

"I checked the doppler online. It'll take about an hour to get to the high point if we walk all the way. The clouds should be starting to build by then. Exciting, huh?"

I smile at him. He's like a little kid. But he doesn't look like a kid on his horse. He's wearing a heavy flannel shirt, a sheepskin-lined vest, and some beaded moccasins. Cloud is skidding around with excess energy and Lew is simply beautiful, somehow gripping the horse with his knees, making it look effortless.

After a few minutes Lew says, "Mira, this horse is squirreling around on me. Don't want him to get Silk riled up. Give me a minute to settle him down. Hold Silk back."

I nod.

He touches Cloud's flanks and they're off like a shot. I remember Lew on horseback last September, but on Cloud he's magnificent. Lew lets loose with a few war cries as he lets Cloud have his head. They race down the tire tracks in the high grass. A half-mile down the road they do a series of figure eights and circles before Lew does a slow canter back.

"That's better. He's listening now. He was being an adolescent. God, I love riding this horse. He's like a volcano."

"You don't look like you're having any trouble."

He looks at me like I was joking. "Trouble? No."

"Can I try a canter? I'll be okay if it's a slow one."

He nods. "Silk has a nice easy canter. I'll hold Cloud back behind you. Do you remember how to trigger that gait?"

"One foot a bit back with pressure to push her onto a lead?"

"I'm impressed. Go ahead. Try a right lead with your left foot back."

It's effortless. It helps that Silk is the best-trained horse I've ever been on. I canter comfortably and don't feel like I need to hang onto anything.

"No fair, Mira," he says. "Now I'm really in love."

I grin back at him.

By trotting and cantering we reach the overlook in less than half the time, pull the horses up together, and look toward the northeast. We've halted on a flat platform of rock that extends out over the lip of the ridge. We keep the horses well back. The drop off below is many hundreds of feet down. Flattening out far below us is the rolling grassy vista of the vast northern plains which extend unbroken to the eastern horizon. Gentle breezes stir the tall grass, making waves in the landscape and constantly changing the muted colors. It's simply breathtaking.

It's been about a half hour when I notice something unusual on the eastern horizon. "My God!" I exclaim. "Look at that."

Lew maneuvers Cloud closer to my side and grins at me. The sky has a greenish-yellow cast. Just forming, but building faster than I could have thought possible, is a purplish-black wedge of thunderclouds. It slants up from the back, pushing the warmer air forward in front of it. You can sense the power being unleashed. The air where we are is suddenly completely still but the hair on my forearms stands up.

"Look, Lew." I lift my arm to show him.

"Just wait," he says. "Any second now."

As he speaks, the grass begins to stir, fluttering back and forth. The horses sense the tension and begin to shake their heads, pointing their ears back. In another few minutes, a strong wind blows in from the north. The giant dark cloud in the shape of an enormous anvil, continues to build, dominating half of the northern sky. The wind builds steadily. The grass is now blown full over, then whips erratically back and forth. I quickly put on the coat, shoving my hair up inside a wool cap. The temperature is dropping with each gust of wind, now howling with an eerie whistle. Lew and I sit in awe as the cloud blocks the light from the sun, and a dramatic gloom overrides the plains. I'm so moved by emotion I can hardly breathe. I whisper, "It's the most overwhelming thing I've ever seen in my life."

He turns to look at me. "It was for me, until I find you sharing it with me." He nudges Cloud next to Silk, and leaning over, far out from Cloud's back, kisses me lightly. Electricity crackles.

We look at each other in awe. I'm not oblivious to the aura of danger and excitement enhancing Lew in this place, his obvious intention. His relaxed feet dangle at Cloud's side even though the horse is constantly moving and shifting in the charged air.

"We'll lose half the grass in this," Lew says, finally. "The grass is so dry the wind breaks it off like dry spaghetti. We better head back if we don't want to get caught in hail and lightning."

"Lightning?" I ask.

"You'll see. Let's go."

We turn the horses and I push Silk into a faster canter than before. I'm screaming with excitement while Lew laughs at me. Just as we make it to Win's porch, the hail reaches us. "Run for the house," he yells. "I'll take care of the horses."

Running up the steps, I watch Lew race for the barn, holding Silk's reins. Win joins me, standing outside under the deep eave waiting for Lew. In ten minutes, he sprints toward us on a dead run. Just as he reaches the porch, a huge pinkish lightning bolt hits the ground about four hundred feet away.

"Perfect!" He yells, shaking ice pellets from his hair and running his fingers through it. "Never cut it that close before. You should have seen Mira. She rides like a warrior. I waited as long as I could. We just made it. a'ka'a'." (Perfect!)

Win is laughing. "Lew," he says, "you're wattsa' pssi." (crazy)

We've had chicken and dumplings and several strong Irish whiskeys. We skipped the cocoa. I'm feeling warm and very good. Very good. I keep laughing and exclaiming, "Wow! I loved it. Wow! This is nothing like DC. My God!" Lew and Win and Lizzie are all laughing at me. I'm probably smashed.

I've really gotten to know Lizzie and Win. It's been one of those perfect days. I feel like a Westerner.

Lew exclaims, still energized, "Why would anyone want to live in the east? I love my job, but this…"

I'm looking at him like I can't take my eyes off him and smiling. I'm sure Win and Lizzie notice.

Finally, Lew says, "Time to go. Mira. Are you ready?"

"Yes," I say. "I can't begin to thank you both for everything. Lizzie, let me help carry dishes to the kitchen first."

Lizzie hands Paulie to Win as we pile dishes and walk to the kitchen.

"Lizzie," I whisper, "I need help. I mean, I really need someone to talk to.

She's serious for a minute. "Yes. Please call or come up. Win's working most of the next few days and I'll be here alone with Paulie. Just call. Or come if you want. Any time."

I give Win a hug and Paulie a kiss and we're off. I haven't even thought about where we're going now.

I pause. "What now?"

"The choice is yours, Mira. It's early. I can take you back to Great Falls. What I want is to take you to Sam's cabin for the night, but I could go back to Win's and spend the night. What do you want to do?"

It's come down to this. Lew has given the decision to me. Was that smart of him? Fair or unfair? I don't know.

"I want you to take me to the cabin and I want you to stay."

"Are you sure?" he says seriously.

"Yes."

We don't talk. There is nothing more to be said. Lew has his arm around my shoulders as he drives.

The key is hidden in a slot between two logs. Lew kneels to light a fire that's already been laid then moves to my side. The fire fills the small room with flickering light as I look into his eyes. The painful truth is hard to face. "I have loved you," I manage to say, "since that first night so long ago."

"Mira…" He brushes my cheek with the back of his hand, so softly. His gentleness makes my eyes fill with tears. They spill over. I cried before when he kissed me. It's like some horrible release of tension, as if I've been holding my breath for months and months. He holds me in his warm strong arms.

I'm better but when he tries to kiss me once more, I start crying again. This will never do.

We lie in front of the fire. It's that old position of me in his arms from so long ago. He's stroking my hair gently, endlessly, saying softly over and over, "I know you're confused. I understand. I understand."

"Lew. I love you and I love Charlie, too. What am I going to do?"

"I know one thing, Mira. Love can't be wrong. We'll figure it out. But know that I love you. It's a given. No matter what you feel and what you say. I love you."

"Should we make love?" I ask, trembling at the implications of the question.

My heart feels as if it's waiting to beat.

"I don't know if I should try to make love to a sobbing woman." He looks at me closely, "And there's a bigger issue here."

Issues aside, I think about the part of him that I want inside me. I want to give him the pleasure I know I could.

"Do you have any idea how I feel?"

"Yeah," he sighs. "I have some idea."

I lie on my back in the thick carpet and reach my arms up to Lew. He lowers himself over me and his kiss is everything I remembered. And this time I don't cry. But I also hold something back.

We spend the night with our arms around each other. Once, sometime in the night, very late or very early, I wake and see Lew watching me. He murmurs something I can't hear. "What, Lew," I ask into the stillness. "What did you say?"

He pauses, then says, "I was just saying, 'at least I'll have this night. No one can ever take it away from me'."

It's after nine when I open my eyes again. Lew is still asleep. It's very cold in the cabin as I slide out from under the comforter, the fire long dead. Tiptoeing to the front door I open it a crack. It's winter outside. It must be close to freezing and the ground is covered with frost and frozen hailstones. When I turn back, Lew is smiling at me. "Woman," he says, "come back here. You're letting in the cold air."

I walk over and slide back under the covers. He puts his arm under my head. "Now what?" he says.

"I know one thing," I say. "I'm tired of crying."

He rolls over on his side, propping himself on one elbow, and looks into my eyes. "Bless Sam for this cabin," he says. "I couldn't exactly take you home and ask Frankie if we could use his room. And it would have been hard to sneak us back to Win's and borrow his tack room bunkbeds. You can see a car coming from a mile away," he smiles to himself. "Besides all the ribbing I'd get."

I stare at him. It's almost embarrassing to be this intimate with my best friend. I feel my cheeks flushing.

"Listen. We could come back here later, but if I don't have time to get my head on straight, I'm not going to stop this time." He starts to rise from me, but I put my arms around his neck and pull him to me.

"You're not making this easy," he murmurs, and slides his hand gently to my breast and strokes it.

I feel my resolve slipping away. We're alone. I can feel my heart starting to race as I run my hands up his chest, caressing his warm skin. Suddenly I'm rolled to my back. His hands continue gently stroking. "Lew, please. Please..."

Abruptly, he stops. "Mira? Have you chosen me?"

I gasp, realizing I've been holding my breath; also realizing I've waited too long to answer.

Lew swings his legs over the side of the bed. "Oh, hell," he mutters.

While I'm trying to calm myself, he suddenly lurches to his feet and almost runs to the bathroom. I hear the shower running then bury my face in my hands. After what seems an eternity, he comes back out buttoning his shirt. "Alright. This is the plan. I'm calling Vinnie and getting an appointment. I give up. If she doesn't have any ideas, I'm immigrating to Australia. And I left you some hot water."

Vinnie answers the door in a faded pink flowered bathrobe with antique cream-colored lace. "I made breakfast, you two. This sounded like a real emergency. I called Kitty at the post office and told her she had to sort the mail by herself today." She looks at both our faces. "What's up?"

We sit silently, reluctant to begin.

Rising, she assembles two plates of scrambled eggs and toast, setting them down in front of us, then brings orange juice from the fridge, pouring it into two small juice glasses decorated with painted strawberries and green leaves. Sitting back down and after looking back and forth at our tortured faces, she asks with an air of expectancy, "Is someone dying?"

We shake our heads no.

"Anything else I can work with," she says. "So...?"

Lew starts to talk then clears his throat several times as I try to frame some sort of reasonable explanation for our visit, bungling the whole thing.

She keeps looking back and forth, then sighs in frustration. "Oh, for heaven's sake, Lew. Did you finally figure out that you're in love with Miranda? Everyone from the res has been watching your evolution with great interest." She shakes her head. "I thought after the Tashi thing, you'd learn to lay it on the line. If the girl's, how do they say it now...? Just not into you, you'd move on?"

After a long period when it looks like he's not going to speak, she zeros in on me. "Hello, Miranda. We met briefly at Win's. I'm not very good at small talk. How's your love life?"

That does it. My eyes mist up with tears, overflowing down my cheeks. The smile fades from Vinnie's face.

"Oh dear," she says, patting my hand. "Hold on there."

"I love you, honey," she says, turning back to Lew's unhappy face. "I have since you were eight and Willie dragged you into my kitchen. You children are still everything to me, the most important people on the planet. Now will one of you please tell me? What's going on?"

I glance at Lew and Vinnie as tears keep streaming down my cheeks.

"Let me," he begins. "The appalling truth is I waited too long. I was—enjoying myself—in my sophisticated new world, until I saw Charlie Curchin make a serious move on Miranda. It was like I was hit on the head with a club. I did everything wrong. By the time I figured out how to talk to Miranda about it, Charlie stepped in and she's... Well. They're very involved. We don't know what to do."

Vinnie looks over at me as I nod unhappily, sniffling.

"Wow!" she says. "Give me a minute."

We sit there waiting. The minutes lengthen.

"Alright. Lew. I don't know this young lady very well and I would like to. Why don't you go visit Bruce? He's painting at his gallery. Of course, they're closed for the season, but go knock on his window. I'll need some time. See you in an hour."

I smile tearfully and nod at Lew. He stands up, gives Vinnie a kiss on her cheek, and leaves.

She turns back to me. "You don't know me, Miranda. It took courage to come here and talk about this with an old woman you hardly know. Shovel in some eggs. I assume you must care a lot for Lew, or you wouldn't be here."

I take a deep breath and then another. "I don't know where to start. Six weeks ago, I didn't know Charlie, and Lew and I were happily coasting along, waiting, honestly, until Lew was ready. I could have laid it on the line, just like you said, but I didn't either. It seems like everyone knew how much we've cared for each other but us. Now I believe I love him."

"So, tell me about Charlie."

I look down. I can't help it. "I know you know him. I've fallen fast and hard, despite his incredible wealth, which is intimidating. He cares for me so much, Vinnie. It's overwhelmed me. If Lew hadn't suddenly declared himself... And Charlie's been horribly hurt before. I can't bear to cause him pain. I love him, too. He's taken me back to meet his parents. They're wonderful real people. They welcomed me." I look up at her and sigh.

We're both quiet. Vinnie's kitchen clock sounds ten o'clock with loud bongs. It seems like forever until it stops.

"I'm not going to give you a lot of garbage," she says at last, "that maybe you don't love either one, or you'll simply have to choose. This kind of predicament doesn't happen very often. The truth is these are two honorable men. I assume you know Charlie was in love with Lizzie two years ago and handled that disappointment with courage and grace. I've talked to him about it. He loves deeply and quickly.

"Lew, as you know, is one of the most kind and caring people I've encountered. Any woman would feel treasured for life. His friends love him. He loves his friends and family completely. In addition, he's had great emotional trauma in his early life, and has come through it with generosity and compassion. But no one is perfect. Everyone has tragic flaws. Do you know how their vulnerabilities might affect you over the long run?"

"I haven't thought about it." The tears well up again.

"Honey. This is no one's fault. In a very short time, two wonderful men have declared love for you and want you to choose. I believe in love at first sight, and it's a glorious thing. It happened to me in my marriage. Sometimes it turns into something that lasts a lifetime. Mine didn't. To tell you the truth, it's very hard to predict who will make an enduring commitment and how much you will love someone down the line. Life is a bit of a crap shoot. Don't let people tell you otherwise."

"Someone is going to get hurt here."

"Probably all three of you are going to be hurt." She pauses. "Let me share something I've figured out during my lifetime. There are four sorrows in life: physical pain, heartbreak, fear, and boredom. There's no easy way to avoid them indefinitely. It would be nice if life wouldn't throw us curve balls, but the only alternative is to hide in our bedrooms and never risk anything. But then, of course," she smiles, "you'd still risk boredom."

I smile back, feeling better that she understands.

"Personally, I'd rather jump off a bridge than hide," she continues. "I love life. I love its challenges. And, young lady, you've got one. But I have one piece of advice. You don't have to choose. Not now, anyway. Why don't you let them woo you? See who has staying power. One or even both might not be able to stand the strain. Or maybe one will be too proud to wait. That won't make either of them a bad guy. But why not have a little fun with this. Stop crying and enjoy it."

"You really believe that?"

"No. Sounded good, though." She chuckles out loud. "But seriously. Neither young man should expect you to make a lifelong commitment after six weeks, for pity's sake. And besides, I can't imagine anything more fun than having two gorgeous men fighting it out over me. Now be honest."

"I admit it. It does feel incredibly nice. When I'm not sobbing."

"Goodness, I wish I was sixty years younger. I'd give you a

run for your money. Lew missed out on early trial and error with women. He's bound to make mistakes. What about Charlie? He seems to fall head over heels in weeks and expects the girl to go along. Do you have any idea why?"

"He said the family wealth has made him paranoid women are after him for the money and lifestyle. When he trusts, he commits. And he's suffered. I don't know if you know about his brother?"

"I didn't know he had a brother."

"He just shared that with me. He had a twin brother who was killed in a plane crash five years ago. They were everything to each other. He's still not over it. He said that's one reason he searches so hard for the real thing. The loss of his brother left such a hole in his heart. He wants to trust so much. He's been betrayed in the past. Vinnie, what am I ever going to do?"

"He's right. Women can fake it, and very effectively, too. I'd want to be sure that he would never doubt your love. It could cause major problems later on. You don't want to feel like he's waiting for you to deceive him."

"I guess I need to take some time."

"And you need to have the confidence that the love Lew feels now is lasting and not a reaction caused by jealousy. He was fine waiting until you pushed the issue. And what about you, honey? What's your Achilles' heel?" What might get you into trouble?"

"I never thought of it like that."

That's why you need time to think. Don't let these guys push you so hard."

"Vinnie, you should give college classes in women's studies. I took one and you just covered most of life's choices in less than an hour. But here comes the biggie. Are you ready to be really challenged? Tell me how to handle this one. I need help!"

"Okay. Hit me," she says.

"Sex."

"What do you want to do?"

"I want to sleep with both of them. I'm dying and so are they, but we haven't done it yet. And if I do it, I don't want to regret it, and I don't want to hurt them."

"Well, good luck with that one," she manages to say. (I've

even thrown Vinnie.) "Miranda, if you figure that one out, put it on Twitter. One word of caution. Once you do it, it's very hard to step backwards."

She takes a minute to study me closely. "My dear Miranda, I love honesty. Every woman seems to want the answer to that one. It doesn't seem to bother men so much. It's a major complication. Men don't take well to sharing, ever. It's a minefield. And women… They like to believe they've been overcome with emotion, but beware. It's a choice like everything else. You'd do well to think carefully. I can't help you there."

"Shoot," I say. "Just when you were doing so well."

Lew picks that moment to storm in. Vinnie's smiling and I'm grimacing at her.

"This is encouraging," Lew says. "No one's crying."

"God love you, Lew, and good luck," she says. "Miranda, keep me posted."

I give Vinnie the most deserved hug imaginable before leaving.

Settling in the car, he looks at me. "Well?"

"She said to go do it twelve times until we're bored with it."

He starts the car.

"Where are we going?"

"Back to Sam's cabin. Right after I order Vinnie a fruit basket. At this rate, I'm going to get a freebee with loyalty points."

I look at him sideways. "Lew, she didn't really say that."

"Never mind. Seriously, that's where I'm going unless you stop me." He looks straight out the front window, waiting for my words.

I hold my tongue, realizing I'm making one of Vinnie's choices.

The sky is slate gray with flakes of snow blowing sideways across the front of Sam's cabin where it's starting to collect in small drifts on the porch.

"Let me bring in a few armfuls of wood, then it can snow all it wants," he says.

Moments later I come up behind him as he's bent over lighting the kindling and put my hand on his shoulder. I expect him to make an offhand comment, but he turns and rises smoothly to his feet. His mood has changed. Obviously, he's made his decision. Possibly he made it sometime in the past. I'm reminded of Lew experiencing the storm. For a brief second, I feel fear. Not of him, exactly... Then I don't want to control anything.

I'm pulled to him. I close my eyes and feel us together. It's so close. All I have to do is let it happen. It's going to happen... Abruptly, I see Charlie's face. It's vivid and tortured. I almost scream out loud. *No! No*, I think again, or did I scream it out loud? Lew has the same tortured look I just imagined on Charlie's face. I pull away to hold my head in my hands.

The passion cools as our breathing slowly returns to normal. I hear Lew murmur something.

"What, Lew?" I ask sadly.

"It doesn't matter. I do love you, Miranda," he says. "Don't doubt it. I swear it on the souls of my ancestors."

We lie in each other's arms. Half dressed, our clothes in disarray, love making not completed. The fire crackles in the fireplace. I take my hand and run it slowly up and down his forearm. My eyes fill with tears.

"What are you thinking?" I murmur.

"I'm afraid I'm killing you," he admits. "It was never my intention to hurt you in any way. Should I leave? I don't know what to do."

"Don't leave, Lew," I plead. "I'm killing you, too."

Sweet despair. We doze eventually.

Eventually, I ask, "Where did you go? Did you see Bruce?"

"Yes. He's a very complicated man. You know the bare bones of his history with the family?"

I nod, avoiding the fact that it was Charlie who enlightened me.

"At one point, I would have strangled him if I'd had my hands on his throat. Now I hold him in awe. His perseverance to survive as a rational person, to be able to have compassion, is simply incredible."

"He seems at peace, with himself, I mean."

"He's an artist now. He told me he's embraced it, in part because it gives him so much time to make sense of his journey. He paints the beauty he could never see before. He told me capturing something that brings pleasure and appreciation of our world to others is soul satisfying—the true meaning of art." He smiles to himself. "It's almost Blackfeet philosophy."

"You identify with him, don't you?"

"It's strange, isn't it? You know how close Paul and Win are. They deeply understand and appreciate each other. I understand Bruce. We've both struggled against terrible family problems. His father was the most soulless individual I've ever heard of. Bruce was alone dealing with it. His mother was so destroyed she couldn't help him. He barely survived it, physically or mentally. I had all sorts of love, as I told you before. Bruce had nothing, but he has come so far." He smiles down at me. "Yes, we're becoming very close."

"All these years, Lew. We've talked about a thousand things and I'm only beginning to know you."

"We've been kids together, Mira. I hope we can be lovers. I hope like hell."

We're quiet for a while and I feel the pull. I reach out for him, and he responds. I thought I knew this man. Vinnie was right. I hardly know either of them. Would it hurt the universe in any way if I physically love Lew? I'll have to choose. Despite what they both say, I know these men won't wait forever. We'll have to talk soon, but now, I roll back and settle into his warm arms.

"Mira?"

"Yes?"

"What did Vinnie really say?"

"She explained this is a horribly difficult problem. Her one caution was to try to take my time, despite the chance of losing one or both of you."

"Then why...? Why did you agree to come back here, with me? Now, I mean."

"I love you, Lew." There, I said it. "This isn't your fault. If making a mistake ruins my life, or all our lives, I'll be heartbroken at my decision."

I see him swallow. "You're going to see Charlie tomorrow. What will you tell him?

His question brings tears to my eyes as I shake my head. "I love him, too. We haven't slept together, and I'll never discuss this again with you. I can't do that kind of intrigue. I'm in pieces over loving you both. I should probably keep you both at arm's length until something changes." Touching his cheek, I add, ""But will I ever have this opportunity again? How could I deny this chance of being alone with you?" I wipe my tears away resolutely. "I don't regret it. Not yet."

Lew is silent. What can he say?

"Vinnie didn't judge. She listened and was honest. She wouldn't take sides, except to say you are two extraordinary men. She said to take my time to know both of you and myself."

He pulls back a little, looking away. "It's painful imagining you'll be with him. But I'll hold on."

"Is holding on unbearable?" I ask.

"Not when the alternative is to lose you." He hesitates, turning back. "What if Charlie insists you choose now?"

"I'm not sure what I'll share," I mutter, fearing Charlie's past suspicions and mistrust.

"Will you tell him we've been together up here? Alone?"

"I don't know."

He rolls over on his back and stares at the ceiling, not touching me. Do I still have a choice to make? I've tried to be honest with Lew. Maybe I'm a fool. Maybe it's impossible for either man to tolerate this. But I don't want to choose Charlie because Lew defaulted.

Maybe my heart is blacker than I imagined. That thought scares me to death.

Some time has passed. "Mira," he begins, "I'll relive the closeness we've had, the time on the bluff, watching the storm together. I'll wait. And I want to tell you a story."

I nod.

"Many years in the past, we call them the buffalo days, a man could have many wives, especially if he was a powerful chief. Many of the most beautiful women were encouraged to marry such a chief because he had much wealth and power and could protect them. That was no small thing in those days. The women's families arranged these unions, mostly to provide safety for their daughters.

"So many young warriors died in battle there were not enough left to take care of the women of the tribe. Many of these powerful men had many wives and were decades older, well past their prime. As you can imagine, many of these young wives deeply loved other younger warriors. If they had affairs and were caught, the woman could be disfigured, even killed, and the young man banished. It depended on whether the old chief was understanding and compassionate.

"One of our legends concerns a young warrior named Scarface. He fell in love with a young woman who was promised to the Sun God, the most powerful God of the spirit world. Nothing could be done, and the young couple despaired. Finally, after much time had passed, an old woman shared the secret if Scarface would travel to the spirit world, far beyond the setting sun, he might reason with the Sun God and persuade him to allow the couple to marry.

"Through many hardships, Scarface was able to meet the Sun God, and by proving himself brave and virtuous the Sun God, through love, was able to give the woman to the young warrior. It showed that love can overcome huge obstacles and that people can love, unselfishly, in many ways. And it's also a story of a woman loved by two incredible men.

"That is part of my heritage. Love is worth it, and has been throughout the ages, not a cause of anguish. You've touched me in a way that will always make me grateful. I want you to know so you won't despair."

It's too late, I think.

Much later I say, "I'll be busy until late Monday night..." I stop as I see him grimace. He knows I'll be busy.

He sighs raggedly. "I'm spending the weekend repairing Mom's porch. Sam designed it and the lumber's been there under a tarp for months. The whole crew is coming to help, Willie, Win, Dave and Bruce. Sort of a porch raising."

"That's good of them."

"Yeah, well, I've been talking about it for the last ten years. It's a great excuse to deserve beers afterwards. Poor Mom. I want to get it done before she has to put a ramp over it for a wheelchair. You'll know where to find me if Charlie fails to show." He sighs. "Probably not much chance, though."

* * *

Lew dropped me off in Great Falls last night around six. Charlie is in the air now, getting in at seven this evening, several hours from now. The earth has shifted. I've mentally played and replayed various conversations, and nothing seems adequate. I've wondered if I could lie to Charlie. I've even speculated that if I did lie, could... Would Lew let the truth slip. And if I fear that, is it a reason not to lie to Charlie? That seems beyond disgusting. Moaning in trepidation, I'm blurry eyed from lack of sleep.

Silently sitting in my living room in the dimming light, I can't make myself move even to turn on a   lamp. The electric heater clicks on and off several times. I leave for the airport in less than an hour.

After much soul-searching, I've decided one thing, I'll never lie to Charlie. The fact that Lew and I didn't quite consummate the relationship seems beside the point. I've definitely cheated. If he asks me directly...

CHAPTER 20

MIRANDA

I'VE BEEN AT the airport for almost an hour, although I know Hugh almost never deviates from his flight plan. He's to drop Charlie off, then fly on to San Jose to pick up Juli.

I wait.

A small kid drops a plastic cup, and it rolls around on the floor. He starts crying loudly and I jump at the sound.

I wait.

At last, the private jet rolls in, parallel to the outer glass doors, close enough that I can see Hugh waving, waiting for Charlie to disembark before maneuvering the plane back toward the runway. Charlie runs across the tarmac, carrying his worn olive-green canvas duffel bag, hurries inside, drops it at my feet, and grabs me, lifting me off the floor with his strong arms. If I thought my encounter with Lew would have changed my feelings for Charlie, I was wrong. His black cashmere sweater carries his individual scent and I understand once more how appalling this is.

"I've missed you," he says. "Don't move away. Not yet." He kisses me, hard and insistently.

Passionate moments later, he says, "Okay, I think I can make it to the truck without really attacking you. That is, if the Green Beast is still running."

"Come on," I say. "Let's go home."

He picks up the duffel and I lead him out. It's very cold tonight, well below zero, no wind, no moon up yet, only thousands and thousands of stars.

"Want me to drive?" he asks, as we approach my truck.

I nod. I'm having trouble speaking normally.

"Come closer, either way, and keep me warm. It's glacial here."

As always, the humbleness of my apartment contrasts with the affluent world that Charlie left when he got off the plane. I wonder if he notices as often as I do. The dinginess of the entryway, the tiny worn concrete steps and the thin hollow front door embarrass me. I feel shabby. I ache with unease, then attempt to cover that up. He's so beautiful... And so innocent.

He pulls his sweater hurriedly over his head and throws it on a chair with a grin. I find myself being partially undressed as I'm maneuvered onto my bed. I've tried to make a decision. To have sex with Charlie and deny it to Lew seems one kind of immoral. But the fact that I didn't sleep with Lew yesterday seems unbearably important. Several harsh words describing myself spring to my mind, which I try to push down. Should I explain to Charlie some of what's been happening? But that seems so cruel. He's obviously so overjoyed to see me I can't bear to ruin it all. My mind careens around in circles. I should be buried in passion. I want to be.

"Miranda," he murmurs. "I need you. I've thought of nothing else."

I move my hands underneath his shirt and run my fingertips up his chest. I close my eyes and try not to feel Lew's skin. I try to bury my thoughts. I want it to be so good for Charlie, but I find myself freezing. I try to bury my guilt feelings, but it gets worse and worse.

"All right, Miranda," he says, finally. "Tell me. What's wrong?"

"I... I..."

He pulls back from me, looking at my anguished face. Finally, "You might as well come out with it."

It's too late. I can't pretend I don't know what he's talking about. I can't cry. It would be abysmally self-serving. I'm thrown into utter silence. Charlie pulls farther away. "Miranda?"

The pain is evident in his voice. He waits. He sighs. And continues to wait.

Finally, I manage, almost choking on the words, "Lew is here."

"I know," he says quietly.

"How...? How do you know?"

"I called your dad before I flew out. He told me about Lew and the Turkish incident."

My chin starts trembling and I clench my jaw to stop it. When I'm able, I begin, "I thought I'd have some time to explain this.

He arrived three days ago—on an emergency break. He called just before he left DC. And I... I had planned to tell him about us, that I'd fallen in love with you." I pause, breathlessly.

"Had planned...?" His face had turned grim.

"Dad told me that Lew was coming out here. Lew admitted that he knew he could have been tortured and killed and was coming out here to get his head on straight. And then I couldn't tell Lew about us on the phone. I just couldn't. When he appeared at my door I fell apart. And... And we've spent some time alone together. You might as well know."

I see him swallow. "Exactly what are you trying to tell me?"

"I..."

"You're scaring me."

I put my hands on his arms. "I... We..."

His voice becomes steel. "Are you trying to tell me you screwed him?"

I look at him. I can't say the words. I just look at him.

"Tell me the truth," he says with unnatural calm.

"Not quite," I whisper.

He rips his arms from me, rolls over, and sits on the side of the bed, facing the wall, finally turning his tormented face toward me. "How could you do that...? After Philadelphia?"

I feel the blood drain from my head.

"I told you I loved you. You said it back. Is this what love is to you? Do you *love* around? Is that it? God damn it all to hell, Miranda." He's visibly trembling.

I open my mouth to say something, but nothing comes out.

"You've told me you love me, but now..." His voice shakes, "And *not quite*. What the hell does that mean? It appears you've gone another way. Doesn't it?"

Now I do start to cry. "Please Charlie. He's made it impossible for me not to love him, too. I had to tell you the truth. I'll probably lose you over this. It's killing me."

He's rigid, staring bitterly at me.

"I do love you. I don't understand any of this, but that's the truth. Let me show you." I reach for him but watch as his body moves imperceptibly away from me. "Have I ruined it all?"

Nothing. Utter silence.

"Please." My voice is almost a whisper. "Hold me."

His voice is icy, remote. "What is it that you want from me? Tell me. Sex? Money? Trips to Europe? Diamond necklaces?"

I wince. "I know you've been hurt before. I'll try..."

His broken stare destroys me. I draw back in fear at his unrecognizable face.

I try one more time. "Please. If you can, give me a chance."

"Just terrific," he mutters brokenly. "Sure, let's fucking do it. Let's have sex. I can do that. I've been there before with women who wanted me, for a variety of reasons." He moves even farther away from me on the bed, groans audibly, then puts his head in his hands. His shoulders appear to shake.

We sit motionless. A thought wells up—I don't want him to cry.

After many minutes he gets up, buttons his shirt, and throws on his down jacket. "I'm going for a run," he says, his voice now under some control. "I'll be back when I can." He puts on his running shoes, grabs a hat from his bag, and dashes out the door.

I focus on the unpacked green bag left by the door, roll over on my stomach, and sob.

CHAPTER 21

CHARLIE

I STEP OUT into the cold Montana night. The wind has come up. It isn't as unrelenting as on the high plains of the reservation, but it's bad enough. I wish I'd dug out my gloves, but know I'll warm up if I run. I turn left toward the river and let go. I can't control much, it seems, but I can run, fast. It's pitch-dark now and soon I reach a trail lit by a just-rising moon. The stars are never this bright on the East Coast.

I've settled into a gentle rhythm and turn my thoughts inward. It's not as if I didn't know this could happen. Miranda's been honest about her feelings for Lew since we started. I took it into consideration from the first night. But damn it! I never thought Lew would come on this strong.

Rational thought aside, I'm furious. I'd like to punch him into the dirt, splatter blood. I smile grimly at the thought, in part because I'm aware he'd probably kill me. I've had martial arts training, could probably do some damage in any kind of controlled situation, but I have a feeling it wouldn't be that kind of a fight.

If I'd pressed for a real commitment from Miranda, would it have mattered? On a gut level, I'm aware I've pushed her very far, very fast, wanting to lock her up. I decided within days of our first date I wanted her, turned on all my charm, did what I swore I'd never do—used the wealth as an incentive, showed her the lifestyle.

Maybe it was guilt, but it seemed the right thing to do to give her some time. It didn't seem such a big risk to wait. But I wonder if I'd pushed it, slept with her in Philadelphia, if she would have, and I can't stand to think about it, "almost" screwed Lew. What exactly does that mean? Did she get naked and roll around with passionate abandon and not do it? And what kind of an artificial line is that? What's okay and what's completely over the line? I'm furious with her. My deepest insecure self says, *See, it was just the money all along. Your girl played you.*

I moan out loud as I run. I love this girl, or who I thought she was? Is she someone I put on a pedestal? Is she really in love with me? I put so much out there, took her home to meet my family, for God's sake, and now I want to run fast and far away, to get away from this pain. I can't go back and pretend I'm cool with it. She'd see through me, anyway. I'm a terrible faker.

I reach the river after several miles. Its water flows through a moonbeam, then leaving beauty behind, it reverts into blackness. I struggle on for a while. Finally, I stop and lean against a fencepost alongside the path. Putting my head down on my arm, I try to hold back the tears, swallowing over and over. *Damn it,* I think. *Damn it.*

Eventually, I head back on the path by the river, walking now, trying to think logically, trying to get some perspective. Forget what Miranda wants, what do I want? I want her. Do I want her enough to try to hang in there? Even with all this agony, I have enough empathy that I believe she's tortured, too. If not, then I've made a mistake of Herculean proportions.

But let's assume she does love me as she says. Do I have the courage to fight down my fury at Lew, and the betrayal I feel, and try to win her? Or should I do what I've always done, say fuck her, and bail out? The bleakness of life without Miranda is a wasteland. She didn't say she loves Lew more. I can imagine her constantly comparing my body, my mind, and my skills in the bedroom. And that tiny voice creeps in again, *You tried to manage her and that never works. Not for long, anyway.*

Well, one decision. I need some control. Let alone self-respect. I'm out of this, as long as there's another relationship looming. But am I cutting my own throat? At the very least Lew and I will both be back east. If he was going to live out here, I'd have to throw in the towel or kill him. I wonder if Lew has figured that out yet? If it was me, I'd get my boss to let me telecommute and... Maybe I should just point that out to Lew. Right.

But can I stay and fight for a girl who has been right up to the line with another guy? Within hours? Should I force her to choose now? It would end the agony. What choices do I have? One, stay in the contest or not? Two, sleep with her or not? Three, try to keep loving her?

I need a trip up to see Vinnie. Ah. Seriously. The bottom line is my girl wants to sleep with another guy. I should leave. In some ways that's the hardest decision of all. I want to feel her arms, see the love in her eyes. It's cold outside in more ways than I can count. But my girl was with another guy. The fact that they may or may not have gone a few extra inches seems irrelevant. I can't stay unless she chooses me. The struggle ends. Coldness descends around my shoulders like the devil's cape. I lean against the fence and dial Hugh's number.

"Hey, big guy," Hugh says. "How's it going in the wilderness?"

"Bleak. Can you stop and pick me up on the way back?"

"What happened?" I hear real concern in his voice.

"It didn't work out. With Miranda."

"I can't believe it. Did you fight?"

Hugh really likes Miranda. "No, Hugh. She's been with another guy."

"Who? Are you sure?"

"Just come and get me. Unless something changes... I'll fill you in."

"If that's true, then screw her. But, for God's sake, think it through."

"I have thought it through. For the last three hours. Just pick me up, damn it."

"Okay. Okay, Charlie. I'll be there with Juli around noon. I'll bring the plane in and wait."

It's apparent that Hugh's upset. He didn't even try any knock-knock jokes.

I walk back toward her house. It's some distance and by the time I get there it's almost eleven. I try the door. It's not locked. I quietly slip in. She's probably been waiting, but I find her sound asleep, kneeling on the floor by the couch, her head resting on her arm on a seat cushion. I stand over her and my heart breaks all over again. I can still see dried tears on her cheeks, her hair in tortured disarray. I ache to touch her. I love this girl. I know I do. With the lightest pressure I touch her cheek. She's curled up with my black sweater knotted in her hands up by her head, using part of it as a pillow. I suppose it smells like me. I'm heartbroken. I believe she's heartbroken by this, too.

I go sit in a chair across the room from her. Physically leaving seems impossible. It's almost an hour before she opens her eyes and sees me watching her. She looks at me for a long time, studying my face, then says, "Tell me."

"You have to choose me, not touch Lew again, or see him alone, or I'm gone."

"I want you," she says. "I ache to have you touch me."

"Then make that choice," I say deliberately. "And mean it."

Anguished, she responds, "I can't do that, Charlie. Not yet."

With as much composure as I can manage, I say, "I need to borrow your truck. I'll have it back by noon tomorrow. Hugh's picking me up at the airport."

"You're leaving?" she whispers.

I stand up, not moving for several long moments, almost weaving back and forth in indecision. I stare miserably at her, holding out my hand for my black sweater.

She slowly hands it to me.

I slowly put it on while staring at her distressed face, hoping she'll stop me. No. After picking up her truck keys from the small table by the front door, I walk into the darkness without looking back.

It's cold and clear out but the wind has continued to build, and I can see entire trees whipping back and forth in the moonlight. I pull the collar of my coat up high around my neck and hurry toward her truck. Pumping the gas pedal twice, I feel the engine catch on the second crank. In minutes, I'm in the grasslands headed north. I wasn't sure where I was going, anywhere away. But now I know I'm headed to Vinnie's. I'll beat on her door if I have to. It's a long two-hours' drive, but the last thing I am, is tired.

My mind is a muddle. This is so far from what I thought I was going to be doing when I left home— driving alone on the high plains in the middle of the night. I wonder who I'd call if the truck died? Some twenty-four-hour gas station, I suppose. I check the gas, over three quarters of a tank. Okay. I should make it. I breathe in and out deeply, trying to calm myself, then sigh from the bottoms of my feet.

It's beautiful in the moonlight. I can see for miles across the frozen prairie. I want to share that beauty. Is that too much to ask? I'm a billionaire, and I believe I'm a good person. Should finding love be this hard? Miranda, I really thought you might be the one. I don't put any music on. I want to feel one with the land. It gives me a measure of peace, lowers my significance a notch.

It's close to three when I pull up at Vinnie's small house. Above all the chaos, one thought stands out. I used to believe that the opposite of love was hate, but I was wrong. I know now that it's loneliness. I sit dejectedly in the dark for some time and consider curling up in the truck, but I need someone to comfort me so much. I finally get out and knock hard on her door. In several minutes, the tiny porch light goes on and Vinnie peeks out.

"Charlie," she says. "Come on in, sweetheart."

"I need you."

"Do you want to talk tonight?" she says.

"Let's try tomorrow. Right now, I want to sleep in a place where someone loves me."

"You've come to the right spot. I do love you. We'll work this out."

Somehow, I believe her as I follow her down the narrow hall and fall into an exhausted lump on her guestroom bed. I sense her covering me with a blanket and kissing my cheek.

* * *

I smell cinnamon rolls and coffee and open my eyes. It takes several seconds to remember where I am. I find the bathroom then stumble out to the kitchen.

"Morning," Vinnie says. "I don't think I've ever had a billionaire spend the night before."

"If you charged what you're worth, you could have a bigger house," I answer.

"Yes, but then I'd have to clean it. I've spent the last five years clearing out cupboards and closets. I'm making progress. Don't want to go the other direction. I've been deciding about a new guestroom mattress, though. The old one is at least fifty years old. How did you sleep?"

"Dead to the world. I don't remember lying down. I remember knocking on your door, vaguely. I'm so sorry to have disturbed you."

"I'm glad you came. Never worry about that."

Vinnie serves up two large rolls and coffee. "So. Charlie. I imagine this is not purely a social call."

Vinnie, do you know what's going on with Miranda and Lew and me?"

"Yes, honey, I do.

"I know you'll keep this between us. Vinnie. I'm lost. I don't know what to do."

"Tell me where we are."

"I flew in to see Miranda. It's been almost three weeks since I'd seen her. I had to work. I had to. When she was with my family, I believed she loved me. I love her. Now she says she loves us both. Maybe it's true, but I can't stay. She... She's been with Lew." I look down dismally.

Vinnie moves to sit next to me on another kitchen chair then leans forward to hold me in her arms. My shoulders start to shake but with some effort I'm able to quiet myself. We're silent together for many minutes.

"Charlie, listen to me," she says finally. "I wish this had not happened to three wonderful people. Some would be quick to find blame, but not me. I don't believe there was intent to cheat or hurt anyone. I honestly don't. Miranda is torn up about this. Lew brought her here and then left. She and I talked for over an hour. This isn't trivial or common. It's happened so quickly no one has had time to do anything other than react."

"How can I do anything other than give up and leave?" I say wretchedly. "I can't stay around and be the other man. I won't." I take a breath. "I can't have sex with her to get even or push ahead in some sordid competition. That would be obscene. And I can't pretend I can love her and not have her while Lew..."

"My darling Charlie, I agree. Miranda is only human. You are only human. It would look weak for you to stay. We're all so intellectual these days, but we're still cavemen at heart. You need to show strength to Miranda, and even if it hurts her, and it will hurt her, you need to go."

"Is there nothing I can do?"

"I'm thinking, Charlie. You are one of the best men I know. You should give love and be loved. I believe Miranda is a lovely, sincere, young woman."

"I wish you would tell me she's not worth it. Maybe it would help. Would you rather Lew have her than me? You love Lew like a son."

"I do, Charlie. He's one of my boys. I desperately want him to be happy. He's overcome so much. He's had so many challenges in his life and has succeeded through great force of will. But that's not it. Besides, I understand you've had great sorrow despite your wealth. I'm deeply sorry, but it's helped make you the man you are today, a man to be proud of. You should consider that a gift from your beloved brother."

At that I finally break down. Looking away, tears well up.

Again, she holds me. When I turn back there are tears in her eyes, too.

"Vinnie? What should I do?" I hesitate. "I want to escape this pain. I want... I need to run away."

She's silent. At last, she sighs. "You have figured it out right. You need to leave and let this play out. It will destroy Miranda. It may ruin or solidify the relationship between Miranda and Lew. There's no way to know how this will end. I wish I had better advice."

"I don't want to destroy Miranda," I say miserably.

"You love her."

"And I hate Lew. I'm not happy with Miranda either. I'm trying not to hate."

Vinnie looks almost as defeated as I feel. I know she's trying to find some encouragement for me. Finally, she takes a deep breath. "This is the way I see it. You have limited options. Miranda knows you—but possibly not completely. You need to talk to her. Try to break down those walls of yours that have kept you alone. Kept you running away. Be courageous. Tell her how you feel. Let her completely know you. Be honest. All three of you will need to make heartbreaking decisions, but you must let her know you." She stops, waiting.

"Yes. I see. It's the only thing..." I groan.

"Charlie, listen to me. This has happened to many people— loving someone and not being able to express it or make it grow. It's called heartbreak and it's terrible. It will get better. You are beautiful in so many ways, Charlie. An admirable woman will treasure you, and it may yet be Miranda. Don't descend into hatred. Go back East and find honor in who you are and bide your time."

"I was hoping for a way to win," I say sadly.

She smiles silently. There really is nothing else to say.

I get up to leave, kissing her on the cheek. "Thank you, Vinnie. I'm one more of us that loves you." I walk to the front door but just as I reach for the knob, the door is thrown open. Lew storms in and we collide hard.

"Charlie?" he gasps. "Bruce saw Miranda's truck and called..."

He sees my face and takes a step backwards. He realizes immediately that I know. His eyes scan the room for Miranda. Before I can think, I pull my arm back and punch him square on the jaw, knocking him back through the door, sprawling on Vinnie's sidewalk. It was a solid blow. For a second or two his face shows astonishment. Fury replaces it. He's on his feet in an instant, rising effortlessly, and standing his ground.

He restrains himself somewhat, growling, "What the fucking hell?"

"What the hell, yourself, Lew," I scream. "You bastard." I throw myself at him and he dodges me easily. I'm completely out of control, rushing him again, but this time I manage to catch his jacket, throwing him off balance, and we end up rolling on the ground, punching in close quarters.

He wrestles away, leaps to his feet, then backs away, waiting for me to get on my feet. This is a Lew I've never seen. He's now a callous fighter, smooth and restrained. I'm calming down from rage and starting to act strategically, trying to make him come at me. We circle each other as I hear Vinnie screaming, "Boys, Stop!"

"I can't do that, Vinnie." I yell. We continue circling. Lew charges me but I manage to duck out of the way, tripping him as he flies by. He rolls on the dried grass and is instantly on his feet again. I dodge and get inside, connecting with a heavy blow to his stomach that doubles him over. I try to follow it up with a sharp uppercut, but he barrels into me with his right shoulder as we both crash to the ground. Suddenly he's on top and hammering me with both fists. I can taste blood. He's doing real damage now. My nose feels disjointed with blood flowing. He pulls back to hit me again but stops and slowly lowers his fist.

"Enough?" He growls.

"Fuck you," I say. He lets me up and we start circling again. This time I feint to his right and rush in from the left, catching his left arm, which I pull behind his back. Sliding my other arm around his neck, I squeeze hard, knowing I'm hurting him. He starts gasping for air and can't move. Abruptly, he falls to his knees as I'm thrown over his head, still hanging on.

BOOM! I hear an explosion of a shotgun blast close in. I shudder and feel Lew convulse. The concussion loosens my hold enough that Lew can squirm loose.

"That is enough," Vinnie yells. "Enough!"

We back away a few inches, glaring at each other. Vinnie calmly steps between us, lowering the gun. With her frail arms she gently starts pushing us apart. We don't move for a few seconds, then follow her wishes.

"Charlie, hit the road. Lew, get in the kitchen and have a cinnamon roll."

* * *

I need to hurry to get to the airport by noon but take a moment to pull over, studying myself in the rearview mirror. My nose has finally stopped bleeding. The left side of my face is swollen, my nose looks like a small bratwurst, and my teeth hurt. I'm going to have at least one black eye. Wiping most of the drying blood off my face with a rag I found under the seat, I'm hoping Lew looks as bad as I do. That first blow to his chin felt soul satisfying. I'm trying to remember when I fought someone in earnest, sixth grade, maybe. God! Vinnie was magnificent with her shotgun.

I feel better. Not great, but better. Not so helpless. Getting out of here is the right thing to do. I'm not feeling like such a loser anymore. I have a lot to offer someone, and if Miranda can't see it... A moan escapes as I feel the rush of agony all over again. I've learned two miserable things in all this. It's not over 'till it's over. And you can't lock a woman down until she's ready.

It's sunny now but haze is developing behind the mountains to the west. It will be past eleven when I get back to Great Falls. I need to drop the truck off and get to the airport somehow. Searching on my cell, I find a local taxi and arrange to have it waiting at her apartment.

I've thought it through—what to say, how to act. The taxi pulls up, just as I'm parking her truck. Grabbing the keys, I walk over to the taxi driver and hand him a twenty, trying to ignore him staring at my face. "I shouldn't be long," I say, "but wait."

He nods, still gaping at me.

This may be the last time I see Miranda. I'm gravitating between love, despair, and everything in between. I knock on her door. In a few seconds she opens it, sees my swollen and bloody face, and gasps. She appears worse off than I feel—red rimmed eyes, ghostly pale, and trembling. I want to take her in my arms and make everything better, but I can't. Not yet.

Trying not to let my anguish show, I ask, "Has anything changed? Will you choose?"

Her eyes say it all. No decision.

I swallow. Then again. "Miranda... I've thought it over. You need to know some things. I've never shared, not completely, how much I fear losing someone I love. You know about Todd. But somehow this is worse."

"Charlie..." Her voice breaks.

"Listen to me," I begin. "I love you. No matter how this ends, know that. I've pressured you hard and fast. I've always known that, and I did it anyway. I tried to tie you down—even before you could really know me. I've tried to keep the illusion going—that I'm perfect, stable, and confident. But inside..."

At that she slides into my arms, pressing against my chest, against my black sweater with blood beginning to dry on the front. She feels so good, so remembered, that I gasp, then hold my breath. I can't completely stop my eyes from filling. Warm, close. I listen to her breathing. Her sighs. I never want to move away. I could stand like this forever.

Dear God in heaven, I think. How to go on? Then I remember Vinnie's words.

Holding her away far enough that I can look in her eyes, I try to continue. "I can't stay here now but know this. I love you. I've tried to let you know me, but I've not let you see my vulnerability. The truth is that I'm destroyed. I'm heartbroken. I have a history of running away from perceived deception—disloyalty. But no more. I'll let this play out. I'll wait for you as long as... As I humanly can."

Reaching up, she winds her hands in my hair. "Don't leave," she pleads, then drops her hands and grabs the front of my bloody sweater, making white-knuckled fists.

But with that, somehow, I manage to break away. "Think it all through," I manage. "I'll be waiting. But you need to decide. I wish..." I turn my head away so she can't see my anguish. Taking a few shallow breaths, I mutter, "I love you so much. Nothing will change that."

As a last gesture, I remove my sweater and hand it to her. "To remember..."

Her hand automatically reaches for it.

As I leave, holding my bag in my left hand, I slam the door so hard it shakes the building. I couldn't help it.

And I walk away from her.

* * *

The taxi ride has been a blur. I pay the cabdriver vastly too much money, grabbing my bag. Fortunately, it's a small airport and I locate the Gulfstream just taxing into the area for private plane access. Pushing through the glass doors, I haul my duffle over my shoulder, and run in that direction.

Hugh maneuvers the plane to a full stop, twenty feet from where I now stand, allowing the engines to whine down. In a minute, the door opens, and Juli runs down the steps, followed immediately by Hugh, who takes one look at my face. "Shit," he says shortly, almost speechless for once.

It took a few minutes for Hugh to file the altered flight plan, currently waiting for confirmation to taxi back out to the runway. Juli and I are sitting together in the back of the plane, me repositioning two ice packs on my face. I wince as I adjust them and spit out some blood as Hugh comes back to join us.

"How's the other guy look?" asks Hugh.

"I got him a beauty on the jaw the first lick, but then I got the worst of it. It was worth it, though."

"Who?" asks Hugh.

"Fucking Lew," I say. "Of course."

"You liked this guy," Juli says. "He's Tommy's uncle. Right?"

I spit out even more blood. "I wonder which side Tommy'll come down on? Lew's been a second father."

"You've been his brother."

"I know."

"What a mess," Juli sighs. "I could hardly wait to meet Miranda. Now I hate her."

"Don't hate her, Juli. She's a special person. Not what you're imagining."

"I won't make any smart comments, Charlie. It's obvious how much this has thrown you. I can't bear to have my brother hurt, that's all."

My cell rings and it's Tommy, so I take it.

"What the hell is going on out there?" he asks. "I just talked to Win who said Lew's jaw is swollen up like a baseball and you did it. What happened?"

"Use your imagination, Tommy. What could have us killing each other?"

"Shit? Are you okay?"

"No. I'm fucking not okay."

"But...?"

"Look. He got me good a couple of times. I think my nose is broken."

"I'm calling Lew next. I'll see you when you get back here. Jesus H. Christ!"

"Later, Tommy."

The radio confirms we're cleared for the approach to the runway. Hugh turns to me. "Can I leave the intercom on? I want to hear the whole story. But I won't if you don't want me to."

"Fine. But no jokes, okay? I'm really not in the mood."

He pats my shoulder seriously and moves to the cockpit as I lean my head against the back of the seat, sigh, and close my eyes.

"Take your time, but catch me up," she says.

* * *

I've gone through the whole story in some detail, starting with meeting Miranda at Win's six weeks ago.

Juli's sitting quietly, shocked. "I knew some of that, but there've been two assassination attempts on his life, plus a kidnapping thwarted in Turkey a few days ago? Plus, Miranda and Lew have been best friends for years?"

"So what?"

"So... He's making a major move on her, and you're surprised she's confused?"

"She would have slept with me two weeks ago. I friggin' put her off, believing I was being a hero to wait and not push her. And now this."

"Did you expect this Lew-person to wait patiently while you tried to lock her up?"

"Jesus. I thought you'd be on my side."

"I am on your side. Any woman would be insane to not grab you. But I have to say... She surprises me. You've been killing yourself trying to find a woman who doesn't want you for your money and this one risks losing you, and all your assets, for an egotistical asshole from no-mans-land?"

"You haven't met this guy. He's brilliant, good looking, and has a wildness I don't have. Women are swooning from Boston to DC over him. Plus, he's a damn nice guy."

"Impressive, but holy crap, Charlie. You're big, beautiful, and reasonably smart."

I glumly roll my eyes at her.

"And you fly around in private jets to top it off," she adds, giving me an impudent glance because she knows I hate that sort of thing. "You'd think that would count for something."

"Damn it. She's not only confused. She's been intimate with him. If not literally then it's only by definition."

She sighs. "Yes, there's no getting around it—that's huge. Sorry, but I do want to kill her. How was she dealing with you walking out?"

"When I told her I was leaving, I thought she was going to die. She was shaking. She said she loves me." I put my head in my hands. "Damn it all to hell."

We're quiet for a while.

"How did you find out about Lew?"

"We, I... was making out with her and she was so distressed, I asked her right out. She told me."

"She didn't try to hide it?"

"No, she said she couldn't lie to me, even if it ruined my love for her. She said hurting me was breaking her heart. She said she loves us both."

"And she wanted to have sex with you, when she didn't with Lew, and you wouldn't do it?"

"I didn't want to do it for a check mate. Of course not."

"Maybe she's made her choice. Maybe she doesn't love you, enough anyway, so she was willing to risk the truth?" She shakes her head. "Truth is what we've been endlessly searching for, isn't it?"

"God, you're brutal, Jules. You could be right. I'm so muddled I don't know."

"What are you going to do?"

"Bury myself in work."

"Not in other women, so to speak?"

"Not unless they're Miranda clones," I say morosely.

She takes my hand. "You do love her, don't you?"

The intercom crackles. "Even I love her. We've got to do something. I'm so upset I can't even think of a joke that applies."

"Well, I'm definitely going to find a way to meet her and this Lew asshole. On the other hand, this might keep Hugh quiet. That's got to be worth something."

The phone rings over wifi. It's Tommy again.

"What?" I mumble angrily, putting it on speaker while adjusting the ice packs.

"Look," he says. "This is hardly Miranda's fault. Lew pulled the Win thing. He took her out riding Cloud. Did the wild warrior demo. You know… Bareback in the wind, hair blowing, galloping horses, weather from hell coming in. Women swoon. And they're old friends, Charlie. All I'm saying is, don't trash this. Give her some time. We all love Miranda. Just don't burn your bridges."

"I know how close you are to Lew."

"You're my brother, too. Nothing is closer than that. One more thing. Lew's been calling her, and she won't pick up. She's probably a mess." He hangs up.

"Charlie?" asks Juli. "Who are these people?"

"Just wait." I sigh resignedly.

ASH

I've been standing in the bedroom doorway for some time, watching her. I've found my hostage to be complicated, and deeply concerned about her friend. When she finally settled down and slept, I thought I could finally relax, but then she started screaming, working herself into such a frenzy I was convinced she could hurt herself. I had to go in and physically restrain her, trying to calm her down. She finally revealed she'd had a dream of us killing Black River... Graphically. That probability made lying to her more distressing. The more I tried to deny it, the more I didn't convince even myself. She started sobbing all over again.

She's finally asleep, which is a relief. I finally had to give her something. She's becoming a tormented flesh and blood person, and it's starting to get to me. That's bad in inestimable ways. I've been too long in the pseudo-normal world of workdays, office politics, and water cooler discussions. It's exhausting staying detached, focused. Loyal. My sharp edge is dulled. My objective is blurring. So far, I've managed to keep it in focus.

CHAPTER 22

LEW

DAMN IT! Why doesn't Miranda pick up? I've been calling her for twenty-four hours. At least she could tell me how she is. She told him, or he found out, about us. It's obvious how Charlie took it. My jaw looks like it could be broken. I don't think so, but I'm drinking meals through a straw. I don't believe he took it out on her, but I need to know. I'm fighting driving down there every minute. I've vowed to let her alone, though. After showing her how I feel, I need to let this play out.

I'll keep to the plan. Everyone is assembling for the great porch project, and I'm going to have to field questions, so I'll wait till everyone gets here and do a press conference.

This is agonizing, for a lot of reasons. I pushed the issue to the brink, literally, and Miranda doesn't seem like a girl who could ignore it—not mention it to Charlie, and have… I'm sure she told him. It wasn't as if we had an audience at Sam's cabin. No one else knew. I hadn't thought Charlie had that level of violence in him. I'm certain I could have trashed him, eventually, but he was surprising. Nothing like a little jealous rage to bring that out. I don't know how he feels about Miranda. I think he loves her, but people always surprise you. Suppose he hurt her?

They're all arriving now, Willie, Win, Bruce and Dave, our police officer-friend. He has the day off so he's pitching in. Maybe he can tell me if I'm agonizing unnecessarily. Win knows, but he told me it was my story to tell.

Mom been making coffee and sandwiches, hasn't seen my face yet. Crap. I might as well get this out of the way.

I lean in the front door. "Mom. Carol. Can you come out here? As they step out on the porch, I hear Mom gasp. "Ahem," I begin. "You may have noticed I've had a face alteration. Um… The bottom line is I spent some quality time with Miranda and… And Charlie didn't like it."

"Didn't like it?" asks Bruce. "And what is quality time?"

I look at everyone and wince.

"Jesus," says Willie.

"Yeah," I say. "We're sort of battling it out." I rub my jaw. "Literally."

"How did Charlie find out?" asks Win.

"I'm not sure. But there were only two people who knew."

Everyone's gotten quiet.

"I know," I say. "This is serious business and I'm a wreck. Miranda and I went over to Vinnie's for an opinion and even she didn't know what to suggest. I've been a numbskull for a long time, and probably shouldn't have tried to play catch-up." I sigh. "But I did. Miranda's in the middle."

"I'm sorry, man," Willie says. "And I'm sorry for Miranda and Charlie. When did this happen?"

"Yesterday morning. I've tried to text Miranda this afternoon, over and over, and she's not answering. Dave, I'm worried."

"About Miranda?" asks Dave. "This is Charlie we're talking about here."

"At Vinnie's. It was a violent fight. It took her shotgun to end it," I say.

"The hell you say," says Willie.

"Yeah. Neither of us would give it up. She came out with her shotgun and blasted it off near us to get our attention. Then she ordered Charlie to leave."

"Jesus," Willie says again.

I look glumly at the ground.

"You really are worried, aren't you?" asks Dave.

I nod.

"Let's do this job and keep texting," Dave says. "Win, you give her a call. She might pick up for you. If not, Les is going to be in Great Falls tonight. I'll have him check on her."

Getting out my pry-bar, I take out my fear and frustration on the porch steps.

Win breaks in. Lizzie just texted. She's been trying to contact Miranda all day. Nothing. That's unusual. Usually, she texts right back."

"Damn it," I mutter. "Damn it."

It's after five when I stand back to admire our work. I've hired Frankie and two of his pals to drag old wood fragments to a burn pile and stack them next to it. It's November so it's getting colder, and the light is dimming. The porch is done, and we're just finishing the stairs, keeping the fire going in the front yard. It's dropped below freezing and I hold my hands over the fire to warm them.

I've called Miranda's number three more times without an answer. She didn't pick up for Win, either. When Tommy talked to Charlie yesterday, he was still furious. He obviously didn't stick around to compete. I feel bad for a lot of reasons and Miranda must be miserable. I'm the cause of that. I hope I get a chance to try to make it up to her, but I'm sick about what I'm putting her through. Classic Lew. Go bulling ahead, then think later. Crap!

As I'm mulling this over, Frankie asks, "Are we done, Uncle Lew?"

"Yep," I say. "You boys have earned your ten bucks." I pull out my wallet and hand each kid ten dollars and am rewarded with war whoops.

"When can we work on my iPad?" Frankie asks.

"We'll be done here in a half hour or so. Go ride your bikes and we'll finish this. I'll help you before we leave for dinner."

Three happy little guys head out. I pause to smile, watching Frankie standing up on the pedals, pumping hard, like an evil spirit is following him. He's a smart kid and I'm proud of him. I pull out my phone. Once again it rings to the voicemail point. Wincing, I head into the house for more Tylenol.

Dave notices. "Les said he'd check around six or six-thirty."

"If I just know she's okay."

We're planning on dinner and a few beers as a reward but, to tell the truth, all I want to do is sit and worry. I really want to drive down there. This is terrible. I don't even know if she wants to see me. Where the hell is she?"

Thirty minutes later Frankie and his pals round the corner, pedaling hard. We're packing up and putting tools away when I hear Frankie screaming from three houses away.

"Uncle Lew! Uncle Lew! There's a man with a big rifle."

Everyone stops. "Where, Frankie? Where did you see the man with the gun?" I ask.

"On the water tower. He didn't see us. He was climbing up the ladder and he sat down on the platform. You can see him. Honest."

I can see the distant tower from here. Mom's house is in direct line of sight, but it's too far to see an individual. Outsiders don't realize everyone on the res keeps an eye out for strangers or locals doing unusual things. We watch each other's backs. It gets old that everyone knows everybody's business, but it can be valuable, too. We have our share of nutcases. Last week's big news—a rancher's son up near the border got drunk and killed all his dad's sheep and chickens. Kept the local gossip line busy for days. He's in jail.

"Lew, grab Frankie," Dave says. "You other boys ride home fast. Go! Everyone else walk inside the house, but don't make it look obvious. Walk slow. Act like you're talking. Tight groups."

He pulls out his cell. "Tom, Dave here." I know he's talking to Tom Mountain Chief, the Browning police captain. "We've got a potential shooter spotted on the water-tower platform. Yeah. Yeah, got it. All units. Behind the firehouse. Silent approach. No lights or sirens until we're close to the tower—right. Call me when you're there. I'll meet you."

I've grabbed Frankie under my arm and leap with him onto the porch. Getting Frankie inside, I give Carol and Mom strict instructions to stay there. They look back at me with wide eyes.

Dave looks to see we're all assembled. His cell rings. "All three. Right. Right. I'll be there. Two minutes."

He turns to us. "Alright. This is police business. Everyone, stay put." He looks directly at me. "Sit tight. Got it?"

He looks at each of us in turn, stopping to stare at each of us until we individually nod, then rolls his eyes.

We all smile benignly as he shakes his head then dashes to his truck.

We wait at least five seconds before sneaking out the back door, down the back alley, and under Red Wolf's carport to the back road. Then, cutting through Maisie New Lodge's backyard shrubbery, we head toward the tower, dispersing near the end of the route. Suddenly the night is full of sirens and blue and red flashing lights. Three patrol cars simultaneously pull up near the tower. Police pour out of their vehicles, training their guns on a solitary man, kneeling on the platform in the near-dark. Putting on a sprint, I slide in where the parked patrol cars are positioned.

"Leave the gun on the deck and start climbing down," Tom yells, using a bullhorn. "Don't think long 'bout it. You have three minutes before we start shooting."

Nothing happens for a minute or so, then the rifle is lowered to the deck. A man starts climbing down.

"Slow and steady. Lie face down on the ground with your hands over your head where we can see them."

The man descends deliberately, reaches the ground, raises his hands, and takes several slow steps away from the tower before lying face down. He's dressed like all of us—hoodie, jeans, scuffed boots. No one standing around knows him.

"Dave, cuff and pat him," says Tom. "Terry, hustle up and get the gun."

"Okay, mister," Tom says, walking over. "What the hell were you doing up the tank with a rifle in the dark?"

He doesn't respond.

"Wait till you see this rifle," Terry yells down. "It's a sharpshooter's model with a night scope. I bet I could hit a target a half-mile away easy."

"What you doin' with that?" Tom asks. "Damn well ain't for rabbit hunting."

Silence.

By this time, my entire construction crew has joined us.

"Let me see that," Dave asks, reaching for the rifle as Terry approaches. "Top of the line. Not for shooting sheep or chickens either."

At that moment his cell rings, and he steps away to take it. "Yeah, Les. Find out anything?"

Dave is completely quiet for several minutes listening. Then, "Yes. Yes, we're on our way. I'll bring Lew and anyone else who wants to come. I know. I know. But ask Fisher not to wait as a personal favor to me. Have him call in the detective squad. We'll meet them at the house. Sure. Sure. I'll put on the siren. Ninety minutes or less."

Everything that has just happened fades into nothing. "What, Dave? What's going on?" I ask, fearing everything.

Dave is studying me. He puts his hand on my arm. "Her truck was there, but she's not. The back door was wide open. They found a sweater, with what appears to be a fair amount of blood on it in the bedroom on the bed. There was a small amount of blood smeared on the spread. Her purse contents were dumped on the kitchen floor. Money was still in her wallet."

"Lew," Dave begins, "maybe you should stay here. You're personally involved, and..."

I respond with a horizontal hand swipe, coupled with a conversation-ending scowl.

To Dave's credit, he made it in an hour and twenty minutes. I've hardly been able to breathe, I'm so terrified. Willie, Win and Bruce have come with us, wedged quietly in the back seat. Dave has been talking to Les all the way down, filling him in about the Browning sniper and getting updates, both about that and the situation at Miranda's. I can't focus on anything other than Charlie's rage up at Vinnie's. What if he turned it on her?

The entire house is surrounded with yellow police tape. Detectives have been there for an hour by the time we arrive. Dave goes inside to get an update. Pacing up and down the sidewalk, I finally end up slamming my fists repeatedly against a tree. Willie and Win are trying to calm me down but I back away from them, holding my hands up. I don't want to hear it.

Her truck is parked several hundred feet down the street. An officer stands guard next to it. More yellow tape surrounds the truck. He shakes his head. I walk back, trying to gather myself. Her front door is still taped so I go around behind. "Don't go in," one of the detectives orders. "The forensic guys have just started."

"Forensic," I scream inside my head. That word doesn't fit with Miranda.

Les and Dave come out, gathering us all together near a concrete wall behind the apartment. "This is all they know," Les begins. "No one in the neighborhood saw or heard anything, but they're still going door to door. They haven't tested for blood residue throughout the apartment yet, but they found an expensive black sweater, with a New York label, with what appears to be a fair amount of blood on it. It hasn't been typed yet."

Blood, I think. *Dear God.*

"We checked her purse contents, but there's no cell phone anywhere in the apartment. We're hoping to triangulate it. The heat was set at sixty-five degrees, the bed was rumpled but not slept in. It's very cold in there so the back door's been open a while. Other than that, we'll have to wait for a more extensive investigation." Les walks over to hug me. I let him. He's been a family friend my entire life. Then he settles himself on the wall, unhappily nodding at everyone else.

"Dave," I say, with barely contained fury. "Call Charlie. He was the last one to see her."

He sighs. "If I let you stay, Lew, you stay seated and not utter a word. If you need to ask something, write it down. And I won't promise I'll ask it. Understand?"

"Yes."

Dave takes a deep breath and punches in Charlie's number. I know it's hard. We're all close friends. Or were.

It's picked up on the fifth ring. It's very late back there, after two a.m.

Dave puts it on speaker. "Charlie. You need to know this is a professional call on the record. Understand?"

"Yes? Sure."

I hear confusion in his voice. My emotions are ragged. If he hurt her…?

"Charlie, Miranda's disappeared. Her apartment was disturbed. Do you know any…?"

He's interrupted by a loud nebulous exclamation, then, "What? What do you mean disappeared?"

"No one's seen her that we're aware of since you left. Lew hasn't seen her. We're investigating. Maybe she'll turn up. Maybe someone knows something, but she hardly knows anyone down here."

"I'll wake up Hugh. I'll fly out now."

"Listen. Come first thing tomorrow. Write down a timeline, every minute until now."

"Who have you called? What are you doing? Who's looking?" Charlie is almost screaming.

"Calm down," Dave says. "We're all working on it. We'll find her, Charlie."

There's silence for a moment. "Alright, Dave. Find her. Find her! We'll be out first light. I'll wake up Hugh."

Scribbling a note on a piece of paper, I hand it to Dave. He reads it and shakes his head no, then crumples it up, before disconnecting his phone.

"Lew," Dave says, "if he was involved in anything, he wouldn't come right back out here."

Staring coldly back at Dave, I mutter, "He's not here yet."

Willie reaches for the crumpled piece of paper, reads it, then returns it to me. I'd written, "Did you hurt her?"

"How did he seem when you saw him at Vinnie's?" Dave asks.

"He was talking with his fists," I say. "I didn't have much opportunity to gage his mood. You should ask Vinnie."

"I'll do that," he says, grimly.

A local policeman comes over to ask if anyone knows next-of-kin. Dave talks quietly to him.

"Should we call Tony?" I ask.

"Let's give it a few hours," Dave suggests, "and hope. I told the officer we'd call her father in a few hours if there's no good news." He pauses. "They don't want to start an official investigation until she's been missing twenty-four hours."

"Damn it, Dave." I'm almost screaming. "We don't know when the twenty-four hours started. For all we know it could have started before Charlie left."

"Jesus, Lew," he responds. "Calm down!"

It's now well past one AM. We're crashing at Jeremy's apartment in Great Falls. He's a good friend, out of town a lot, and Win has a key. We've spent the last hour hashing out ideas as I sit brooding in a corner, repeatedly scanning my friends' faces before asking, "Could Charlie could be involved with this?" I'm specifically asking Bruce, who was at one time intimately familiar with murderous rages.

He smiles grimly. "If you're asking, can anyone really know what someone else is capable of? I'd have to say no. You all know what I did. If you put enough pressure on someone or take away something that is everything... Charlie's been deceived before. If he believed it was happening again...? Well, you can't know for sure."

"Willie. Win. You guys are good at reading people. Have you seen anything in Charlie that could lead to violence?"

Willie slowly shakes his head.

"Win?" I ask.

"Never. No. And I've seen him seriously thwarted. He was a gentleman as far as Lizzie was concerned. No. I just can't see it. They need to explore all possibilities."

I don't want to hear it. I keep seeing Charlie's furious face.

The hours are lengthening. "Dave," I plead, "there must be something we can do."

He starts to shake his head. We've been through this conversation several times before.

"Damn it, Dave. We have to call Tony. If she was going to call anyone, it would be him. I don't want to upset him either, but…"

"No," he sighs. "You're right. It's time. He'll have to know soon, anyway."

"I'll do it," I say.

It rings and rings then goes to voicemail. "He's not answering," I say. "It's after three a.m. back there."

Suddenly my phone rings. It's Tony, calling back.

"Lew," he says, slightly breathlessly. "I'm on the way to the airport. Charlie filled me in. They're picking me up soon. Hugh's flying him down from Philly with his sister Juli, and an ex-FBI, lawyer friend. We'll take off from Dulles little after four our time and be out there around six your time. Where should we go?"

"Tony wants to know where to go. Charlie is flying them out. They'll be here about six."

Dave holds out his hand for the phone.

"Tony. Dave here. Go directly to the Holiday Inn, downtown Great Falls. It's four blocks from the police station. By the time you get checked in, it'll be after six-thirty. We'll meet you at the station. No. We don't know anything yet." He glances at me. "A lot of strange things happening up here today." A long pause. "Don't panic, Tony. Could she have called her sister? You have? No. Yes. Yes, tell Charlie that will help. Yeah, see you there."

Dave turns to us. "Charlie has sources working on tracking Miranda's cell. They're breaking laws right and left. He told Tony they'd pick up the pieces later. They should have a phone log by the time they get here. Hopefully, she has her phone with her. Also, they'll trace any calls she's made over the last few hours. This doesn't sound like a guy who has anything to hide."

I'm not ready to let him completely off the hook, but he's been a friend. I don't want him involved with anything. I don't hate him. He has more cause to hate me. I just want Mira somewhere safe. I'm sick. She didn't temporarily drop out. She wouldn't do that to her dad if nothing else.

Willie comes over to sit by my side. "Turn your brain off for a few hours. We can't do anything till morning. Go in one of the bedrooms and lie down. I'll call you if there's anything."

I nod. I'm so exhausted my thoughts keep circling anyway.

CHAPTER 23

JULI

WHEN CHARLIE woke me up just after three, I couldn't believe it. After adjusting yesterday to the stunning news that Miranda had in effect dumped my beloved brother for a rural Mensa Indian, it now seems she's disappeared. Charlie's apparently a suspect in her disappearance, and he wants to run back out there to try to find her. Maybe I'm still asleep. I pinch my forearm and it hurts.

Dad and Mom met us in the hall after hearing us banging around, throwing clothes in suitcases, and making phone calls. They asked a few questions but went back to bed when Charlie put them off, convincing them to wait until later to be told the whole evolving story. He'd already talked to them about Miranda's *recent struggles*. His discolored face made that necessary. But he hasn't told them about her sudden disappearance. It would have caused too many questions that Charlie didn't want to discuss. They'll have to wait longer. He promised to call with new developments.

I'm grateful he trusted me with the news, allowing me to go along for moral support. Charlie, Hugh, and I are back in the car in the middle of the night, being driven to the airport by long-suffering Stosh, on our way to our small jet. We'll stop in DC to pick up Miranda's father, then fly west well before dawn.

I was looking forward to meeting this girl, even liked her on the phone the two times I've talked to her, but now I'd merely like to have her found alive. I want Charlie off the hook. I'm tempted to kick this Lew guy in a vulnerable place. I have a lot of leg strength. You don't destroy my brother and get away with it. I understand he's a big guy so I could probably do some damage and not be charged with anything. And, anyway, we have good lawyers.

* * *

In the back of the plane, Charlie sits staring fixedly at Tony Flynn, as they have remained for the last two hours. They both look scared and shocked, so it seems inappropriate to walk back and talk about my on-going murder fantasies. When I met Miranda's distraught father, the gravity of the situation finally began to hit me. I need to take this seriously. What if something terrible has happened to her? That would deeply wound my brother. From what little he's said, I know he's devastated over this. He believed himself to be genuinely in love with this girl, at least until twenty-four hours ago. Unbelievable.

Instead, I go up to the front of the plane and speak through the intercom to Hugh, asking permission to sit in the co-pilot's seat. I always ask. It's his domain.

"Come on in, Juli," he says.

I settle myself and turn to him. "Is this girl worth all this?" I ask.

He glances at me, sighing deeply, "This must sound like high drama to you. I don't understand this myself. It seems beyond belief anyone would target Miranda. She's a conventional, appealing, intelligent girl, but there are things you don't know. The same guys that have made several attempts on Lew's life have threatened her indirectly, possibly to get to him. This could be the real thing, and potentially deadly. I'm very concerned."

"Do you like her, Hugh?"

Staring fixedly out the cockpit window, he sighs. "More than that. Enough that I'll take this very personally if something has happened to her. I could have been interested myself, but I would have had to get in line."

"Seriously?"

"Yep."

"But I don't understand. How could she go off with this... This interloper?"

"She hasn't gone off. I talked to him just before we took off. Miranda was so distraught he was leaving her alone to sort out her feelings. Now he's frantic."

"If he's so assassination-prone, why did he go out there and endanger her?"

"I suppose he didn't consider that. I didn't either. We all thought she'd be safer in Montana."

"Why was she out there alone if she'd been threatened?"

"The government people didn't feel it was a serious enough threat to keep her under constant surveillance. She wasn't mentioned by name, and they couldn't turn up any concrete connection although they're still searching. Besides, it's almost impossible to guard anyone 24/7. And for how long?"

"I wonder if Charlie's thought of this?" Should I bring it up?"

"Jules, it's only been five hours. Hold on. Let's see what the police have come up with. We'll be landing in forty-five minutes."

"Alright, but this Lew-guy sounds like an egotistical, self-indulgent asshole. He's hurt a lot of people. I don't care what you say. Whether he's arrogant or just plain stupid, he better stay away from me."

"Honey. You just don't want Charlie hurt again."

"He's been through enough pain. We all have, God knows."

"Let's just hope this is a false alarm. I want her found." He gives me a weak smile, then turns to gaze out at the Rocky Mountains just appearing on the horizon.

I give Hugh a kiss on his cheek then head back to sit with my tormented brother.

CHAPTER 24

LEW

ENTERING THE GREAT Falls police station, we're quickly ushered into a conference room. Charlie sits quietly, but extreme tension shows on his face as well as utter fatigue. On his right is a stranger, a corporate type, looking intensely concerned. On his left side sits a young woman I've never met. The woman is beautiful in a natural unadorned way with a wavy jumble of reddish-brown hair, freckles, and green eyes. She's also notable because she's blatantly glaring at me. She must be Charlie's sister. Next to her sits Tony.

I walk to Tony's side. He stands and we tightly wrap our arms around each other, holding each other for several minutes. He looks like death as he whispers to me, "It's what I feared." I love this man like a father and his pain compounds mine.

Finding a chair opposite Charlie, I cross my arms, and study my rival. It gives me some satisfaction that his face looks worse than mine, although my chin is deepening purple. I wonder idly if they'll offer us some ice with the coffee as we continue to stare coldly at each other.

A fiftyish man with a short crewcut enters and closes the door.

"I'm Captain Stu Fisher. I'll be heading the investigation," he begins. "I know some of you here personally. Dave, of course, and Win and Willie. And I've met Lew on occasion. I've mentioned this to Charles Curchin and his associates. It does not cause them a problem. We're not over the twenty-four-hour limit since Miss Flynn was discovered missing, but with Dave's strong backing, we've decided to proceed with greatest haste. Especially with the disturbing discoveries in the young lady's apartment. Dave will act as professional liaison."

Absolute silence.

Fisher continues. "There's no designated crime yet. We're in very early stages. I understand from talking to Mr. Curchin that he will answer any questions and provide any assistance. He's offered to take a lie-detector test immediately if we deem it necessary. He's provided us with his timeline, and I want to go over these details with you. Possibly add some parallel timelines. Let's go around the table first and introduce ourselves."

We do that quickly. Peter Rathbone is introduced. He discloses that he was formally employed with the FBI and is now under the employment of Curchin Ltd. Charlie's sister, Juli, doesn't say a word other than her name. I'm trying to appear composed, but I find myself coldly staring at Charlie. Often, I find him glaring back at me.

"Mr. Curchin," Captain Fisher begins. "Let's go over your past twenty hours. You may be the last person to have seen Miss Flynn."

Charlie clears his throat. "I've discussed this with my associate. He understands that I will volunteer everything I know without reservation or evasion. He will immediately offer any relevant expertise to the investigation." His voice is an authoritative monotone I've never heard from him before but his shoulders droop as he runs his hand through his hair and sighs.

He passes out paper copies of his whereabouts in Montana. "As you can see," he says, "I wasn't here long." He frowns briefly, looking concertedly at the paper. "I arrived in my private jet, which was piloted by Hugh McManus, at six p.m. on the evening before last, Friday. Soon after my arrival, Miranda and I had a serious disagreement. At approximately seven, I went for a long run to... Clear my head.

"At about ten-thirty p.m. I contacted my pilot, who had flown on to California to pick up my sister, requesting him to stop on the return leg and pick me up. The call can be documented." His voice briefly trembles. "I had decided to return to Philadelphia."

Many people around the table show compassion with Charlie's pain. His sister reaches over to touch his arm.

He continues. "I returned to Miranda's at approximately eleven-thirty p.m. and left her apartment an hour later, borrowing her truck. I drove directly to East Glacier, to the home of Vinnie Long, and knocked on her door at approximately three a.m. I slept at her house. At about seven she fed me cinnamon rolls and we discussed some things."

"Our Vinnie," Captain Fisher interrupts. "That Vinnie?"

"Yes," Dave asserts. "Willie's grandmother."

People glance at Willie who smiles back.

"I've spent some time visiting Vinnie's kitchen myself," the police captain says. "Go on, Mr. Curchin."

"Well, anyway, we discussed my relationship with Miranda. Just as I was getting ready to leave, Lew Black River showed up. I punched him. We fought. Then I left."

There's silence around the table for several long moments.

"Well?" Captain Fisher asks finally. "Who won?"

Everyone is looking at our discolored faces. We're now glaring openly at each other.

"I guess it was a draw," I mumble, as Charlie stares fixedly at me.

"Continue, Mr. Curchin," Captain Fisher says more seriously.

With effort, I see Charlie turn his stare away from me. "I drove straight back to Great Falls but stopped at the Chevron on Vaughn Road to fill the truck with gas, then drove on to Miranda's. I had arranged for a taxi to meet me there at eleven. I made it with about five minutes to spare. The taxi driver pulled in just as I arrived. I went inside her apartment, kissed her, and left for the airport."

"Any idea how blood might have gotten on a certain black sweater?"

"It was my sweater. I had blood on me from the fight with that fucking asshole." He glares at me again.

It's everything I can do not to go over and cave his face in. I feel Willie tighten his hand on my forearm.

"So... When you dropped off the truck, you took off your sweater?"

Silence. Everyone looks at Charlie.

"I wanted her to have something to remember me by. I left it with her."

"A bloody sweater?"

He pauses. "Yes."

His voice had risen at that last word defiantly. I leap to my feet and start launching myself over the table when Willie grabs me by my belt, trying to pull me back into my chair. Peter Rathbone is wrestling similarly with Charlie.

We both struggle for a moment or two then give it up. I sigh repeatedly as Charlie sits down fuming. The sister is still standing, fists clenched, at Charlie's side, glaring at me. We're given a few minutes to calm down. I glance at the man accompanying Charlie as he puts his arm around his shoulders, whispering something. Charlie nods over and over until he whispers, "Thanks." They must have more than a professional relationship. I remember Miranda mentioning the Curchins don't have traditional employees.

"Let's continue," Captain Fisher interrupts. "About the blood on the black sweater?"

"I was wearing it when I kissed her. That's my blood on my sweater."

"We'll be testing the blood."

Charlie looks him straight in the eye. "All I know is that's my blood on the sweater. Possibly some of his," he says, pointing at me.

"Has anyone else seen or talked to the young lady after eleven-fifteen yesterday morning?"

Silence.

"Did the taxi driver see her when he picked you up?"

"No. She was inside when I arrived. I slammed the door hard when I left, just so you know."

"So... You can't prove she was alive at eleven-fifteen, and neither can anyone else that we know of?"

"Yes. I suppose that's right," agrees Charlie.

"And, in fact, as far as we know now, no one else saw her alive after you got to her apartment at six the previous evening."

"Yes, but..."

That silences the group.

"Dave Miller said you were working on phone records?"

Rathbone breaks in. "We arranged for the results to be faxed to your office. They might be here by now, including the triangulation of her cell phone."

"I'll be right back," Fisher says.

Fidgeting in my chair, I'm seething. No one says a word. I'd begun to believe Charlie couldn't have been involved, but I understand you can't really know people. And people can change. Just look at my friend, Bruce. Juli takes Charlie's hand. He tolerates it for a few seconds, then impatiently pulls it away.

Captain Fisher returns with printouts.

"Unfortunately, there are no phone calls from her phone for the time in question. I'd hoped someone could establish that Miranda is alive, at least until eleven-fifteen yesterday morning. In fact, no calls were made after four p.m. the previous afternoon so it will take further investigation. Also, there have been no new calls, except numerous attempts to call hers."

"I called many times to check on her." I explain. "No answer."

Captain Fisher continues. "She has a pattern of averaging five or so calls a day, but there has been absolute silence. Perhaps she's upset and has isolated herself, but it's unusual. How was the apartment when you were there last, Mr. Curchin?"

"Fine, normal. We didn't physically fight."

A uniformed police officer comes into the room and hands a paper to Captain Fisher. He studies it briefly then nods to the officer who leaves.

He looks up. "A bit of good news, Mr. Curchin. Your blood-type and only your blood-type was found on the sweater, type O. Miranda is blood type A. Also, the preliminary investigation shows no other blood in the apartment except the bedspread, also type O."

Despite himself, I can see Charlie heave a sigh of relief.

"This is the situation." He turns to Charlie. "I can't completely rule you out as a suspect, but I don't have any direct evidence or professional inclination to hold you. Not now, at any rate. And we may need your resources to help in the search effort. The cell data shows her phone was triangulated to an area north of Highway 2, just west of Cut Bank, and east on 444. That's your jurisdiction, Dave." He turns to Charlie's side of the table. "It's mostly wide-spaced large land holdings and ranches in the midsection of the reservation, extending to the Canadian border."

Win adds, "Lew, Willie, and I know a lot of people who live in the area, my Aunt Jeanette, for one, and many friends and acquaintances. We all know the area thoroughly. It's part of my fire-fighting grid."

"Okay. I don't want to waste time," Captain Fisher says. "Mr. Curchin, you've been forthcoming with information. It's possible you are involved in Miranda's disappearance. A lot could have happened before driving on to Vinnie's, getting there by three in the morning.

Charlie's face flushes with anger, starting to say something. Fisher interrupts, holding up his hand. "But let's assume nothing criminal happened. We need to make a concerted effort to find her and find her quickly, using any available resources. Is anyone aware of anyone else who may have cause to hurt this young lady?"

Dave, Bruce, and Willie immediately turn to stare at me. Tony also reacts in horror. I hadn't consciously connected... I'd been so focused on hating Charlie... His kid sister reacts, shooting visual daggers in my direction. And Charlie almost rises from his seat.

Bile rises in my mouth. "Yes," I admit. "There've been several attempts on my life. And... And there's a guy in custody right now in Browning..." Nausea threatens me again. "It's conceivable... I mean, it's possible someone took Miranda to silence me."

A hush dominates the room as my heart pounds rapidly.

Fisher stands suddenly. "Hold any conversation," he says, and walks out the door.

We sit in silence for several long minutes. I hear doors opening and closing somewhere outside. Voices raised. Then several more minutes pass. It's all I can do not to groan in frustration and fear. Assuming Charlie had nothing to do with this, no wonder Charlie has reacted with such fury. Not only did I try to take his woman, but I may have... I can't go there. But I may have...

Fisher returns. "All right, then. The tribal police are bringing their prisoner down here. After initial interrogation, there are indications that this may be a national or international issue. We'll be holding him down here and calling in the FBI. Meanwhile..." He starts passing out papers with a map of the area west of Cut Bank. "We've got search dogs coming. Let's get some bodies out and start searching. I want this entire area combed structure by structure."

"Two Fire Service helicopters are on loan to help," Charlie says. "My pilot, Hugh McManus, is going to fly one. They're being flown up from Missoula."

I see Captain Fisher grab a pen and start scribbling. "We've got four all-terrain patrol cars available and four patrolmen, plus two patrol helicopters. It's light now. Let's divide up into four flight teams and start rolling. We've got a rectangle of twenty miles east to west and ten miles north and south. There's two hundred square miles to cover. I'll divide you up with a ground vehicle paired with each helicopter and divide the total area into a grid. We'll have four five-by-ten-mile sections. The helicopter crews can scout and locate structures where someone might be held, then direct in the ground units. We'll have additional patrol cars search the area along Highway 2 and they'll transport search dogs. If anyone needs backup, they can call in the additional cruisers. We'll divide up. Charlie, those two Forest Service helicopters are under your authority. Do you want to go up with your pilots?"

I notice he's now being called "Charlie" instead of Mr. Curchin.

"No, I want to be on the ground, in one of the cruisers along Highway 2, in case anyone turns up something."

"Okay. Give me a minute." He starts scribbling more lists.

"This is how I see it," Captain Fisher says. "I've got everyone paired up with one pilot and one of my troopers who knows the area in question. If your Forest Service pilot flies one of the helicopters from Missoula, the extra patrolman can stay with him and act as an additional spotter. He'll know the area better. We'll pair up a local trooper with each one of your guys, Dave. That will free up one of our boys to go with you, Charlie. Those of you in helicopters head out to the airport now. The rest of you study the lists and pair up. I'll be in command in the other cruiser on Highway 2. Check in every fifteen minutes or so. You can all listen in on Universal 16 for updates. Any questions? Suggestions?"

"Yes," Charlie says. "I'm putting my sister in Hugh's helicopter for more eyes in the sky. Pete, here, is a Gulf War Veteran. He'll go up in the other helicopter piloted by Bill Walsh from the Forest Service."

Charlie seems to be able to function. I'm staggered that I may be the cause of Miranda being taken. I can't allow my mind to fully complete the thought. I'm also amazed Fisher could put this together in less than an hour and a half.

I'm terrified for Miranda and trying to put my hatred for Charlie aside. As I glance at him, I can see his hands are shaking. He's a controlled train wreck. It takes one to know one. But he could be on the edge because of the unthinkable. I know one other thing. If he hurt her, I'll recreate my ancestors' atrocities.

I hurry out the door and run smack into Charlie's sister. We literally throw each other off balance, wedged together in the small space.

"Excuse me," I say automatically, and take a step backwards.

Her green eyes flash. I can see her biting her words. Neither of us says anything or moves.

Finally, she utters in a distinct whisper, "Get—out—of—my—way!"

I stare her down, not moving for several seconds, then step sideways. My mood is dark. What I wanted to do was push her against the wall.

"Asshole," she mutters, as she blows by me.

"Obviously good breeding got lost in the last generation," I retort loudly, glaring at her back.

She pauses, then storms ahead. I guess we're not going to get along.

* * *

I'm paired up with Dan Strickland, a Great Falls cop, and Bill Walsh. It was pointed out I would be safer in the air—one more personal blow. We hustle out to my truck to head for the airport. Those in the patrol cars are speeding north now but our helicopters will pass them on the way up. The cars will have on their flashers, but it will take them an hour and a half or more to get to the search area. Our helicopter unit will have the most easterly location. I have a look at the map, noticing the red bullseye of the phone triangulation, but there's a large margin of error.

It's colder now with a weather system rolling in, originating from a band of low pressure moving counterclockwise in from the northeast. The wind is already becoming more northerly, beginning to jostle the helicopter. Our usual prevailing winds are from the west, but the jet stream is dropping down overtop of us. Visibility is good for now, but there's some overcast increasing to the north. If only rain or snow would hold off.

I know Dan slightly. He has some Blackfeet blood, but his family has lived off the reservation for a generation. We check in with Fisher and keep the channel open. Dan has relatives in Cut Bank so is very familiar with our section. I'm happy to be in the air checking structures. The men in patrol cars will circle buildings and investigate sites on foot. Other pilots are communicating with ground vehicles, making plans and connections like we are. It took us a while to get in the air, but we're passing the cars now on their way north, tipping our rotors as we fly by overhead.

The land is beyond familiar. I've been on these roads hundreds of times. Friends and extended family members own some of the buildings along highway 15, increasing the closer we get to Cut Bank. I don't have the composure or energy to explain details to Dan other than to say Miranda and I are close friends. He understands enough not to push it.

In the back caverns of my mind, I worry that she's already been killed as a threat to me, to remove me from security work. The acceptance that I, not Charlie, am probably responsible for her abduction fills me with black despair.

It's only ten in the morning. Fisher put this together in record time. I no longer believe this is a result of jealousy-produced rage. I believe Charlie loves her, as do I. What a fucked-up mess. I no longer want to hurt him, unless... My mind is circling. I'll be glad to concentrate when we get to the search area. Anything to move ahead.

I wonder about Charlie's sister. As far as I know, Miranda's never met her. Charlie is usually even tempered unless he's trying to kill me. This sister obviously is more on the edge. What a witch. I remember she's a professional soccer player. Fine, just keep her away from me. It would be appalling to get in a real pushing match. At least if I'm furious, I'm not so frantic.

Miranda? Where are you?

* * *

It's after three in the afternoon and everyone is discouraged. I've switched to a ground unit. We've investigated many isolated sites but turned up nothing. I've been in and out of the car, jogging to various sheds and old barns, anywhere a person could be held. The wind is beginning to howl. I've needed my heavy jacket.

The intercom crackles, "Attention all units."

It's Fisher. I recognize his voice now.

"The Browning sniper is providing some important information. The incidents are connected. He's admitted knowing no specific details, but someone was to be held hostage. He swears he knows nothing else but admitted that Lew was his target."

"This appears to take the heat off Mr. Curchin, but the young lady remains in serious trouble. We're hoping these guys don't decide to terminate and leave the area. Does anyone have any comments? Any reason to change our current course of action?"

Silence, as we digest this. This is on me. Doom descends.

An unfamiliar voice asks, "Has anyone re-triangulated the cell phone?

"No results. Nothing," Fisher says. "They haven't even been able to duplicate the original data. Possibly the phone has been destroyed. Keep searching. I've called in more police units from Missoula and Helena. We only have three hours of daylight left."

I reach for the radio. "Fisher, Lew Black River here. Find out what kind of vehicle the guy was driving. See if he rented it and if so, where? Find out if there were other vehicles rented near the same time by individuals for similar periods of time. Maybe we can get an idea of what to look for."

"Great idea. I'll pass it along now."

Yeah, great idea. But I'm dying here.

* * *

Every outbuilding structure in the grid areas has been searched by hand. Our small army is now talking to all the homes and ranch houses in the area to see if strangers or unusual activity have been observed. So far nothing. The overcast is increasing with a low ceiling and almost dark. The helicopters will have to return soon to Great Falls for refueling, anyway. For now, we've congregated in a field behind the Cut Bank medical clinic as we sort out ground searchers and vehicles for a final effort. None of us want to quit, but there isn't much we can do in the dark.

Charlie's friend Peter, several pilots, and most of the police force personnel, are returning to Great Falls for the night, intending to regroup up here at seven tomorrow morning. Dave's decided to drive to East Glacier to spend the night with his family, taking Juli and Tony home with him. Bruce will also drive home. Hugh will accompany the helicopters to refuel and watch over them, camping out at the airport.

We're left with the core group including Charlie. He's unequivocally been accepted back into the family, although he and I are sitting as far apart from each other as possible. He's known all along he had no part in this. No wonder he hates me, currently sitting isolated in his own world; scared.

Win adopted Charlie for the night. Both will spend the night with an aunt of his. I'll go with Willie to a friend's house just out of town after dinner.

Over orders of meatloaf and mashed potatoes, we try to imagine what else we could do. We're all tired, talking quietly, and trying to relax. Willie turns to Charlie, who hasn't said a word, and asks how he's doing.

He raises leaden eyes to Willie's face, then mine. "I keep hoping...," he manages. "It's so cold out there tonight. Do you suppose they gave her a blanket?"

Charlie's simple statement of concern produces goose bumps on my arms. Our eyes meet with new mutual compassion. He's forgiven me, even though I'm at fault. He's been a better man in all ways from the beginning. It's not about who gets her anymore. Just let her be alive. The agony has taken away our hatred. Friends put arms around each of us. There doesn't seem to be anything more we can do.

We're almost done eating when Willie's cell phone rings. "It's Dave," he announces. "Maybe he has information on the rental cars."

Willie listens intently. "Okay. Okay. I got it. Yes. Yes. First thing. See you at seven."

"This may help," he says. "The shooter rented a SUV from Avis at the airport for seven days, two days ago. Within the same half hour, two guys rented two additional SUVS for the exact same period. Their IDs don't check out. They're all silver Ford Explorers. Dave says we should be on the lookout for them tomorrow, at houses or otherwise, and the ground units can knock on doors."

I'm thinking hard. Something almost rings a bell.

Willie and I take one cruiser to the home of an elderly lady who tends to mother him. I snuggle down on her couch, but only doze intermittently. I keep picturing silver SUVs.

CHAPTER 25

LEW

ABOUT ONE-THIRTY I snap awake out of a sound sleep. Now I've got it. When we flew over Richardson's isolated ranch house early yesterday, I remember seeing a new SUV parked outside their dilapidated barn and thinking, *I wonder if ol' Stretch won the lottery.*

"Willie. Willie?" I shake him awake.

"Yeah," Willie says as I start to explain. "I know them well. They're in Arizona until March. Grandma mentioned it. They're in a reading group together. They closed up the house for the winter."

"Willie, I can't wait till morning to check it out. Are you game? You got your gun, right?"

"We should let Dave know and the Cut Bank police," Willie grins. "We shouldn't storm the house. But we could sneak around in the dark to see if anything looks suspicious. Check license plates. We're Indians, at least you are. Come on."

Willie is bursting with enthusiasm. Typical Willie.

"Listen," I say. "Don't go off half-cocked. I keep getting friends in danger. You've got to promise me."

"I promise. I promise. Call Dave."

Dave's having a fit, but we're going. We're supposed to call the dispatcher at the Cut Bank office every ten minutes to check in. We absolutely promised not to do anything more than scout from the exterior of the house. The cut-off road to Richardson's is only three miles west of town, but the primitive dirt road then extends across a five-mile-long rolling prairie landscape headed north. We know we can get to within a mile of the house with running lights on, but once we get up to a high grove of trees, we'll have to let our eyes acclimate and drive in the dark.

The grass is mostly long and dry, even after the big wind and hailstorm a few days ago. After parking Willie's truck an eight of a mile from the house, off the road in a dip in the plateau, we jog the rest of the way. There's hazy overcast but it's not difficult to see. A half-moon is low in the sky behind the cloud cover, providing diffuse light. We find two SUVs. Just as we get within two hundred feet of the house the front door opens, and we hunker down hastily in the grass. The bright glow from the inside room throws a shaft of light out onto the frozen front yard.

A man steps outside, stops halfway to one of the cars, then calls back over his shoulder. We can just hear him over the sound of the wind. "Stop bitching. I'm getting it. She's asleep, anyway. So's the boss."

He goes to the nearest vehicle and returns to the house with a paper bag.

We've learned a lot. First, these guys are not the Richardsons. And second, there's a female inside. We're both armed. I start fingering my gun. "Willie? What should we do?"

"We have to look, don't we?" Willie asks. "At least look in the windows around back of the house?"

I nod. We give the front a wide berth and work our way through the dried grass to the rear of the house. The windows are small and high, but the curtains aren't closed. Willie leans against the wall with his knee bent and when I stand on his leg I can peer in easily. Someone is awake in the bed in the first bedroom, reading a magazine. I can see him easily by the light of a small bedside lamp. I signal one finger to Willie and use primitive sign language to indicate a male.

We move to another window. Again, I climb on Willie's knee. It's dark in this room, but the door is slightly ajar, allowing just enough light into the room so I can see. A man is sitting in a chair almost directly under the window. I can see only his back in silhouette. Miranda is lying on the bed with her hands bound together. She appears to be asleep. I get so excited I almost fall off Willie's knee. I nod frantically and mouth, "Yes, it's her."

We creep far enough away to talk. The wind is continuing to build so we're not worried about noise. The clouds are now racing by overhead, but I can still see in the moonlight. In a lowered voice, Willie says, "We have two choices, call for back up or go get her now."

"Let's do both," I reply. "Call Cut Bank. Then you go out behind the barn and create a diversion. I'll be ready, and when they're distracted, I'll get her out of there. We'll all hide in the tall grass back behind the pump house. Tell the Cut Bank boys that's where we'll be."

"Dave's going to have a shit fit."

"Willie, I don't want to risk you. Maybe this will backfire. I'm too involved to judge."

I can see Willie's broad grin in the moonlight. "Oh, what the hell," he says.

We call the police to check in. The Blackfeet word for crazy, ahwahtsouptsii, is shouted until my ears ring. That phrase is now part of my working vocabulary in several languages. They're screaming bloody murder as we hang up. I know a couple of the guys, one's a cousin. They're on the way but it'll take them fifteen minutes to get here in the darkness. Willie next called Win but got a busy signal, so he called Charlie. They're closer, only minutes away. Willie gave him directions and headed for the barn.

I return to Miranda's window, climbing up on an overturned five-gallon bucket. The window is cracked open. All I need to do is remove an old screen. I'm ready. The man in the chair stirs, stretches, and walks over to her sleeping form. He stands motionless at Miranda's bedside. I'll slit his throat if he touches her.

An enormous explosion rocks what seems like the entire nearby county. Jesus H. Christ! I said a diversion, not strip mining. It works, though. The man races out of the room.

Slipping in through the window, I put my hand over Miranda's mouth in the dark. She jerks away then recognizes me as I undo her hands, moving her to the window. Sliding out first, I yell, "Jump!"

She does, and I catch her on the way down.

"Run. Run for the pump house," I whisper as loudly as I dare, pointing it out for her.

She's stiff from being tied up but gets going.

A shot rings out. "Go. Go. Go," I yell. More shots.

Kneeling in the grass, I return fire, trying to cover her escape.

Several men are firing at me, running my way. Standing, I pump
out a barrage of bullets then start to run toward our truck, diverting
them away from the pump house. More bullets hit the ground just
to my side when a sudden hellish pain in my left leg staggers me.
My leg folds up, collapsing me on my stomach in the grass about
two hundred feet away from the main house. The pain is horrible.
The bone feels shattered.

Bullets fly from another direction. Willie's trying to keep them
away from me.

Managing to rise enough to kneel on my one good leg, I stabilize
one arm with the other and get in one good shot. One shooter falls,
manages to get up, then begins hobbling toward the SUVs.

The other two make a run for it, intercepting the limping third
man, then haul him between them.

Willie runs up to me, brandishing his gun.

I can see Miranda approaching behind him. "Get her out of
here," I yell. "I have a gun. They're bailing, anyhow. Go! The
police are coming."

One of the SUVs is already racing away in the distance down
the two-track, its headlights flashing by our truck hidden in the
darkness. Moments later, the second SUV moves a short distance
away from me, then stops.

Willie nods, grabs Miranda, half-carrying—half-helping her
run, and takes off toward his truck. Moments later, another car
is seen heading this way. It abruptly cuts off the road and heads
directly toward the pump house. The headlights suddenly point
straight down. It must have gone over a small ledge. Steam rises in
the headlights. Win and Charlie emerge then begin running back
toward Willie and Miranda who are nearing his truck.

They make it just as Charlie and Win approach them. Win helps
Miranda inside, throwing himself in after her, while Willie yells
something, pointing toward me in the darkness. Doors slam and
Willie guns it away as Charlie starts running in my direction.

Just as Charlie reaches me, a glow appears from the area of the
second SUV, five hundred feet away. A lone guy is starting a grass
fire, the strong wind fanning the flames. In seconds the blaze grows
with fierce intensity, reaching twenty feet in the air. The wind is

blowing the fire directly at us. Even in the winter, these grass fires can burn twenty or thirty miles before you can stop them. *My God,* I think. *I'm dead.*

Charlie reaches for me, but I yell at him. "Run, Charlie. Get out of here. You can make it." He stops for an instant, then starts running full out toward his steaming car three hundred feet away.

I'm alone. The fire is bearing down on me. I hear the roar over the sound of the wind. I have two minutes to live. Charlie's going to get the girl. He couldn't do anything, but I wish he'd tried. I want a hero for Miranda. I turn to face the fire. Not a good way to die. I'll try to make my ancestors proud.

Unbelievably, more fire begins burning in the direction of Charlie's car. The wind drives it in the opposite direction away from us. Charlie is racing back to me.

The fire is close, seventy-five yards. Sparks fill the air, starting to burn my face as I try to swat them away.

He's here. Hauling me up to standing, throwing me over his shoulder, half carrying-half dragging me, he heads back toward his fire.

The grass fire is close behind us, bearing down. Fifty yards. Twenty-five yards. Ten yards.

Somehow, we make it to the newly burned-out area of the backfire. Charlie's exhausted and stumbling. He staggers fifty feet inside the smoking blackened grass and collapses.

We both turn on our stomachs and put our arms around our heads.

"Face in the ash," I hear Charlie yell. "Face in the ash."

Fire diverts around us.

Gradually, the air cools.

After five minutes or so Charlie yells, "Okay."

We sit up coughing and wheezing. "Damn, Charlie. I'm surprised you could haul a big lug that far."

"Yeah," he says, coughing some more.

"You saved my life, Charlie."

"I fucking did, Lew. I'll deserve a blue necklace for that."

"I'd vote for you," I say, then cough my lungs out.

He pulls out a cell phone. Presently, I hear someone, probably

Hugh, yelling happy expletives. Charlie tells him our location then clicks off the phone.

"They'll wait until the smoke clears and the fire dies down enough for them to land. Fifteen minutes or so." He answers my unasked question. "Yeah. He's already in the air."

We're silent for a while, adjusting to this. Breathing deeply. Coughing a lot.

Finally, when I have some breath, I mutter, "I thought when you set that second fire you were trying to kill us faster."

"James Fenimore Cooper. Rescue fire. 1827.

"What?"

"It was first discussed in James Fenimore Cooper's novel, *The Prairie*—how settlers lived through grass fires. We wildland fire fighters are trained to use rescue fires in extreme situations." He takes off his belt and wraps it tightly around my thigh which is still oozing blood. "Win knows."

We cough some more.

"Did you realize if I was charcoal, you'd get the girl?"

He turns to me and says with a wry half-smile, "No. I wish I had."

We shake our heads.

"What happens now?" I ask.

"We catch the bad guys, tie them up, and burn a fire over them."

"After that," I ask.

He looks at me seriously. "I'm going back East. No other option that I can see."

"She loves you."

"It appears she loves you, too. I'm not inclined to battle it out again. With my fists or otherwise."

"This is a real fucked up mess."

"Yeah, well," Charlie sighs, then adds, "You forced the issue."

We sit silently. There really is nothing further to say, but finally I ask, "Two years ago, when Win had disappeared, if you could have slept with Lizzie... At the critical stage, would you have?"

He sighs. "As you can imagine, I've thought about it recently."

"Well?"

"If Lizzie could have been persuaded...? I really did love her.

It's taken me two years to get over her, and we never even went on a real date. But in answer to your question. There was one night... I'll never know what might have happened in the long run. She was still so much in love with Win, I thought it would torment her." He looks away. "Anyway, I backed off." He turns to stare pointedly at me. "And here I am again."

"You're the better man, Charlie. I wanted Mira more than I've ever wanted anything in my life. It seemed like my best shot. I hadn't thought pushing it..." I glance at him and see anger emerging. "...That pushing it would hurt her. I should have played it with more class. For her sake." I wait a moment then finish my thought. "I had my opportunity and blew it."

"Damn it," Charlie says, "I'm not the honorable hero. I'm playing the game, too. As hard and as deliberately as I can. Shut up now, will you?"

My leg begins to throb badly.

Ultimately, I ask one last question, "Do you still love her? Will you keep fighting to get her back?"

He winces. "I'll say this, and them I'm done talking. I don't know if that's possible?"

"Just so you know," I say, feeling his pain. "I love her. I wish I hadn't hurt her like this. I wish like hell. But if she'll have me, I'll make it my mission in life to make it up to her."

"I love her, too." Charlie replies, giving me a long frigid stare as the wall goes up between us. "I planned to marry her."

* * *

We sit waiting in silence. Soon, I hear the rotors. Someone shines a spotlight on the ground, finding us easily. Charlie waves them down. Dust and smoke gust into the air as the helicopter comes in for a landing a hundred feet from us. The rotors remain turning as a policeman jumps out and runs over. He and Charlie help me to my feet, and I sling my arms over their shoulders. The three of us make it to the helicopter where I'm loaded in on the floor. We're airborne in several minutes, heading toward Great Falls. Now that the heat's off, it's everything I can do to not scream out in pain during the rough ride. The wind is howling, throwing the helicopter from side to side, occasionally dropping it like a stone. First trying deep breaths, I resume panting, attempting unsuccessfully to relax.

Someone up front yells back they caught two bad guys. They're on their way to jail. I'm glad, but my leg is on fire. One more big jolt and I hear myself screaming.

ASH

Damn my hired sharpshooter. If he'd managed to get Black River from the tower, none of this would have happened. I rehearsed him over and over. 'Wait 'til dark,' I said. I must have repeated it twenty times. Then I'd waited, hoping I could just let the girl go if our target was already dead. If only...

After many minutes of agony, and repeatedly disinfecting the blade with my lighter, I manage to dislodge the bullet. Tearing my shirt into long strips, I wrap them over the oozing bullet hole with a wad of material, putting a pressure dressing on the wound. I'm sick unto death with fatigue, pain, and loss of blood.

If he still survives, I'm just blowing that fucker out of the water. I feel myself losing consciousness. Blacker edges surround objects in the dim light. Maybe the fire did the job on Black River, but even that sickens me. I hate desperation moves. The darkness closes in on me. They'll either find me or they won't. Maybe I'll die here.

CHAPTER 26

CHARLIE

I'M BACK RESTING in the emergency room area at Great Falls General where I was seen, treated, and released. Fortunately, I was offered a shower in the ambulance crew's quarters, several serial showers, and got most of the smoke and burned black off me. Hugh and Juli brought me some clean clothes. I look like my normal self except for the first and second degree burns to the backs of my hands and neck, and a little singed hair. My burns have been covered with antibiotic ointment and wrapped in gauze. Lew's leg has been x-rayed and he's now waiting for an operating room to be available in the surgical suite. I stood with him in the outer area of the ER until several minutes ago when they wheeled him into the inner area.

To say I have mixed emotions about Lew is an understatement. All of my preconceptions are in turmoil. Lew's still in a lot of pain. Moments ago, they gave him a shot of morphine and it's beginning to ease off. He gritted his teeth the whole trip down. I felt compassion for him. Some of the time.

I'm feeling good about the rescue. Lew's a big guy, carrying well over two hundred pounds on a six-three frame. It was close. Stumbling would have been a tragedy. We both would have been dead. If I hadn't had experience in the fire world, known about rescue fires, there would have been nothing to do but wait and die with him or run away. I didn't have matches or a lighter with me and had to bet everything on the disabled car's lighter working quickly enough. I lit some paper in the car and used that to light the second fire. I was lucky. And, as they say, luck is better than brains.

I'm waiting for the rest of my friends to be driven down in patrol cars, Miranda included. I don't know how much she knows. I suppose someone told her about Lew being shot. If things had been different, I would have had Hugh fly me up there, put my arms around her, and never let go. I'm frantically concerned about her. If those thugs hurt her, touched her... I'm experiencing an overwhelming desire for vengeance but overriding even that is the pain of loss. I haven't a clue what my emotions will be when I see her. She'll probably run to Lew to comfort him. I don't know if I can stick around for much of that.

Moving around a corner, I can see through glass doors leading into the surgical area. Lew is lying on a stretcher waiting with his arm over his eyes in the bright light. They had to call in an orthopedist, who talked to both of us about the extensive repair, bone grafts, metal plate and pins, and a long rehab. I check the wall clock for the hundredth time. They should be arriving any minute.

There's noise in the corridor beyond the outer doors. Willie and Miranda come running in with several cops. She sees me and stops in her tracks. Her hair is wild, her face blotchy. I can't tell what's in her eyes.

"Where's Lew?" she asks desperately.

I try to keep myself unemotional and point through the doors. She runs in that direction while Willie walks over to me.

"How is she," I ask him, attempting to control my voice. "Is she hurt?"

"She has some abrasions on her wrists. That seems to be the worst of it."

"And emotionally?" I ask.

"She cried a few times, but I think it was relief, not something more serious. She said they didn't hurt her." He studies me closely. "She'll be okay, Charlie. I don't think she's covering up anything terrible."

I turn my head away, sighing deeply several times, trying to relax. Willie puts his arm around my shoulders, saying quietly, "I took care of her. I held her all the way down. She wasn't alone."

I nod and turn back to look at him. "Thank you, Willie."

He stands up. "I'm going to check on Lew."

I stand up, too. I need to see her face. We walk around the corner and through the doors I see Miranda with both of her hands holding one of Lew's. They're both very serious as I see her bend down and kiss his cheek. He reaches up for her. I can't bear any more of this. Turning back around the corner, I walk some distance down the hall and lean against the wall. Tears come to my eyes. All I hoped for. All I believed to be true was a fantasy.

Resentment wells up, replacing compassion, a familiar coping mechanism. I knock my head back against the antiseptic pale-yellow tile, several times. The pain feels good. The loudness of the hit surprises me, causing me to stop. The hospital hall is silent. Sterile. Empty.

Fuck it all, I think. *Fuck it all*. Maybe there is no one for me. Maybe the family fortune Dad put together is a curse for his children. I add Miranda's face to a gallery of faces, receding into my past.

Pull yourself together, I tell myself. *Find Hugh. Get away. I want to go home.* Almost running, I reach the main lobby where Hugh sits, shoulders slouched, looking at his hands. He looks soberly up at me and starts to stand.

"Yes," I say. "I'm ready."

We reach the outer doors, when out of the corner of my eye I see movement. Screaming begins as Miranda runs up and physically pushes me away from Hugh. "Wait. Stop. Stop. I need to tell you something. Alone."

My gut freezes, eyes narrow, and I take her arm. "Okay, Miranda," I manage. "What do you need to tell me?"

I see her chin shudder then she tries to calm herself. "I have to tell you. When I woke up, I was so scared. I started screaming and thrashing. The man… The leader… He said if I continued to struggle, he would have to drug me."

My heart lurches but keep my face a mask. She's been running the words together, finally taking a gasping breath.

"Do you know what got me through it? Your face. I kept seeing your face. Not Lew's. I kept saying to myself, over and over, 'If I can live to see Charlie, tell him I love him. Just that. Just so he knows. I have to stay alive.'"

My throat is locked. I don't know what to say anyway. For hours, I've been fighting off images of her fighting for her life while trying not to descend into pure hysteria myself. Exactly what she said. Trying to stay alive.

"Please, Charlie, can you try to forgive me? You're the one. I was sure then. I'm sure now." She finally stops, overcome with emotion.

I try to understand what I'm feeling. A part of me wants to turn on my heel, make a sarcastic comment, and leave her hanging. But she's been hurt so much already. I want to help. I want to bring her to a warm place and forget all this.

"What about Lew?" I manage.

She swallows. "I won't see him. I promise. I just told him, Charlie. I told him I love you. That I need you." She pauses. "He'll always be someone I deeply care about, but he's not backup. If it doesn't work between us…" She puts her hand on my arm. "I won't run back to him. I'll have to earn your trust. I've broken it."

I can't reach out to her. I want to, but my arms feel infinitely heavy, frozen in place. I can't see her well. She seems to be offering me everything I hoped for, but how can I believe it? The hideous doubt has returned. I thought I'd finally banished it. Her voice seems far away. I can't hear her. There's a roar in my head and I take a step away.

"No. Don't do it, Charlie," she pleads.

I raise my hands to my head as if to ward off the noise.

"Don't give up on us," she pleads. "You came back to find me. You must care."

I fall away another step. My old words resurface. *Do you love around?* My feelings are ash, burned out—cold coals. Maybe past fanning to life. I look past her toward the front door and see Hugh, thirty feet away, frozen in place, watching.

Charlie," she says, grabbing my jacket lapels, shaking me. "Maybe... If you just go through the motions. Maybe it will come back."

That focuses me. I look back into her eyes. "Sex?" I mutter. "Is that what you're saying? Just like turning on a key?" I'm watching this conversation from a spot above myself, watching a play. I have no idea what the ending will be. I'm finding it hard to focus on the plot. "What is it you want me to do, Miranda?"

"Just don't leave, Charlie. Not again. Can't we go somewhere? And talk?"

I'm trying to think. It's hard with the roar still swirling in the background. I look at her face, blotchy red and pale at the same time. I seemingly loved this woman, minutes ago. But I can't feel it. I keep seeing her kiss Lew's cheek. Looking at him lovingly... Strangely, consigning Miranda to the fading pictures of has-beens is what hurts the worst—all those faces disappearing into my past. I look over at Hugh. He looks in pain. I can't understand why.

"Give me a minute," I say flatly.

I walk over to Hugh. "I need some time here. Can you fly Juli and Tony back to somewhere? DC? Somewhere?"

I get the feeling there is a lot he wants to say as he takes a few steps toward the parking lot. He stops. Abruptly he turns, walks back to me, and grabs my arm. "Remember what the Knight Templar said in that Indiana Jones movie? 'He chose poorly.' Try harder, okay?"

"Okay," I repeat mechanically, my brow furrowed.

"Be smart," he says. "Be fucking-ass smart."

I watch Hugh walk to the rental car and get in. Trying to gather my wits, I walk back to her. "I want to leave. But I guess I owe it to someone to figure this out."

"Thank you," she says quietly.

"Don't go back to that unequal place," I burst out. "I don't want that either."

She winces. I can't bear to look at that. She stands there silently. Waiting.

"Let's go to a hotel. I can't think beyond that."

"I'll need to talk to Dad first."

"Hugh's flying him back to Silver Spring."

"Dad won't go. He understands we need to resolve this. He'll wait here until… He's afraid for me. He wants to be here."

"He's a very good man."

"Yes."

We check into a local hotel. Neither of us is hungry, but I order some food brought up. I don't want to leave this room for any reason, not until we understand each other.

We sit in chairs across from each other as she waits for me to say something. It takes some time to organize my thoughts. At least the roaring in my head has stopped. "I was afraid," I hear myself saying coldly, "when I thought you might be dead. I didn't know if I wanted to try to have a life if you were dead."

"Charlie…?"

"But now everything has changed. I don't want to look at you. I despise you somehow. I want to get away from you."

"That's because I've hurt you so much."

I nod. The lack of emotion is horrible. I feel coldly sick.

She gets up from her chair and kneels on the floor in front of me. "Charlie, you've got to believe me. You were right. I don't want to be the bad guy, the guilty one. I've done nothing wrong except to try to find love. I never wanted to hurt anyone. I've done my best. I never asked for the life I've lived these last few weeks. I've felt great love for two men." Her voice rises. "I've discovered I want you enough to risk hurting you. I won't let you walk away again easily. If you leave this time, you'll know what you left on the table."

"Do you understand," I mutter, "how deeply you hurt me?"

"Will hurting me now make that any better?"

"Maybe."

She inches a little closer to me and lays her head on my leg.

She closes her eyes and sighs. I can't bear to reach out to touch her, but her warm cheek on my leg feels so good. I hear a voice in my head saying, "She's faking this, it's the money after all," but I push it down, and down again. Instead, I say coldly, "Miranda, go lie on the bed."

She stands up and goes to the bed and lies down. Her eyes lock on mine.

I stand over her for several minutes. Finally, I sit beside her, lifting one hand to her cheek, stroking it mechanically as I move my other hand to her leg. She's not the woman I love, she's a phantom. I search her face for another betrayal, moving my hand up her thigh, higher and higher. I pause. This feels immoral. An assault.

"Go ahead, Charlie," she says. "I can wait to see the look in your eyes when you love me. I'll hang on."

I look down at her, hardly breathing. I feel so cold and alone. If she does really love me, I could kill it now, no matter what she says. My hand on her leg starts to shake. Finally, I manage, "Dear God in heaven, Miranda. Can you hang on? Please hang on." I force my arms up to and around her shoulders. I pull her slowly to me. I feel her arms wrapping around my chest. We hold each other silently for many minutes.

"How long can you hang on?" I ask. "I'm going to take a hell of a lot of convincing."

"Until we are old people," she whispers.

I cover us both with a warm blanket and we huddle together, each with our own fears and memories of the last few days, but at least we can begin to comfort each other. It's enough for now.

CHAPTER 27

LEW

I'M LYING ON the stretcher waiting for the orderly to wheel me into surgery. My leg hurts like hell, compounding my pain over losing Miranda. *God*, I think, *at least she exists in the world*. At least that. Willie is standing with me, being a pal. And I need a pal. Somehow Willie always knows that. I hope they put me under anesthesia soon. Loss of consciousness is appealing.

Groaning, I reposition my leg to relieve the pain, but it makes it worse, and I begin panting. As I look up, I see Charlie's sister, glaring at me from the doorway, her long reddish hair glowing under a ceiling spotlight. I shut my eyes for a long moment then open them again. She's still glaring. I'm livid.

I motion to her to come closer, but she only stares frigidly, not moving a muscle. I gesture repeatedly until she saunters over.

"So, what the hell is your problem?" I ask.

"No problem," she answers. "I was enjoying the view."

"You like watching people in pain?" I snarl.

"Depends on the person. I like it when the universe evens things up."

I glance at Willie, who I see is beginning to enjoy himself.

"Look, Lady," I say. "You don't know anything about the people here, what we mean to each other. Why don't you take your billions and go annoy someone else?" My leg feels like it's falling off, tearing tissue as it goes.

"I know enough to know when someone's been a real top-of-the-line ass," she says. "You're a real winner. Charlie used to talk about you, considered you his friend. Not only did you try to seduce his girl, you come out here while people are trying to kill you and endanger everyone."

It takes a lot to get me really riled but I feel myself crossing that line. Besides, she's hitting very close to home. "God damn it,"

I mutter. "Who elected you judge of moral behavior?" I pause to gather my wits. "What's your problem? Is the professional women's soccer circuit lacking in real men? Are you frustrated? With all your money, can't you buy a little sex?"

Willie's sipping coffee and spits out a mouthful at that.

"You pompous moron," she slashes back. "I'd hate to be your bodyguards. I bet you go around doing dangerous things for fun, letting those poor suckers dodge your bullets. If you're so important, why don't you go sit on a throne at the NSA and give everyone else a break?"

That does it. Besides, I remember Aamad, who I did put in danger, and of course Miranda. Rising up on the stretcher, intending to shake my fist in her face, I wrench my leg instead and end up screaming in pain.

She smiles sadistically and walks away.

"Wow!" says Willie, as I slump back on the stretcher in a cold sweat. "Impressive dame."

"Impressive, my ass," I say, still panting in agony. "She's a rich bitch who likes stomping on people's faces."

"At least she's loyal to her brother," Willie responds. "Besides, all that energy could be redirected." He raises his eyebrows suggestively.

"In my next lifetime." We hear footsteps coming in our direction. "If she tries to go in the operating room after me, shoot her. I don't want her anywhere near me when I'm unconscious."

I wake up in the recovery room and blink my eyes. Two muscular men in suits with obvious shoulder holsters and alert looks stand near the door. At the end of the bed Ross hovers.

"Boss? What?"

He shakes his head. "I've got to keep a lid on this before I start getting movie offers. Do you have any idea what *low profile* means?" But his smile takes the edge off his words.

My lips are dry as I try to clear my throat to speak.

"Lew. Lew. Lew. God love you, but this is the way it's going to be. You will be guarded 24/7 and you will come back to DC and remain in protective custody while your leg heals up with all the high-level medical care we can arrange. Do you have any problem with that?"

"No, sir," I mumble, sleepily.

"We should have our entire network developed and ready to start training foreign allies by the late spring with your help. Until then, get used to guys with guns in your bedroom. Get it?"

I nod seriously.

"All right then. As soon as your brain works, I want to hear the entire story. I mean, did you really rescue the girl out a back window and hold bad guys off with a gun while they were shooting at you? And what about the dynamite?"

Oh, I think. *That was what Willie used.* I grin sheepishly at Ross.

He pulls over a chair and sits at my side. "Lew," he says, "I admit it. I care about you on a very personal level. You're an old-fashioned hero, and a breath of fresh air in the morass of the capital. I don't want anything to happen to you."

"I can't believe you flew out here, sir," I say.

"I can't believe I did, either. But I wanted to make sure you were okay. Just rest and get well."

I try to organize my thoughts, then add contritely, "You were right. I should have stayed away." I pause. "I'm really sorry."

"Yeah. I let my sympathy get in the way of my good sense. Doesn't happen very often."

"Did they get the bad guys?"

"We interviewed Miranda. There were three men involved. The youngest one seems to be the ringleader and we don't have him in custody yet. We have a good description. It seems you may have shot him. We found a great deal of blood. The other two were apprehended. It's possible they were set up as decoys while the main man got away. It appears it was the Russians or surrogates who were behind the scenes on this."

"When can Miranda be safe?"

"You need to get your head straight and finish this project. Should take several months. Now that the whole thing is out in the open, she shouldn't be vulnerable as a bargaining chip, but we won't guess on that. She'll have around the clock protection. We've talked to Tony. He's an NSA guy. He understands and isn't completely horrified."

"I wish you had the last kidnapper."

"We'll get him, Lew. The entire Federal network is working on this, CIA, FBI. We'll get him."

"He'll be desperate. If it is Russia, they don't deal generously with failures."

"Try to relax and get well. Miranda will be guarded like Princess Di."

I try not to point out how that turned out.

"Don't worry about anything. We'll look after your girl. I promise."

I wince at that last comment. I can't help it. My eyes close and I hear Ross stand up. I feel him pat my shoulder as he leaves.

It's early the next morning and I've pushed the magic morphine machine, feeling it start to work, when Charlie walks in alone.

"Still alive, I see," he says.

"Not much competition, though," I say. "And anyway, Miranda told me you won."

"We have a long way to go, Lew, before anyone wins."

"Still, you have a chance. I was told I didn't."

We're quiet together thinking.

"We're flying back East as soon as I leave here," he says finally. We're going to try our hardest to make it work. It's probably me fighting myself that's the problem."

"Charlie, listen to me. Despite what she said, she does love me. And the fact that she loves you more means a hell of a lot. She told me not to hope, that she was going to risk everything for you. I'd give anything, anything, to be in your shoes. Don't blow it. But I won't exist for her on this planet while you try to work it out."

"Okay, Lew. I get it."

"But it's not all or none."

"I don't understand."

"Love is a gift, Charlie. You don't win it all and get to keep it. And you can't lock it up. It just is."

He looks at me for a long time. Finally, he nods.

"Charlie, listen. Miranda's at risk. You have to help her be safe. I'm out of commission here and I'll be guarded 24/7. They won't be able to take me out now." I pause. "Getting at Miranda is still their best chance to influence me." We look at each other with shared anxiety.

"Ross and the FBI have already talked to our family," Charlie explains. "If they need us, we'll coordinate efforts. Hugh's ready to sleep in a bag on the floor by her bed if it would help."

"One more guy with the hots for Miranda," I mutter sadly.

Charlie nods and gives me a wry smile.

"I wish you well, then," I say.

"I almost believe you mean it."

"I almost believe it, myself."

CHAPTER 28

MIRANDA

HUGH IS FINISHING his pre-flight check and the plane is full of jet fuel. I've called my almost-new boss at home to put the job on hold until this situation is resolved. He was gracious about it. Said they'd take me whenever they could get me. But he also admitted that having a new employee with lingering issues like mine could be a problem. Let alone the bodyguards with guns.

Hugh is wearing his usual professional uniform of a pilot's tailored blue suit coat with gold shoulder bars, and shorts. He even tried to get me interested in a joke about a farmer's daughter and a pilot, but I put him off. We're both feeling better. I even told Hugh that he should stop flaunting his muscular hairy legs. Charlie and I agreed he's coming around. He's been very depressed—for Hugh. This whole affair has apparently been very hard on him. I've been told he gave Charlie six months to resolve our situation, or he was going to make a move on me, himself. Charlie agreed that seemed fair. He also said he didn't think it was a joke, although with Hugh it's hard to know for sure. Charlie appears much like his old self, but I continually catch him sighing, over and over, and staring fixedly at things.

I'm going back to stay at my parents' house but with security outside 24/7. Besides, I'm not sure if I'll be welcomed back with open arms at Charlie's. Everyone in his family knows about my indecisiveness. Also, we're going to be under enough pressure to sort out our feelings.

I'm looking forward to sleeping on the plane with Charlie's arms around me. I'm tired and restless. If I let my eyes close, I immediately have bad dreams. It's mid-morning and we'll be in the air soon. Charlie just got off the phone with the orthopedist who did Lew's surgery yesterday. It went well. Dad will stay in Montana for several extra days, to be with Lew. I've discussed with Dad Charlie's and my decision to try to make it work, so he decided Lew needed his support more.

In addition, Lew's mom is down from Browning. He'll stay two more nights in the hospital, and then, if he's well enough, will be flown directly back to DC together with Dad on a military plane. Ross, Lew's boss, told me he'll be sequestered with more bodyguards until the project completion sometime in late April. In the meantime, he'll start on rehab with a private therapist.

Charlie's sister, Juli, will stay out here for a few days. The Curchins have family friends near Missoula, and, frankly, I don't think she wanted to make small talk with me on the flight back. I got the impression she was not too happy with me in our first short encounter.

Sitting alone in the back of the plane, I'm mulling over my conversation with Hugh. He sat me down and told me how Charlie saved Lew in the fire. I've always known what a quality guy Charlie is, but it made me feel this is an impossible uphill fight. I remember how I felt in those early days when I felt unequal. Now I feel unworthy. Why would he even want to give me a second chance, especially considering his past?

Charlie approaches from the cockpit after a discussion with Hugh, smiling down at me. "All set?"

I nod uncomfortably.

"What's up?" he says.

"Why, Charlie? Why have you decided to risk it?"

Sitting down beside me, he buckles up, then looks at me seriously. "Because it's extremely difficult to find what Juli calls a special person. My history has been to run when I'm convinced I'm being used. You know that. We've talked it into the ground," he says, taking my hand. "For once, I'm not going to run, Miranda. If it doesn't work out it doesn't but I'm going to find out the old-fashioned way. If I get hurt, it can't be any worse than what Lew's going through. Besides…" he smiles. "I wanted at least to get some sex out of the deal."

I smile back. "I thought that was probably it. When can we start?"

"Ten minutes after takeoff. That's what the back room is for. And one more thing. You've behaved strangely for a woman who is pretending to love me and is really after my money. Outside of kicking me in the groin, you've done everything humanly possible to discourage me, turn me off. You must really like me."

"Yeah, Charlie. I really like you."

Before I know it, Charlie is unbuckling. "Come on, kid," he says. "I'll race you."

I sit down on the bed then lie on my back. The low hum of the engines and the soft vibration of the aircraft produce a soothing insulated backdrop. We probably should take more time, but now it seems like I've been waiting my whole life. I guess we'll see how it goes. Charlie switches off the intercom. His eyes are soft and warm staring down at me, yet suddenly somehow distant.

"I've waited so long," I say. "I'm exhausted waiting. Please kiss me."

His arms hang at his side, his face undecipherable. "I don't know how to begin," he murmurs. "We've been so close to it, and we've been through hell. It's almost too much."

"How do I prove I love you? Maybe I should beat it into you with my fists." I laugh softly at the image. "But I'm not a very violent person."

He leans over me and touches my cheek with the back of his hand. "I feel like I'm diving into a dark pool. I don't know how deep I can go and survive."

I reach up to brush the hair out of his eyes. "Vinnie told me to be sure you would fully trust me—that down the line it could cause serious trouble. For once I'll disagree with her. Even if you can't be completely sure, I'll risk it." I search his eyes. "Because I'm sure of myself."

He looks at me for a long time, sitting quietly, his face showing anguish. I want to take his hand and hold it to me, but I hold off, waiting. He looks at me, frozen in time and position.

"Tell me," I say softly.

"I want to believe you," he says. "I want to believe you so much."

I ache with the pain he's keeping alive. Finally taking my hand, he turns it over and kisses my palm deeply, his eyes smoldering over its edge. Reaching up, I pull him slowly down to me until our lips touch. I don't feel the passion I've been searching for so desperately. Running my hands up his body, I start unbuttoning his shirt. His eyes finally begin to darken with desire. Still his hands remain distant.

Taking his hand, I place it on my chest where I'm sure he can feel my heart pounding. His other hand moves behind my back, pulling me up to him. I want to give him pleasure. I would do anything for this man. But more than that, this man deserves everything I have to give. His eyes burn, holding mine, not yet letting go. Not yet giving in.

Please, Charlie, I think. *Trust me.*

Time is altered, stretching and shrinking, a plane flying through time zones, adding to the unreality of our situation. Moments pass until I realize I'm holding my breath. At last, his face relaxes, relinquishing the tight control he's held himself in. "Miranda," he confesses, "I do love you. God help me."

Clothes are shed. His hands unrelenting, as they move to the center of my desire for him. I rise up against him. No hesitation at last. Yes. He fills me forcefully. I feel the explosion building inside me as I give myself over to pure passion. And fly over the edge.

Afterwards, I fall into a deep sleep with his arms around me. My sleep is untroubled, safe, and when I near wakefulness, I feel him next to me.

Later we're talking the simple nonsense of lovers, my body constantly touching his as I wrap my leg over his, holding him. "Charlie, I promise. We can make the miracle work."

He touches my face. "Did I ever tell you about Juli's and my agreement?"

I shake my head.

"Right after Todd's death, we agreed to meet if we were still alone in five years to help each other find special people. She has the same problem I have trusting. I'm hoping I won't have to show up," he smiles at me.

"She's so vivacious and beautiful. I can't believe she can't find her own men."

"That's not the problem, of course. The guys she might be seriously interested in often run the other way. She's intimidating as it is, plus the assets and the looks. Maybe she could use some help. She hasn't had a serious relationship in years."

"I'll give it some thought later. For now, I'm going to use all my extra energy convincing you her help won't be necessary." I reach up for his neck, attempting to pull him down to me.

Despite himself, he grimaces, unexpectedly serious. "I've been through hell too, you know. Both the kidnapping and the thing with Lew."

"Remember you asked me to choose? I thought I couldn't live without you, but I'd just hurt you, I wanted to be completely sure. The thought of causing you enduring pain... Well, I just couldn't, and then I almost died of the agony I caused both of us. I've made a real mess of this. I'm so sorry."

He nods, then smiles at me. "And now I have debts to pay."

"Debts?"

"Well, I don't know if you've talked to Vinnie, but she helped me through the deep hole. I'm getting her a new mattress for her guestroom. Besides, knowing you, I might need it again."

"What else?"

"Win's aunt's car is toast. It was a 1974 Pontiac Catalina and will be hard to replace so I told her to pick out a new car, within reason, of course. A Bugatti would stand out in Cut Bank. She's looking at a Volkswagen Jetta Hybrid."

I snuggle against his strong chest and feel safe.

He sighs deeply. "Tell me what happened? With those men."

"I tried several times to talk to them, become a person to them, hoping it might make a difference down the line. Two of them were emotionless, almost never said anything to me directly, one-or-two-word orders." I stop to think a minute. "But the leader. I still can't figure him out. He was frightening, but never cruel."

"Tell me more. Frightening?"

"He was almost protective, made me believe he could be reasoned with. He asked personal questions about my family. He even tried to figure out my relationships with both of you. He seemed especially troubled when I told him about Lew's past—how important he was to his family. How his father died when he was young, and he had to become the man of the house; and about his older sister who acted like a mother. He became increasingly affected, so I kept trying. I thought I'd found a soft spot. Then suddenly, like reaching some limit, he became extremely upset, leaving abruptly, and slamming the door."

Charlie shudders. "Did they…take care of you?"

"I had energy bars and juice, and I was warm. Willie told me you were terribly worried about that."

"It tormented me. I kept seeing you shivering in the cold."

"I love you," I respond.

He rolls my hand over and kisses my fingers. There is so much feeling in it that my eyes fill.

"What did the leader say to you?" he asks.

"Like I said, he was the scariest because he could make me relax and talk to him. Then he'd suddenly clam up and turn cold. He was so changeable. At times he seemed almost scared. He told me over and over, more times than were necessary, that he'd let me go. He promised me. Like he really meant it. But if I pleaded with him to spare Lew, he…disconnected."

He hesitates, then asks, "Do you want him dead?"

"He may already be dead."

"Still…?"

"He's trying to kill Lew," I vent with sudden passion. "Yes. I want him… Gone."

After several moments of silence, Charlie gathers himself. "I have to ask, Miranda. Did they…?"

"No, Charlie. Rest your mind on that. No one touched me or hurt me in any way. But they made no effort to hide their faces. Despite what I'd been told, that made me terrified they'd kill me. But maybe I didn't matter after all. Maybe I was just a means of getting to Lew. He was the one they wanted to kill. Early on, the other two men talked about killing him as if I wasn't there. Details. Can you imagine hearing that? That's what made me hysterical."

"I won't stop worrying until they get the bastard; or hopefully find his body. Even then…" I see him swallow. "When? How, did they get you?"

"It was right after you left, several minutes, like they were waiting for you to leave. I'd gone into the bedroom and was lying

face down on the bed, crying. I heard a sound behind me, and…
And I thought you'd come back." I can't look at him. "Someone
held me down on the bed with his knee and put a needle in my leg.
I never saw his face. I woke up in that room where Lew found me."

"I should have stayed. I shouldn't have left you alone."

"You would be dead if you'd stayed. Those guys were going to
get me, one way or the other."

He's quiet for a long time. "It took Lew to find you. If there was
justice, he should…"

"Look, Charlie," I interrupt him, "I'm not a prize in a war game.
I'll always love him and be grateful, but it's you I want to share my
life with. If you'll let me."

He presses his lips to my neck, sighing, and pulls me to him
again.

* * *

Sometime later, I hear the buzzer that Hugh wants to talk.
Charlie flips the intercom switch. "Yes, Hugh?" he asks.

"We're about twenty minutes away from DC, about ready to
start the descent. Any further instructions?"

"Let me," I say.

Charlie gives me a look of surprise, then nods.

"Captain McManus," I say formally.

"Yes, ma'am," he replies.

"We're having a nice time back here. I want you to change the
light bulb."

I leave the intercom on to hear Hugh laughing. Charlie gives me
an odd look as the plane banks sharply to the left.

PART III

CHAPTER 29

LEW

AFTER THE LAST six months being in relative lockdown, and the completion of our international security project, I'd been looking forward to two-weeks vacation. Surprisingly, Ross called me into his office to suggest I take a full month to relax and recharge. I could have kissed him. On many levels I needed it. He knew, but then he's been in the boilermaker for twenty years. I decide to drop in on Tony to celebrate.

I deserve a party now that my high-level contribution to international hacking security has been launched. The monitoring grid I helped develop is firmly in place with international covert acclaim. Ross believes the fait accompli, as he puts it, removes me from the targeted position. It feels fantastic! I love my job, but I need some wild time.

I haven't been home to the reservation since we rescued Miranda last November. Of course, she wouldn't have needed rescuing if it wasn't for me. I'm still living with guilt over that. The difference between recreational sex and what I felt for Miranda was so great I've more or less given up women to figure it all out. I laugh at myself. I'm not completely virtuous. My shattered leg took a long time to heal and the boys with the bulging shoulder holsters definitely put a crimp on my love life.

They never caught the third kidnapper. It seems reasonable that he was spirited away to Russia or some such place. That's what Ross believes. Spies are professionals and don't generally hold grudges. Danger is part of their job description. I could have gone home before with protection, but I didn't want to endanger anyone. I hate it that Juli, the fire-breathing dragon, was the one who pointed it out to me.

We all, including my bodyguards, carried computer-generated pictures of the guy Miranda described for months—a series of photos with the guy in multiple disguises. Nothing. I wish they'd caught him. They found an extensive amount of blood at the scene, and neither of the guys they caught were injured. They also found the second rental SUV with significantly more. They can't imagine he got away on his own after losing that volume of blood. He must have had help. I don't like loose ends, but Ross says that's typical. It's relatively easy to spirit one guy across our porous border. Or maybe the guy really is dead.

Tony told me that Miranda doesn't have nightmares anymore and for that I'm grateful. I know from talking to Tony and Tommy that Miranda and Charlie seem deeply in love. I've kept my promise to stay away, planning to fake casual friendship when the need arises. If I could find someone to care deeply about, maybe it would help, but other women I've met recently seem two-dimensional.

As I pull around the last corner, I see a new Tesla parked in Tony's driveway and my heart sinks. Maybe I should keep driving. I haven't seen either Charlie or Miranda since last November, although I've talked to Charlie on the phone. He seems normal to me, no longer holding a grudge. But why should he? He won.

With concentrated effort, I pull in the driveway, take a deep breath, then walk up the sidewalk to the house. I often spend time at Tony's, watching sports, hanging out. Until today, I had to drop in with several bodyguards who hung out on the porch while I visited. I'm so used to being escorted that I wait for the boys, then laugh to myself when I remember I've been allowed off the leash.

Yelling the Blackfeet greeting, "Oki", like I usually do, I take the three front steps in a single leap. My leg's coming back.

"Come on in, Lew," I hear Tony yell back. "I've got company."

I walk in self-consciously, trying to appear relaxed. It's hopeless. Charlie stands, walks over to me, and holds out a hand. We shake. Besides my own personal turmoil, I've always liked Charlie a lot. And he did save my hulking self in the fire. Miranda tries to keep seated on the couch, finally gives it up, and runs over to give me a big hug. I put my arms around her, glancing at Charlie. He nods. We're cool.

It's been a long time, so we start to catch up.

"Where are your buddies?" asks Tony.

"Hopefully following some other clueless fool. I'm just starting a month's leave. The boss insisted. I'm planning on spending most of it in Montana." I grin. "Besides, now that the Rena spy-complex has been busted, they consider me in the green danger range rather than red. That's even below yellow which means I'm not considered an active target."

We all shake our heads. I was barely avoiding assassination because Rena unknowingly supplied my location. Stephanie, her roommate, turned out to be an informant. When Rena discussed my plans or whereabouts with her new friend, she immediately contacted her network who targeted me. Jeez. You can't make this stuff up. Stephanie's disappeared and Rena's sorry.

"How's your leg?" Charlie asks.

"It still aches at night if I overdo it but I've started running. What are you doing here, Charlie? It's fire season."

"Miranda and I are back, just over the weekend. It's Mom's birthday tomorrow, and we're flying up to Philly tonight after watching Juli's game this afternoon. Come with us. We have V.I.P. passes."

"I'll pass on that one. She's ahwahtsouptsii."

"What?" asks Charlie.

"Crazy," I say, with an appropriate facial expression.

He laughs and we all join in.

"Your sister and I don't have a relaxed relationship," I say. "The last time I saw her I was lying on a hard stretcher awaiting surgery, and we were screaming insults."

"Come on, Lew," Charlie says. "You have seventy pounds on her. I doubt she'd beat you up. You don't have to run onto the field and be her best buddy. She won't even notice you." When I hesitate, Charlie adds, "Tony's going too. You've been a model ex-boyfriend. I'm not worried."

"Thanks a lot," I say with an edge to it. We all laugh.

"Come on, Lew," adds Tony. "I'll buy you a beer. It'll be fun to see her play in person."

"I was coming over here to watch the game. Oh, fine. Besides, I need to get used to seeing you two together sometime."

"Atta guy," says Miranda. "We'll have a great time, and you

can hide out in the car if we go over to say hi."

We sit down and trade stories about our extended family of friends. "What are you doing, Miranda? Workwise?"

"I've been doing consulting work for the law firm in Great Falls. They're always over-loaded with plenty of work for me, but I'm considering going another direction."

"Bruce said something about working on an inmate rehab project together."

"We've been tossing some ideas around over beers and reached the point of having some serious discussions. He and Alec thought this up and they could use a lawyer to handle some of the foundation paperwork and various contracts. I'm very excited. The Curchins may get involved at some point, but I don't know if you're aware that Alec, himself, has substantial assets. They came indirectly from Bruce's father."

"I remember hearing something about that, but none of us ever knew any details."

"Alec has, how shall I put it—a legacy that he wants to put to some noble use. Bruce, as you know, has intimate experience with the prison system. He's the one who thought this up. Alec has training in the legal profession, but he doesn't want to draw attention to his past by doing the legal details."

"So? What are you considering?"

"You may not know that this country has the highest percentage of incarcerated people in the world, with Russia and Rwanda running a distant second. That's deplorable. Our country has essentially thrown away hundreds of thousands of lives, even turned prisons into private for-profit businesses. What we're planning is a joint pilot project with the Montana prison system. We want to create a structured, tiered parole system that selects deserving individuals and provides in-depth education, specific training, and a jobs program. We want to start with young men who got into trouble at a very young age and never had a chance."

Once more I'm overwhelmed with who I let slip through my fingers. "Mira, that's just incredible. I'm so proud of you."

"Well, we haven't gotten very far yet, but that's what I'll be doing while Charlie's doing fire work. We're flying out Monday."

"You want a lift, Lew?" Charlie offers. "When are you going out?"

"I'm open. I'd love a free ride. Sure."

"And you'll come to the game?" she asks.

"If Tony will protect me."

"Stick with me, Lew. I've got mace if the worst happens."

"I'd kind of like to see that," I say, "but I won't get my hopes up."

* * *

We join the crowd pouring into the stands and find a spot in a roped off area near the mid-field line. I easily spot Juli's reddish hair, braided in a thick pigtail down her back. Charlie mentioned she's a co-captain, so she's running around happily yelling encouragement and warming up with goal kicks. Charlie goes down and leans over the railing, trying to attract her attention. When she's not disturbing my peace with expletives, she can be charming, I guess. And I suppose she had cause to hate me. Just one more lesson in the world of women. I'm thirty-one as of last month. Too old for stupid mistakes, plus I get very little sympathy.

The noise from the stands increases as both sides line up for start of play. I've seen Juli on TV several times. She's magnificent. She has incredible leg strength, can kick distance with accuracy, plus she's a strategic player. And she has one of the most accurate corner kicks I've seen a woman do. Also, I enjoy grinning to myself when she gets flattened occasionally.

CHAPTER 30

JULI

I HEAR MY NAME called and see Charlie leaning over the rail, grinning. After I blow him a kiss, he points into the stands until I see Miranda waving wildly with Tony next to her. Next to him sits another tall man. When I focus on him, I utter an expletive under my breath. It's an automatic thing I do whenever I think of him. It's that damn Lew Black River, probably my least favorite person on the planet.

Even I know it's gotten irrational. Charlie and Miranda are blindingly happy. There's no need for me to defend and protect my brother from Native American seductions if there ever was. All the same, he triggers strong emotions—like the desire to kill. I have no idea why he's here. The feeling is mutual. Miranda admitted to me recently on the phone that everyone makes a concerted effort not to mention his name around me and vice versa. We both go ballistic—her words.

I used to feel pretty much the same way about Miranda, but she won me over. She has this understated but persistent way of calling me out on my negative emotions, even directed at her. We started laughing about it and never stopped. I gave in. Charlie's right. She's family now and I love her. Simple.

This other jerk though… Everyone tells me I should let it go. Even Charlie has been encouraging Miranda to get us together, for fireworks if nothing else, which says everything about how confident he is in their relationship. I just hope Black River doesn't want to bond after the game. I decide I'll channel my disgust onto the field. I'm thinking I'm going to have a great first half.

We've got a minute or so before taking the field and, against my will, I resume dwelling on Michael Meredith. Last week I pulled the plug on yet another relationship. I'm still bummed about it. He'd been the first serious relationship I'd had in—well—a long time. I even called Charlie.

"Hi, kid. How's your love life?" His standard opening.

I started to tell him, then surprisingly couldn't talk.

"Jules?"

"I ended it, Charlie. With Michael, I mean."

"What happened?"

"That's why I called."

"Go ahead."

"We were just leaving Mom and Dad's. We'd had a nice dinner, and then we were on the way to the airport so I could fly down here for the game. We started talking about general stuff, you know, a vacation to Italy in the spring. I wanted to do some hiking in the Italian Alps before settling in at a resort and…"

"Yes?"

"He kept redirecting the conversation to working for the firm. That's okay. It was in the works. Dad and I've talked about it several times. Michael was…is talented. He was going to start in a training position. Dad liked him."

"You liked him. It's been going on five months now."

"I think I misjudged him."

"Are you sure?"

"Listen. See what you think. I wasn't in the mood to talk much about him working for Dad, so I'd let him ramble about it for a while, then changed the subject back to Italy. Several times. He called me on it. We got into a fight about me always having my own way, not listening, dominating our conversations.

"It got worse and worse. I was losing it, too. It wasn't only him. Anyway, it escalated. It was like a dam blowing out, maybe for both of us. I've been trying to keep my temper capped. I've wanted someone to care about me. You know that."

"I know, Jules."

He pulled the car over to the side of the road. We were yelling by that time."

"Juli, everyone has fights."

"You and Miranda don't."

"We don't talk about it. Miranda was yelling at me last night about not fighting. She said I'm a wuss."

"You are. Do you ever even raise your eyebrows at Miranda?"

"She's so cute she makes me laugh at her."

"Damn it, Charlie. Just listen."

"Sure. Sorry."

"I was trying to do what I always tell you, trying to look at things his way. But he kept pushing it. The fight got personal. Things were said. He… Charlie, he grabbed my arms and squeezed. Hard, for a long time. He was furious. I have bruises. I was scared."

There's silence on the phone.

"I'd been terrible. Yelling. Maybe it was my fault. I don't know. And he's been calling, every hour. What do you think?"

"Don't ever see him again."

* * *

I snap back to see Charlie winding his way back through the crowd to Miranda and find Black River standing next to her. I grit my teeth, mostly from habit. Why I'm holding to such extreme animosity for him mystifies me. I'm the one who's vulnerable. My perspective on things is suddenly muddled. Maybe hating Lew has been a diversion from other more fundamental issues.

CHAPTER 31

LEW

THE GAME HAS stayed close with the lead switching back and forth. It's now inside the last few minutes, tied 2-2, when Juli takes a pass on the right side of the goal, positions the ball, and plants her left foot to cross the ball to a forward in front of the net. A defender from the other side comes in to block the shot, loses her balance, and falls into the side of Juli's planted left leg. Both women go down, but Juli doesn't get up.

"Shit," Charlie mutters under his breath.

The coach and a trainer come running out. After several minutes, they get her to a sitting position but even from this far away I can see her grimacing.

Now she's up on one leg with her arms around two trainers' shoulders as she's assisted off the field. I know enough about sports injuries to know that holding a leg up in the air is not a good sign.

In several minutes, the play resumes. One trainer has already assisted Juli onto a stretcher and transported her toward a waiting ambulance. Charlie has gone over to talk to the emergency crew, putting his head inside in the back door to talk to Juli.

It takes off, no siren, and heads towards the center of town.

"I need to be with her," he says, running back. "Can we all drive to the hospital, and you can drop me off? You can go back to Tony's, and I'll catch a cab when I know what's going on."

"What do you think is wrong?" I ask.

"She thinks it's a cruciate. She's had one torn before. If so, it's nine months or more of rehab. I don't know if she'll want to try to play at this level again. Damn it all to hell. She's such a beautiful player."

Miranda takes his hand. "Come on, Charlie. Let's go."

"Maybe it was just stretched," I say. "Let's hope."

We follow the ambulance route to the hospital. Miranda is

driving while Charlie is on the phone with his folks. Tony and I are sitting in the back seat quietly listening.

By the time we park the car, Juli has been taken in through the ER entrance and Charlie runs in to start talking to the doctors. Miranda and I enter and remain just inside the outer doors.

Minutes later he joins us. "It's torn," he says, shaking his head. "You can move the lower leg all over the place. They're calling in Fred Haring to do the surgery. He's one of the team doctors and top of the line. He's hoping to do it in a few hours. Might as well get it over with."

He walks back to join Juli, who's still lying on the stretcher outside an adjacent exam room. Through the archway I see her reach up for him, her shoulders shaking, and I hear crying. Charlie is holding one of her hands and stroking her hair. Miranda joins him, bending over to give her a gentle hug.

In a few minutes, Miranda returns saying, "Dad, let's get the car." Charlie's disappeared, apparently arranging for the surgery and signing papers. "Lew, can you wait here to see what Charlie wants to do?"

As they hurry away, I sit down in the large ER waiting room, hunkering down behind a pillar, hoping she doesn't notice me. I wouldn't be any comfort to her. A few people come and go. Juli and I are essentially alone.

She starts crying again. I'm sure she doesn't know I'm here. Peeking around from behind the column, I watch as she folds both arms over her eyes, sobbing. Despite my dislike for this girl, I feel terrible. I know how hard she has worked to play at this level. In a few minutes the crying stops, and she lies there quietly, sniffling occasionally. I can't stand it anymore. She's alone. Reluctantly, I get up and walk over to her.

She hears me, turns, and notices me. Sighing, she lies back down, looking straight up at the ceiling, then closes her eyes, dismissing me.

After several minutes she cracks open her eyes.

Yeah, I'm still here, I think.

"Who won the game?" she asks, finally, in a flat voice.

"The bad guys," I say, "three to two."

She grimaces and closes her eyes again. I stand there awkwardly for several minutes.

"Looks like the tables are turned," she mutters, keeping her eyes shut.

I remember her spitting hatred when I was the one lying on a stretcher with a gaping gunshot wound to my leg, minutes after Miranda told me she was in love with Charlie. It was a low point, and now I haven't a clue what to say to her. Finally, "I'm really sorry about your knee."

She pauses and sighs again. "I don't think I can come back. Not again."

"You were magnificent out there," I say.

She winces. "Yeah, well…"

"We could rehab together," I manage. Now why in the hell did I say that?

"Go away, Lew," she mutters.

I turn to walk away. "Hey," she says.

I turn my head back.

"Thanks, anyway."

"You're welcome," I say, making a pathetic effort to smile, then return to hiding behind the pillar.

Why does she put herself through all this? She's rich beyond imagination and she's out trashing her leg, playing her guts out. But then, look at Charlie. He's out battling forest fires because it gives his life meaning. I suppose rich is a hollow pleasure unless you care about something: family, friends, or a piece of land to take care of, something bigger than yourself. I don't see much difference between them and me. Taking one last peek around the pillar, I find Juli staring in my direction. She's got a hard road for a while.

Charlie appears, coming over to inform me he's planning to stay until the surgery is over. His parents will be here in an hour or so. Then he returns to Juli, taking her hand. Miranda comes over to get me as she waves at Charlie. "Let's go," she says.

In the car on the way back to Silver Spring, I ask, "What's she like, Miranda? We had a very rocky start."

She thinks a minute. "I remember Lizzie telling me once,

something Vinnie told her—that passionate people were like red and yellow birds in a flock of brown sparrows. Well, Juli is a peacock."

"Passionate?"

"She's got passion trumped. If she likes something, or someone, or a cause, she's in completely. Of course, if you're on her shit list…"

"I get it. I'll give her a wide berth."

" 'Course, passion is passion."

"Yeah. Willie pointed that out to me when she was yelling at me on that stretcher. I'll pass."

"Hmm?" Miranda murmurs.

"Don't go there, Miranda," I warn. "I'll be glad to be across the country from her."

She gives me a calculating smile.

"Stop it," I say.

CHAPTER 32

LEW

I'M COMING HOME. Hugh is piloting, making the final approach for the landing in Great Falls. His plan is to park the plane and spend a few days with our friends on the reservation. He and Miranda and Charlie will all stay at Win's. It's going to be a great month. I have cases of beer and twenty pounds of my favorite ribs, special order, in the hold of Charlie's plane. We're planning a huge party tonight.

Charlie and Miranda are dropping me off in Browning to see my family before I drive my old beater pickup out to Win's. I'm feeling good!

Hugh ambles back to say hello after taxiing to the holding area. He tries a pilot joke on Miranda, who promises she'll listen later in the car, but he looks so deflated we have to all sit and wait for the joke about a chicken and a pilot. The pilot always loses. I glance at Charlie who's smiling with an indulgent look at his friend. It's hard not to really like Charlie. I suck it up, again.

Willie and Win surprise me at the gate. That's more than nice. We yell Blackfeet greetings and dissolve into hugs and backslaps. That's all it takes. I'm home.

* * *

I'm relaxing with Hugh on Win's porch, overlooking Two Medicine River as the sun descends toward the Rockies. We're groaning from eating too many ribs and many helpings of the potato salad Lizzie and Win's mom made. I'm trying to put the mass of friends in some sort of order for him with the interlocking relationships.

"I can't quite understand how Charlie fits in with all this?" he asks. "Originally, I mean. And the entire extended family?"

"Yeah, well, you know he fell in love with Lizzie after Win disappeared. Even though he lost out, we all sort of felt close to him when he saved Lizzie's life. That was, of course, before we both fell in love with Miranda, and he was on probation when I thought he might have killed her. Does this make any sense?"

He shakes his head.

"I didn't think so. I'll back up. Going on four years ago, the brothers, Sam and Paul Thomas, got to know Willie and Win and they became close friends. I got involved. Women got involved. Paul met Ellie and her sister is Lizzie and... I give up. Pretty soon we were all inter-connected."

Hugh is rolling his eyes at me.

"Just know this," I continue. "We know how special this group is. We are a family. We try very hard not to let anything mess that up." I glance across the yard at Miranda. "Grudges just aren't worth it in the long run. You could say the whole is bigger than the sum of its parts."

"Speaking of grudges," Hugh says seriously. "Is there any new information on the third man— Miranda's kidnapper?"

"Nope. He disappeared into the woodwork. Ross and I've discussed it several times. I've been worried she might still be at risk. Ross believes, since she and I are no longer involved, she's not in danger." I hesitate. "I suppose I agree. If so, that's one good thing to come out of all this."

"Did they find any matches of the blood found at the scene? I know they tried for a long time."

"Nothing. No match to any DNA on record. Not even distant relatives. Ross thinks that he might be dead after all. There was a massive amount of blood."

"And the two guys they caught wouldn't tell the interrogators anything?"

"Wouldn't or couldn't. They hardly knew each other, not even names, if that can be believed. They cooperated to create a composite of the guy, but even that was a problem. He had a light beard and short brown hair. He could have changed his looks dramatically, and he was average in most ways, height, weight, hazel eyes. Nothing that would help identify him."

"Was she to be exchanged? Or killed if you didn't surrender to them?"

"All they knew was that I was to be eliminated. They were the muscle. I guess that's common in the spy world. Need to know—to protect the higher-ups. They were questioned vigorously. I'm just hoping he's long-gone for all our sakes. Or dead."

"It's been a long time now—six months."

I study Hugh. "Did Miranda ever talk about it? Was she assaulted in any way?" I pry awkwardly. "I've wondered for a long time and couldn't ask."

Hugh turns to meet my gaze. "Put your mind at rest. Charlie and Miranda talked extensively about it, and I asked her myself once when I had an opportunity. The guy in charge got away, but he kept himself and the other two under tight control. He didn't allow any personal contact." He looks at me. "Charlie was convinced. I was too. I'm positive she wasn't just trying to protect us from the truth."

I look out over the river. I can let it go.

"How are you dealing with the Miranda thing?"

I turn back to him. I trust Hugh.

"It's been hard," I answer. "But she loves these people, too. Her father has a connection that goes back to the First Gulf War. I watched Charlie be in my place when he lost Lizzie to Win. He's class, Hugh. I expect you know that." I sigh. "And it's worked out well for him."

"Yes, he is class," Hugh says. "And I know what you mean about family. He and I have been family since we were little kids. I was with him when we found his brother's plane. Todd was central in my life."

"I've met Charlie's family several times, mostly involving my nephew, Tommy. They've given him a life of endless possibilities. He could have gone another way. That's another reason for me to do everything I can to let Miranda go. Besides, she's so happy."

We both look at her standing with Charlie, who has his arm around her. She's laughing with Win and Lizzie.

"Yes," agrees Hugh. "It's better to keep peace. And maybe there's a special person around a corner for you."

"And you, Hugh. What's your story?"

He smiles. "You might as well know," he says, "everyone else does. I was in love with Juli for a long time when we were much younger. It's been over for many years, but I never found any woman who measured up."

I turn to stare at him. "Really?" I ask. "She's scary."

"You don't know her," he says. "She has walls, just like Charlie. Inside she's a marshmallow. We dated in high school and my first year in college, but after I went away to school it never really worked. I feel bad for her she can't find someone. And I feel bad for myself, sometimes. I guess I need to look around. That's what Charlie keeps telling me." He takes a large sip of beer. "I've dated around for years—macho pilot. You know, no commitments." He sighs. "But something's missing in my life. Did Charlie tell you I was giving him six months to work it out with Miranda or I was going to step in and take her away from both of you?"

"Were you kidding?"

"Nope. She's easy to like. But look at them now. Both of us will have to try harder."

"No one tempting you?"

"I'd like to find a great girl, but maybe I enjoy being abused too much. Speaking of abuse, why don't you give it a shot with Juli?"

"No offense, but I go for more sensitive women. I always get the idea she could take me out and is waiting for an opportunity."

He laughs. "She has plenty of other attributes. I should know."

We're quiet for a while sipping our beers.

"Do you ride?

"Horses, you mean?" Hugh grins. "Sure. Did you ever hear the one about the cowgirl and the pilot?"

"Come on, Hugh. You need some exercise to clear your head."

I'm smiling when Hugh and I ride out. I asked if anyone else wanted to go for a ride and Charlie answered, "Forget it. That got Miranda in a lot of trouble last time."

He was right. There's nothing like a wild Blackfeet on a big horse, riding bareback to woo women. It almost worked, too.

Win encouraged me to take Cloud. No other horse I'd rather ride. I put Hugh up on Arrowsmith, Win's mom's horse, a big chestnut. I didn't put a saddle on Cloud. He's a horse that's fun to feel through your knees. It's a beautiful June evening and, even though it's after nine, the sun is just setting. The horses are standing in deep grass at the edge of the mesa as we look down at the river cutting through the grasslands. It's close to the same place I took Miranda to in the storm. I take breath after breath of the pristine air. It's my country and my soul, too.

"It's beautiful, Lew," he says. "Incredible."

I nod. My land.

Hugh's cell rings. "Hi kiddo. How 'ya feeling? He did, huh. Yeah, we're on horseback. Your favorite Blackfeet." Hugh breaks out in raucous laughter. "Not nice, Juli. Besides, he's bareback, you ought to see him. Hot."

I groan and roll my eyes at Hugh.

He laughs. "Glad you're keeping the doctors on their toes. Yeah, I'm sure your mom likes spending her birthday visiting you. Here. Say hi to your buddy, Lew."

Shit. I try to wave him off.

He's almost doubled over laughing. "No. Chill out. He's dying to say hi. Here's Lew."

I hear her screaming as Hugh holds the phone away from his ear. "No, Hugh. You friggin' jerk…"

I look daggers at him as he passes the phone to me.

"Oh, hello," I say in my best artificial voice. "How's the leg?"

A pause. Then, "Not too bad." Another pause. "I was bored, so I called Charlie. He told me where Hugh was."

"He said you had a horse when you were a kid."

"Yeah, I did. I'd rather be on a big wild horse, not in this stupid hospital bed. Tell me what you're looking at and the horse you're riding so I can picture it."

"I'm sitting on Win's horse, looking down on Two Medicine River. The water looks like liquid silver, winding through the Park valley, seven hundred feet below us. Beyond the river, the sun is just setting behind the Rockies."

"What colors are the land and the mountains?"

"The grass of the plains is still greenish gold and long. They had a lot of rain last spring. The foothills are bright orange in the setting sun and the mountains are navy blue."

She doesn't say anything.

"Juli?" I ask.

"It sounds so beautiful. I wish... I wish I could see it."

"I wish you could see it, too," I say, surprising myself that I mostly mean it. I like to show off my country.

"Tell me about your horse."

"He's the best horse in the area. Tall, over sixteen hands. A coal black quarter horse, typical muscular hindquarters, and a handful. He's shimmying around, having fun trying to unseat me but he can't. I'm having fun with the battle, so I haven't bothered to show him it's hopeless."

"Is that the horse you rode with Miranda? I heard about that horse."

"Yeah," I say, grimacing. "Same one."

"Hmm. Now I really wish I was there."

I don't have anything to say to that. "Do you ride well?" I ask instead.

"Yes," she says. "I do."

Humble, I think.

Hugh is holding out his hand.

"Take care," I say, rolling my eyes as I hand the phone back to Hugh.

"See," he says to her, starting to laugh hard at something she says, then disconnects. "That went well," he says, grinning at me.

"Yeah," I say. "No direct threats."

"To you, anyway. I forced her on the phone."

He's looking at me with this know-it-all look.

"Okay, I admit it. She can almost sound like a human being when she really tries."

His grin gets larger.

"You know," I say. "You really need to spend more time with Willie. He's a Goddamn know-it-all, too. Together you'd know absolutely everything in the universe."

He keeps smirking that stupid grin as we head back.

CHAPTER 33

LEW

I'VE SPENT A lot of time with Mom, Carol and my nephew, Frankie. He just had his tenth birthday and I made it a point to take him places, to expand his world a little, and be a father figure. We went to Missoula for a weekend, saw movies, played video games at an arcade, and ate at some decent restaurants. I showed him how to order off a big menu. We talked about what he wants to do when he grows up.

Frankie won't have to learn from his mistakes like Tommy did. He's smart in that way. He knows just how far to push adults, so they stay on his side. When he wants something badly, like a new video game, I'm a sucker. We talked about choices. Drove him around to see what hard work could accomplish. I don't see him as going down a bad road, but I want to be there to make sure.

Win and I worked hard on his ranch, shirtless in the hot summer sun, hauling hay. For a break we rode horses into the backcountry, packing in for several days, rifles suspended loosely on our saddles as we hunted for game. He and I took little Paulie down to Win's great grandmother's deserted cabin on the riverbank, watching him splash in the water. It was looking back in time. Almost thirty years ago Win and I were little boys playing in the same shallows. The ghost of Great Gramma Birdie was laughing down at us.

Hiring on with Willie, I acted as a guide on several backpacking trips. He and Susan are talking marriage. He wants to have a family and is trying to persuade his wild woman to settle down.

I stayed until after the mid-July pow-wow and just got back to DC. I found my Blackfeet-self again. Win and I talked about getting the whole extended family on horseback next July and riding in the summer pow-wow parade. Paulie will be almost two and Win would hold him in front on his saddle. Lizzie would love it.

I dressed in old t-shirts and frayed jeans, ate fry bread, and rode bareback in my bare feet, even letting my hair grow longer. I'll be coming back in September for the annual reunion at Win and Lizzie's. I shouldn't need a bodyguard, but Aamad would love it out here. He might even like riding a horse if people weren't shooting at him.

My leg is doing well, not completely back, but coming. I still automatically favor the other leg and I want to continue the rehab until that stops. Since I've been back, I thought about calling Juli to check on her leg, just to be polite, but I never did it. The truth is she still grates on me. I'm too close to the edge with her. I'd be tempted to trip her on crutches. I smile at my mental image of her splatting on the ground. 'Not nice', I say to myself.

I'm planning on watching baseball with Tony as I pull my M3 in his driveway. God! I love this car! Whoever said money doesn't bring happiness. "Oki" I call out, leaping on the porch.

"Hey," he yells back. "I got subs and beer."

"You're the man."

We settle in on the couch with our feet up on the coffee table to watch the pre-game. "I just saw Juli," he says. "She stopped by with a present from Miranda. Hugh brought it back on his last trip out."

"Yeah? What'd you get?"

"A painting Bruce did of Two Medicine River. See there?" He points over the fireplace.

"Nice." I nod appreciatively. "I have a similar one over my bed."

"She had a message for you."

Grimacing... "Juli?"

"You know," he grins. "You may have misjudged that girl. I think she's *darling*."

"You're full of it," I say.

"You doth protest too much," he says.

"Hamlet?"

Tony nods.

"So... I'll bite. What was the message?"

"She was on a cane. She said she's using the gym at Georgetown.

Her soccer team uses it for their home gym. Anyhow, she said if you want to use it, you could. Miranda told her you live in the neighborhood. It was Miranda's idea."

"I need to tell Miranda to butt out," I mutter. "She's got some crazy idea I'd like to tame that wild woman. Definitely not my type."

"You missed my point," says Tony. "Have you seen some of those other ladies? Gorgeous. You might shop around."

"Hmm?"

"See," Tony says. "Just looking out for your best interest."

* * *

Okay. This could work out. This is my third visit, and I haven't seen Juli, but I have noticed Rachel. Six feet one inch of beautiful and obviously interested. I haven't been involved since Miranda, but this girl makes celibacy seem wasteful. I'm about to firm up an intimate dinner out, when the door opens and Juli breezes in, carrying her gym bag. She acknowledges me briefly then starts stretching. I throw my towel around my neck and walk over.

"How's the rehab coming?" I ask.

"Improving. I can get my leg back in good shape. That's not it. I can't decide if I want to do what it would take to try for a comeback."

"Can't help you there," I say. "It was a pleasure watching you, though."

"Thanks," she says shortly.

"Oh, and I appreciate using this gym. My apartment is a quarter mile from here. It's perfect on the way home."

She smiles dismissively, so I head over to talk to Rachel, who's more welcoming.

"Hello," I say. "How's the beautiful left wing?"

"It's too bad you did basketball," she responds. "You would have been a great keeper."

"I've been told that before. I have great hands."

"Do you now," she smiles suggestively. "I've been thinking about dinner. Let's make it short and sweet then watch a movie at my place."

"Works for me," I say, then happen to glance over at Juli, catching her grimacing at our conversation. Obviously, I'm still on her shit list. It's been over six months and despite myself I wish she could let it go. I don't do polite well.

* * *

Four days later, I stop at the gym after work. The soccer team left town to go on the road and have a game televised tonight at eight. I've met at least half the team and Tony was right. I'm rapidly becoming something of a team mascot. Rachel and I did have dinner and it led to other things. Well past time I got back in circulation. And she loves me being six-three because she can look up at me. I'm thinking a lot about her looking up at me from a variety of positions. Tonight, though, the gym is almost empty, not unusual for a Friday night with the soccer team out of town. Juli walks in soon after me.

"Hello," she says briefly, and slips into the shower area to change. We work out in relative silence, occasionally catching each other's eye, smiling guardedly. She seems like an ordinary nice person, but then I've seen her when she's upset.

We're both working hard. She impresses me, working so diligently, all business. Finally, she says, "That's it. I'm ruined. Besides, I want to get back to my apartment to see the game."

Before I have time to think, I blurt out, "My place is just around the corner. I could order a pizza. Want to come over and watch it together?"

I see her pause. "Okay. Sure. That would be fine."

"I'll shower here and wait for you. Sausage and mushrooms work for you?"

"Perfect. Give me twenty minutes."

I'm sitting on a rock wall outside the gym when she comes out. "I'll follow you," she says, walking quickly toward her Audi. I feel very odd, nervous. Strange. Oh, yes. I remember. We're supposed to hate each other. I shake my head already regretting my impulse.

* * *

We've each finished a couple of beers and the game is going well. I'm feeling good and so is Juli. In fact, I'm feeling very good. We're kidding around a bit. It's halftime, still tied zero to zero, and it's gotten dark outside. I get up and turn a small lamp on low. When I come back, I sit closer than I had before. I'm feeling even better. I put my arm on the top of the couch behind her shoulders. She hadn't dried her long hair and it falls in long reddish disarray. I find myself wanting to weave my hands in it.

Finally, I do it, turn her head toward me, and gently lean in and kiss her. It's a test kiss. I have no idea if she's going to melt in my arms or push me away. I get the impression she's not sure about that either.

So far so good, I think, smiling to myself. I take my other hand and weave it in the waves on the other side of her head, pull her toward me, and really kiss her this time. I feel myself react physically. I mean the whole deal.

She freezes. "Okay," she says.

"Okay?"

"I better leave," she says, standing up and looking around for her cane which is propped by the door.

"Look, Juli. I'm sorry. Stay and finish the second half. I didn't mean..."

"I just came over to watch the game."

"You did. I read you wrong. No harm. We can just be friends."

"We're not friends, though, are we?"

"Well, I thought..."

"I know what you're capable of."

"What do you mean by that?" I'm starting to get mad and stand up to face her.

"You take advantage... You hurt people."

Abruptly I'm coldly furious. "You mean Miranda?"

"And my brother."

"I loved Miranda. I probably always will." I'm crossing a line. It's like a stripe on the floor. I step over it. "Who are you to criticize me? At least I feel things. My pain. Other people's pain. Can't you feel anything for anyone?" I glare at her sanctimonious face. "Maybe you're just angry at the whole world."

She gives me a tortured look. Grabbing her backpack and whirling around, she catches my small lamp, sending it flying through the air.

I manage to catch it before it hits the ground as she storms out the door.

"Jesus H. Christ," I growl to myself.

After stewing for several minutes, I reposition the lamp then go over to lock the door, finding her cane still leaning against my wall. Pulling the curtain aside to glance out the window, I find her car still parked in front of my apartment under the glow of a streetlight. I can make her out inside. She's leaning forward, her head on the steering wheel, appearing to be crying. I almost go out to her car, standing with my hand on the doorknob for a long time. Finally, after resisting the impulse to throw the cane in her direction, I prop it against the outside of the house and return to the couch. Leave it alone, I think. We're oil and water.

The second half has started so I settle in to watch it. After several minutes of having my eyes locked on the screen and seeing nothing, I get up, walk to the front window, and pull back the curtain. The cane's still there. She's still there.

Damn it. I slip on my moccasins, grab her cane then pad out to her car, knocking on the window. She looks up, winces, then puts her head back on her hands clenched on the steering wheel. I knock again.

"What?" she asks through the glass.

I hold up the cane.

She ignores me, glowering silently.

I motion for her to roll down the window. Frowning and hesitating, she finally starts the car, and the window begins to drop. "What?" she asks again, holding out her hand for the cane.

"You might as well come back," I say, sliding her cane in the window. "We need to talk."

She looks straight ahead as I stand waiting, finally turning the car off, and opening the door. I walk back to my front porch. When I glance back, she's following, stony faced.

It's still warm outside so we sit on the steps in the darkness. "Okay," I say. "Can we at least try to be friends?"

"I don't know," she says, then admits. "I'm afraid of you."

"Afraid? Do you think I could hurt you? I've haven't hurt anyone in decades other than Charlie, and he was hurting me first." I pause. "And 'course, the guy in the hospital..."

"Are you dense. I don't mean physically."

"Hey," I say. "No need to get insulting. At least we can be polite."

"You're right," she sighs. "I'm sorry."

"Alright then. What do you mean?"

"And I'm sorry about the lamp."

"I caught it. So...?"

"I mean... I mean..."

"Juli?"

She grimaces and moans. "I'm attracted. Obsessed, damn it. And I don't trust you. At least I don't understand you. I should stay very far away from you."

Ah, I think. *Is that what's been going on here?*

"Juli, what exactly are you afraid of?"

She sighs. "That I'll get hurt, obviously."

"So. Do you want to get in the game or hide and be safe?"

"It's not a game. Not to me."

I pause, trying to organize my thoughts. "You bring out strong emotions," I admit. "And I'm not sure what I'm feeling. I don't trust you, either." I turn to face her. "I put my heart on the line recently and had it crushed. But I know one thing—if you don't risk anything, you may miss everything."

She looks down at her hands as I stare at her. She's silent for several minutes. At last, I see a small smile. She turns and looks up at me, reaches out, puts her hand around my neck, and softly kisses my lips. It's another test kiss. I know one when I feel it. I put my arms around her and all the passion I hadn't recognized ignites. Pulling her to me, I slide my hands up her back, kissing her neck, and dropping lower. "Juli," I manage, moving my lips to the rise of her breasts, exploring with raw desire. We devour each other's mouths, groaning. My hands slide under her shirt as I massage her soft skin. My entire body suddenly radiates heat.

Finally, she pulls back, panting. "Lew. What is this?"

"I hardly know." We look at each other in the dark.

"I don't think this is friendship," she says. "But it's something."

"It seems important to think this through." I manage, leaning slightly away from her. "Besides, I want you so much, this second, I might hurt you."

She gives me a look. "Or I might hurt you."

I touch her lips with my finger. "How about one more test kiss?"

We dissolve into each other again. *My God*, I think, pressing her body to mine. I feel the roar inside me building again. This time I barely manage to back away. "It's everything I can do not to haul you over my shoulder, throw you on your back, and ravish you," I mutter. "I could use a little help here."

She moans. "You seduced Miranda, why not me?"

"You just told me you didn't want to be hurt. I'm trying."

"But now I'm hurting for a different reason."

"How about a very cold shower?"

"Together?"

"Juli!"

"I know. I know," she manages with a half-smile. "Maybe I could like you. It's possible."

"Does it matter?"

She's suddenly serious. "Yes, it does. I'm going home. I need to think."

"Are you going to get any sleep?"

"I doubt it." She gets up and walks purposefully back towards her car. "I'm still scared," she calls back over her shoulder. "But I'm beginning to think it might be worth it."

She throws the car in gear, guns the engine, then I watch her drive away. I know one more thing. She's not the only one who's scared.

CHAPTER 34

JULI

I'M FORCING my mind in other directions. It's all I can do to make it home. I drove two blocks past my driveway. The duplexes we lease for home quarters are only two miles from our home field and an equal distance from the gym. My world has just fallen in again. First, my knee ligament tear and resultant surgery has left me examining my life. I was hoping to play another two years then retire, find a new life's goal. But now I'm faced with attempting the elite rehab, reconditioning, and all it entails, for one more year on tour. Moreover, I want my life to mean something. Going to charity events and getting photos in "Town and Country" isn't really my thing. I shudder at the thought.

And now there's this damn Blackfeet. It was much easier to detest him when he was ruining my brother's life. But like Lew just pointed out, it's about taking risks. Charlie fought down his trust issues and laid his soul on the line. Miranda is worth it. And I never want to get into a similar tug-of-war like she found herself in. In the dark of night, I think about it. After too many long empty nights, I'd love to have one man I could care deeply about. But there's that same old issue.

My parents have a great marriage after thirty-five years. Mom said it was a little rocky at first, until she convinced Dad she wanted and deserved to be a true partner in the family enterprise. I doubt he'd considered all her intellectual abilities initially, and they probably blew him out of the water, but he survived. Now he bursts with pride. And no one can say all of us kids haven't had a loving, encouraging family.

That's why I can't figure out why I have so much trouble with men. I've dated at least five impressive guys for significant periods of time. Things start out well, but they end up leaning hard on me for a career push. Either that or we end up fighting it out for dominance. The thing with Michael… That was the worst yet. He stopped calling eventually, then switched to vague character assassination through mutual acquaintances. There must be some quality guy out there who could feel secure enough to care about me and not use me or try to subdue me—who I could trust for the long haul.

I've parked in my usual spot and finally allow my thoughts to go where they want—toward this intellectual bumpkin. What am I ever going to do about him? I'm tempted to run, but now I simply want his body. Is that horrible? Maybe. Despite my loyalty to Charlie, I've finally come to believe Lew was deeply hurt, and I don't like using people either.

I've fought off bedtime fantasies involving him for some time now. It has something to do with the fact that he's not trying to control me. Most of the time he basically ignores me or is polite. Until tonight, of course, he barely tolerated me. He doesn't seem to care about my family…situation. And Charlie says he's a damn nice guy, too, which made him such a dangerous rival. He calls things the way he sees them without manipulation.

I bet he looks great naked. I'm supposed to be finding a long-term relationship and I keep fantasizing. I should ask Miranda. I know she's seen him au natural, or at least close. Oh, crap. I think I'm going crazy. He has this beautiful black hair and tan skin and an untamed look about him. I want to see him on that black horse on the Northern Plains with the mountains in the setting sun. Sigh. I seriously need a tranquilizer.

I'm still sitting in my driveway with my brain circling when my phone rings. "Hi," he says. "I called Tony and got your number. Do you want a nightcap with me?"

"I've got to be honest. If you come over here, I'll want more. I'm fighting this." I take a breath. "This is insanity. Don't you remember? I'm the rich bitch who said all sorts of horrible things to you. You're a Blackfeet and I'm a condescending zillionaire, and I probably still hate you in my DNA."

"Exciting, huh? Unless you forbid it, I'm coming over. You have ten seconds."

"Are you insane?"

"Absolutely. Address?"

I give it to him. "But you can only come on my porch. I can probably handle you outside in public."

"Good enough. I'll be there in five." He disconnects.

What am I doing? I'm tapping my foot, that's what.

He made it in four. His black M3 screeches around the corner and comes to a stop with a lurch. Lew leaps out with a bottle of champagne and two glasses. "I didn't want you to risk going in the house," he says with a lecherous smile.

I grin helplessly up at him. "I've lost my mind, but you are one gorgeous guy."

"Juli," he says. "Maybe we could go for pure lust."

That hurts me suddenly, deeply. My eyes tear up. "You see," I say. "You see. That's what I'm afraid of. I can't do it. Not anymore. I thought maybe I could but... I don't want superficial. Not with you."

He looks confused.

"It's not your fault," I say hopelessly. "I'm not sure what I want. But that's not it." I bury my face in my hands.

He moves over to my side of the porch and puts the bottle and glasses down on the step. "Juli, that's not what I want, either. It was a bad joke. I was nervous. I want something more, too. Please. Let me start over." He puts his fingers under my chin, lifting my head up so that our lips can meet. He gives me a warm gentle kiss. It lasts for some time.

"Could you put your arms around me and hold me?" I ask.

He looks into my eyes, pulling me to him. I feel his lips in my hair. I understand what Miranda must have been feeling. I feel— overwhelmed, and sigh from my soul.

"Why don't you hate me anymore?" he asks.

I shake my head in confusion.

He doesn't say anything else, waiting.

"As I got to know Miranda, I realized she was worth fighting for. How you must have felt. Then I didn't blame you as much."

When he doesn't say anything, I continue, "The hatred died gradually. It's gone. And I've come to love Miranda."

He can't help it. He winces.

295

"You still love her, don't you?"

"Yes," he says simply.

"Do you think you'll have room in your heart for anyone else?"

"I hope so," he says quietly. "Sometimes you have to move ahead on faith."

I pick up his hand. "I hope so, too."

We sit quietly for several minutes, adjusting to new emotions, when I notice a man in a parked car, pulled over in deep shadows in a nearby driveway, possibly watching us. I imagine I can see a glimmer of light, a reflection on glass. "Lew, look at that man." I say, pointing at the darkened car a half block away. As soon as Lew turns to look in that direction, the man lowers what appears to be a pair of binoculars, quickly turning to look away.

He sighs. "One of my bodyguards."

"What? You're sure?"

"Yeah," he says. "Depending on what the CIA turns up, they intermittently put a tail on me. They're supposed to be so good at it that I don't notice. To tell the truth, I'm so oblivious I usually don't. It's irritating, though. It can interfere with personal relationships."

"Are you that important?"

"To my mother."

"Lew?"

He kisses me and looks back toward the neighbor's driveway.

The car abruptly pulls onto the street, turning away from us. We both watch its taillights disappear into the darkness.

He turns to look at me carefully then sighs. "I'm not supposed to talk about it. But yeah. I'm good at what I do. I see patterns, anticipate linkages, steps that aren't in existence yet."

I study him. I never thought.

"What about you?" he asks. "What's your life story? Have you ever had your heart broken?"

"You're changing the subject. About the bodyguard..."

"Tell me."

"Only once," I say quietly. "When my brother died."

"What was he like?"

"He was like watching a beacon of light. He brought us all joy. When he was in the room, he made everything exciting. Everyone else worried about him, but not me. He was a daredevil. Always walked the thin line, but I never for one second imagined he could die. It wasn't possible. Not Todd. Then, from one second to the next, he didn't exist. It's been five years."

"I knew about it, but I've never heard Charlie talk about it."

"The three of us were very close. Charlie and Todd were twins, and I'm only thirteen months younger. Charlie is the only brother I have left. I suppose that's why I feel so protective of him."

"Kiss me again," he insists, pulling me to him. Opening his lips, he touches my tongue with his. This doesn't feel like pure lust anymore. I see him glance down the dark street.

"Bring the glasses inside, Lew."

We're crossing another line. I lie on my couch and reach my arms up for him as he kneels on the floor at my side, leaning over me. His lips are at my throat, running up and down. When he nips my earlobe, my body explodes in wanting. My hands seize his t-shirt, wrestling it off. I couldn't wait. He's the most beautiful man I ever saw, broad shoulders, tight skin, and full sensuous lower lip.

I run my hands along the tops of his shoulders, feeling the ridges of the muscle fibers. There's so much strength there, more than enough to protect me. I surprise myself. Never have I fancied that I wanted or needed to be protected. I smile in astonishment.

"What?" he asks.

I won't admit that thought. Instead, I answer, "Just another reason to love my brother. He rescued your body."

"He did that," Lew admits. "You should have seen him scrambling along with me draped over his shoulders."

His hands become gentle as he strokes my breasts then leans back to look into my eyes. "So beautiful," he whispers. "You're so beautiful." He laughs. "Even when I hated you, I thought that."

I run my hands up his chest, stopping to run my fingertips over his small brown nipples. "You too," I say. "You're the most beautiful thing I ever saw." That makes him laugh loudly.

I pull his head down to my belly and stroke his hair, running my fingers through it. "Do you think we should sleep together?" I ask seriously.

"I want that. I can't believe how much I want that."

"What about Rachel?"

"I'm a terrible liar, but that's good. You can trust what I say. I admit I've begun," he leans up, smiling at me, "a less-than-serious relationship. But now… I'll tell her immediately."

"What exactly do you want?"

At that, he looks seriously in my eyes. "That's surprising," he murmurs.

"What, Lew?"

"I suddenly want to take care of you," he says. "We should wait until I'm sure of the way to do that." He shakes his head. "There. I've learned something."

"Maybe we can take care of each other," I say with equal surprise. "Just don't leave. Not yet."

He moves his thumb across my lower lip causing me to jump at the sensation. "I'm not leaving you."

"Lew…?"

"Hmm?"

"What if I don't want to wait?"

There, I've said it, surprising myself again.

He looks like he's been struck in the face. Then a slow smile washes across his face.

"I'd try not to hurt you," I say, trying to keep pleading out of my voice.

His eyes change. Their intensity almost makes me turn away. For a brief instant, I wonder if I can cope with this. His words come back. "If you never risk anything…"

He stands deliberately. His arms encircle me. I'm lifted and carried into my bedroom, carefully not to hurt my leg. My head is awash with astonished delight as he lays me on the bed. For the first time in possibly my entire life, I give it up. All of it. The thought, the control, the calculation, the fear. I want him. More than that, I want to be a part of him. I hear my name whispered, "Juli. Juli." A glorious sound coming from his lips.

"Finish it. Please."

The muscles in his arms are strong, the flawless body, the molding of his chest. Our energy is unleashed—two bodies together. I'm lost in his beauty and my lust. Call it what it is.

CHAPTER 35

JULI

IT'S BEEN A wonderful summer, probably the best period of my life. I laid some old ghosts to rest. Gradually, I've let myself believe in this incredible guy. It took us several weeks to decide how to handle it all. The pull was so strong, but Lew had been severely chastened by his previous impulses. It was his trust in his impulses that was the hardest. Strangely, once Lew explained the point of hiding being the worst risk of all, I was all in. It's funny looking back on it, but I ended up being the seducer and Lew, a frightened warrior, trying to be cautious.

I never saw the bodyguard again. I looked. Lew never does. But once or twice, when we were in an isolated place, I thought about it. Once, he caught me scanning the nearby woods and laughed about it. "Juli, I'm not that important. Even Ross thinks I'm off the hit list."

"I just don't want anything to happen to you, I said. "You don't have a boring recent history. What would I do?"

"We Blackfeet have nine lives," he said, lightly. "Didn't you ever hear about Custer?"

"Were your ancestors in that battle?"

"No," he said, suddenly serious. "We'd all been massacred six years before that."

I gave him a horrified look.

"It was in 1870. Look it up on the Internet, The Marias River Massacre. We Blackfeet call it The Bear Creek Massacre. After years of hostilities, including killings on both sides, army soldiers were looking for a small party of natives who had killed a white man after he severely beat and humiliated several Blackfeet. Instead, they stumbled onto a large encampment on the Marias River that had been under government protection. They knew they were innocent people, but their blood was up. They slaughtered them all, well over two hundred women, children, and old men in a matter of minutes."

"But how do you know if…?"

"My grandparents shared with me and my cousins how our direct ancestors and a few others were able to escape by running to the trees and hiding in the river's overhanging bank. It happened in the dead of winter, the river was frozen, so most of the others who escaped died of cold and exposure. My great, great, great grandparents were some of the very few survivors."

I gasped, beginning to understand his precarious heritage, so different from mine.

"And I'm here aren't I?" he stressed, cutting the dialogue off. "It's not a pretty story."

Putting my arms around him, I thought, *just take care of yourself.*

There were joyous times, too. One of my favorite memories was the night that started with a bet.

We were down on the dock at Charlie's Chesapeake Bay cottage. It was a warm summer night with a strong breeze keeping the bugs away in the deepening darkness. There were dim lights in the distance and back at the cottage porch, but the dock was hidden in blackness. A fingernail moon hung low over the western horizon.

It had been a beautiful day. I was teaching Lew how to sail a twelve-foot sailboat. We were currently stuffing ourselves with chicken sandwiches and cookies, while chugging white wine straight out of the bottle.

"Lew," I began, "I bet you ten bucks you can't fight off my passion tonight."

"Easy. I'll remember you insulting me while I lay on that stretcher with my leg half blown off. It'd work like a bucket of ice water dumped in my lap."

"Hmm," I murmured. "Sounds like a challenge. What are the ground rules?"

He grinned. "Okay. You can't touch me below the waist, and you can't tie me up. Other than that, go for it."

"How will I know if you surrender?"

"You'll know," he said meaningfully, "but I don't like to lose bets." He rolled over on his back on the thick blue towel on the dock and put his arms behind his head.

"Do your worst," he said.

I unbuttoned his shirt slowly and laid it open. I started kissing his neck and slowly worked my way down his chest. I glanced at him. He looked up at the sky and started whistling.

"Nothing," he said.

I sat back on my heels and started slowly unbuttoning my shirt. The whistling got louder.

I leaned forward and started touching his chest with my breasts. He closed his eyes and shuddered.

"What?" I asked.

"I was just imagining that ice water hitting me in a variety of private places."

I sat back on my heels on the dock and looked down at him lying there with his eyes closed, a small smile on his face. "Lew?"

"Yes?" he replied, without opening his eyes.

"I'm in love with you. I want you to make love to me."

I saw him swallow as he opened his eyes. We looked at each other for a long time. "Hell," he said finally, "it's only ten bucks."

The moon dropped lower in the sky. The sounds of the bay, the waves lapping against the dock, an occasional gull crying in the darkness, all provided the backdrop. The gentle breeze cooled our heated skin. We removed our clothes and explored every part of each other. My world narrowed to his body and my sensations. We touched with our hands and lips, slowly, tenderly. We'd had more wildness, but I sensed something different. I gently kissed his skin. I knew instinctively that lovemaking with Lew was giving. Each sigh of his desire was a gift he gave to me. Never in my life had I experienced that kind of pleasure. I felt his hands exploring, wanting me. I moaned at his touch and felt his pleasure. I guided his body to mine, taking the separate me and making me part of him.

Later he turned on his side, looking at me in the darkness. "Juli," he murmured, "can it be true that you feel the way I do? I'm a simple man. I don't ask much in this life, but if you do love me, I'll spend my life showing you how much I love you back."

"It's been four weeks, Lew. How can you be sure of that?"

It's only been the same four weeks for you. I could ask you the same thing."

"There probably isn't anything sure, Lew. Maybe in a few years, you'll revert to thinking I'm the biggest bitch of all time."

"I admit that's possible, but I know one thing for sure." I could just make out the intensity in his eyes. "I'm all in." He reaches out for me. "Kiitssiikahkoomiim. I love you."

I slid over to him and put my heart in his hands.

* * *

I could spend hours watching him doing little things, wash and wax his beloved car, squirting himself with the hose just to make me laugh, or putting together peanut butter and jelly sandwiches for picnics in the local park. Bliss is having him lie with his head in my lap, feeding him grapes, like Cleopatra feeding Caesar. I don't know myself.

It's been our own private secret that we're in love. Lew says he's so happy he doesn't know what to do with it all. He told me he was motivated to share his happiness by giving homeless people bags of hamburgers and helping little old ladies across the street. He almost died helping one very large old lady when he got tangled up with her cane, tripped and almost fell in front of a bus. "Jeez, Lew," I said. "Even super-heroes watch the traffic."

And then last week, Lew and I were doing our slow jog in the park, that is, I walk fast, and he jogs. I'm not allowed to do any impact activities yet. Still, three times a week we do our thing and reward ourselves with a picnic. Besides, I love to watch Lew run. There's something wild about it. I squint my eyes and see him running on the plains over a hundred years ago. When we're alone, he embellishes with a few war-whoops. It turns me on, as if I needed any help. No one in my life has seen me a pile of mush like this. I giggle like I'm fourteen.

We were sitting on a bench near the rose garden as I pulled out our lunch. Lew scanned the nearby area. "What's up?" I asked. "Looking for Custer?"

"I was talking to Ross yesterday and mentioned the man you

thought you saw last month. He assured me no one is currently guarding me. Other targets are more important right now. He was mystified. He seemed somewhat concerned and it surprised me. Said he'd check into it. Ask around."

I felt a chill. "Who might it have been?"

"You have any disgruntled exes?"

"Not recently. The last one didn't have the gumption to hold a grudge. How about you?"

He shook his head sadly. "Rachel was too nice. It was disappointing."

Ash

I survived in anonymous seclusion for the last six months. Having doggedly endured half of my lifetime in a covert existence, waiting for the call which finally came, I failed. I've searched my soul endlessly for understanding. Am I a dud, a fake, a born loser? In the last analysis, am I a fraud? After several months of bungled assassination attempts, kidnappings, and a near-mortal wound, I was cast out. Or rather, I cast myself out. Completely. Even my handlers thought I was dead, and I wanted it that way, while I was trying to stay alive in the physical and metaphorical wilderness, decoupled from everything that gave my life purpose.

I have no real friends, am isolated from my remaining family, and worst of all I have no future. I failed my country, my handlers, and myself. In desperation, I finally decided to risk existence again. At long last, I made myself known. They may ultimately have me killed after deciding I know too much. I offered, pleaded, to be allowed to attempt the big one—the objective I missed. They want him badly. They've decided to let me try, almost admitting they have nothing to lose. If I can just pull this off...

CHAPTER 36

LEW

JULI IS OFF visiting her parents in Philly. I've been putting in twelve-hour days and needed a good workout. It's late in the evening, just before real darkness, and the park where I run is almost deserted. Glancing at my watch, I see that it will be closing soon so I increase my pace, and head back to my car. Faint thunder booms off to the west and it feels like rain. They have world-class thunderstorms back here and I smile with anticipation. The humidity has risen off the charts so I'm looking forward to a long shower, a cold beer, and putting my feet up to watch the end of the ballgame. It's late and I'm too bushed to drive to Tony's, but

I might call him and get in a wager if the score isn't already too lopsided.

My vague headache is gone. I'm feeling pleased with my faster pace, and as I pull out my phone to call Tony, I notice a man approach me out of the near darkness. He passes by as we give each other a passive smile.

"Get in that car, Lew," he says quietly from behind my back. As I turn, he points with one hand to a tan sedan parked close to mine. With the other, he presses a gun into my back.

Startled, I focus on the unremarkable man holding the gun. He's several inches shorter than my six-three and not superficially threatening except for the piercing dark eyes. The gun is cold and hard, and he looks like he knows how to use it.

He's chosen his spot well. No one else is around, only distant taillights far down the road. What I do in the next several seconds could mean life or death. I'm alone. My first thought is that Ross is going to be sorry. I'm breaking new ground at work, exploring important new territory. For once, I'm scared shitless. I've been vaguely surprised Ross has been so accommodating, letting the bodyguards slide for now. I'm not sure even he understands the kind of cyber protection we're going to need in this new cold war. He's over forty.

All that rumbles through my head, as I decide what options I have. Not many. I can feel the cold steel still rammed up against my back. He hasn't shot me yet and he could. He'd simply have to dump my body in his trunk and drive away. That means someone must want me alive.

"You have ten seconds," he mutters. "It would be far easier to kill you. You must know I'll do it. First your spine, then your head. We're alone. Decide."

I swing my leg into the seat well and feel a sting. I know what's coming. Juli is going to be panic-stricken. Strangely, my last muddled thought is wondering what Ross will think when they find my deserted car. I slump into the seat as everything goes dark.

When I come to, it's pitch-dark. I believe I'm now in the trunk of a car. My mouth is duct taped. Maybe he's going to kill me after all. I break out in a cold sweat. I'm wedged in tightly with my knees forced up and against my chest; the floor and surrounding space is hard and metallic. When we go around corners, my head is wedged into a small spot, shifting around painfully. My hands are handcuffed behind me. I'm terrified. I'm afraid he may never stop, but I'm afraid when we do stop, he may kill me. Suddenly the brakes are slammed on, throwing my whole body forward and causing severe pain in my head and shoulders. "Keep your wits about you," I think to myself.

Suddenly the trunk lid is lifted, but before I can think, another needle is shoved in my thigh. Darkness.

* * *

I hear the pulse of an overhead fan before I see anything. I'm in no hurry to open my eyes and listen carefully. Very slowly I crack them open enough to see. I'm handcuffed to a very sturdy bedframe with two sets of handcuffs, keeping my arms wide apart over my head. I'm completely helpless, held in a sixties-style bedroom with aluminum-framed windows, slid open for breeze. Warm air flows in through a screen, fluttering cheap, white cotton curtains. The duct tape is gone, letting me assume I'm somewhere I can't be heard.

My shoulders hurt, and as I shift to reduce the discomfort, the man sitting in a chair across the room raises his eyes to me.

He doesn't say a thing nor do I. Finally, I ask, "Now what?"

His unresponsive expression tells me nothing. "You're going on a trip."

"Where?"

He smiles coldly. "I'm buying my way back in."

"Excuse me?" I mumble.

"I'd be extremely careful," he says, quietly. "You almost ended me last fall. I didn't enjoy taking that bullet out of my leg."

"You're the third man," I say, then am silent for a while, considering. "Are you going to let me live?" I ask finally.

"We'll see," he says, flatly. "If I can deliver you, you'll be worth more. But then, you're worth a lot dead."

My head continues to clear. Damn it. I remember the torture videos. I imagine it could be sophisticated torture. I have no idea what I could withstand. Could I fake going along? How long? I wet my lips. "Could I have some water?"

He looks at me, considering my request.

Walking to a counter, he brings back a plastic bottle of water and holds it to my lips as I guzzle most of it.

"Thanks," I say.

No response.

"And thank you for not hurting Miranda," I say. "Back then."

That seems to jolt him out of his shell. "All she did was worry about you," he replies. "Finally, I had to drug her to get her to shut up."

I swallow. We stare at each other. "She told me you talked about me, about my family."

"Seems we have a lot in common. My father died of guzzling booze. Yours did, too, if I remember correctly. Cheap whiskey, in his case, instead of vodka." He laughs, roughly. "Half a world apart. Both sons-of-bitches."

"Is your mother alive?"

"Shut up, Black River. I don't want to bond with you. We're just killing time here."

"How long?" I ask.

He smiles that cold smile again. "You don't need to know."

After attempting to control my fear, I'm able to study the man. On closer inspection, he's younger than I originally judged—maybe late thirties or so, not that much older than me. His rumpled, loose-fitting shirt and jeans disguise a fit man. And he's smart, careful. I watch him studying me back. Nothing wasted here, no information, no movements.

He crosses to the one lamp and turns it off. It's now profoundly dark so we must be far out in the country. The louder thunder rolls on and on, with lightning frequently illuminating the room. The curtains start whipping in the increasing wind. A huge bolt of lightning hits so close to the house that I can smell the ozone. I try to think of options, any opportunity. Time passes. I assume he's dozing in his chair but then he shifts the gun on his lap, staring straight at me. A warning.

I'm scared.

More time passes.

I have no idea where I am or whether this guy has help or is winging it alone. I'm less terrified. He said I'm worth more alive so if I make it easy on him, he'll probably keep me that way. Escape. It's my constant thought. If he can get me out of the country, I'm as good as lost. I have to get loose from these handcuffs. That's the primary thing. I'm sure the guy knows that, too. He's no amateur.

Russia is threatening again. The deciders upstairs don't see the ominous signs I do. They keep talking about mutually connected financial benefit being a deterrent to unchecked aggression. I see it in another way. This is personal. Putin's ego is on the line. He doesn't want his country, the obvious extension of himself, to be seen as second tier. He's a very savvy dude with a strategically long horizon. He'll grab what he wants now and pick up the pieces later—work out his best deal after he's won some of the marbles. He doesn't need to win it all, just cause chaos.

It seemed so simple to me that I've kept it as my major focus. Sometimes, I think the academic types make it complicated so they can justify their expensive educations, but it boils down to a chess game. Russia also excels at that.

My mind has been wandering to avoid what I need to accept—that, unless I can figure a way out of this, it won't matter what the hell I think.

* * *

It could have been hours or several days for all I know. I've been knocked out periodically. If it's only hours, no one will have missed me yet unless they found my car and checked the license. Juli will reach out when I don't call her. I think tomorrow is Monday, but I'm not sure. Someone at work will try to get a hold of me. Where are my friggin' bodyguards when I need them? Aamad went to the Jersey Shore with Giti. He's been complaining they're talking about reassigning him to some young techy kid about twenty-two. He even tossed out the idea that we should fabricate an incident to keep the big guys on their toes, so they worry about me. It's not all kidding. Aamad's been concerned. Well, incident made to order here.

I'm trying to remember what I know about Houdini. Something about tightening the wrist muscles then relaxing them for some maneuvering room in handcuffs. Maybe next time. Maybe a bathroom break? I'm uncomfortable and I'm mad. I'm even mad at Ross for not worrying about whether there was something to worry about. 'Course I would have laughed at him. Well, I'm not laughing now.

A light goes on in the room, a wall switch turned on a small bedside lamp and Bozo is looking at me. "We're moving," he says. "You can use the john. Just remember, I really don't mind if I kill you. It'd be a hell of a lot easier." He unlocks one of the handcuffs, then relocks my right hand behind my back to my belt and walks me into the bathroom with the gun shoved in my back. I might have had an opportunity a second ago, but now that's passed. I decide not to try anything here.

* * *

We're in a car on the freeway headed north and have been driving for two hours. It's still the middle of the night and there's almost no traffic. We seem to be headed for the Jersey shipping docks. I'm uncomfortable. My hands are handcuffed behind me, and I'm strapped tightly in a seatbelt. A filled syringe lies on the console between us—a threat if I consider causing a problem.

I've thought frantically, trying to think of what I could offer, something to get me out of this mess. I'm running out of time. I think of Juli, Miranda, and all the people I love, fighting off despair. They can't help me. I need to think of something.

The guy is a good driver. He's doing nothing to attract attention, cruising along at the speed limit. Several police cars pass us going the other way, but I have no way to alert them. Unless... I have very long legs. If I could reach my left leg up and entangle my foot in the steering wheel, I could cause the car to crash or at least be noticeable. I start looking for another police car. I'll have only one chance at this and may get shot in the attempt.

I consider my options. This is dangerous. The car could explode. But I really don't want to get drugged, loaded into a packing crate, and mailed off to Timbuktu. I decide to go for it.

I'm somewhat familiar with the area. Soon we'll be turning off toward the waterfront. The car clock says 3:45. Minutes are ticking away. If we get off the main highway, my chances of finding any police plummet to zero. "Please. Please," I say to myself. I can feel my heart racing from the adrenaline.

Way up ahead I see flashing blue lights on a car, coming from the opposite direction, moving fast. Now or never. I wait. And wait. When the police car is almost next to us, I see Bozo's hands tighten on the wheel and make my move. Leaning over far to my right, I bend my knee up, hook my foot in the wheel and pull as hard as I can. The car swerves sharply to the right, crashes into a cement barrier, rolls onto its side and slides along the concrete. The sound of screeching metal fills the air. The sparks shower blinds me, going on for God knows how long, until the car finally flips over on its top and stops. The last things I remember seeing are the flashing blue lights turning around. I close my eyes.

I never completely lose consciousness although I'm thoroughly stunned. My heart is still pumping from the adrenalin. The night is suddenly full of sirens, police radios, and loud talking as I slowly orient myself. The air is full of acrid smoke. Someone is removing the handcuffs as I lie on my side on a stretcher by the side of an ambulance. When I can, I roll onto my back, but as I try to sit up strong arms keep me in place, so I wiggle individual body parts, deciding I'll live.

An officer approaches me. I smile weakly at him as he smiles back. "I imagine you have a story to tell," he says. "Why don't we start with your name?"

I take a deep breath. "My name is Llewellyn Black River," then take a second to spell my first name. "I work for the NSA and my boss is Ross Clopton." I give him both Ross's office and home numbers. "Whatever you do," I caution, "don't talk to Dolly, his secretary. She'll have a heart attack."

After several minutes of questions, the trooper leaves to call Ross. I'd give anything to listen in to that conversation.

I lie quietly for several minutes trying to orient myself. Finally, lifting my head off the stretcher, I look around. At least six patrol cars are assembled with lights flashing and a crowd of uniformed police milling around, plus two fire engines with motors running loudly. I can also make out Bozo sitting in the back of a police cruiser. Two more officers stand just outside his open back door talking.

Without asking permission, I sit up suddenly and hop awkwardly off the stretcher. "Gotta ask a question," I explain to the surprised attendant, and before he can object, jog stiffly toward the cruiser. "A minute, officers. I've got to know something."

They shrug but listen in as I bend over the open door.

My kidnapper glances briefly up at me before staring fixedly at his handcuffed hands.

"Why?" I ask. "Why didn't you just kill me?"

Bozo gives me a disgusted look, not answering immediately as if deciding whether it's worth the effort to tell me.

"I should have," he finally mutters, shaking his head and ultimately looking me in the eye. "I don't know. Maybe I wanted the big payoff. I wanted to see their faces when I delivered you hog-tied. It would have been a huge deal." He turns away, pauses, then looks at me again. "Or maybe it was because that girl cared so much." He glares dejectedly at the seat back in front of him.

As I lean away, I hear him mumble to himself, "Goddamn Blackfeet warrior."

* * *

Deja vu. As I wake up early the next morning, there stands Ross—again—at the end of my hospital bed, with two armed guards stationed at the door. When we make eye contact, he starts shaking his head.

"Hi, Boss."

"Hi, Lew," he says with mock patience.

We grimace at each other.

"How's the third man?" I ask finally.

"Unhappy. He knows he's not going anywhere soon. Still, he's not a murderer that we know of. Even he knows that counts for something. And it turns out, he was an NOC, a mole for years, waiting to do the big job."

I lick my lips and Ross hands me a glass of water. "How am I?" I ask, stretching. "I feel pretty good."

"You're fine. That hard head of yours is still beautiful—that one cut on your forehead didn't need stiches They put on steri-strips instead. You can use it to get sympathy. Dolly's been hysterical. That's been the worst of it."

"Did you call anyone of mine?"

"I'll let you handle that. They're discharging you as soon as you get dressed and the doctor signs you out. She'll be here in a few minutes." He smiles encouragingly. "Go home, Lew, and relax."

"Are the bodyguards going back on? I really dread that."

"We're meeting this afternoon to discuss it. So far everyone thinks this was an isolated incident—a guy trying not to be eliminated by the mother country for a massive screwup. We're reactivating Aamad as your private bodyguard, at least for the time being. He's on his way in, barely controlling his enthusiasm. Said you can watch torture videos together."

I nod vigorously. "Thanks for coming."

"Sure. I had nothing else to do. The Middle East has been relatively quiet for an hour or so. Oh, actually..." He smiles. "I did call one person. She's just outside."

I watch as Ross motions to the guards who follow him out into the hall. A familiar face peeks around the corner.

She approaches my bedside, tries to speak, then starts to cry.

"Come on," I say. "You're going to ruin your reputation as a hard-hearted bitch."

"Just call me Marshmallow," she manages.

CHAPTER 37

JULI

THERE WAS A small part of me that still wondered. I found myself waiting for him to profit from my connections or control me. I finally asked Lew about it. We were spending the early evening at a small café across from our park in DC, just before we left for Montana. Our bench rested under the striped green and yellow awning out in front, and I sat by his side, my head on his shoulder, running my fingers up and down his forearm.

"Juli, what are you thinking? You seem far away."

"I was wondering... If you really knew me, can I be what you want? I'm a strong-willed lady. It can get aggravating. I'm trying to let you know the real me, to show you my worst self, but I can't seem to find it around you."

"Hugh told me once that you were a softie. I don't agree. I think you're tough, but incredibly sweet. To me anyway."

"You don't worry I'm too domineering?"

He turns to look seriously down at me. "Do I let you beat me up? I'd hate to think I was a lap dog."

"I absolutely adore you, Lew. I'm the lap dog here. You don't have a worst side."

He shakes his head in disagreement. "You already know the worst about me. I have absolutely no imagination outside of the computer world. I have no common sense to the point of fumbling into catastrophic messes. I'm hoping you can look out for me, keep me safely out of trouble."

I grab his arm firmly and ask, "One other thing. Don't you want to use some of the family fortune to further your career? Isn't there a part of you that's very glad to have access to all this money?"

"Why?"

"Why?" I look up, giving him a wry smile. "You really do have an abysmal lack of imagination."

* * *

Everyone is gathering for another family reunion on the Blackfeet Reservation. The area surrounding Win's barn is full of trucks and cars and he's half-joking about getting a parking attendant next year.

Charlie has been encouraging our parents to come with us to Montana and meet his adopted family and Lew has been pleading with me to make the same trip. I didn't need any encouragement. Besides, I've been waiting for months to share the view on horseback with him. Ever since that long-ago phone call in which we gritted our teeth to be nice.

Hugh flew Charlie and me out yesterday morning with Mom and Dad. Aamad, the happily reconstituted bodyguard, flew out separately with Lew. As far as anyone out here knows, Lew and I wouldn't be caught dead on a plane together.

I stroll over to Hugh who has his arm locked around Katherine. I've been acquainted with Hugh's skill with women for years. I was one of his first successes, even though the mutual attraction wore off a decade ago. Seeing them together, I laugh inwardly at the familiar outcome. Hugh brings out wantonness in women.

"Hello, you two. You better watch it. This western lifestyle puts men in a romantic mood."

"That's what I've been warning Katherine," replies Hugh. "But she says not to worry. My humor puts her off."

She smiles. "I survived the knock-knock jokes, but the pilot and the farmer's daughter put the nail in the coffin."

Lew and I are acting like we hate each other. So many people were pushing us together it seemed like losing to say, "Yeah, you were right." As far as we can tell, no one knows anything although Tony has probed a lot. Lew's been reluctant recently to discuss female exploits, so he's suspicious. If Lew comes near me, I automatically leave the area, frowning disgust, and have been teased about it. I always did love acting.

In the few months we've been together, I'd never seen the laid-back western person emerge completely. I've loved watching Lew and his best friends interacting.

Several of us went out last evening on horseback. Lew, Win, Willie, and I rode out to see the view. It was very warm that evening and the guys were shirtless with similar blue beaded necklaces. I'd been told it would take a full evening to tell the stories behind those.

We all went bareback. I've been enjoying Lew's surprise that I'm a wild woman on a horse. I spent a lot of my adolescence on my own horse, and ride like... Well, like an Indian.

Lew and I got into one-upping each other with faked lethal hostility. We kept moving our horses as far away from each other as possible. No one can figure us out. Willie, who I just met, kept ribbing Lew about my superior equine skills. Lew glared at him, added several choice expletives, told Willie to give it a rest.

We silently lingered to watch the fiesta-colored sunset, the four of us together, our horses standing in formation on the rim of the high river canyon. The underlying whisper of the long grasses added magic to the evening with the occasional call of a hawk soaring over the valley floor. I'd waited a long time. The mountains really were navy blue as the sun dropped behind them. The lower slopes glowed red and looked like they're burning. We lingered a long time, savoring the dusk. I've been looking forward to sharing it alone with Lew, but that will have to wait.

* * *

It's Saturday night, the climax of the reunion. We've just finished a steak dinner cooked on a giant grill, set up over Win's fire pit.

The light has faded. Several of the men move to build up the fire. Sparks fly high in the air against the darkening sky as wood is thrown on the embers. Sam and Bruce are starting to play guitars with the crowd settling down in a satiated state of contentment.

I look over at Lew and nod. It's time.

We're both are sitting far apart, but get up simultaneously, making our way, meandering independently, to the huge tub set off on the side of the yard, containing ice with pop, beer and wine. We look in different directions at the last minute, bumping accidentally into each other.

"Excuuuuse me," Lew says, his voice low but dripping with sarcasm.

"Just friggin' get out of my way," I hiss.

"Sure. Make way for the princess," he says loudly. Everyone is starting to look at us.

"You cretin. You can't even pretend to act like a human being," I mutter, my voice rising to match his.

"You... You entitled loser," Lew spits out. "Who invited you here, anyway. You don't belong with my people."

People are anxiously whispering. Willie stands up. So do Charlie and Hugh.

"You... You..." I'm screaming and stammering now. "No wonder Miranda chose my brother!"

Many people are gasping. More people are starting to stand up. Charlie starts toward us. Lew looms over me, pretending to grab my arm roughly.

"Lew," Charlie yells angrily. "Hands off."

Reaching out, I grab Lew's left arm, turn and flip him over my shoulder in a self-defense maneuver, catching him off balance. He lands flat on his back on the ground in a halo of dust.

"Take that, you disgusting mound of buffalo shit," I shriek.

We both end up on the ground, protecting my leg as we practiced, rolling over and shoving ineffectively at each other, and appearing to pull hair.

I'm screaming.

People start running toward us, yelling frantically.

Lew flies to his feet, pulls me up on mine, bends me over backwards and kisses me like—Like no one else is there.

Everyone running toward us screeches to a halt.

Lew and I start laughing hysterically. He pulls me up in his arms and swings me round and round in a circle.

Absolute silence, except for my mother who's still screaming.

"Gotcha!" yells Lew.

I look around. At least half the people have their mouths hanging open.

"My God," gasps Charlie. "I thought I was going to kill Lew after all."

"Yeah. Well," Lew explains. "We decided we'd fall for each other just to keep the peace."

He takes me into his arms again, starting to kiss me, but suddenly pulls away. "Mound of buffalo shit...?"

"Wait. Wait," I say, laughing. "Before I do anything else, I want to meet Vinnie. I've been faking it—wanting to murder Lew. I wasn't sure I could fool her, so I've been avoiding her."

I go over and give her a big hug. She's shaking with laughter.

Pulling over an empty chair, I settle next to her. "Well, Vinnie. All's well that ends well."

"This is the best, the most wonderful-best. Oh, how fun!"

"Vinnie, I'm so glad to meet you. Everyone loves you. Even my brother had to drive up at three in the morning to get perspective. I hope you'll be happy about us. We're crazy about each other," I beam. "And we had a lot of fun practicing."

"Honey, you have no idea. This situation with Charlie, Lew, and Miranda has kept me up nights. I've been so worried about Lew. He's so brave and wonderful. I've hated to see him so unhappy."

"Vinnie," I say seriously, "I agree. He deserves every wonderful thing I can give him."

"Well, welcome to the family," she says. "And that last activity... Well, I'll be awake all night, laughing. You were both very convincing." She pauses. "I expect you know Lew is a spectacular guy, one in a million, but he needs a skillet to the old noggin occasionally, to focus his attention. I think it's the techy thing. You seem like just the right person to do that."

"Vinnie, it was me. I'm the one who needed my point of view adjusted. I really did want to kill him not so long ago. Together, we had barely enough smarts to figure ourselves out. We may need a lot of counseling."

"Well," she smiles conspiratorially. "My kitchen door is always open if things get dicey. But you'll have to make an appointment. I've been upgraded. Charlie got me a new mattress for my guestroom, and Lew's making me a website for sign-ups and a blog."

The End

Made in the USA
Monee, IL
10 May 2023

33472127R00181